# The Mammoth Book of
# Sherlock Holmes Abroad

# The Mammoth Book of Sherlock Holmes Abroad

## Simon Clark

ROBINSON

RUNNING PRESS
PHILADELPHIA · LONDON

ROBINSON

First published in Great Britain in 2015 by Robinson

A CIP catalogue record for this book
is available from the British Library.

ISBN 978-1-47211-882-0 (paperback)
ISBN 978-1-47211-883-7 (ebook)

Typeset in Plantin Light by Hewer Text UK Ltd, Edinburgh
Printed and bound in Great Britain by CPI Group (UK) Ltd., Croydon, CR0 4YY

Robinson
is an imprint of
Constable & Robinson Ltd
100 Victoria Embankment
London EC4Y 0DY

An Hachette UK Company
www.hachette.co.uk

www.constablerobinson.com

First published in the United States in 2015 by Running Press Book Publishers,
A Member of the Perseus Books Group

Books published by Running Press are available at special discounts for bulk
purchases in the United States by corporations, institutions and other organizations.
For more information, please contact the Special Markets Department at the
Perseus Books Group, 2300 Chestnut Street, Suite 200, Philadelphia, PA 19103,
or call (800) 810-4145, ext. 5000, or email special.markets@perseusbooks.com.

US ISBN: 978-0-7624-5617-8
US Library of Congress Control Number: 2014954821

9 8 7 6 5 4 3 2 1
Digit on the right indicates the number of this printing

Running Press Book Publishers
2300 Chestnut Street
Philadelphia, PA 19103-4371

Visit us on the web!
www.runningpress.com

# Contents

# Contents

# Acknowledgements

It's only right that the acknowledgements section contained in an anthology of Sherlock Holmes stories should begin by recognizing Sir Arthur Conan Doyle. This medical doctor turned writer created one of the most enduring fictional characters of all time. It's a fair assumption that at any given moment someone somewhere is watching a Sherlock Holmes adaptation, and who knows how many people will be reading about Holmes and Watson investigating another exciting case?

My thanks go to the Sherlock Holmes expert Charles Prepolec. Thank you, also, to Mike Ashley for his encouragement and help. Mike edited *The Mammoth Book of New Sherlock Holmes Adventures* (Robinson Publishing, 1997); in doing so, he set a very high standard in the finding and the gathering together of "lost" cases. And much gratitude to Duncan Proudfoot, Emily Byron and Georgie Szolnoki at Constable & Robinson for making this anthology possible in the first place.

I would like to thank you, the reader, for your undiminished appetite for new Holmes and Watson adventures. Happily, I share that appetite, too. I also whole-heartedly thank my wife, Janet, for her advice and feedback as I recruited such a fine team of writers and compiled this volume that you now hold in your hands.

All of the stories in this anthology are in copyright. The following acknowledgements are granted to the authors for permission to use their work herein.

# Introduction

*Holmes and Watson run across the moor. Fog swirls. The eerie howl of a gigantic hound ...* Mystery and excitement all but crackled from the television screen, and I, at eight years old, sat on the edge of the chair not wanting to even blink in case I missed one marvellous second. The film and television adaptations of the Sherlock Holmes stories provided me with my first introduction to Sir Arthur Conan Doyle's legendary detective – and the film that long ago captivated me and transformed me into a devotee of Sherlock Holmes was the 1959 Hammer production of *The Hound of the Baskervilles*, starring Peter Cushing.

A few years later, I began to read the Conan Doyle stories in a little old book with red covers that I found in a tin trunk at my grandparents' house. I still have that book, *The Adventures of Sherlock Holmes*, published by T. Nelson & Sons. It's here beside me on my desk as I write this introduction. A handwritten note on an otherwise blank page before the title page tells me that the book was bought by F. Audsley on 20 May 1918. The red volume's diminutive size suggests it was specially produced for those serving in the military, so it could be slipped into an army overcoat, perhaps, before its owner headed out to the trenches of the First World War in Europe. In my mind's eye, I can see Mr Audsley finding a few precious moments to escape his nightmarish surroundings by reading exciting adventures, involving a man with a twisted lip, or the red-headed league, or a scandal in Bohemia, while artillery thundered, and bullets flew overhead.

I don't know who Mr Audsley was, exactly, who indirectly bequeathed me *The Adventures of Sherlock Holmes*, but the book has been a good companion to me over the past forty years or so. I loved the adventures that Holmes and his friend, the ever-loyal Doctor John Watson, embarked upon. Yes, I liked the parts where Holmes receives visitors to his Baker Street rooms, and makes his astonishing deductions based on how the sole of a boot is worn, or the singular position of an ink stain upon a sleeve. But what really made my blood race with excitement was when Holmes would urge Watson to pack his bag, collect his revolver, and check the train timetables for some destination where the drama would explode from the page.

Holmes would then unravel the mystery and identify the culprit, with, as likely as not, an arrest to follow, bringing every-thing to a satisfying conclusion. When Holmes and Watson ventured to remote parts of Norfolk or Devon these would, to many readers of the time, seem quite outlandish and strange – places that could contain lurking danger in the form of ominous figures prowling the countryside, or oozing marshes that might claim the city gentleman who wandered too far away from the path.

Holmes travelled further afield, too, of course. "The Final Problem" sees him venture across the sea to mainland Europe, eventually reaching the terrifying Reichenbach Falls in Switzerland – it is here where he experiences his fateful and seemingly catastrophic encounter with the evil Professor Moriarty.

It was this notion of Holmes travelling away from the cosy surroundings of 221b Baker Street that prompted me to suggest to the publisher of this book that I compile an array of short stories that sends Holmes out of London and away from Britain to countries overseas. The exotic places would provide an unfa-miliar setting for mysteries that would test Holmes's ingenuity. What's more, the very landscapes themselves would test him, too, when he found himself in extremes of heat and cold, and, perhaps, faced by local populations that were hostile to the Englishman.

The publisher liked my idea and gave me the go-ahead for *The Mammoth Book of Sherlock Holmes Abroad.* I immediately invited a range of authors who I knew could pen fiction that was entertaining as it was imaginative and would still be respectful towards the legacy created by Sir Arthur Conan Doyle, and satisfyingly echo the style of the original works. I recruited writers, however, that would be prepared to take risks, and transport Sherlock Holmes "abroad" in, perhaps, more senses than one. Consequently, not only does he travel to exotic locations in these pages, he also encounters mysteries that are equally exotic, and severely test his powers of deduction.

Within this book you will find several tales that are very much traditional Sherlock Holmes adventures, in the sense that they wouldn't have been out of place in *The Strand* of a hundred years ago, the magazine that first featured Sherlock Holmes. Others in this volume will challenge the reader, just as certain Conan Doyle tales would have raised eyebrows and increased the temperature of the flesh beneath those stiff collars of Victorian and Edwardian Britain.

It must be said that our detective hero also experimented with drugs. These, on the whole, were legally obtainable in Sherlock Holmes's "time". It wasn't until the Dangerous Drugs Act of 1920 that a wide range of narcotics, including cocaine and opium, were banned in Britain. Therefore, we can easily imagine Holmes "travelling" to fantastical destinations without ever leaving his armchair. Indeed, Doctor Watson observes his friend rising "out of his drug-created dreams" in "A Scandal in Bohemia". Where the drugs carried Holmes in those dreams we don't know, but in this volume you'll find him, on at least one occasion, "transported", let us say, and possibly influenced, by certain chemicals that he was so fond of injecting into his veins, or smoking in his pipe.

Other writers in this volume give Sherlock Holmes more conventional modes of transport: locomotives, horse-drawn carriages, sailboats and steamships. Nonetheless, these convey him to faraway realms where he encounters mysteries and adventures galore.

I hope you enjoy accompanying Mr Sherlock Holmes, as he steps out from his rooms in London's Baker Street, and ventures abroad on these extraordinary journeys.

*Bon Voyage*.

Simon Clark
September 2014

# The Monster of Hell's Gate

## Paul Finch

The sun dipped as we approached the mountain range. The rugged peaks of the Nandi Hills glinted flame-red, lilac shadows flowing like ink across the flat green/gold scrubland lying betwixt us and the eastern slopes of those majestic highlands. Of course, beauty is in the eye of the beholder, and all the time I'd known him, my friend, Mr Sherlock Holmes, had never once been stopped in wonder and awe by anything picturesque. Even now he leaned against his armrest, absorbed in thought, the dusty white brim of his homburg pulled down over his eyes, drawing on a cigarette he'd unconsciously taken from the engraved silver case donated to him in gratitude after the stressful business at Mortmain Manor.

In truth, the romance of our setting could be exaggerated. The last two days had been arduous even by the standards of our recent travels. The horse that pulled our trap was a bony nag, its sagging posture and stick-like ribs suggesting a painful need for food and water. As such, we made laborious progress even though our road ran straight as an arrow. This was a service road, and better than many others we'd encountered in the East African Protectorate. It ran parallel to the railway tracks, only a dozen yards of dry earth separating us from the neatly arrayed sleepers and sun-gleaming metals. If nothing else, this was a welcome trace of modernity in a hot, harsh wilderness; firm evidence that civilization, at least as we British knew it, was finally pushing north through the Great Rift Valley. But it also underlined the sheer vastness of these spaces, and answered the oft-asked question as to why so mammoth a series of tasks had ever been undertaken in East Africa in the first place.

The Ugandan Railway, as the press at home christened it, had been completed five years earlier, forging an unbroken line of communication for almost seven hundred miles between Mombasa on the Indian Ocean and Kisumu on the east shore of Lake Victoria, to much acclaim but at staggering cost. This new branch line, originating at Kalawi Junction, a middle-of-nowhere former army outpost now turned crossroads town, drove away from it at a right angle towards Lake Rudolf, and had encountered similar problems: swamp, jungle, rocky ridges minus tunnels, depthless ravines minus bridges, and of course fierce wildlife and hostile tribesmen.

The portion of the route we were traversing now, which one could probably characterize as savannah, was less overtly dangerous, but, though scenic, monotonous. It changed little as we traversed it hour after uneventful hour. Our driver didn't help. His name was Jervis, and he'd been a lance corporal in the King's African Rifles. Now – at sixty-five, I estimated – he was too old to be of service. That notwithstanding, he'd remained here in the Protectorate, seeking what work he could, and as such was completely acclimatized. Even in the raging heat of a bone-dry February, his short, stooped form was shrouded in a double-caped overcoat, with a scruffy, moth-eaten cap hanging sideways from his head. He was a pucker-mouthed, pockmarked man, wizened and browned to the texture of a walnut. I'd attempted to engage him in banter, regaling him with a few military quips of my own, but his monosyllabic responses had not encouraged me to continue.

I adjusted my position for what seemed the eightieth time. It wasn't easy finding comfort on a wooden plank only thinly clad with ox-hide. I irritably addressed the yellowed copy of *The Times* I'd managed to acquire at Kalawi. It was dated December 1905, which meant it was only three months out of date – something of a blessing in this part of the world. But its front page made the usual gloomy reading.

SOUTH AFRICAN COMPENSATION BILL
TO REACH £10 MILLION

As a continued aftermath of the Boer War, the reconstruction process was costing the British taxpayer ever more money. Not only had the initial three million pounds allocated to cover the resettlement of Boers displaced from their farms in the Transvaal or the Orange Free State, or interned in those terrible prison camps, now been used up, another three million had been earmarked in the way of interest-free loans to provide landowners with the means to replace their crops and livestock; and now it seemed another two million was to be forwarded as compensation to neutral foreigners and native blacks who'd also suffered. As a prominent MP who had opposed the South African campaign said, who knew where it was going to end?

"What did you make of Meinertzhagen?" Holmes asked me, unexpectedly.

I shrugged. "I imagine he's the kind of chap who gets what he wants."

"Most certainly." Holmes relapsed into thought again, though my brief, rather inane observation couldn't have added much fuel to that process.

The Meinertzhagen in question was Colonel Richard Meinertzhagen, under whose remit protection of the new railway project fell. On first meeting him at Kalawi, I'd thought him a rather typical pillar of colonial officialdom; an army officer by name, but in reality occupying that mysterious middle-ground between soldier, bureaucrat and sportsman that one tended to find over here. He was tall, straight and handsome, civilized in all his manners, undoubtedly well bred, and yet an unbending kind of man, with hidden depths of toughness. We'd met him in one of the stable paddocks attached to the Kalawi barracks. He'd been clad for the outdoors in a staff officer's fawn tunic, jodhpurs and tall, well-polished riding boots, and was standing legs apart and crop in hand as he barked instructions at a group of boys engaged in breaking a succession of spirited horses. Almost inevitably, he'd seemed unflustered either by heat or dust.

"Is he the sort of man," Holmes said, "who would stay his hand if . . . say, if it came down to it?"

"Well, it *has* come down to it, hasn't it?" I replied. "And he didn't."

Holmes acknowledged this without speaking. I was referring to the events of five months previously, when twenty leaders of the Nandi nation, the native occupants of this region, having risen under arms against the railway's intrusion into their tribal homeland, had been lured to a peace negotiation by Meinertzhagen, only to be machine-gunned en masse. A single bullet fired from Meinertzhagen's own Mauser pistol had claimed the life of Koitalel Arap Samoei, the Nandi's supreme leader.

"That said," I ventured, "the publicity was hardly good. I doubt he'll want any further kerfuffle with these local chaps. Which I presume is why *we've* been called in."

"Well, of course." Holmes's tone implied surprise that I thought this a remarkable enough point to raise. "I've no doubt that very fact lies at the root of all these recent murders."

"Not this mysterious monster we've heard so many mumblings about?" I said.

"Oh, I wouldn't be sure of that, Watson. You've travelled the Empire to its limits. You don't need me to tell you how intimately involved with colonial politics monsters can be."

"Pleased to meet you, Mr Holmes . . . it's a great honour."

The overseer's name was Alex Butler, and again he was just what I'd expected a white settler to look like out here. He was deeply tanned, and though a head taller than either myself or Holmes, burly with it – to the point of being four-square. He had a bull neck, a jutting jaw and a thick black beard. His weatherworn khaki tunic fitted him tightly, though his sleeves were rolled back to the elbows, exposing ham-like forearms covered in brush-bristle hair. He wore a wide-brimmed bush hat, tied under his chin with a leather thong, and two criss-crossing bandolier belts filled with ammunition. What looked like a beaten-up Martini-Henry rifle was slung at his shoulder, twenty or so tiny notches etched into its butt, a huge acid scar on its lock. Despite his ferocious appearance, Butler grinned broadly, showing even rows of white-yellow teeth. He shook our hands with strength and vigour.

"Welcome to Hell's Gate – at least that's what the boys have been calling it, thanks to us losing so many souls as we approached. Its official name is the Tungo Gorge."

For the last twenty minutes, Jervis had driven us virtually alongside the railway, up a shallow gradient through a forest of whistling-thorn so closely interlaced that the setting sun had barely penetrated it. Above, the entangled spiny boughs had formed a low ceiling, which I fancied would claw the paint from the roof of any passing train. Immediately after that we'd entered the aforementioned gorge, a colossal crevice in the Nandi Hills running south–north, which we'd traversed half the length of before we'd finally encountered the construction crew.

It was well after dark, but in the infernal firelight of multiple torches, rugged walls of red rock rose sheer on either side. Only a slice of star-speckled African sky was visible overhead.

"Your boys don't seem to care for it very much," Holmes remarked, thinking on the groups of native men we'd seen headed east on foot, weighed down with tools and backpacks, as we'd finally reached the whistling-thorn. Those gathered around us now numbered only thirty or so, the African features of the Nandi alternating with the paler Asian faces of coolies imported from the Subcontinent. To a man, they looked tense, nervous, and yet their eyes shone with fascination at the sight of Holmes. His arrival had no doubt been trumpeted for several days.

"That's easy to explain, gentlemen," Butler said. "There were two more murders this evening. That makes sixteen in total in the last month."

"Are the corpses still lying where they were found?" Holmes asked with immediate interest.

"Afraid not, Mr Holmes, sir," Butler said. "Leave dead meat out here for long, and the scavengers are all over it. McTavish has assigned one of the tents at the far end of the works as a temporary mortuary."

"McTavish?" I asked.

"Our chief engineer, Dr Watson." Butler said this with a degree of disdain, which he quickly realized we both had noted. "Forgive me, gentlemen. Robert McTavish clearly knows how to build a railway ... but, well, I sometimes wonder if this is really the place for a minister's son."

"You think he'd rather be saving souls than hammering spikes?" Holmes asked.

Butler smiled to himself. "I wouldn't go that far, Mr Holmes, but there's much of East Africa still needs taming, and sometimes that requires a firm hand. Anyway, you must look at the bodies ... of course you must. But if you feel like resting first, that might be an idea, especially if you're planning on eating."

"No time for rest," Holmes said, indicating that I should take care of Jervis, who, once I'd paid him, stated flatly that he was heading home straight away and wouldn't be returning. Apparently supply carts arrived from Kalawi Junction on a two-weekly basis. When we were done, we'd "need to hitch a ride back with one of them".

"And who's to worry if we must first dawdle around here a few days," I said, in a huff, as Holmes and I, laden with bags, followed Butler along the remainder of the gorge on foot.

"I doubt there'll be much dawdling, Watson," Holmes replied curtly. "The fear in this place is palpable."

The few labourers remaining made space for us as we walked through. Some wore shorts or loincloths, though most were clad in loose-fitting rough-wear. Even though it was night-time the heat was unrelenting. Drab, dusty tents were everywhere, along with piles of raw materials, filling the gorge on both sides of the railway. There was also the construction train itself. This consisted of at least twenty open wagons loaded with metals and timbers. Though the locomotive was located at its rear, it was turned around, the idea being that it would push the train forward slowly as the tracks were laid, so the cargo was always delivered to the point of need most swiftly. As we passed the footplate, the driver and his mate, both Indians, remained onboard, watching us warily. One wore a Webley pistol in a harness, while the other clung to a two-handed spanner.

"They are not happy," I agreed.

"What do you know of the Nandi Bear, gentlemen?" Butler asked over his shoulder.

"Precisely nothing," Holmes replied. "Please feel free to enlighten us."

"In Nandi mythology, it's a great brute of a bear . . ."

"Of which there are no known wild species native to any part of Africa," Holmes said.

"Correct, Mr Holmes." Butler sounded impressed. "But even if wild bears were found in this part of the world, that'd be irrelevant. The Nandi Bear is a kind of spirit beast."

"A tribal totem?" I suggested.

"A bit more than that, Dr Watson. A guardian spirit. At least, in the Nandi belief."

We'd now reached the end of the train. Beyond it, the gorge was filled with opaque blackness. But initially our attention was drawn elsewhere – to a large tent on our right, standing separate from the others.

"It's this beast," Butler said, lifting the tent flap, "which, according to the rumours, is killing our workforce."

We entered and, by the light of a suspended lantern, saw two naked corpses lying on parallel tables. Both were local Africans: tall, well-built chaps. Butler told us the one on the right was Torokut, who had been the construction camp foreman; the other was Abasi, one of his labourers. Both had been terribly mutilated, their bodies slashed and torn from head to foot.

"I'm afraid you can't see the others," Butler said. "We've either sent those back or had them buried along the way. Local sensitivities and all that."

"Have only Nandi workers died?" Holmes asked, assessing the evidence in his usual unemotional way.

"No, Mr Holmes. We've lost several coolies too."

"So this is a message for everyone," Holmes said under his breath. "You say these two attacks occurred earlier this evening?"

"Shortly after eight. We've been falling behind badly. Torokut took it on himself to put in extra time. He and Abasi were working alone just a way up the gorge from here, trying to clear scrub that we'd torched during the day. A couple of the other boys heard their screams, but they were too frightened to investigate. I was down the other end of the train at the time. When I got there, it was all over."

"Well, these fellows *haven't* been murdered," I said, and I honestly believed that at the time. "They're clearly the victims of an animal attack. I'll need to make a proper examination to ascertain the exact cause of death, but at first glance there are any number of possibilities. Throats bitten, skulls crushed, evisceration of the lower abdomen. The signs are obvious."

"And that can't be unusual in a region like this?" Holmes said, posing it more as a question than a statement.

Butler shrugged. "Unusual enough for Colonel Meinertzhagen to have paid your fares all the way down the east coast and across the interior. Unusual enough for him to have sent to Mombasa for additional troop numbers, once they're available."

"You don't have lions and leopards in this part of the country?"

"We certainly do, Mr Holmes. The lion attacks at Tsavo impeded the mainline railway's construction for quite a few weeks. But there's no evidence there are big cats in Tungo Gorge. Or that they've attacked any of our men. Big cats kill to eat – even if disturbed, they drag their prey away afterward, or devour as much as they can on the spot. None of our casualties were in any way eaten. On top of that, I've farmed several thousand acres in the Lumbwa highlands for quite a few years now; I've guided prospectors, hunting parties, missionaries. I know my lions and leopards. I'm used to their spoor. I'd stake my life on there being no big cats around here at present. We even set lion traps when we were out on the plain, but caught nothing."

"Even so," I protested, "this is a dangerous place. I'd expect every man to carry his weapon of choice, and yet I only saw one of your chaps armed with a gun."

Butler shrugged again. "We have to be wary of that, Dr Watson. Some of the boys we know and trust are allowed guns. Mainly coolies. The problem is the Nandi. They were in open revolt only recently. To equip them with firearms would be a big risk. As an extra precaution, only I have keys to the ammunition store, which is the compartment right at the front of the train. No one else is allowed in there but me."

"Not even Engineer McTavish?" Holmes asked.

"McTavish has his own little kingdom – the explosives store."

"You'd think a king with explosives to hand would be a force to reckon with, eh?" came a feeble-sounding Scottish voice from the entrance to the tent. "Truth is, I feel anything but."

This was our introduction to Chief Engineer Robert McTavish. And a less than inspiring one it was. My immediate impression was of a fussy man who back in civilization would be preened and dapper, and yet here had allowed heat and exhaustion to get the better of him. Like Holmes and me, he was clad in tropical whites, though they were grubby and creased. He was of short, tubby stature, his paunch hanging over his belt buckle from an open waistcoat, his hair a greasy red-grey thatch, which hadn't seem a comb in days. The top of his lengthy nose was pinched by a lopsided pair of pince-nez, but perhaps the most startling thing about him was his half-beard. He had a full red moustache, but only one side of his lower face wore whiskers, though these were dabbled in lather, so he'd evidently been in the process of shaving. The other side of his jaw was clean, but cut in several places, blood dribbling freely onto his collar.

"Apologies for my ghoulish appearance, gentlemen," he added. "I only just heard you'd arrived. Plus—" he offered us a shaking hand "—I'm not as steady as I once was."

Formal introductions were made, at the end of which McTavish shook his head wearily. "So what do you think of our horror show?" he asked.

"I suspect an animal attack of some sort," I stated again.

McTavish smiled. "You think we've never experienced that kind of thing out here, Dr Watson? Trust me, I wish that was the answer, then we could snare and shoot the rogue beast respon-sible, just as they did on the Tsavo River."

Before I could reply, Holmes spun to face Butler. "You told me these men were heard screaming as they died. You didn't mention any animal sounds – no roars, snarls?"

"Nothing of that sort, Mr Holmes," Butler replied.

"Nothing," McTavish echoed disconsolately.

Holmes gave this brief thought. "And that's something we can't disregard, Watson, no matter how it may muddy our waters."

I had to admit, this odd fact needed explaining. In India, I'd known tiger attacks where the predator made no sound initially, but if it turned into a struggle, as this one surely must have with two victims involved, there were almost always growls. Besides, there are no tigers in Africa.

"Time we looked at the murder scene," Holmes said.

Butler took the lantern, and we moved out of the tent. Much of the camp now lay at our rear, but was largely deserted, the major-ity of the workforce having retreated to their beds. Alongside us stood the front three carriages of the train. The first was a rudi-mentary but fairly standard railway compartment, which, after its years of service on these sun-wizened hinterlands, looked under-standably weather-worn. According to McTavish, this one contained the works office. The second compartment was sealed, its few windows shuttered and bolted, the shutters bearing warn-ing insignia for explosives, though several of its air vents were fixed open with screws. The third and last, the ammunition store, bore no markings but this too was closed up except for several air vents, which had also been screwed open.

Our eyes had now attuned to the equatorial darkness, and we could see that north of this point, the railway line ended in dust. From here on the gorge was filled, initially with burnt and black-ened vegetation, but beyond that with lush, tangled thorns and deep grasses, some reaching to shoulder height and above. We advanced into this along a footpath flattened through the stub-ble. Butler led the way with lantern held high and rifle unslung. On reaching the clearing where the double attack had taken place, it immediately struck me as worrying how close it was to the main camp. Thirty yards from the end of the train, no more. Here, the burned foliage thickened up again, interspersed with patches untouched by flame, but it offered no real screen. It seemed that only superstitious terror had prevented the rest of the workforce coming to the doomed pair's aid.

On entry to the actual clearing, it didn't require Holmes's sharp eye to conclude that violence had been done. Both charred and fresh vegetation alike had been trampled and torn, the sun-baked earth kicked up in divots. And there were spatters of gore everywhere.

"So close to safety and neither one of two strong men was able to escape," he remarked, thinking aloud. "Our assailant came upon them with great speed and ferocity."

"Every death has been like this," McTavish said in the tone of a man at the end of his tether. "Some poor fellow out alone, or even two, usually after dusk, assaulted with brutal savagery, left dead in a minute or less. And yet our sentries never see anything, sometimes it's the sentries themselves whose lives are taken."

Holmes was no longer listening. He'd slipped on a glove and was in the act of pulling several yellowish strands from an acacia bush.

"Straw?" I said. "Is that important, do you think?"

He pursed his lips as he slid the strands into a small envelope that he'd taken from his pocket. "Look around, Watson, you'll find dried grass aplenty, thorns, twigs. But no fresh straw."

"I don't wish to spoil any burgeoning theory, Mr Holmes," McTavish said, "but it's likely the two victims brought that here themselves. Probably bedding from their sleep mats."

Holmes nodded, acknowledging this, but pocketed the envelope anyway.

For several seconds, we stood in silence, letting the heat seep through us. Even the usual trilling of night insects was absent, which was perhaps a little strange,

"It's the ultimate double threat, of course," Holmes eventually said. "This Nandi Bear story. Not just a fear the beast will kill you, but a fear it will kill you because you've trespassed on ancient tribal land. So if you fall victim to it, not only does your body perish in this life, your soul perishes in the next. Considerable motivation to abandon a job halfway through."

McTavish shook his head in despair. "But I can't understand why anyone would want to scuttle this project. We all stand to gain. It's economically and strategically vital for the whole Protectorate, it helps us defend the source of the Nile, opens up new markets to British goods in the African interior, will enable us to transport troops into the Sudan via Lake Rudolf . . ."

"Will the Nandi see the same advantages?" Holmes wondered. "They certainly didn't when the mainline was run through their lands to Lake Victoria."

"But they paid a price for that," McTavish argued. "They even lost their beloved leader."

"Which could be why they're now fighting you in this clandestine manner," I said, though personally I still felt we were dealing with an out-of-control animal here.

"Pretending there's a monster when in fact it's they themselves?" McTavish shrugged. "You're not alone in that suspicion. Butler thinks the same."

"It's plain as the horn on a rhino's nose," Butler chipped in from the far perimeter, where he was standing with his rifle across his chest.

"But you don't, Mr McTavish?" Holmes asked.

The engineer shrugged. "I've spoken with the Nandis at official level, Mr Holmes. I negotiated agreements with them. Not just in regard to this railway, but to the previous one too. Look, they're an honest set of fellows. Hard-working, affable among themselves—"

"But not with outsiders?"

McTavish looked irritated by that. "Not initially, no. When we first laid the parent line across their pasture, they called it the 'Iron Snake'. It was a gross intrusion into their privacy. But they've grown accustomed to the idea now. They can see the benefits, the trade—"

"But there could still be some latent hostility?" Holmes asked.

"That would be an understatement, Mr Holmes," Butler interrupted again. "The Nandi hate you." He hawked and spat. "They don't want us anywhere near this place."

"They don't *hate* us, Butler!" McTavish retorted. "If they did, their young men wouldn't have come and laboured for us. They can see the pay is good, and I think, after the death of Samoei, their elders have reached a decision that this kind of progress can't be halted."

"But discontented individuals remain?" Holmes persisted.

"Perhaps one or two," McTavish admitted. "Not the sort to wage this kind of guerrilla war. Murders like this were not the Nandi way before, so why should they be now, especially when the victims are their own people? No Britons have been killed, you'll notice. On top of that, when these crimes began, I had meetings with the Nandi members of our workforce, and they were sure their own kind couldn't be doing this. They say they'd have heard if there were any rumours."

Even though, as Holmes always instructed, I was determined to be open-minded about this, I felt a growing sympathy with McTavish's position. En route here, we'd passed several Nandi settlements, and had seen only pleasant folk leading quiet lives in grass-roofed villages. Their children had even come rushing out to see who we were, waving, calling to us.

Holmes didn't appear to share this view. Not entirely.

"It has struck you, McTavish, that by insisting our killer is the Nandi Bear – a mythical tribal monster – the Nandi might simply be resisting blame, refusing to face an unpalatable truth about themselves? Much as those Londoners did who insisted Jack the Ripper had to be a Jew or a Red Indian, or some drooling, wild-eyed maniac?"

"I think you're crediting the Nandi with too great a sophistication of feeling, Mr Holmes," McTavish replied with a sad smile. "They have a very simple view of right and wrong, good and evil – there are few in-betweens to them. Hence the ease with which Samoei was lured and killed by Meinertzhagen. But, whatever the truth of it, I don't see how we can carry on much longer. Every time there's a death out here – and Lord knows, there are deaths enough already – accidents, fever, scorpion bites – it's more than just a personal tragedy. With each actual murder, we lose a percentage of the workforce. They flee, terri-fied. You've seen for yourself, we have only a handful left now, and progress was moving at a snail's pace as it was. For the sake of the rest of us, we may have to abandon this place, maybe as soon as tomorrow."

"Abandon the whole railway?" Holmes asked, eyebrows arched above his lean face.

"Temporarily maybe, until we can recruit new labour else-where." McTavish shivered. "But Heaven help us, the whole thing is already running drastically over budget. A big delay would be a disaster in itself, and would reflect very badly on Meinertzhagen, who'd be absolutely furious."

"And would blame the Nandi no doubt," Holmes said. "And attack them again."

"Exactly. We'd have another war on our hands."

Holmes pondered this as he turned and headed back to the camp.

Before I followed, I surveyed the foliage to the north of us. It was lush, dark. Again the silence out there struck me as odd. Nocturnal insects in the Tropics are notorious for the racket they can raise. The only occasions in my experience when they fall silent is when something very dangerous lies close at hand.

"It seems obvious to me, Holmes," I whispered, as we headed back.

"Indeed?"

"There are still resentful Nandi, who are prepared to do anything they can to prevent this railway reaching completion."

"You forget one important detail, Watson – the teeth and claw-marks on the bodies. Were those the work of Nandi spears and machetes?"

"Couldn't the murderers have fabricated claw-like weapons? Fitted teeth into clubs, that sort of thing?"

"An interesting conjecture. But I've already decided to check the bodies again."

On return to the camp, McTavish climbed into the works office to provide us with any official paperwork that might be of use, while Butler said he would see about arranging sentries for that coming night. We took the opportunity to re-enter the mortuary.

The bodies lay as before, brutalized and dismembered. This time I stripped to my shirtsleeves and made a more thorough examination.

"Any obvious man-made injuries?" Holmes enquired. "Incisions, stab wounds?"

"There is *this*." I indicated something I'd noticed before but had thought irrelevant. "Among his other injuries, this chap Torokut has lost two toes from his left foot. The more I look at it, the more I think they were cleanly severed, as though with an edged implement."

Holmes drew his magnifying glass and crouched to examine the wound. "Unfortunately, Watson, I suspect this injury is somewhat older than the rest."

"Not much older surely? It's almost fresh."

"Yes, but it's been dabbed with iodine. In addition, there's a sticky residue along the sole of the foot, implying that some kind of gluey bandage was bound here."

"That's correct, gentlemen," McTavish said, entering the tent behind us. "Foreman Torokut was hurt yesterday morning when they were clearing ground cover. One of his co-workers accidentally caught his foot with a machete."

"Are you telling me this fellow lost a couple of toes, and you put him straight back to work?" I said.

"It was Torokut's own choice, I assure you," McTavish replied. "I suggested he take some time off. But, like I said earlier, their world is changing, particularly for their ambitious young men. He didn't want to languish without pay in the sick tent, and he's not the only one. A bush railway is a difficult and dangerous environment. A few weeks ago we had a man – a very stout fellow, Kiprono. He fell on his own pick, punched a hole in his groin, would you believe. It was a shocking wound. But he insisted on returning to work that same day, though he was hardly fit." McTavish shook his head. "By the following morning he was dead too."

"Blood poisoning?" Holmes asked

"Not a bit of it, Mr Holmes. This same beast – the Nandi Bear. But this was a few weeks ago, as I say. The latrines were still outside the camp. It was sometime after midnight, and Kiprono limped out there alone. The thing took him while he was relieving himself. Poor devil. Anyway . . ." McTavish knuckled at his brow. "I'm for bed now. It's early, I know. I hope you'll forgive me, but it's been another terrible day and I need to sleep if I'm to resolve this problem satisfactorily tomorrow. I sincerely hope that won't mean you've travelled all this way for nothing, gentlemen, but with these latest deaths I don't see how we have any choice."

We accompanied McTavish as he walked through the camp, elaborating as he did on the other murders and handing us documentation to this effect – official reports, witness statements and the like. By now, most of the campfires were dying and, as we'd seen earlier, the bulk of the workers were inside their tents. McTavish's own quarters were several hundred yards along, but before we reached this point, we passed the cook tent, where Butler was briefing two nervous-looking coolies, both armed with breech-loading shotguns.

"We place one chap at either end of the train," Butler explained, after the Indians had set off to take up their night-time posts. "One advantage of camping in a gorge: the enemy's angles of attack are limited."

"Yet still he comes," Holmes said, unimpressed by this simple logic. Apparently, two other men had died in the gorge prior to Torokut and his work-mate. The killings hadn't just happened out on the plain.

"We do what we can, Mr Holmes," Butler replied. "With so few boys remaining, we can't put entire gangs out on watch. There'd be no one to work during the day."

"Might we see the tent belonging to the unfortunate Torokut?" Holmes asked.

Butler looked surprised. "You don't want to eat first? It's been a long day, surely?"

I did, as it happened, so first we went into the cook tent, where we were treated to a rather marvellous curry. After that, Butler escorted us through the camp to the billet where the unfortunate Torokut and the other victim, Abasi, had lodged. There wasn't a great deal of space, so Butler remained outside while we entered – only to find that it contained very little: tools, some rough clothing (neatly folded), a few pathetic personal belongings, two simple foldaway truckle beds made from wooden frames with ox-hide strips and, crammed into a corner as though awaiting disposal, a crumpled heap of deeply bloodied bandages.

"That foot wound must've bled profusely," I remarked.

"And still he went back on the job," Holmes said. "McTavish is right, if some of these people are so dedicated to working with the railway company, is it truly conceivable that others among them would oppose it with criminal violence?"

"Society takes all sorts, Holmes, even simple rural societies like this."

"And yet the Nandi in the workforce don't think this could be the case. Is there anyone better placed than men like those to make such a judgement?"

"More questions here than answers, Holmes, that's for sure," I said.

"I quite agree."

"Of course, if McTavish reaches the decision I suspect he will tomorrow morning, this investigation will have finished before it's even begun."

Holmes seemed unperturbed by that. "My dear Watson, the murders may not yet have finished, let alone the investigation."

That night, we were allocated a tent close to the centre of the train. We were both bone-tired, but as I suspected, sleep was to prove elusive. It wasn't just the intense heat; those wood and leather truckle beds were damnably uncomfortable. Unable to rest, we spent a slavish extra hour perusing the documents McTavish had given us, but to my eye at least they contained little of value

"Well," I grunted, after we'd extinguished our lamp for the second time, "we haven't learned much so far."

"On the contrary, Watson, we've learned a great deal." Holmes reclined on his bed, but, from the dim firelight outside, I saw that he'd taken the envelope from his pocket and was re-examining it. "Wherever our assailant lurks, there is fresh straw."

"The straw bedding," I replied.

"Is there any straw bedding in here?"

I felt at the truckle bed on which I was lying: hard-wearing wood and ox-hide, but no straw, no bedding. "Well, it might not be the same in every tent."

"Granted, but it *was* in the tent belonging to the two most recent victims. I'd imagine these foldaway items are the easiest kinds of beds to transport, and railway construction crews are forever on the move."

"That means McTavish lied to us," I said.

"Or wasn't thinking straight. He's clearly a man on the verge of nervous exhaustion."

"Also, he seems . . . well, he seemed a trifle guilty, I'd say."

"How astute of you to notice, Watson."

"He *is* a minister's son, I suppose."

"And perhaps is torn about his duty," Holmes added. "Wondering if the imposition of the British way on these people is actually good for them."

"You think that may have unbalanced him somehow?" I asked.

"You mean is he a suspect? No. But I can't help wondering if this torment has blinded him to the nature of the opponent we're facing."

"You suspect the Nandi then?"

Holmes pondered his. "Were it not for the Nandi fatalities suffered here, I would leap to that conclusion. In the meantime, I'd prefer to sleep on it. McTavish isn't the only chap who's tired."

But, as it would transpire, neither we nor the worn-out Scottish engineer would get any kind of rest that night. Only two hours later, we were woken by a frenzied shrieking and shouting. I'd only slept lightly, and jumped up with such force that I struck my head on the canvas. Of course, Holmes was already out and through the tent flap. I staggered outside after him.

To our left, by the fading glow of the campfire embers, other men were emerging from tents, half naked, fuddled with sleep. It was the same on the right, with one additional detail – on this side, the men fell back in horror from a central figure, which stumbled in our direction from about forty yards away.

"Great Heavens," I breathed. "McTavish!"

As we dashed forward, we were overtaken from behind by Butler, minus hat and tunic, but with rifle in hand and heavy boots clumping the ground.

"Robert!" he bellowed. "*In God's name!*"

But even Butler came to a sliding halt when the bloodied shape of McTavish slumped to his knees in front of us, and then fell face first in the dust. The rest of the workforce crowded in. It was all Holmes, Butler and I could do to fight our way through. We turned McTavish over, to general gasps. His face had been gouged to ruin by what must have been a monstrous set of claws, and his throat slashed repeatedly. His torn shirt revealed ribs laid bare by multiple lacerations.

"He's dead," I said dully, after dropping to my knees and, rather pointlessly it seemed – no man could have survived those wounds – checking for vital signs.

Butler rose to his feet, his face a livid purple. Frothing into his beard, he turned his Martini-Henry on the gathered labourers, who slowly retreated.

"Where did this happen?" he demanded. "*Damn it, one of you must have seen!*"

"Easy, Butler," I cautioned him.

"Devil take you, Watson, how am I supposed to react?"

As one, the frightened labourers shook their heads.

"You see!" he roared. "Right in the midst of us! And this lot quivering in their tents like terrified rabbits. Not one of them saw a thing ... well, I don't believe that. One of these damn cowards surely saw what happened!"

"We *know* what happened," Holmes interjected. "The same assailant that killed Torokut and the others has now killed Robert McTavish. We're all on the same side here, Butler."

"Robert was too understanding with these blasted Nandis!" Butler retorted. "That was his main mistake. His job here was to build a railway! Nothing else! And damn them and their kind to hell in a hand basket if they objected!"

"Think straight, Butler," I urged him. "These chaps wouldn't be here working for you if this was their true face."

"Well, we're running now," Butler said, still shaking with rage. "That's all there is to it. This has done for us. But I'm damn well not leaving here until I've found out who's responsible for *this*! Someone bring me those damn sentries! If they were asleep, I'll thrash the living hides off the pair of them."

Happy to send the blame elsewhere, the rest of the workforce were quick to grab the two coolies who'd supposedly been on guard duty, disarm them and hustle them forward, forcing them to their knees – at which point Butler questioned them viciously, repeatedly threatening them with his rifle. I watched uneasily, while Holmes held some more discreet enquiries of his own. At first he examined McTavish's tent, which hung in blood-soaked ribbons, and then circled among the frightened onlookers, speaking quietly with those who understood English.

The sentries assured everyone they were innocent of wrongdoing, which Butler dismissed out of hand.

"At least consider that they may be telling the truth," I said.

"Don't be a fool, Watson. One had the north end of the train, one had the south. A narrow field of vision by any standards. They claim they didn't sleep, but how could that be if someone or something slunk past without their noticing?"

"Because the attack didn't come from either end of the train," Holmes said.

He now stepped forward in the company of two other labourers. One was a very aged Nandi, white-haired and white-bearded, who I'd noticed assisting in the cook tent earlier. He was clad in a knee-length shift and leaning on a twisted stick. He

ambled forward with the assistance of a taller, much younger
Nandi dressed only in shorts.

"And what's this?" Butler snorted.

"A witness," Holmes said.

There was an amazed muttering.

Butler's eyes flicked from the old Nandi to the young, and
back again. "You saw something?"

Slowly, uncertainly, the old fellow commenced a rambling,
low-voiced monologue, which I could make neither head nor
tail of because it was in the complex Nandi tongue.

Butler's harsh voice cut across him. "Enough gibberish! Can
anyone here translate?" He turned to the younger one. "You . . .
who is this imbecile?"

"My father, *bwana*," the young Nandi replied in faltering
English.

"What's he saying?"

"He say, half-hour ago, he not sleep. He hear 'bang'."

"Bang?" Butler said. "You mean like a gun?"

The young man queried his father, who responded by shaking his head.

"He say, something hit wood."

"Like a thud or bump, you mean?"

The younger Nandi nodded. "He think strange. He come out.
See nothing. Eyes . . . not so good. Fires low."

I glanced around. Only now were the campfires being
restoked. Again, they cast that wavering hellish light up the
rugged canyon walls.

"He see," the young Nandi added. "On . . . train."

"On the train?" Butler replied. "What do you mean?"

The young Nandi pointed to the train roof.

Butler looked incredulous. "On the roof?"

"Yes, *bwana*."

"Something jumped down onto the train roof?" I said, equally
astonished. Overhead, the walls of the gorge rose tier upon tier
into fire-tinged darkness. "That'd be a devil of a leap for any
living creature."

"*What* jumped?" Butler asked impatiently.

This time the old man lowered his head, and shook it.

"Well?"

The young Nandi asked the question again, but, as before, the old man refused to answer.

"My dear fellow," Holmes said, stepping forward, "if you're too frightened to give a name to this thing you saw, perhaps you could tell us whereabouts you saw it? Which part of the train?"

Somewhat reluctantly, the old one turned and pointed.

"The north end of the train?" Holmes said. "Where the explosives and ammunition trucks are?"

The young Nandi nodded, explained that this was close to where his father's tent was located.

"Good God!" Butler shouted, dashing down there to check those two vital compartments had not been compromised. He returned just as quickly, assuring us they were still sealed, and then resumed his interrogation.

"No more of this stupid native superstition," he barked at the old man. "You need to tell us what you saw. We have to know what we're dealing with here."

Still the old man refused, but now Holmes approached his son.

"Young man, you should know that we are leaving this cursed place as soon as first light tomorrow." Holmes glanced for confirmation at Butler, who sullenly nodded. "By mid-morning, you and your and father will be far from here. This thing will not be able to harm either of you. But it's important he speaks to us now. Or other Nandi may come here at a later date, and they won't know the danger." He indicated McTavish's mangled corpse. "Does your father want more of his people to die like this?"

Again the young man relayed the message, and this time, reluctantly, his father responded.

"He say . . ." The young man struggled to find the words. "Is . . . forbidden to say. But he will draw."

Brief confusion reigned, before Holmes ushered everyone back. The old man leaned down and, with the end of his walking stick, inscribed a shape in the dust.

It was a crude depiction of an animal, something on all fours, with powerful front shoulders, a sloped back and long, muscular forelimbs. Its head was flat and square, and its mouth gaped, exposing huge incisors. Unmistakably, it was a carnivore, and a large specimen at that, because while his father was drawing, the young Nandi explained that it was "more big than two men".

I expected Butler to scoff, to resume shouting. But for the first time that night the overseer himself seemed lost for words. If it was possible to tell in that firelight, he even blanched.

"The Nandi Bear, I presume?" Holmes said.

Butler chewed his lip. "Every description I've ever heard, every wall and cave painting I've seen . . . that's exactly what it looks like."

He turned his narrowed gaze on the old Nandi, and was about to speak further, maybe to advise him that if this turned out to be a lie, he could be arrested as a conspirator in these crimes, but the rest of the crew had now had a chance to absorb the image – an apparent confirmation of all their worst fears – and a gabble of panic-stricken voices erupted. Coolie and Nandi alike began scrambling back and forth, shoving each other aside, rushing to their tents.

Only three deafening gunshots, fired into the air from Butler's Martini-Henry, brought them to order.

"Where do you think you're running to?" he shouted, address-ing their rows of sweat-shiny faces. "It's twenty miles to the near-est village, and sixty miles to Kalawi Junction. You think you'll make it that distance in the dark, with this thing, whatever it is, on your tail? Listen, it's three hours to sun-up, at which point we will leave this place together, on the construction train. You men can ride on the cargo wagons. Nothing will assail you there."

Mutters and mumbles followed this, and nods of frantic agreement.

"Very well," Butler said. "But we do this in calm, sensible fashion. We pack up as if moving on to the next camp, and leave nothing behind of value."

The throng dispersed reasonably quietly, each man heading off to pack his personal equipment. This seemed a good plan even to my ears, but the lack of a rational explanation was more than frustrating. It only surprised me that Holmes didn't appear to feel the same way.

He lit another cigarette and smoked as he watched them go about their business.

"My apologies, gentlemen," Butler said, approaching us. "I hope Colonel Meinertzhagen paid your fee in advance. It seems you've wasted your time out here."

"Butler," I said, "you're surely not giving credence to this Nandi Bear nonsense?"

"Dr Watson, those canyon walls are over a hundred feet high. Nothing, neither man nor animal, could have jumped down from up there without killing itself."

"A spirit-bear might," Holmes said.

Butler eyed him curiously. "I don't believe in ghosts and demons, Mr Holmes."

"Neither do I," Holmes replied.

"But what you and I believe is not the issue here." Butler shrugged with regret. He walked over to McTavish's body and sighed. "Whatever this thing is, whether it's the work of the Nandi, which I still suspect, or some other saboteur, there are things here beyond our control. In any case, as I say, without the brains of our operation, we've no choice. We *must* turn back."

Holmes nodded.

Butler slung his rifle over his shoulder and, calling a couple of the boys over, supervised the removal of the engineer's body to the works office. He turned back to us.

"There are no actual living quarters on the train – the boys are on the wagons, as I said, and I'll bunk in the ammunition truck, but for you the office will at least be comfortable. Plus you'll have privacy. Aside from Robert, of course. I don't like asking you to ride for an entire day in the company of the dead, but it's needs must, I'm afraid."

"The living, in my experience, are infinitely more troublesome than the dead," Holmes replied.

Butler nodded, and strode away. We, too, went to gather our things.

"I'll admit I'm confounded by this," I said, as we entered our tent. "But one thing's clear. If the failure of this railway doesn't work to turn Meinertzhagen and his paymasters against the Nandi people, the death of Robert McTavish certainly will."

"Without question," Holmes replied. "It amounts to a declaration of war. Which is exactly what the murderer wants. And which is also the reason we too must head back."

"You have a theory . . .?"

"Later, Watson. When we're on the train. Even canvas walls have ears."

One and a half hours later, Holmes and I were ensconced in the office, where there was now a melancholy air. The long, narrow desk was strewn with paperwork, which the unfortunate McTavish would never again need. The same applied to the charts and diagrams on the walls, and the various books and hand tools littering the surrounding shelves. If nothing else, the deceased engineer's decanter of Armagnac was something Holmes and I could put to use – and we did, purely for medicinal reasons of course. We were both heavy-limbed with fatigue, and yet there was no possibility of sleep.

In that regard, the presence of McTavish's corpse did not help. It was laid on a trestle in the corner, and with its shroud-like wrappings blotched through with blood, was hardly a pleasant sight. On top of this, as the heat of the day increased, it would likely become pungent, especially in the enclosed carriage. But Holmes had already put this from his mind. He sat by the window, lifted the blind and gazed along the firelit gorge. The eastern strip of sky was slowly turning violet. Shouting voices could be heard further down the train as the last of the workforce climbed aboard with their packs and bundles.

The south door to the office, the one connecting with the open-topped wagons, was closed and locked, so it was through the north door that Butler now entered. His rifle was still at his shoulder, but he'd removed his hat and was dabbing at his sweaty face with a cloth. Even Butler – a solid, sun-hardened fellow if ever there was one – looked harrowed by these events.

"We're done at last," he said. "The locomotive will be running backwards of course, so it'll be a slow journey. But I'm all in anyway, and am going to try to sleep. You gentlemen should do the same. By the time we wake up, we'll be at Kalawi Junction. And then, I fear, our problems will really begin."

Holmes nodded, and Butler withdrew, closing the door behind him.

The train juddered to life, commencing a slow crawl backwards, though over several minutes it gradually accelerated to a respectable thirty or so miles an hour, swaying and rocking along the new-laid rails.

"Quite the actor," Holmes commented.

"Who?" I enquired.

He remained glued to the window. "Butler, of course."

"Butler? I don't follow."

Almost unconsciously, Holmes filched a cigarette from his silver case. "Nice bit of melodrama he put on back there, I thought."

"Melodrama?"

"That terrible outpouring of anger and grief for the loss of his friend, whose very name he sneered at when first we arrived here."

I was bemused. "You think he was pretending?"

"Maybe, maybe not." Holmes lit his cigarette and exhaled a stream of smoke. "But do you imagine they'd be close friends, a minister's son with clear liberal tendencies, and a hardy bushranger? We certainly didn't see much sign of it before."

"We haven't been here very long, Holmes."

"But do you consider it likely, Watson?"

"Whether I do or don't, that hardly proves anything."

"Not on its own, I grant you. But let's look at the larger picture." He pondered for a second, blowing out more smoke. "Mysterious and violent deaths have occurred on this railway for the last month or so, in short, ever since it entered the lands belonging to the Nandi people. All the victims appeared to have fallen prey to a vicious animal."

"Correct."

"Discounting the mythical Nandi Bear, we are left with several possibilities. Either the beast responsible, whatever it is, was simply defending its own territory, which is unlikely, as the work party always moved on to territories new within a few days. Or it followed the work party, which is also unlikely, as many miles have been covered since the first death, and no wild animal would stray over so vast a distance? Not easily."

"A predator might," I countered. "If it thought it had found an easy food source."

"And yet none of those killed were even partially eaten."

"That is a problem," I conceded.

"In which case, we must consider the third possibility – that we are not, in fact, dealing with a wild animal at all."

"So, again it comes down to the Nandi?"

"Not necessarily. We've already noted how Nandi men have died too, while McTavish advised us that wiser heads in the Nandi tribe have realized further resistance may be futile."

"We said it before, Holmes, rogue elements . . .?"

"And as McTavish said before, Watson, those Nandi friendly to us would surely know about that, and would bring it to our attention if it were the case, certainly they'd do that rather than blame some tribal demon. However, let us focus on our friend Butler, if that is his real name."

"His *real* name?"

"Do we know it's his real name, Watson? Do we know *anything* about him?"

"Only that he works for Meinertzhagen . . ."

"As do hundreds of other men, all swiftly recruited, no doubt, when contracts were signed for the construction of this railway. Do you imagine the good colonel checked all their antecedents?"

Again, I was lost. But now Holmes was in full flow.

"It seems likely, does it not, that for a killer to most effectively strike again and again at this train's workforce, he would actually be travelling with it? He can hardly have travelled on foot."

"Yes, but . . ."

"Hear me out, Watson. Butler has not been entirely truthful with us, so why would he have been truthful with Meinertzhagen. For example, he claims to have farmed this region for many years. And yet he couldn't translate a word the old Nandi man said to us."

I shrugged. "It's not inconceivable that he hasn't learned the language."

"'The Nandi hate *you*'. Those where his exact words at the scene of the double murder. Not 'the Nandi hate *us*' . . . they hate *you*'. Then he corrected himself and added: 'They don't want *us* anywhere near this place.'"

"A slip of the tongue?" I suggested.

"Or an unguarded moment, one I find rather telling. It indicates that Butler does not consider himself one of us, as in one of us British."

"Well . . ." I shrugged again. "These colonials, you know . . ."

"But we already suspect that he isn't a local man. And if that's the case, and he isn't one of us either, what exactly is he?"

"By his accent he's a fully naturalized Anglo-African. I mean . . .' A new thought left me thunderstruck. "Good grief, Holmes, you don't think he could be a Boer?"

Holmes regarded me with a pensive smile. "It isn't implausible."

"If so, he's a very long way from home."

"So are we, Watson. So was McTavish."

"But, Holmes, the South African issues are settled . . ."

"To the satisfaction of some. Maybe not all."

"This is all supposition, surely?"

"Not quite, Watson. You observed the notches on Butler's rifle. I counted at least twenty."

I had, as I've already mentioned. Personally, I'd always considered it a distasteful practice as it appeared to celebrate the act of killing. It was a typical affectation of bushrangers and other border ruffians, and yet, on reflection, even by those standards twenty notches seemed rather excessive.

"Quite a scorecard," Holmes added, "for a supposed civilian. On which subject, if you look at Butler's rifle, you'll actually notice that it isn't a standard Martini-Henry of the sort produced in the Royal Small Arms Factory at Enfield."

"So . . . it's an imitation?"

"More than that, Watson. It's a Peabody-Martini-Henry, of the type made by the Americans and purchased by the Turks, many of which, as you know, found their way to the Boer Republics. I fancy the acid burn on the lock is all that remains of a telltale crest. The Ottoman star and crescent perhaps?"

"By Jove, Holmes," I said. "This blaggard _is_ a Boer. But couldn't he just be . . . well, a good Boer?"

"I imagine they all consider themselves good, Watson. The question is why would he be conducting murder and sabotage?"

I shook my head. "It makes no sense. Especially when the British government's in the process of authorizing enormous compensation payments."

"Revenge is often irrational," Holmes replied. "What I mean is, how can atrocities like this, terrible to those present yet minor in the great sweep of things, really be of gain to a foe of the British Empire?"

"Well . . . we know the costs of the Ugandan Railway have spiralled. But it's seen as essential work."

"Exactly," Holmes said. "As Engineer McTavish said, the project _must_ continue. The money will need to be found, no matter how crippling the burden on the Treasury. But this won't reflect well on Colonel Meinertzhagen. It will be another disaster on _his_ watch."

"He'll attack the Nandi again," I said. "We know he's sending for extra troops. Perhaps this time he'll do a real job of it. Not just kill their leaders but incarcerate their warriors in prison camps, like those in South Africa."

"And anti-British feeling abroad will be further outraged," Holmes said. "British brutality overseas will draw ever greater criticism, further alienating her from friends and allies."

For a brief time, I was dazed. Yet much of this was conjecture. And there were holes in it.

"There's a clear motive," I said. "But if it *is* Butler who's committing these crimes, how does that explain their animalistic nature?"

"If Butler was a Boer commando, Watson, he'll have fought tough campaigns on arduous landscapes, and will have much experience of hand-to-hand killing."

"So are we disregarding everything the old Nandi told us? About the figure jumping down onto the roof?"

"On the contrary, Watson." Holmes removed his homburg and his grimy white jacket, then took the Webley revolver from his holster and checked it was fully loaded. "I disregard nothing."

"But what about that terrible shape he saw?"

"As his son informed us, the old man's eyesight is poor." Holmes crossed the compartment, and commenced a quick, cursory examination of McTavish's desk, pulling out various drawers. "In addition, the campfires were low. Would you rely on such a witness testimony in a court of law back home?"

I still struggled with this. "Whoever our killer is, he ... *it* attacked with terrifying speed. More than could be explained by Butler's commando experience in the Boer Army. It brutalized McTavish to death as he lay in bed, and was gone before anyone could intervene. It simply vanished."

"It didn't simply vanish, because such a thing is impossible," Holmes said. "And no one tried to intervene because of superstition. The moment they heard McTavish scream, they hung back in their tents, terrified. The Nandi Bear, or at least the Nandi Bear legend, was responsible for that much."

This at least made sense. With the rest of the boys so frightened, the assailant may well have had time to leave McTavish's quarters and duck away – maybe to the rear of the tents, skirting the canyon wall as he slipped back through the shadows. "But, Holmes, there is still the question of those terrible wounds, which no man could have inflicted."

Holmes glanced from the window. The walls of Hell's Gate gorge rolled past, dappled orange-yellow by the rising sun. "This case is full of deceptions, Watson. Nothing is what it seems. Seeing isn't always believing. A man can murder without inflicting *any* wounds."

"I don't understand."

"Understand this, stored ammunition does not need to be ventilated the way stored explosives do."

"Of course, but—"

"What time do you make it?"

I checked my watch. "Almost seven."

"Approximately one hour since Butler turned in."

"Agreed," I said.

Holmes nodded. "The time is now. Further delay will serve us nothing."

I stood up and drew my own revolver. "Hopefully, he'll already be asleep. We can take him into custody without a shot being fired."

"He won't be asleep, Watson. If Butler is who we suspect, he's a very resourceful and dangerous man. On top of that, he isn't here alone."

Before I could query him further on this, Holmes strode to the north door, opened it and stepped out onto the running board. Warm, gritty wind swirled around us as we peered across the narrow gap above the couplings to the door to the explosives store. I fully expected that to be locked, but Holmes produced a key, which I realized he'd taken from McTavish's desk.

"I anticipate no opposition in this next compartment, Watson," he said, his voice raised above the din of the wheels. "Keep your pistol drawn, but exercise caution. I've no desire to get blown to kingdom come."

"Erm . . . no," I agreed, bringing the weapon to my shoulder, careful to unhook my finger from the trigger.

That next compartment was a dim, narrow space, rendered narrower still by the crates stacked along either side of us. I wasn't sure what explosives McTavish had used, or how volatile they might be, but with the constant swaying and jolting of the train, it was a relief to see that most were caged as well as boxed. We reached the north end of the compartment safely. Holmes stopped in front of the door. Now he spoke quietly.

"It's rare I offer advice such as this, Watson, but today it might be a case of shooting first and asking questions later."

I objected immediately, pointing out that the sum total of our suspicions against Butler were, in police terms, circumstantial at best.

Holmes waved this aside. "When we enter the ammunition truck, we will know where we and Butler stand. As I say, be ready to open fire instantly. If so, shoot straight and clean. Our lives may depend on it."

He stepped over onto the opposite running board, and I with him. More heat and wind blew around us. The next door connected with the ammunition truck, the final compartment on the train. Here, Holmes levelled his revolver on the lock.

"You sure you want to do that, Mr Holmes?"

The pair of us jumped with fright. We turned our faces upward, but Butler, perched on the edge of the compartment roof, already had his rifle to his shoulder and was training it firmly down at us, at Holmes in particular. His big machete knife was fastened into its sheath, and he'd donned his bush hat again; despite the shade of its brim, his strong white teeth stood out in a V-shaped grin.

"Keep your guns where I can see 'em," he said. "Either of you makes a sudden move, Holmes is a dead man."

We stood rigid, aside from the swaying motion of the train, our pistols clearly visible.

"That's it . . . now release them," he said. "Just let them go."

With no option, we dropped our firearms; they clattered down through the couplings and vanished. Butler kept his sights locked firmly on Holmes.

"Interesting thought, eh?" he said. "If I fire on you now, Holmes, could my bullet travel the full length of you and still pack enough punch to sever the chain holding these carriages together? If so, it'd save me the trouble of uncoupling them manually."

We regarded him in silence as he climbed down the ladder alongside us, the rifle perfectly balanced in the crook of his arm. From his manner alone, we had no doubt he could operate the weapon single-handed.

"You see," he explained, "this ammunition truck can never reach Kalawi Junction." His boots thudded onto the running board alongside us. "But I suspect you already know that."

"It would make sense," Holmes said coolly.

"What . . . you intend to leave it out here?" I stammered. "What is this? Are you trying to arm the Nandi?"

Butler sniggered. "Why would I? The Nandi don't want to fight."

"But all along, you've been insisting—"

"They'd still find it, of course," Holmes said, addressing me, though his gaze was fixed on Butler. "There'd be no reason for them not to take advantage."

"Good Lord!" I replied. "Then it would *look* as if they want to fight. It might look as if they'd attacked the train themselves."

Butler sniggered again. "You'll make a detective of him yet, Mr Holmes."

Holmes shook his head. "Sadly, Watson, I fear this will be as much about what *doesn't* reach Kalawi, as what *does* get left out here."

"Ah," I said. "Us, you mean?"

"That will be part of it—" he replied.

"Enough talking, gentlemen," Butler interrupted. "Up you go." He gestured with his rifle. "On top of the ammo truck. You first, Watson."

We scrambled in single file up the ladder. On the roof, we were neither of us as surefooted as Butler, who'd clearly practised this before. We tottered forward with arms outstretched, convinced we were about to overbalance. Hot, dusty wind gusted over us even more fiercely, though we weren't even out of the gorge as yet. Our captor followed at a crouch, rifle levelled on our backs. When we'd made it perhaps twenty yards, almost halfway along the roof, he called us to a halt.

"Turn around, gentlemen," he said.

We did so.

"This is absurd, man!" I shouted back at him. "Utterly pointless. Even a Boer must get tired of revenge at some point."

"As you're *not* a Boer, Dr Watson, how could you know?"

"You think we British haven't suffered in war?" I demanded.

"If so, it doesn't stop you starting more wars. Not that I've any reason to disbelieve you personally. But no matter, in a few minutes we'll be in the whistling-thorn, and all your pain will end."

I suddenly remembered the dense thickets of thorny trees that overarched the train's roof shortly before the entry to the gorge. "We'll be swept to our deaths, is that the plan?"

"Of course, and when they find your torn, twisted bodies, they'll think it further work of the Nandi Bear. I mean, who here will say different?"

"And you're so sure we'll die?" Holmes wondered. "You won't be able to get off to check."

"Oh, you'll die, Mr Holmes. If not from the fall, from what happens next. It's sixty miles to Kalawi Junction. You'll have no water, no food, and most likely you'll both be injured. If the sun doesn't finish you, the vultures and hyenas will. But even then it'll be a quicker death than that endured by my mother and sister in Bloemfontein concentration camp."

"This won't bring them back, Butler," I said.

"Brandt, please. That's my real name – Ernst Brandt."

"Of course it is," Holmes said. "You'd need a fake English name to enlist in Meinertzhagen's service."

"I have a full set of fake English credentials, Mr Holmes. It would amaze you how thoroughly corrupt your imperialist bureaucracy can be."

"I assure you it wouldn't."

"And soon, I understand, there'll be even more money with which to bribe your greedy, self-interested officials."

"That compensation comes from the British public," I asserted heatedly. "Who were appalled by the treatment of your people."

"How generous of them," he retorted. "As they are waited on at breakfast in their Hyde Park addresses. But it isn't Britain's public I'm at war with, Dr Watson. It's Britain's government, her military, her industrialists, her economic powerhouse – all those elements that drive Britain's endless conquests."

"You think that by starting another war between the British and the Nandi that will harm those interests?" I scoffed.

"That isn't the war he's trying to start, Watson," Holmes answered.

Butler, or Brandt as his name apparently was, laughed. "You really are as astute as they say, Holmes. Watson, you don't recall how close the German Empire came to intervening during your country's South African adventure?"

"But they didn't intervene," I replied brashly, yet a slow, terrible understanding was dawning on me. The Germans had been particularly vociferous in their condemnation of Britain's South African policy – to the point of open belligerence. Still, I tried to brazen it out. "If they didn't support the Boers, you think they'll support the Nandi?"

"The difference is," Holmes said, "here in East Africa, the German Empire has real and expanding interests."

"Exactly right, Holmes," Brandt said. "To answer your question, Watson, no, I don't think this new war in East Africa will embroil the German Empire. Not on its own. But you need to face facts. A war between Great Britain and Germany is coming soon, for all sorts of reasons. And if I've contributed just one of them, I'll go to my grave a happier man."

"And unfortunately," Holmes said, "go to your grave is what you now must do. Come, Watson, now we know exactly what's what, the game's not just afoot, it's right in front of us."

He lurched forward towards Butler, who levelled the rifle again.

"Easy, Holmes," I cautioned. "He has the advantage."

"An advantage he won't use," Holmes replied with confidence. "Bullet-riddled bodies are no use to him. Even Meinertzhagen will realize those aren't the work of the Nandi or their spirit bear, especially when his experts identify a Peabody rifle as the culprit. I rather suspect there's only one of those in use along this section of branch line."

"But Holmes, if he has to shoot . . ."

"Oh, if he *has* to, yes, but he's a big chap. I'm sure he'll fancy his chances first."

"Bloody *idioot!*" Brandt snarled, slipping again into Afrikaans.

Instead of firing on us, he swung his rifle like a club. Holmes ducked and caught him with two solid punches to the body. Brandt was a doughty sort – he only slightly tottered, but now I came in too. Despite my military days, I was less of a pugilist than Holmes, who'd been an excellent boxer in his youth. However, Brandt didn't wish to lose his rifle, and so took half a moment to loop its belt back over his shoulder, which afforded me a chance to throw my first punch. I caught him smartly on the jaw. Holmes threw a third, pounding his kidneys. Brandt twisted in pain, but lashed at me with a boot, and struck at Holmes with a heavy backhand. I caught my blow on the thigh. Holmes evaded again, though this allowed Brandt to draw his machete, a foot of gleaming, razor-edged steel.

"Holmes!" I shouted.

"I see it, Watson!" he replied.

We circled him, but as the train jolted, all three of us staggered. For a second, Holmes was teetering on the very edge, his heels in mid-air. He righted himself in time to avoid a slashing blow from the knife. I feinted with my left and threw a right. Brandt blocked it with his meaty forearm, and drove the knife at my throat. I was able to catch his wrist, but his strength bore me backward, and suddenly I was at the other edge of the roof, arching over. All Brandt needed to do was push me and I'd go crashing to my death, but I clutched onto his sleeve, and now Holmes grappled with him from the side. Brandt spun back, his elbow caught Holmes a hefty wallop in the side of the head – Holmes slumped down onto his thigh. As Brandt turned to face him, I leapt onto his back.

"Damn you, Watson!" Brandt growled.

Toppling forward, he flipped me over his shoulder. I landed heavily, my spine slamming the sun-dried timbers. Brandt sagged briefly to one knee, but before he could stand again, Holmes struck his wrist with a sharp, flat-handed chop. Brandt's hand opened in a spasm, and the machete clattered loose. Holmes snatched it by the hilt and, in the same motion, slashed it across Brandt's shoulder. Thanks to the Boer's thick bush tunic and leather bandolier belt, it only superficially wounded him, but the blood surged through the rent material. Brandt barely seemed to notice this, pulling his rifle around again as Holmes backed away, lugging me by the collar. As he did, we passed a trapdoor in the roof I hadn't previously noticed. Holmes scrabbled at the bolt holding it closed. Brandt, still struggling to untwist the rifle strap, broke off to bellow: "Don't open that, Holmes! Don't be a damn fool!"

The bolt slid loose, and the trapdoor exploded upward in a blur of matted brown fur and the most terrifying ivory teeth I'd ever seen, curved like sabres and framed in a blood-red maw. With insect-like speed, the huge, hideous thing didn't just emerge, but found a static perch on the edge of the trapdoor – where it squatted, slowly turning its hellish head in our direction.

"Behold the Nandi Bear, Watson!" Holmes said, still retreating, still lugging me along. "Surely you didn't think even Ernst Brandt could have left those corpses so ravaged!"

"Good grief, Holmes . . . an ape?"

"A baboon!" he corrected me. "To be exact, a Chacma baboon. One of the largest, most aggressive species in Africa, and, it won't surprise you to learn, a native of the Cape region, in particular the Transvaal and the Orange Free State."

Even by Chacma standards, this thing was enormous. Not far off the height of a man, and maybe three feet across the shoulders, its torso wedge-shaped but immensely thick and compact, its long arms heavy with muscle, the black fingernails on its shovel-sized hands crooked into vicious, jagged talons. Its long, grey, sloping face bore multiple aged scars, while its pelt was caked with dung and dried blood, and covered with fragments of straw. With fevered intensity, it fixed its dark, red-rimmed eyes upon us, and gaped again, those murderous teeth bared, and yet it made no scream – just a prolonged, snake-like hiss.

"Good Lord!" I said again. "Good Lord in Heaven."

At the other end of roof, Brandt looked equally alarmed. He'd finally untwisted the rifle strap, and backed quickly towards the top of the ladder.

"He's been using this beast as a weapon?" I said, stunned.

"Without doubt," Holmes replied. "It attacks on command. Most likely, the unbolting of the cage is the signal."

"But how to unleash it on specific targets?"

"Fresh blood, Watson. What else?"

My thoughts raced. McTavish with his ragged razor cuts, the two labourers with their sliced toes and punctured groin. Good Lord, how many others working on this railway had suffered minor cuts and abrasions without realizing they constituted a death sentence that would be enacted that very night?

"The scent is enough to drive most animals mad, Watson," Holmes added. "But when a beast has been trained to it . . . maybe on the battlefields of the Boer War."

"Good Lord," I said again. "But, Holmes, *why have you let this devil out?*"

"Because, Watson, we aren't the ones who are wounded here."

And now, slowly, like some demonic statue creaking to life, the thing switched its attention away from us, pivoting round until it faced Brandt, whose tunic of course was drenched in blood.

He pointed his rifle at it, shouting something in Afrikaans. I'm no expert on that tongue, but it sounded like: "Back, Caracalla!"

"Caracalla," Holmes breathed. "A suitable name for an unthinking killer."

Brandt shouted again, so frenzied his words that I lost track of their meaning.

In response, it sprang, gambolling along the roof with such speed and agility that Brandt only managed one shot, missing widely, before it struck him head on, hurling his rifle away and smashing him down with both its fists, at the same time tearing and mangling his flesh with its snapping jaws. Fleetingly, his shrieks were lost in the rattle and clangour of motion, before it raised him with both hands and brought him down with shocking force across its knee, and that sound at least – that *crack* of bone and gristle – we heard. It hurled his corpse away like a broken doll, a final offering to the gods of Hell's Gate, for now at last we rumbled out from the flame-red cradle that was Tungo Gorge, the whole of the East African plains spread in front of us.

Wildly the beast spun, its eyes glaring with feral madness. It focused on us, and came pounding back along the roof, still in silence, but with ribbons of crimson froth dangling from its jaws.

"Down, Watson!" Holmes shouted. "On your face!"

I felt certain we faced death, but dropped to the woodwork anyway, Holmes alongside me – though now he was holding something aloft, something small but bright. Caracalla was no more than ten yards away when the sun struck Holmes's silver cigarette case properly, its dazzling rays reflected straight into the brute's eyes, bewildering it, frightening it, blinding it.

It reared to full height, arms across its face – a near human gesture, I thought.

And then with a tumultuous thrashing and crashing, multiple thorny boughs rushed past us, skimming over our prone forms by inches, but sweeping into the baboon, tangling it up and carrying it backward, turning and twisting it, hammering its frantic form along the roof of this final compartment – before it was gone. Gone from the train, gone from sight, gone for good amid the endless interlaced branches that sped on and on over us in a natural arcade.

Holmes and I lay flat, faces hard on the juddering wood, heat and sweat seeping through our dusty clothing. It was another ten minutes or so, forest shadows rippling over us, twigs whipping our backs, before the train pulled clear of the whistling-thorn, and rolled out into the vast emptiness of the Rift Valley.

We made an exhausted, bedraggled twosome as we clambered down between compartments, crossed the explosives store and re-entered the works office. Here, Holmes slumped behind McTavish's desk. He watched grimly as, with shaking hand, I poured us both another brandy.

"No one will believe *this* adventure," I advised him.

"You said that about the Hound of the Baskervilles, did you not?" he replied. "Another case wherein man brutalized a beast until it would do his dirty work for him."

"You think that terrible creature was made during the Boer War?"

Holmes mused on this. "The Boers formed effective guerrilla bands. Caracalla would be ideal for their purpose, especially at night, against fixed positions. Maybe against wounded men."

"Gad!" A nightmare image flooded my mind: of this silent, ruthless predator ranging across darkened battlefields at the end of an action, tearing and savaging our injured.

"Perhaps it was trained from infancy to that purpose," Holmes added. "Certainly someone with knowledge – a vet or doctor – ensured its silence, presumably by cutting its vocal cords."

I shuddered at the thought of such callous ingenuity.

Holmes sipped more brandy. "Whether it became Brandt's property when he joined that guerrilla band, or whether it was his to begin with, who can say."

"Either way, it was a fearsome weapon to use against the railway," I said.

"Fearsome and criminally indiscriminate. Once released, the beast would use the darkness to prowl the outskirts of the camp, following the scent of blood. It didn't matter which unfortunate it was drawn to. All Brandt needed was a violent death every few days. That would soon create panic. And if at any stage, it was seen, or even shot, the explanation would be simple: a displaced wild animal had stalked the camp. An oddity perhaps, but no blame on any man."

"But how did you deduce in the first place that an animal was being used?"

Holmes smiled tiredly. "You mean aside from the claw marks identified by my ever-reliable medical friend, Dr John Watson? Well, the straw used to line the beast's cage, the location of which was given away by the fixed-open air vents in the ammunition truck. One needs constant ventilation for the storage of explosives. But for basic ammunition, there is no such requirement. The impact on the train roof was another clue. You heard Brandt back in the gorge. The rocks towering above us were a hundred feet high. No animal, no matter how dexterous, could survive such a leap. And even an animal with hands could not climb up it again. Not so quickly that it wouldn't be seen."

"So the thudding the old Nandi heard was the sound of the trapdoor opening?"

"That was a reasonable conclusion. If the thing didn't come from above, it must have come from below."

"And your suspicions about Brandt's heritage made him the prime suspect?"

Holmes shrugged. "Only Brandt had access to the ammunition store. And when he insisted on returning to Kalawi and locked us in the works office, that was the final evidence."

I indicated the south door. "Only *that* door was locked, Holmes. The other was open."

"The other door was the door Caracalla would use when he came in here to finish us off."

Despite everything I was startled. "Brandt planned to murder us from the beginning?"

Holmes nodded. "Most certainly. Both our deaths and the death of Robert McTavish would have provoked a savage response from Colonel Meinertzhagen. On top of that, the loss of the ammunition truck in Nandi territory would have served two purposes: to throw almost irrefutable suspicion on the Nandi themselves and, more practically, to enable Brandt to free Caracalla into the wild and presumably dismantle its cage – thereby removing all trace of what had really happened. After that, no doubt, he'd evacuate the scene on foot. I'd imagine a man like Brandt could survive in this wilderness more easily than most."

"But even if Caracalla *had* come in here," I said, "neither you nor I were bloodied . . .?"

Holmes nodded to the far corner, where McTavish lay under his crimson sheet.

"The beast killed the labourer working with the site foreman," he explained. "Even though it was the foreman whose foot was wounded. We were attacked on the roof simply because we were there. All those bloodied were condemned to die – along with all those in their company."

"A madman," I said. "Brandt . . . a sheer madman."

"If so, Watson, a madman we created."

"The deuce with that, Holmes! This fellow was . . . well, he was what the French call a terrorist. A small-minded nobody using death and mayhem to try and destabilize civilization."

"Well . . ." Holmes sipped his brandy again. "One man's civilization is another man's barbarism."

"And who should make such distinctions?" I finished my drink in a gulp. My blood was up, I freely admit. "Not these deranged voices out on the margins, where no one is even listening, I'll tell you that."

"Hmmm," Holmes replied. "Quite."

# The Case of the Maltese Catacombs

## William Meikle

My good friend Sherlock Holmes does not take to enforced rest, not even when ordered to by his doctor. Our holiday in Malta was but two days old, having taken lodging in the naval officer's mess in Valetta harbour. Holmes had already solved two cases of smuggling, proved the house guilty of rigging the gentle games of bridge played of an evening, and ousted the nightwatchman of the main dock, having showed him to be guilty of neglect during an illicit liaison with a lady of the night. It was not so much that I decided to retreat to the Army garrison at Mdina, more that we were asked to leave an hour before the request would have become somewhat more forceful.

At least the stifling heat away from the coast did much to ensure that Holmes's enthusiasm did not overreach his physical state. Once we arrived in the ancient city, the Captain of the Guard's hospitality stretched to an immense breakfast of eggs, ham and fresh bread, a gallon of strong sweet tea, and as much local history – mostly of the religious variety – as either Holmes or I could stomach.

Indeed, the young officer seemed rather nervous and excited that he had such an august personage as Holmes under his roof.

"My sergeant-at-arms was beside himself, Mr Holmes," the man said, as he poured another cup of tea. "To hear him speak you are up there with Nelson and Wellington in the ranks of the great. He is all a fluster – and, as a Scotsman, he is not normally a man given to frippery."

The Captain, despite his nervous demeanour, was obviously one of those chaps who liked to hear himself talk, and given his head he went on at quite some length. After a while, Holmes feigned tiredness and excused himself. I was offered a smoke – and more of the Captain's rather dull history lessons – before I was able to extricate myself from the table. I finally gained some relaxation on my own part on the battlements of the old walled city, looking out over the length of the island while sipping a most welcome gin as the sun went over the yardarm.

Holmes sat in what little shade could be found against the wall, smoking a cheroot and staring out, unseeing, at the view. To my trained eye he seemed to have some of the colour back in his cheeks, and his eyes were sharp, no longer clouded by pain. The affair of the Scottish Stone, the wild hunt for it across the Highlands, and its subsequent return to Westminster Abbey, had taken a great deal out of my old friend – more than he would admit. His health would suffer for it for some time yet, although I was now hopeful that this holiday might be just the tonic he required – if I could only get him to keep still.

It was to prove a fruitless hope. After barely half an hour of sitting, Holmes tapped me on the arm.

"You know I appreciate your concern, old boy," he said. "But I cannot sit here idle – I could have done that just as easily in Baker Street, sitting in my chair with *The Thunderer*. Since we have come all this way, what say you that we do some exploring? There are thousands of years of history underfoot – let us see what the epochs have to tell us, shall we?"

In truth, I had been rather hoping we would find time to delve under the old city. Holmes had spoken true; the foundations on which the ancient settlement had grown were riddled with tunnels and catacombs in a vast necropolis, which had been expanded and extended over the centuries by each occupying force – of which there had been many. The tombs had lain unre-marked for many centuries before being opened up and exca-vated in 1894 by Dr Antonio Annetto of Caruana, but even his enthusiasm had barely scratched the surface of the wonders that were yet to be recovered. I felt quite giddy at the prospect of discovery that awaited us.

I went in search of some help, and found the aforementioned Sergeant-at-arms at the door to the Captain's quarters, as if he had been standing there watching us, perhaps too shy to intrude. He, too, seemed rather excitable for a seasoned soldier, but I put that down to his reaction to having Holmes in such close proximity. He went quiet, almost tongue-tied, when Holmes joined me at my side, and chose to direct his attention to me rather than my illustrious friend. At my request, he opened up the heavy iron gate that led to the passages under the citadel. He would not accompany us, refusing point blank, and indeed making every attempt to divert us from our chosen path.

"Are you sure you gentlemen wouldn't rather just have another gin or twa? You wouldna get me doon there for love or money, sirs," he said, a broad Scots brogue coming through. "Not even in the daylight."

Holmes did not reply – he was looking the Sergeant up and down and I knew that look only too well – my friend had spotted something that had caught his attention. Whether it was of any import remained to be seen, but to Holmes almost everything was of import in one way or another.

"There's no need to be afraid of the dead," I replied for us both as Holmes took a lantern from the side of the door and lit the wick. "It's not as if they're going to rise up and attack us."

"I'm not so sure about that, Doctor," the big man replied, and up close I saw something in his eyes that I took for fear. "Come and stand night watch by this door for a few weeks and you'll soon change your mind. There's terrible sounds comes up from the deep places – moaning and groaning as if the dead are in pain – and a foul stench that no amount of ale can wash away. No – you wouldna get me doon there."

He would not be drawn further, and Holmes had already started to make his way through the doorway. I quickly forgot the conversation as I followed him down into the tombs.

\*    \*    \*

The air grew colder, and dryer still than the hot wind above. Large, canopied burial chambers dominated the main corridors of the complex, their high arches and supporting pillars providing an echoing, almost sepulchral backdrop to our wanderings in the labyrinth. Dried husks of long dead bodies lay in carved-out hollows, swaddled in cloth as thin as tissue paper, and the only sound was the padding of our footsteps on the stone.

Holmes seemed quite delighted with the sheer variety of funerary practices to be found. He tapped the wall beside several tombs as we passed by, descending ever deeper into history.

"Renaissance Italian, Moor, Roman, Greek, Phoenician, if I'm not mistaken, and now more Roman. All these peoples, once at each other's throat, squabbling and fighting over land, religion, money, and now all together in their final peace. A few days spent here would serve to deprive any man of the notion of his own importance in the grand scheme of things – wouldn't you say so, Watson?"

I was about to reply when Holmes put up a hand to stop me.

"Do you smell that?"

I was about to reply in the negative when I did indeed notice a faint odour – and one with which I was all too familiar.

"A foul stench indeed. Putrefaction – there is something dead down here – I mean, apart from the obvious."

Holmes nodded, and his mood was suddenly sombre and attentive.

"Stay close, Watson, and keep your wits about you. There is more here than meets the eye."

I knew better than to argue, although I was at a loss to see where any danger to us might come from in this place.

As it turned out, it was not danger that concerned Holmes. We turned a ninety-degree corner into one of the larger of the burial chambers. The air filled with the stench of rotting flesh, and I tried to breathe shallowly to avoid exposing my nasal passages to its assault.

Three bodies lay in the hollowed-out surface inside the chamber – all swaddled in the old dusty material that was by now familiar. Holmes handed me the lantern, stepped down and examined the dead more closely. When he turned back to me I saw immediately that he had found something, and that he was not greatly displeased at having done so.

"We will need to get somebody down here," he said. He rolled the rightmost cadaver over – and a young man dressed in what I took to be workman's clothes fell out of an outer layer of the older cloth, his all too recently dead eyes staring up at us. Even from where I stood I could see that the whole left side of his head had been caved in above the ear. He'd been struck – with quite some force – and to my eye it looked far from accidental.

"There's not enough blood," I remarked. "He was killed elsewhere."

"And placed here in this fashion in the hope that he would not be noticed among the other dead," Holmes agreed. "Indeed, if we had not decided on a visit, he may have lain here for the rest of time – once the stench dissipates there will be little to distinguish this corpse from any other in this place."

Holmes was no longer on holiday – if he ever really had been – I saw the tension in him, and the rising excitement. This is what my friend lived for; we had a mystery on our hands, and a crime to be solved.

"Let me have the lantern," Holmes said. "I must study the scene before all and sundry are trampling through here."

I did as I was bade, and stood above him as Holmes made a minute study of the body and the area immediately around it. The stench of corruption was stronger still now, but Holmes's full concentration never wavered from the task at hand. He pointed out several things to me over the next few minutes – a rosary clutched in the lad's left hand, his ginger hair and, in a battered leather wallet in his pocket, a pressed leaf of what I took to be clover. There were also traces of grey dust ingrained in his trousers at the knees, and more of the same in the turned-up material around his ankles. When Holmes finally stood and passed the lantern back to me, I saw only steely determination on his face.

"It is murder, Watson – grim and calculated. Let us go and inform the chaps up above and get things moving. It seems our holiday is over."

Knowing the military mindset, I was not at all convinced that even Holmes would be able to persuade them to allow his participation in any investigation. But such considerations became moot as soon as we reached daylight up on the battlement.

The Sergeant-at-arms was standing in the doorway, as if waiting for our return.

"You must come," I said. "And bring some help. There's been a murder."

The big man laughed. "Oh, I doubt that, sir. There's nobody missing up here, and there was nobody down there but you and Mr Holmes. I can't see how a murder could possibly have happened, unless you two gentlemen had something to do with it."

Holmes looked the big man up and down. "Yet I assure you, there is a body lying down there that is most recently dead. And if you do not come with us this very second, I will call for your captain, and let him see what is to be done."

The Sergeant finally relented, although he continued to exude an air of faint amusement. But despite his earlier protestations to the contrary, he showed little hesitation in descending with us to the chamber where we had left the murdered lad.

There were two bodies lying there, but only a faint lingering odour of corruption to show where our murdered boy had lain. Both the body and the cloth it had been wrapped in were gone, leaving no other proof that he had ever been there at all.

The Sergeant laughed nervously at our bemusement. "I told you this place was tricksy, sirs," he said. "Now, tell me again about this murder?"

"He was here," I said. "And you can still smell him."

"I smell no such thing," the Sergeant replied. His amusement had vanished, and he seemed most keen to depart from the spot. "It's a damned tomb – it's supposed to stink."

"And yet there was indeed a body here only ten minutes since. You must report this, man," Holmes said.

"Exactly what must I report, sir? That two fine gentlemen got themselves spooked on a tour of the facilities? I shall get on to that right away."

He left us there in the tomb, and we heard his footsteps – almost running – echoing away, leaving us once again in the quiet dark. Holmes turned and started heading in the opposite direction, deeper into the tombs, and, as he had the only lantern, I had little choice but to follow him.

"Where in the blazes are you going, Holmes? Surely we must report this to that man's superior officer?"

"Not yet, Watson. There is more going on here than meets the eye – and as no one passed us on the way up or down, it can only mean that there is someone still in here with us, or that there is another way out. In either case, I mean to get to the bottom of it."

We spent the best part of an hour in the tombs, with Holmes studying every foot of the way. He remarked twice on things of interest – one was a small red smear on the wall, no bigger than the nail on my little finger, which might have been blood, and another was a tiny scrap of dry cloth, lying on the floor in the centre of the corridor. Beyond these two things there was no sign that anyone but Holmes and I had been in these corridors recently. I was almost ready to give up, but Holmes refused.

"The lad did not just fall down and die, Watson. And he was in here for more reason than to just get killed. The answers are here – we just have to root them out."

I still thought his search would come to naught, until, right at the deepest, darkest part of the caverns, we came upon a much larger and more ornate chamber, roughly hewn from the bedrock. The entrance to this chamber had but recently been opened, the evidence of which was plain in the paler scars of fresh rock workings on the walls and the grey dust and rubble that lay in piles on either side.

"I think we have found where the lad got the dust on his trousers," Holmes said, and led me into the chamber itself.

A single stone sarcophagus sat in an otherwise empty area dominated by five large, ornately carved pillars that reached from floor to roof. Each pillar had a single word carved down its length, the letters having been worn by age but still distinctly readable. Holmes spoke the words as he passed each pillar.

"*Sator, arepo, tenet, opera, rotas* – Early Christian iconography – I have seen these words before," he muttered, but he did not at that point in time let me in on his thinking. "And look, Watson," he continued as he stepped around the tomb itself. "It seems someone has been attempting to defile this resting place."

I walked round the far side of the sarcophagus to join him. Two picks and a shovel lay on the ground, one of the picks having been broken at the haft. Holmes bent closer.

"And we have our murder weapon," he said. He lifted the shovel into the light.

Blood glistened on the dull blade.

"But where has the body gone?" I asked.

Holmes smiled. "I can think of one obvious place."

We turned our attention to the sarcophagus. It seemed to be carved from one single block of stone, the lid being a remarkably tight fit and unmoving despite no amount of straining and pushing from us both.

"I can see why they tried the picks," Holmes said sardonically. "No, our missing boy will not be in there – this lid has not been moved for many a long year."

He studied the top of the stone. There were a series of abstract carvings of what might be a horn in the shape of a crescent moon, a babe in arms, a spoked wheel, and something that looked like a donkey – or an ox – it was hard to tell given the poor condition of the stone.

"I do not recognize the provenance," Holmes said. "But it is clear that this was made to hold someone of some importance."

"One of the Knights of St John perhaps?" I said. "Surely that is most likely, given our location?"

"Certainly not," Holmes replied, somewhat abruptly. "That order did not arrive on the island until the sixteenth century – this coffin is older, far older, by ten centuries and probably more." He ran his hands over the carvings. "This means something, Watson. There is a good reason that our quarry has targeted this burial in particular. We have more than one mystery on our hands."

"And speaking of mysteries – where in the blazes is the dead boy if he's not in there?" I asked again. "No one passed us, and we've been over every inch of this place."

Holmes shook his head. "As yet, I cannot tell you. But there are only so many answers to questions posed by a murder in a sealed area, and I have not yet had time to consider all the possibilities."

"Shall we inform the Captain of our find?"

Holmes shook his head again. "Not until we are sure he is not also involved in the criminal activities underfoot. Let us head up into the light – this calls for a smoke and a think."

When we once again walked up out of the catacombs into daylight I was surprised that the Sergeant was not there waiting for us, but when I remarked on this to Holmes he merely smiled thinly and did not reply. At least the Captain of the garrison had remembered our presence and showed his hospitality once again.

As he welcomed us in to his quarters he enquired after our visit to the catacombs.

"I need to find time to get down there myself," he said. "The men are full of tales of ghosts and ghoulies of course – you know what a superstitious cove your squaddie can be. Did you find anything of particular interest?"

Holmes kicked my ankle rather unsubtly under the table when I thought of replying, and turned the talk away from the tombs onto local history – a topic on which the Captain was only too happy to expound for the duration of our lunch. We had a small mountain of sardines and fresh bread, washed down with bitter, cloudy ale that had not survived the journey from home as well as it should have, after which we returned once more to the veranda on the battlements.

It was only then that I tried to get Holmes to expound on his current thinking.

"I have not yet formulated a hypothesis, Watson," he said, lighting up his travelling pipe. "But, as I said, there are a limited number of ways of pulling off a sealed-area mystery. I think we can rule out any subterfuge regarding the lad himself – we can both agree he was quite clearly dead. What we have left to consider is how the body was hidden in the little time it took us to ascend and descend again with the Sergeant. That, and the matter of the tomb where the murder occurred is what I must concern myself with, if I am given some peace and quiet."

I knew a rebuke when I heard one, and refrained from any further attempt at questioning Holmes as he settled in his chair and fell quiet.

I have plenty of experience of watching Holmes think – usually in the aforementioned Baker Street apartments. What with the stifling heat, the black flies and the memory of the dead boy at my feet, I was rather pining for the comforts of hearth and home that afternoon on the battlements of the old city. I even remarked on the fact to Holmes, but he was as immobile as any of the dead who slept below us; he only moved to puff at his pipe and occasionally scrape a new match alight to get his smoke going again.

After an hour of this, I grew restless and, leaving Holmes to himself, went in search of the Sergeant-at-arms, intending to report on what we had found in the deepest part of the tombs. I found him in the small scullery near the armoury but I did not intrude, for it was immediately clear to me that he was in angry – albeit whispered – conversation with a small, obviously local, chap. I stood by the open door, but was unable to hear much of what had transpired. I caught a single name – "Black Mary" – and some of the gist of the rest by observing the local man's hand actions, in particular the ones he made to mime the act of striking someone hard about the head.

I had to scuttle away sharpish to avoid being detected as the conversation abruptly ended and was dashed lucky that the Sergeant did not look in my direction. He did not notice me though, and it was obvious he had other things on his mind – his face like thunder as he strode off down the corridor at some speed. I considered following him, but decided that bringing Holmes up to speed on this new development was more important.

As I returned to the battlements, Holmes was rising from his chair, his shadow thrown long by the sun that had begun its descent into the sea far off to our west. He left a scrap of paper on the table and I saw he had been working on some kind of word puzzle that seemed to relate to the words we had found carved on the pillars in the tomb.

| S | A | T | O | R |
|---|---|---|---|---|
| A | R | E | P | O |
| T | E | N | E | T |
| O | P | E | R | A |
| R | O | T | A | S |

I immediately spotted the alignment of the letters, which read the same up and down the five columns.

Holmes saw me looking.

"It is called a Sator square, Watson," he said. "I believe it to hold an answer to at least one of my questions. But that will be of little importance unless we can identify our grave robbers. I see you have news. It will have to wait. If we are to stand vigil tonight, we must be there early to avoid detection."

"Vigil?" I asked, but I had a sinking feeling that I knew exactly what he was proposing.

"They will return to the tomb tonight, I am sure of it," Holmes replied. "I believe that our very presence here has precipitated matters towards a rapid conclusion. They have little option left open to them but to make a desperate attempt to win their prize. And we must be there waiting for them."

I resigned myself to a late supper and, with a heavy heart, made a quick detour to our room where I picked up my service revolver and fresh smokes before rejoining Holmes. He stood at the battlements, looking down to where the road below snaked away into town.

"How high would you say we are here, Watson?" he asked, as I went to his side and looked over.

"Twenty-five feet, at a guess?" I replied, and he nodded, as if I had confirmed his own view. Without another word, he made his way to the iron gate that led to the catacombs.

He had a lamp in his hand already – the one we had used earlier was back in its place by the door.

"I took this from the Captain's quarters while you were gone. No sense in alerting anyone that comes here to our presence in the tombs," he said with a grim smile as he lit the wick.

Once again I followed him down into the darkness. We descended in silence until we reached the spot where we had found the boy's body.

"However they spirited the body away, it had to be close by. Give me a second, Watson, it is past time we had a good long look around," Holmes said, and left me in the centre of the chamber while he circled around the perimeter of the area with the lantern. The lamp cast flickering shadows that did little for my feelings of calm detachment there in the silent dark. The flickering did, however, seem to please Holmes somewhat, as he had a smile on his face when he returned to my position.

"It seems we have solved one of our problems," he said.

"We have done no such thing," I started, but he stopped me by putting up a hand.

"What if I told you we are approximately twenty-five feet below our position where we stood on the battlement?"

I finally caught his drift. "You have found a hidden passageway?"

"I believe so," he replied. "There is enough movement of the air to cause the lamp to flicker when I move over to our right, so there is definitely another corridor off this one, and it is at street level – they must have taken the body away through there. Come, Watson, lend me a hand."

I followed him over to what at first glance seemed to be merely a patch of wall in an alcove that sat in deep shadows. Holmes waved the lantern in front of his face. The light flickered in a faint but now noticeable breeze. He handed me the lantern, stepped forward and put his shoulder to the wall. At first I thought he had been mistaken, but then there was a loud scrape of stone against stone and a portion of the wall swung away from him, revealing a corridor beyond from which fresher air blew. I stepped up alongside Holmes, my hand on my revolver in case of a sudden attack.

The corridor he had uncovered was mostly empty. Faint light some twenty feet away showed that there was an exit, of sorts, in that direction, but my attention was taken by a body on the floor – the young man lay bundled there, discarded like a broken doll.

"At least that mystery has been solved," Holmes said, stepping back and letting the false wall swing back into position. It closed with a soft scrape.

"We cannot leave the lad there—" I started, but Holmes interrupted me.

"We shall see to him soon enough, Watson. Let us descend to the lower chamber and wait. I believe we shall have some action this very night that will bring this case to a swift conclusion."

I followed as we went down the rest of the way in silence. When we reached the lowest chamber, I made to light a smoke. Holmes stopped me.

"There is not enough movement in the air I'm afraid, Watson: the scent of that tobacco might give away our position should they come along too soon." He led me to a recessed alcove where we could watch proceedings from the shadows without being seen. "We cannot have this either," he said and, without warning, doused the lantern, plunging us into total darkness.

I waited for long moments for my eyes to adjust, but there was not a speck of light for them to latch on to.

"Dash it, Holmes. You could have warned me you were going to maroon us in a crypt in the dark."

I heard my friend's soft laugh from beside me.

"We have nothing to fear, Watson. Remember, we are the hunters tonight."

"At least tell me what you have surmised," I replied, keeping my voice soft – anything louder than a whisper sent most disconcerting echoes ringing around the chamber.

Holmes replied equally quietly, "I thought it might be more of the same kind of thing I found in the naval officers' mess. Given the age of the tombs, I suspected some kind of smuggling ring dealing in antiquities, but there is more to this matter than that – the murder of the boy speaks of darker motives. You know, of course, that the lad was Irish – his dental work was most distinctive in that regard."

"I know no such thing—" I started, before being interrupted by another laugh.

"The shamrock in his wallet, and the rosary in his hand might have given it away, don't you think?"

I was too abashed to answer as he continued. "And given our Sergeant-at-arms's subterfuge and crude attempts to hide his own origin, I started to develop my theory."

"Subterfuge? What are you getting at, Holmes?"

"Why, his accent of course. I thought an old hand like yourself would pick up on it – he's another Irishman. Oh, I have no doubt he has spent much of his time in Glasgow, but beneath that there is a most distinctive underlying twang that tells me he hails, not from the banks of the Clyde, but from Ireland – and the west coast at that. Cork probably. You did not notice that – or the faint but unmistakable grey dust that he had tried, unsuccessfully, to clean from the knees of his trousers – but surely you noticed just how keen he was to warn us off from venturing down here?"

"Yes, I'm not quite that dim-witted. But what would the Irish want with a tomb on Malta?"

I heard the smile in Holmes's reply.

"I have my suspicions, but no proof as yet. That is why we are standing here in the dark surrounded by the dead. But hush – someone is coming."

Seconds later, the pad of footsteps on stone echoed around us. Dim light flickered in the main corridor, strengthening as the grave robbers approached.

Their accents were noticeable even before I saw them. Two Irishmen – one of them was indeed our Sergeant-at-arms – and the local chap I'd seen in the scullery came into the chamber. It was immediately obvious that there was some disagreement among them.

"You didn't have to kill the boy," the Sergeant said – and now I could clearly hear the Cork man behind the façade. "He wasn't doing any harm."

"He was taking feart," the other Irishman replied. I had not seen him before, but he wore the uniform of a squaddie, so I guessed he belonged to the barracks. "Screaming about how this wasn't right, how we should let her rest in peace – daft talk about blasphemy and sacrilege. I just gave him a wee tap on the head to quiet him down. Well, maybe a bit more than a wee tap. We're just lucky I was able to hide the body in time."

"But not before they found it first."

"How was I to know they would be down here today? You told me you'd stop them. 'Fill an Englishman up with gin and he'll sleep the day away,' that's what you said.

The Sergeant merely grunted in reply.

"Well, it can't be helped now. But those two snoops won't give up – and our story won't hold water for very long – we need to get this done quick."

They set about attacking the sarcophagus with pick and shovel, but it was obvious from the profanities and cursing that they were making little headway.

"We have to get in there," the second Irishman said. "If she is what they say she is, and has what they say she has, then we'll need it for the cause."

"We'll not do it with these tools. We need a hammer – a bloody big hammer," the Sergeant said.

The local man intimated that he knew a man who knew a man, and all three made to leave the chamber. I slid my revolver from my pocket, and waited for Holmes's signal for action. But no signal came, and the three men left, the diminishing light bobbing up and away, their footsteps fading into the distance until we were left once more alone in the dark.

A full minute later Holmes lit the lantern.

"I believe we can chance a smoke, Watson," he said. "We have a respite, a pause for thought."

"Why didn't we take them?" I asked.

"I need a closer look at that tomb," Holmes replied. "Given what we have just heard, the occupant may be even more important than I first surmised."

"I was going to tell you what I saw in the scullery," I told him as he left the alcove and went to bend over the sarcophagus. "At least we know they did indeed kill the lad. But there was also a name spoken. I don't know how it fits, but it might be of import. They mentioned a woman – Black Mary. Perhaps she is a local with knowledge of this place?"

Holmes laughed. "Watson, you never cease to amaze me. 'Black Mary' indeed – I should have seen it sooner. It all makes sense now."

"I wish it did to me," I replied. "I'm still none the wiser."

"Let us have a smoke then, and I'll see if I can enlighten you," Holmes replied.

He was still inspecting the top of the sarcophagus as I passed him a cheroot. We lit up, and he finally included me into his thinking.

"Some words have more meaning than others," he said, as he lit up. "And where you say them can invest that meaning with even more depth and import. 'Black Mary' are two such words here on Malta. Have you heard tell of the cult of the Magdelene?"

I nodded.

"I have seen the Black Madonna icons – all visitors have."

"Good – then you have probably heard the story – how she escaped the Roman tyranny to bring Christ's message to these islands?"

I looked down at the sarcophagus. "You don't think this is her?"

"It really does not matter what I think – it is what these robbers think that matters. They are Irish, they are talking about the cause and they are intent on raiding a tomb in search of what it might contain. Imagine it is the Magdelene, and that she has something of import buried beside her. Imagine the focus a religious icon or relic would bring to that country and their cause. History has many examples of religious fervour driving cultural change – few of which have ended without mayhem and bloodshed. It is a happy coincidence that we are here at the start of the matter to nip it in the bud before it can flower."

Holmes continued to study the sarcophagus, then took the lantern over to have a closer look at the letters on the five pillars. When he returned to my position he was smiling again.

"Well, Watson, I do believe our holiday has done some good after all – I think our visit precipitated these men into a course of action for which they were not fully prepared, leading them to make clumsy mistakes. And I also believe I now know what might be inside this stone tomb. But that will have to wait – I think our friends are about to return. Quickly, let us melt into the shadows again and see what transpires."

I did as I was bid, doused my cheroot and joined Holmes in the alcove just as he extinguished the lantern. Seconds later, we heard the sounds of the robbers approaching.

I was worried that the smell from our smokes might have lingered in the air and given us away, but on their arrival the robbers wasted no time. They set about attacking the sarcophagus with a sledgehammer so heavy that even the Sergeant – the largest of the men – struggled to wield it. Despite its obvious weight and heft, it made almost no impact on the stonework beyond sending a few loose chips flying. The Sergeant grew weary long before the stone did, and neither of the other two men could manage more than a few feeble swings before they too had to desist through fatigue. Only when it was obvious that they would make no further headway in their attempt to open the tomb did Holmes tap me on the arm.

I had my service revolver in hand as we stepped out into the light.

"Kindly desist, gentlemen," Holmes said, his voice ringing and echoing in the chamber.

The three men turned as one to look in our direction. The look of surprise on the big Sergeant's face would have been almost comical in any other circumstance. He hefted the sledge-hammer like a weapon until I showed him the pistol.

"Be a good chap and put that down, would you?" I said, and was mightily relieved when he complied.

"We're not doing anything wrong," the big man started, until he was stopped by a harsh laugh from Holmes.

"Despite evidence of grave robbing and bloody murder to the contrary?" Holmes replied.

"You have no proof."

Holmes laughed again. "The boy's body is in the corridor behind the false wall," he said. "I doubt if you have bothered to move him. And we have your tools here with the lad's blood on them. Proof enough for even your captain to take action, I should say."

The Sergeant's bluster fell away as fast as it had come, to be replaced by a look of animal cunning I had often seen on the faces of Holmes's cornered adversaries.

"We are all men of the world here," he said softly. "We could share the spoils?"

Holmes laughed again. "I have many faults, but greed is not one of them. I am, however, frequently guilty of curiosity, so I have a mind to show you what you have missed before we hand you over to the authorities. Watch them, Watson, please."

Holmes strode towards the sarcophagus and ran a hand over the scarring on the stone brought about by the men's crude attempts at opening it.

"Brute force always bows before the intellect," Holmes said. "And had you any spark of original thought of your own, you would have seen that the answer was written before you this whole time."

He pointed at the tall pillars, and the writing thereon. Holmes was in his element – he had an audience, and an explanation to provide to them.

"*Sator, arepo, tenet, opera, rotas.* Watson has already seen how these words can be aligned into a palindromic square, but they are more than that. The square itself has been used over the centuries as both a warding spell to keep away evil, as a prayer, and, as you will see in this case, the words can be a coded message that will allow me to open the casket where your thuggery has failed."

He ran his hand over the carvings on top of the stone.

"If *arepo* is taken to be in the second declension, the 'o' ending puts the word in the ablative case, giving it a meaning of 'by means of *arepus*'. This produces the rough translation 'Mastery comes by turning the wheel'." He pointed at the carved wheel in the centre of the casket. "See how simple it becomes when you pay attention?"

He reached over, gripped the stone in both hands, and turned the wheel.

The lid of the casket popped open with a hiss of escaping air, showing a defined gap that had not been there mere seconds before.

Unfortunately, Holmes's performance had taken too much of my attention, and I had dropped my guard. I was dismayed to see the big Sergeant make a leap for Holmes, even as the other Irishman threw himself across the room towards me. I could not bring myself to shoot an unarmed man, so I stood my ground, sidestepped as he grabbed for me and gave him a sharp rap on the head with the pistol's butt that sent him sprawling on the stones. The local man had not moved, and crouched by the wall with his hands in the air, staying out of the fight.

Holmes had worse luck of it. The Sergeant pressed a swift attack, a flurry of hefty punches that had Holmes on the retreat before he found a spot to stand his ground. Even then he was hard-pressed against a bigger, stronger opponent not hampered by a recent illness. Still, Holmes's innate fighting skills stood him in good stead. He danced out of the Sergeant's reach, feinted left, went right, and put in a body-blow combination of punches that sent the big man to his knees. But that only served to put the Sergeant once again within reach of the sledgehammer. His hand curled around the handle, and I clearly saw that Holmes would have no time or space to evade a swing that would crush his bones to powder.

I steadied myself and took the shot.

The Sergeant was dead by the time I walked across the room to check on him.

"Why would he press such an attack?" I asked. "He must have known that, having the pistol, I would always have the upper hand?"

"Desperate men do desperate deeds, Watson," Holmes said. "Let us see what fuelled him."

The man I had felled was still out cold and the local chap still crouched by the wall, so I joined Holmes in pushing aside the lid of the sarcophagus.

The skeletal remains of what I believed had once been a woman lay inside. Any clothing she might have been buried in had long since rotted away.

"This could be anyone," I said.

"I think not, Watson," Holmes replied. "What these men were after was indeed to be found inside. You see, there is another legend associated with the Sator square – of how relics of the crucifixion were saved and brought out of Jerusalem by the Magdelene – nails that were given names."

He leaned forward and gently eased open the skeleton's right hand.

He pointed to the five black iron nails that lay there, naming them in turn.

"Sator, Arepo, Tenet, Opera, Rotas."

# The Adventure of the Colonel's Daughter

## Denis O. Smith

"Now, here is something a little *recherché*," said Sherlock Holmes, as he opened his post at the breakfast table, one bright morning early in June 1886. I looked up from my newspaper and saw that the letter he was reading was adorned with a large coat of arms. "It is from the Russian Embassy," he remarked as he passed it over to me, "but is not very informative."

The letter stated simply that the Ambassador's representative, Mr Alexander Illyanov, proposed to call that morning at half past ten, on a matter of great importance. It added that they remembered with gratitude the part Holmes had played in the Lamyashin case, and hoped he would again be able to assist them.

"There is nothing in the papers this morning which mentions the Russian Embassy," I remarked.

"Perhaps it is some business that has not yet become public knowledge," returned my friend. "No doubt our curiosity will soon be satisfied," he added with a glance at the clock.

Our visitor arrived on the stroke of ten thirty. He was a smartly dressed man of medium height, with a broad, intelligent face. He took the chair Holmes offered him, put down the leather satchel he was carrying, and launched straight into his account.

"It is a serious matter, Mr Holmes. A popular military officer has been murdered, and a young man has been arrested for it."

"I have heard nothing of it."

"That is not surprising. The events took place far away from here, in my homeland. Even in Russia itself it has aroused little interest, for the place it occurred – Krasnoi – is a small provincial town, almost three hundred miles south-east of Moscow. There has, however, been a significant development: his Imperial Majesty, Alexander III, has decided to take a personal interest in the matter. The young man accused of the crime, Michael Vorovny, is the son of one of his Imperial Majesty's closest advisers, Count Vorovny. He protests his innocence in the strongest terms, and all those who know him swear that such a fine young man could not possibly have committed such a dreadful crime – and yet the evidence against him seems conclusive.

"His Imperial Majesty sent a special investigator down to Krasnoi, to look into the matter, but he was unable to discover anything which might prove the boy's innocence. Then it was recalled what a great service you had performed for us a few years ago, in the case of Igor Lamyashin, and word was at once sent to London, to see if you might assist us again. Mr Holmes, the boy's innocence must be proved! You are our only hope!"

"With all due respect to yourself, to his Excellency the Ambassador and to his Imperial Majesty," Holmes responded after a moment, "I cannot prove that right is wrong, or black is white. If the young man is guilty, and such facts as I uncover indicate that to be so, then that is what I must report. The station in life of those I investigate is of no consequence to me; I seek only the truth."

"Of course, that is perfectly understood. I did not intend to suggest otherwise. The problem is that everyone who knows Michael Vorovny believes him innocent but no one can prove it."

"Very well. When did the events in question occur?"

"Two weeks ago."

"Hum! The physical data on which I might found my case have probably been obliterated by now, which makes the task much more difficult, and perhaps even impossible. Still, it can do no harm for us to hear the details. Do you have all the facts?"

Our visitor nodded and, opening his leather case, took out a sheaf of documents. "These papers arrived in London only yesterday."

"Then let us have as full an account as possible," said Holmes, leaning back in his chair, putting his fingertips together and closing his eyes.

"The town of Krasnoi lies about two hundred and eighty miles from Moscow, on one of the main railway lines to the south-east," began Illyanov after a moment. "It is a pleasant enough place, but is undistinguished save by one fact: it is there that the home depot of the Kursakov Regiment is situated, in which young Vorovny serves as a lieutenant. The Kursakov Regiment has a long and proud history, and the senior officer, Colonel Korniev, is a man whose honour and bravery are recognized throughout the Russian Army. He is a married man, with one child, a daughter, Olga, who is twenty years old. She is, all agree, a young woman of quite exceptional beauty. It is not surprising, then, that the young officers all take an interest in her, or that she is known generally as 'the sweetheart of the regiment'. But she is an intelligent girl, as sensible and well mannered as she is beautiful. While no doubt enjoying the admiration of the young men, she has never done anything to lead them on unduly, or to favour any one of them over another. Nevertheless, certain rivalries and jealousies have arisen among the men on her account. At a ball held two months ago, Michael Vorovny danced with Miss Kornieva several times. He was not the only young officer so honoured, but the general opinion was that she esteemed his company higher than that of any of his fellow officers, and that his feelings for her – which were obvious to everyone – had perhaps begun to be reciprocated. This judgement appeared to be confirmed in the following weeks, when Vorovny and Miss Kornieva were seen promenading about the town together on more than one occasion."

Illyanov paused for a moment before continuing. "Of course, such affairs of the heart never run entirely smoothly. Problems and setbacks are only to be expected. In this case, such a problem arose in the person of Dmitri Drachkov, another of the younger officers. Drachkov was several years older than Vorovny, and considerably more experienced, both in military matters and – if I may so express it – in the art of paying court to young ladies. He also outranked Vorovny, being a captain, and had the reputation of being a dashing daredevil, a gambler and boon companion, fearless in the face of danger and ruthless in the pursuit of his aims, be that aim to destroy an enemy, win a game of cards or secure the attention of a young lady.

"Drachkov called upon Olga Kornieva on some pretext or other, and by the use of that charm which came naturally to him, evidently succeeded in gaining a place in her affections sufficient that she accompanied him to a concert or two in Krasnoi. This seems to have hit young Vorovny hard. His friends report that his face became quite a degree paler, he lost his appetite, and lost, too, all interest in the usual pastimes of the young officers. The general opinion seems to be that Vorovny felt unable to compete with his older, more experienced and far more pressing rival, and had lost all confidence in his own good qualities.

"One evening in the officers' mess, a quarrel broke out between the two men. This, all are agreed, was begun by Vorovny, who had had far too much to drink. He made a clumsy verbal assault on Drachkov, which the older man easily rebuffed. Not satisfied, Vorovny returned a few minutes later to where Drachkov was playing cards with some of his companions, and made a further verbal sally upon his hated rival, to which Drachkov responded vigorously, in words which were insulting and humiliating. Inevitably, perhaps, Vorovny thereupon launched a physical attack upon Drachkov and, perhaps equally inevitably, Drachkov responded in kind with a more efficacious assault, leaving young Vorovny laid out on the mess-room floor. 'Take this stupid boy outside and throw a bucket of water over him,' said Drachkov, and returned to his cards. This incident was witnessed by nearly all the young officers.

"I come now to the events of Tuesday, the week before last. Before I do, I had best describe to you the place where the murderous attack occurred. The army camp covers an area of about twelve acres, although not all of that is actively used, some of it remaining as farmland and woods, as it was before the army camp was established there, and some as an exercise area for the horses. It is situated on the outskirts of the town, but as the town is not a large one, it is only a ten-minute walk from the main gate of the camp to the centre of town. The camp itself is much as you would expect. There are sentries on the gate, and a wall or fence surrounding the whole area. There are a great number of buildings, some large and some small, with much open space between them. Over at one side of the camp is the main supplies building. This is generally known as 'the tower', as it is taller than most of the other buildings. It is constructed of stone, and has a very large water tank on the top. Below that are three floors, which hold the miscellaneous supplies for the regiment. Apart from specialized items, such as ammunition and explosives, and equipment for the horses, which are kept elsewhere, these include almost everything imaginable. On the ground floor are stored the larger and heavier items, on the floor above a miscellany of items, including all sorts of weaponry and tools, and on the top floor smaller items.

"In charge of all these supplies is a non-commissioned officer, Sergeant Azzarudin, who has one or two men to help him. At twelve o'clock every day he goes to the canteen for his dinner, and the tower is locked up. However, following an incident a couple of years ago, when some officer required certain items urgently and could not get into the building because Sergeant Azzarudin was elsewhere, all officers of the rank of captain and above are issued with a key of their own.

"On the day in question, Azzarudin and his assistant had gone to dinner as usual, and the building was locked up. Nearby, forty large artillery pieces were lined up, and three men were employed in giving them a fresh coat of paint. They, too, had had dinner at the canteen, but they had left half an hour earlier than Azzarudin, and returned while he was still away. They have stated that that part of the camp was very quiet when they returned, and there was no one about. After a few minutes, however, they saw Captain Drachkov, whom they all knew by sight, approach the supplies building and let himself in with his key. A few minutes later, Lieutenant Vorovny approached them and asked if they had seen Captain Drachkov anywhere about. They told him that Drachkov was in the tower. He thanked them for this information, and then proceeded to walk backwards and forwards across the open space in front of the building, as if deliberating something in his mind. Eventually, as if he had at length reached a decision, he stopped, turned and made his way to the tower, where he pushed open the door and went inside.

"Scarcely two minutes later, Vorovny re-emerged from the building, but in that short space of time his appearance and manner had changed utterly. He had entered the building in a silent and purposeful manner; now, as he emerged, he appeared wild-eyed and hysterical, and scarcely in control of himself. There was blood dripping from his hands, and smeared all over the breast and sleeves of his tunic. He staggered forwards, towards the painters, and cried something incoherently about 'murder' and 'retribution'. One of the men later stated that Vorovny appeared to be smiling broadly as he spoke, but the others disagreed, stating that the expression on his face was more like a rictus of shock or horror, as of something terrible he had done or had witnessed. He did not linger there, but turned and ran off, waving his arms about in the air wildly. Naturally concerned, the painters went over to the tower, pushed the door open and went in. The ground floor was deserted and in perfect order, but when they mounted the stairs to the first floor, they found things in some disarray, with boxes and packages scattered on the floor as if a fight had taken place. In the middle of the floor, Captain Drachkov was lying on his back in a pool of blood, the handle of a knife protruding from his chest.

"One of the men ran off to get help from the infirmary, which is not far away, but he had not got halfway there when he met the medical officer, Major Grigoriev, hurrying towards him in the company of Lieutenant Vorovny.

"The next part of the testimony," Illyanov continued, after he had consulted the papers in his hand for a moment, "is taken from Major Grigoriev's own report on the matter. He states that when he reached the tower he found Captain Drachkov still alive, but only just, his heart beating very faintly. It was clear that he had lost an enormous quantity of blood, and Grigoriev doubted that he would survive. He did all he could to staunch the flow of blood, but it was a hopeless task, and he judged – which proved subsequently to be correct – that the knife blade had severed the aorta. Vorovny, he states, was so beside himself as to be almost witless, so he sent him to notify the military police, whose station was not very far away. At that point, of course, Major Grigoriev did not know what had occurred, and had no idea that it would be Vorovny himself who would be charged with the crime. He sent two of the painters to the infirmary to get a stretcher and more bandages, but by the time they returned it was too late. Drachkov had passed beyond human help. A few moments later, Vorovny returned with a policeman, who took charge of the situation.

"That afternoon, the prosecuting officer of the military police, Major Kratusov, interviewed everyone who had seen Drachkov since the morning, to gain a clear picture of the day's events. Eventually, concluding that no one but Vorovny could possibly have murdered Drachkov, they arrested him that evening. By this time he had recovered a little of his composure, and protested his innocence in the strongest possible terms. According to Vorovny, when he had entered the tower he had found Drachkov just as he was later seen by the others, lying on the upstairs floor, the knife protruding from his chest. He had at once knelt down to see if he could do anything to help, which is why he had become so covered with blood.

"He was then informed that he had been seen following Drachkov around earlier in the day, and asked why he had done so, and why he subsequently followed him into the tower if it was not to attack him. His answer was that he had been trying to pluck up the courage to apologize to Drachkov for his recent behaviour, which he felt had been stupid and unmanly. It was pointed out to him that he and Drachkov had been in the officers' mess at the same time when they were eating dinner. Why, he was asked, had he not spoken to Drachkov then? Vorovny's answer was that he was embarrassed to be seen apologizing to Drachkov in public. Besides, he added, Drachkov was not alone, but sitting with companions, and Vorovny thought that if he approached him, Drachkov might have spoken brusquely and insultingly to him before he could explain himself, and made it practically impossible for him to apologize for what had happened before. As an answer, this seems plausible to me, but the prosecuting officer was not impressed and Vorovny was formally charged with Drachkov's murder and has been held in confinement since. You can see how dark the evidence looks against him, Mr Holmes."

"Indeed. Not all points are against him, however. For instance, he asked the painters if they had seen Captain Drachkov, they told him Drachkov was in the tower, and he thereupon entered the tower himself. Surely it is inconceivable that his intention then was to murder Drachkov, when there were three witnesses stationed close by, and he had, moreover, specifically drawn their attention to his presence and to the fact that he was following Drachkov into the building."

"This was a point that his Imperial Majesty's special investigator made, but Major Kratusov conjectured in response that Vorovny had perhaps entered the tower simply to have words with the other man over their rivalry for Olga Kornieva, but when the discussion became heated, Vorovny lost his temper and struck at the other man."

"Whose was the weapon?" asked Holmes.

"It did not belong to anyone," Illyanov returned, "but was from a stack of such knives lying on a shelf in the storeroom. It must have been seized on the spur of the moment."

Holmes nodded. "Is there any way into the building other than by the main doorway?" he asked after a moment.

"No."

"The windows?"

"There are two ordinary sash windows on each floor, one at the front and one at the back. But those on the ground floor cannot be opened; they have been stuck fast in the closed position since the last time they were painted, about a year ago. The upstairs windows can all be opened, but rarely are, and in any case were all found to be securely fastened on the day of Captain Drachkov's death."

"I suppose if there are a lot of miscellaneous supplies in the building, it might be possible for someone to hide somewhere, behind a crate or something similar?"

"Yes, his Majesty's investigator considered that that might be possible, although there was no evidence to suggest that it was in fact the case."

Holmes appeared to be about to speak, but Illyanov hurriedly continued: "I know you must have many such questions, Mr Holmes, and I will do my very best to answer them, but first I would like to know if you will take the case."

Holmes hesitated for a moment. "I am inclined to do so," said he, "but would not wish to raise expectations only to disappoint them. Tell me, sir, what final conclusion did the Tsar's special investigator reach?"

"He was convinced that the young man was innocent of the crime, but could see no way of proving it."

"And you?"

"I?" responded our visitor in surprise. "I, too, am utterly convinced of his innocence, but—" He broke off and did not finish his sentence.

"You were about to confess that your opinion is not entirely unbiased," said Holmes. "Well, well, that is understandable."

"What do you mean?"

"I do not know what claim you may have to the name of Illyanov, but I very much fancy that I am in fact addressing Count Vorovny himself, father of the accused young man."

Our visitor sprang to his feet and paced about the floor in agitation for some time, his chin in his hand. "You are quite correct," said he at length. "How did you know?"

"On the flap of your leather satchel is a coat of arms and a large Cyrillic letter which I know is pronounced as 'V'," said Holmes. "I observed when you entered that you kept that side of the satchel turned away from us and laid your gloves over the top of it to cover the monogram. That of course served only to draw my attention to it, and when you opened the satchel to get your papers out, I saw what it was you were hiding from us."

"Your powers of observation are as keen as I have heard, Mr Holmes," our visitor remarked, resuming his seat. "I am sorry to have practised this little deception upon you, but I was concerned that if you knew I was Michael Vorovny's father you might dismiss what I told you as nothing but the fond hopes of a misguided parent."

Holmes shook his head. "You need have no concerns on that score," said he. "I have had considerable experience of sifting genuine evidence from wishful thinking."

"There is another reason for my pretence. It is not so very long since our two countries were in conflict. I myself had personal experience of it, being a young subaltern at the siege of Sevastopol. Now, by virtue of my rank, I am Colonel-in-Chief of the Kursakov Regiment. I thought if you knew of my connection to the Army, you might feel disinclined to take the case."

Again Holmes shook his head. "In a better world, the conflict to which you refer would never have occurred. It was the occasion of great valour from the troops on all sides, and an equal amount of blundering from our ministers and diplomats. Let us honour those to whom honour is due, and leave the matter there. I have decided to take the case. When do you wish us to leave?"

"Could you possibly leave today?"

"Yes, if you wish it."

"I have, in anticipation of your agreement, already made all necessary arrangements for the journey. Can you be at Victoria Station by two o'clock?"

"Certainly. But I would wish my good friend and colleague, Dr Watson, to accompany us. His presence has frequently been invaluable to me. You have no objection to coming, do you, old man?" he continued, turning to me.

"None whatever," I returned. "On the contrary, I should be delighted and honoured to accompany you."

"The travel arrangements I have made can readily accommodate Dr Watson," said Vorovny, rising to his feet once more, "so all is settled. Two o'clock at Victoria Station!"

Both Holmes and I were experienced travellers, able to pack a bag and make all preparations in the very minimum of time, and, after a hurried lunch, we reached Victoria at the appointed hour, and caught a fast train to the south coast. We crossed the Channel in the afternoon, and arrived in Brussels late in the evening, just in time to catch the overnight train to Berlin. There we were met by staff from the Russian Embassy, who whisked us off to a nearby hotel for an excellent breakfast, after which we just had time to stretch our legs in a brief stroll round the centre of Berlin, before catching the late morning train to Warsaw. There, we dined in the evening at a hotel by the station before settling into our compartment for the long onward run to Moscow, which we did not reach until the following evening. That night we put up at a fine hotel in the city centre, which I think was a relief to us all after such a long and tiring journey. My room was silent, and the bed very comfortable, but as I drifted off to sleep it seemed I could still hear the sound of railway wheels clattering along the track, and still feel that I was swaying back and forth with the movement of the train.

The following morning, refreshed by a good night's sleep and a hot bath, we set off upon the final stage of our long journey. Our train slipped smoothly away from the bustle of Moscow and south through the picturesque suburbs, and soon we were speeding along across broad plains of farmland, dotted here and there with clumps of woodland, groups of cottages and barns, and frequent brightly painted little churches, with their characteristic onion-shaped domes upon the roof. What struck me most about this countryside was the utter vastness of it. On all sides, these plains stretched away as far as the eye could see. Sometimes, far in the distance, a line of low hills would be discernible, but we never seemed to reach them. Rather, they passed from sight and their place was taken by other hills, which seemed just as far away.

Throughout this journey, the three of us went over and over the evidence which had been accumulated about the murder of Dmitri Drachkov, including the lengthy report of the Tsar's special investigator. Drachkov, it seemed, had a long history of both gambling and the pursuit of the fair sex, to both of which activities he applied a ruthless determination. To Drachkov, it seemed clear, a rival or opponent was an enemy, to be crushed without mercy. And yet a certain forceful charm, the same charm that had made him so successful with the opposite sex, had enabled him to retain a wide circle of male friends, even among those who now supplied this information against him. It was said of him that he could be very open-handed when he wished to be, often buying drinks for others in the officers' mess, especially when he had had success at the card table. These bursts of flamboyant public generosity were remembered by many. But it seemed that such apparent open-handedness was very much on his own terms. He disliked being imposed upon, and more than one man who spoke to the special investigator mentioned that Drachkov was not so generous in private: of those who had approached him for a small loan or some other favour, not one had been successful, and one man had described him as utterly unsympathetic to anyone else's difficulties.

One unusual occurrence that had come to light in the recorded testimony, although no one was prepared to give any details, and the testimony had only been given on the promise of anonymity, was that four years previously, when the regiment had been stationed in the southern Caucasus, a duel had taken place between Drachkov and another officer, although such things were strictly forbidden by Army regulations. The issue between the two men had been their rivalry for a local girl, and the weapons of choice had been sabres. The other man had been badly wounded, and his second had conceded defeat on his behalf. This had saved his life, if not his honour, and the whole affair had been hushed up.

The Tsar's special investigator had also asked several of the officers about Drachkov's gambling. To judge from his questions, his thought seemed to be that if Drachkov had been outstandingly successful, this might have excited resentment, especially if there had seemed anything unfair about his success, or if he had won large amounts of money from his fellow officers. These conjectures proved without foundation, however: the general consensus of opinion was that Drachkov was not markedly better or worse than anyone else at cards or other gambling activities. The only resentment he aroused was at the way he celebrated his victories, tending to crow about his successes and dismiss his failures as sheer bad luck.

On Drachkov's dealings with the fair sex, however, feelings were somewhat different. There was a general grudging respect for his success in this regard, but some expressed distaste at his treatment of women, describing it as callous or manipulative. This might have seemed like little more than envy, but several of the officers had personal reasons for resenting Drachkov. More than one had remarked that anyone hoping to impress a young lady might as well abandon such hopes if Drachkov were present, as he would be sure to cut one out, sometimes by such crude tactics as positioning himself in such a way as to block the lady's view of anyone but himself.

All this testimony certainly illuminated the character of the murdered man, but cast no light at all on what had occurred on the day of his death, or on the possibility that anyone but Michael Vorovny could have murdered him. Drachkov had been seen to leave the officers' mess just before twelve forty, which accorded with the testimony of the men engaged in painting the artillery pieces, who reported that they had seen him enter the tower at a quarter to one. The two officers with whom he had dined both stated that their conversation as they ate had been fairly trivial and that Drachkov had not appeared to be preoccupied in any way. What Holmes might make of any of this, I had no idea, but I confess that the more details I heard of the matter, the less confident I became that he would be able to prove Michael Vorovny's innocence.

Our train made a couple of brief stops at small wayside stations and a longer stop, of about forty minutes, at the station of what appeared to be a fairly substantial town. There we took lunch in a large dining room attached to the station, the meal consisting of some kind of smoked meat, potatoes and pickled cabbage, followed by several cups of tea from a huge and ornate samovar. As we ate, we were entertained by two musicians playing those strange triangular-shaped string instruments they call *balalaikas.* They were very tuneful, and seemed to be well appreciated, for the cap they placed on the floor was full of coins by the time we left. Having rejoined our train, we continued our journey across the seemingly endless southern plains. The weather was very fine now and the air very clear, with just a few fleecy white clouds drifting across a sunny blue sky. Eventually, as the afternoon was turning to evening, we reached Krasnoi and alighted at an attractive station.

In the yard outside, a fresh-faced and smartly dressed young officer was waiting for us beside an open carriage. He introduced himself as Lieutenant Plyanki of the Army legal department, and informed us, in perfect English, that he had been assigned to be our guide for the duration of our stay.

"What are your wishes, Excellency?" he asked, bowing as he addressed Count Vorovny.

"Never mind the formalities, Lieutenant," returned Vorovny in a dismissive tone. "I am not here as the head of the regiment, but in a purely private capacity – as the father of a boy who is charged with murder. It is the wishes of these English gentlemen that are important. Do you understand?"

"Yes, sir."

"I think it is a little late in the day for you to begin your inquiries," Vorovny continued, turning to us. "What I therefore propose is that we show you to your hotel and you can begin your work in the morning."

"Is it far to the hotel?" asked Holmes.

"Not at all. It is in the centre of the town, just a short distance from here."

"Then I should prefer to walk," said Holmes. "I feel the need to stretch my legs, and there is nothing like a walk to stimulate one's intellect."

I heartily agreed with this proposal. Our luggage was therefore sent ahead in the carriage, and the four of us set off to walk to the hotel.

"May I speak, Excellency," said Plyanki, as we made our way along a pleasant tree-lined thoroughfare in the warm evening sunshine.

"I've told you, Plyanki," returned Vorovny, "forget the formalities. Treat me as you would any other officer."

"Then, sir, may I suggest we walk through the park? It is the most pleasant route to take."

We all agreed to this and, a few minutes later, turned into an attractively laid-out park, where the pathways wound between lawns and flowerbeds, bright with the blooms of summer. Somewhere in the distance, a band was playing, its melodious strains seeming to float on the soft, early-evening air. Lieutenant Plyanki had begun to tell us something about the band, when he abruptly broke off.

"Why, here is an odd chance," he remarked, drawing our attention to three elegant-looking ladies in light summer dresses, walking on another path, away to our left. "That is Madam Kornieva, the Colonel's wife, and her daughter, Olga. The lady between them is Madam Grigorieva, wife of the regiment's chief medical officer. They have probably come to hear the band."

The paths we were on converged and crossed a little way ahead, by an ornamental fountain. The women were in animated conversation and had not noticed us, but Count Vorovny called a friendly greeting to them and they stopped and turned.

"Excellency!" cried Madam Kornieva in surprise, bobbing a little curtsey, as did her companions.

"No formalities, ladies, please," said Vorovny. "I am here in a purely private capacity."

As they spoke, I found my gaze drawn irresistibly to the face of young Olga Kornieva, focus of the rivalry between Dmitri Drachkov and Michael Vorovny, of whom I had heard so much. She was certainly remarkably pretty, and I could readily understand how such a face might arouse the strongest passions in a man's breast. Her sharp, bright eyes, pert nose, full red lips and the blush on her cheek like the bloom on a rose were such as men have died for since the dawn of time. But, even as I gazed on this vision of beauty, I found myself wondering whether there were not perhaps something a little hard-hearted in this young lady, to be promenading in these pleasure gardens while her chief admirer was in a prison cell, about to be tried for the murder of his rival. Next moment, this thought was dashed from my head, as Miss Kornieva burst into floods of tears, and it was evident that she was in a very fragile emotional state. Her mother turned to Plyanki and spoke crossly, and he looked a little abashed.

"What did she say?" asked Holmes.

"She says they have spent all day trying to cheer Miss Kornieva up and persuade her to take a walk, and I have ruined all their efforts by mentioning the purpose of your presence here."

Holmes patted Plyanki on the arm. "Do not be too down-hearted," said he. "Your intervention has at least served to show us the depth of Miss Kornieva's feelings."

"One thing is clear, anyway," said Count Vorovny, as we left the ladies and resumed our walk across the park. "My presence, and the formality it causes, can only hamper your investigation, Mr Holmes. I shall therefore remove myself from proceedings. I shall send you a document in the morning, authorizing you to go anywhere in the camp and interview anyone you wish, but I myself shall remain at Colonel Korniev's house, and keep out of your way. However, should you require my presence for any reason, a note will bring me at once."

The following morning, Lieutenant Plyanki arrived at the hotel just after breakfast with Count Vorovny's signed authority. As we set off for the army camp in the carriage, Holmes asked Plyanki his view of the affair, and the young man expressed his strong conviction that Vorovny could not possibly have been responsible for Drachkov's death.

"Would you consider yourself a friend of Michael Vorovny?" Holmes asked.

"Yes, I would. We trained at the officers' college together. But it is not simply our friendship that leads me to believe in his innocence. Everything I know of his character makes it practically impossible. Why, I have never even seen him lose his temper in the slightest degree; the thought that he could stab a fellow officer is inconceivable."

Holmes nodded. "And Miss Kornieva? What do you make of her? You may speak as freely as you wish to us, Lieutenant. What you say will not be repeated to anyone."

"I understand. She is very pretty – that is undeniable – and her character, too, seems an attractive one. But there is something aloof in her manner, which can put a man off."

"You have never entertained hopes in that direction yourself?"

"No," said Plyanki, shaking his head. "I may have admired her from afar, as it were, as I am sure most of the men do, but she has always seemed beyond my reach. Besides, there is another girl, a local girl, on whom I have had my eye for a while. I think we all thought when Vorovny began paying court to her that he was perhaps being overambitious, but she did not rebuff him, so he perhaps has some qualities the rest of us do not."

"I see. Do you have an opinion about Dmitri Drachkov?"

Plyanki considered the question for a moment. "He was a man of very forceful character," he said at length, "no doubt a fine officer, a fine swordsman and, altogether, an imposing presence."

"But you did not admire him?"

"No. I know that some of the younger men were in awe of him. He was, in a sense, a centre of attraction, like a sun about which lesser planets revolve. But there was something in his character that prevented one liking him wholeheartedly. He was a great raconteur, with an immense fund of droll stories and witticisms, but he had really nothing to say about life itself. And, for all his ostentatious displays of friendship, one knew instinctively that he would drop one like a stone if it suited his purposes."

"Do you know anything of his family?"

"Not really. Their circumstances are modest ones, I believe. I seem to remember hearing that his father held a minor clerical position of some sort in Minsk."

"What do you know of the duel he is said to have fought in the Caucasus?"

"Officially, nothing. Unofficially, I know it was with Captain Baturin, a former friend of his. I believe they later overcame their differences – at least, I have often seen them playing cards together. Of course, the duel is never mentioned by anyone."

At the army camp we were admitted without demur upon showing Count Vorovny's signed authority, and Plyanki conducted us to the low building that housed the regiment's legal department. Holmes enquired if any record had been made of the contents of Drachkov's pockets at the time of his death, and, in answer, a small wooden tray was produced containing a miscellany of small items: coins, a pipe and tobacco pouch, matches, a key ring with two keys on it, a small notebook and pencil and so on. For a few moments, Holmes sifted through these small objects, then he picked up a small triangle of paper, which I could see was smeared with blood.

"What is this?" he asked Plyanki. "It looks like the corner of a banknote."

"It is," returned the other. "It is the corner of a twenty-five rouble note. It was found clutched in Drachkov's hand."

"What does the prosecuting officer make of it?"

"Major Kratusov does not consider it relevant to his case, and does not intend to mention it at the hearing. If the defence counsel brings it up, the Major will argue that Vorovny had probably offered money to Drachkov, either in restitution for the attack he had made upon him in the officers' mess, or in an attempt to persuade him to cease his pursuit of Miss Kornieva, and that after he had stabbed him he had pulled the money from his hand, without noticing, in his haste, that he had left this scrap behind."

"Hum! Was the banknote with the missing corner found in Vorovny's possession?"

"No. It is believed he had disposed of it somewhere."

"I see. Is Captain Baturin in the camp at present?"

"Yes, he is employed in the Chief Paymaster's office."

"Then I think I should like to speak to him."

A short walk brought us to another low building, where, after a few moments, Plyanki brought Captain Baturin out to speak to us. He was a thickset, dark-haired man, with a straggling moustache, who faced us with a look of sullen intransigence upon his features. Holmes explained the reason for our presence, and asked him about the duel he had fought with Drachkov, but his face remained impassive.

"What of it?" was his only response.

"I suppose you subsequently made up your differences?"

"Then you suppose wrong."

"And yet I hear you often played cards together."

Baturin let out a harsh, unpleasant laugh. "One might play cards with the Devil himself if it were the only way to pass the time," he said at length, "but one would still detest him." He made to turn away, but paused. "Whoever murdered Drachkov has done us all a favour," he said in a bitter tone. "Let me know when you've decided who it is, and I'll come and shake his hand." With that, he turned on his heel and went back into the building.

"A pithy individual," remarked Holmes in a dry tone. "Let us now inspect the scene of the attack."

We walked round the perimeter of the parade ground, where a large number of soldiers were undergoing drill instruction, and made our way to the far side of the camp. There, just in front of a thick belt of trees, stood a tall, stone-built structure which I recognized from its description as what was known as "the tower". All around the base of it, bright yellow flowers had been planted. Plyanki pushed open the door, and we followed him inside, where he spoke to a short, broad-chested man who was leafing through some papers on a counter, and showed him Count Vorovny's signed warrant. All around the walls were wooden shelves, piled high with miscellaneous items of every shape and size. In a corner, a second man was stacking some large boxes.

The short man was introduced to us as Sergeant Azzarudin, who was in charge of the stores, and, at Holmes's request, he conducted us up a steep wooden stair to the first floor. This was laid out similarly to the floor below, with shelves on every side, the only difference being that the items on the shelves in this case were smaller. A dark stain on the bare boards of the floor was pointed out to us by Azzarudin as the place where Drachkov had met his death.

"The knife that killed him was one of these, I take it," remarked Holmes, indicating a large stack of flat cardboard packets on one of the shelves. "Let us take a look!" He picked up one of the packets, which was about an inch in thickness and seven or eight inches long, and began to open the flap at one end. Azzarudin made some remark, which Plyanki translated for us as a warning to be careful, as the blade was very sharp. Holmes nodded as he withdrew the contents of the packet, which was wrapped in some sort of heavy, greased brown paper. This he carefully unwrapped, revealing a large-bladed knife with a wooden handle. For a few moments, Holmes examined the knife, then he carefully wrapped it up again in the paper and slipped it back into its box, before replacing it on the shelf.

"Where was the box that had contained the murder weapon found?" he asked.

"On the shelf beside the other boxes."

"And the greased paper?"

"In the box."

Holmes then examined the windows. The one at the front of the building looked out across the camp, the one at the rear onto the belt of trees that ran to right and left in front of the boundary wall of the camp. They were both sash windows, and Holmes lifted up the lower half of each in turn and leaned out, looking about for a few moments. Evidently satisfied, he closed the windows again and refastened them, then he led the way to the top floor, where he again made a careful examination of the whole room, including the windows, before we descended once more to the ground floor. There he questioned Sergeant Azzarudin about the system of documentation used in the stores building.

"He says," Plyanki relayed to us, "that anyone wishing to get something from the store must present a requisition form detailing what is required, and the form must be signed by an officer."

"And if he and his assistant are absent?"

"Then senior officers, who have a key, may let themselves in and take what they require, but they, too, must always leave a signed requisition form on his counter detailing what they have taken."

"Were there any such forms left on his counter when he returned from lunch on the day of Drachkov's death?"

"He says not."

"Can you ask him if there are any problems with petty pilfering? Tell him he must answer honestly. He himself is not being accused of anything."

"He says there has been very little since he took over the work. It is a source of pride to him. During his predecessor's time there were a lot of mysterious shortages, items going missing and so on. It was particularly bad during the time the regiment was stationed in the Caucasus region, four or five years ago."

"What became of his predecessor?"

"He was eventually convicted of gross negligence, demoted and sent to a fort near Irkutsk, in Siberia."

"Was anyone else involved?"

"Yes, but nothing could be proved, as some of the records were missing. Azzarudin says that his superior at the time, Major Bannishevsky, was very angry at what had occurred, but the lack of evidence meant he could do nothing, and the matter was closed."

"When did Sergeant Azzarudin leave for lunch on the day of Drachkov's death?"

"About ten past twelve."

"Did his assistant leave at the same time?"

"No, he had left five minutes earlier. Azzarudin had stayed behind to finish posting some entries in his daily logbook."

"Please ask him if he thinks it possible that anyone might have been hiding in the building without his knowledge when he went off to lunch."

"He says that that is almost impossible. They had not been very busy that day, and he is sure he had seen everyone who came and went in the course of the morning."

"Very well. I think I should like to speak to the medical officer now. Could you ask him to come over here?"

"Of course," said Plyanki. "Count Vorovny's signed warrant gives you the authority to summon anyone you wish. Would you like me to fetch anyone else?"

We had left the building as they were speaking, and emerged into bright sunlight. Holmes stood a long moment in thought before replying, then he took Plyanki off to one side, pointed at the men painting the artillery pieces in the distance, and issued some instructions, but I did not catch his words.

"Now, Watson," he said, turning to me, as Plyanki strode away, "I would like you to help me look for some flowers in the woods."

My companion led the way round to the rear of the building and into the wood behind it. As far as I could see there were no flowers among the trees, but he proceeded very carefully and methodically, peering closely around every tree he passed. Gradually, we worked our way to the left, and edged our way a little deeper into the wood, my friend's back bent over as he scrutinized every square foot of ground.

"I don't really know what we are looking for," I said after a while, "but there are the remains of some flowers here, Holmes. They're dead, I'm afraid."

He came over to see what I had found, and let out a cry of triumph as he stooped down and picked up a small heap of faded brown foliage.

"Well done, old man! It was a long shot, Watson!" he cried as he rose to his feet, a gleam of satisfaction in his eye. "A very long shot, but it has hit the bullseye! Would you do me the great favour of holding these leaves?"

"Certainly," I said, taking the dull-looking little bundle from his hand. I said nothing more, although I confess that the thought passed through my mind that my friend had temporarily lost his sanity.

As we emerged from the woods, Plyanki was approaching with a dapper-looking, middle-sized man whom he introduced to us as the chief medical officer, Major Grigoriev. He shook Holmes's hand and, at the latter's request, we returned to the tower and ascended to the first floor.

"This is where Drachkov was lying when you found him?" Holmes asked Grigoriev.

"That's right," replied Grigoriev via our translator.

"He was still alive then?"

"Yes; there was a faint, slow beat from his heart. Had the wound been a little to the side, the blade would have penetrated the heart, and he would have been dead already. As it was, the wound was to the aorta – as I surmised from the large quantity of blood on the floor – and I thought it unlikely he could survive more than one or two minutes at the most. Of course, I did what I could for him, but I couldn't save him."

"The fact that no one could survive for long with such a wound suggests that the attack had been made only a few minutes previously, then?"

"Yes, five minutes at the most, I should say."

"Is there always someone on duty at the infirmary, in case of such medical emergencies?"

"No, not always. When we are on home soil, such emergencies are thankfully few and far between."

"So, in a sense, Vorovny was fortunate to find you there, considering it was dinner-time?"

"That is true. My assistants had gone off to dinner and, ordinarily, I would have done so myself. But there were some medical records I wished to complete, so I told them to bring me something back on a plate."

"And when Vorovny burst in?"

"I was still working on the records. Vorovny was practically incoherent, and I couldn't make out what had happened, but I could see from his manner that it must be something very serious – moreover, he had copious amounts of blood on his hands and tunic – so I didn't even bother to get fully dressed. I just seized my medical bag and dashed off with him at once, in my shirtsleeves."

"How long did it take you to get here?"

"Less than a minute, I should say. The infirmary is not far from here."

"And then?"

"Of course, I didn't know then exactly what had happened, but I could see that Drachkov was dying. I sent Vorovny to bring one of the policemen and tell the men that were painting the guns to fetch a stretcher at once. But just as they returned, Drachkov breathed his last."

There had been footsteps downstairs as Grigoriev had been speaking and I turned to see, to my great surprise, Count Vorovny himself, followed by Captain Baturin and a tall, distinguished-looking officer with a large moustache, whom Lieutenant Plyanki introduced to us as Major Kratusov, the chief prosecuting officer. At Holmes's request, Sergeant Azzarudin was also called upstairs to join us.

"I got your message," said Count Vorovny to us in English. "What is it you want?"

"To explain to you all what really occurred here on the fatal day," said Holmes.

"What! But you have only been here a couple of hours!"

"The truth of a conclusion is not dependent upon the time taken to reach it. If you will act as interpreter, Lieutenant Plyanki, I will begin.

"The first thing to note is that Drachkov did not bring a requisition form with him when he came here on the day he died. No such form was found in the building, or on his person. We must conclude, therefore, that he did not come here to collect some item from the store, but for some other purpose, probably to meet someone privately, at a time when there would be few people about.

"The second point is that when Michael Vorovny arrived, he did not know that Drachkov was in here, but had to ask the painters if they had seen him anywhere about. Nor can it plausibly be argued that Vorovny's ignorance on the point was feigned, as such a pretence could serve no conceivable purpose. All it achieved was to draw the attention of the men outside to his presence here, and to the fact that he had entered the building. Therefore Vorovny was not the person Drachkov came here to meet.

"We now come to the weapon that killed Drachkov, which was one of the knives on the shelf here. I have unwrapped one myself, and do not believe it can be done in under twenty seconds. Twenty seconds may not sound very long, but it is an appreciable length of time when two men are standing side by side. Drachkov could not possibly have been unaware that the other man was unwrapping and extracting a knife if he was here when it happened, even if an attempt were made to distract him, by handing him some money, say, or dropping some money on the floor. Therefore the knife had been unwrapped before Drachkov arrived. This is also suggested by the fact that the empty box was on the shelf with the other boxes, with the greased paper stuffed back inside it, as if to prevent Drachkov from noticing that one of the knives had been removed from its wrapping. As Vorovny arrived after Drachkov, and was in this building for barely two minutes, it could not have been he that took the knife from the box."

At this point, after a brief delay for the translation to be given, Holmes was interrupted by Major Kratusov.

"You give an interesting alternative view of the matter," he said via Plyanki, "but it is not conclusive. Perhaps Drachkov himself unwrapped the knife, either to inspect it or simply to pass the time, and Vorovny subsequently took it from him, either by force or duplicity, before using it against him. I am aware that Drachkov did not have a requisition form with him, but he may simply have forgotten to bring one, or perhaps, as you say, he had not come to requisition supplies, but to meet someone, that someone being Vorovny. As to why Vorovny spoke to the men outside, there might be many reasons. Perhaps he simply wanted to know if Drachkov had arrived yet or not."

Holmes nodded his acknowledgement of these points, but remarked in an unruffled manner that he had only just begun his account.

"I come now to the money involved in the case," he continued after a moment. "That there is money involved is a certainty, for the corner of a banknote was found clutched in Drachkov's hand. I understand it has been suggested that Vorovny might have been offering this to Drachkov for some reason, but this strikes me as very unlikely, and does not accord with human nature. The issue between the two men was a personal one, concerning an affair of the heart, about which Vorovny had felt both resentful and humiliated. But perhaps he had come to realize that, although few admit it, most men lose out to a rival in love at least once in their lives. If so, he may have accepted that his behaviour was wrong, and concluded that he should apologize to Drachkov to heal the rift between them, as he maintains. This strikes me as eminently plausible, as such an apology would demonstrate clearly that Vorovny was more mature than had previously been apparent, and this would help to repair his injured self-respect. But to suggest that money might play a part in this is surely absurd: such a transaction would, on the contrary, tend to confirm, both to himself and to others, Vorovny's position of relative weakness, and would thus damage his own self-respect yet further. Moreover, it seems highly perverse to suggest such a thing when there is a far simpler and more likely explanation:

"It is common knowledge that Drachkov was frequently open-handed in the officers' mess, and always seemed to have plenty of money at his disposal. There seems, though, something of a mystery as to how this could be. I am informed that he was not from a wealthy family and that his gambling activities were not notably more successful than those of anyone else. It seems likely, then, that his pay was supplemented by some other income, possibly of an illicit nature. One might suspect that he was profiting at the Army's expense, by pilfering army property, selling it elsewhere and pocketing the proceeds, although Sergeant Azzarudin maintains that there has been little pilfering from these stores since he has been in charge. There is another possibility, however, which is that Drachkov was not engaged in such theft himself, but knew who was, or who had been in the past. If he had evidence to prove such criminal activity, he would thus be able to extort money from those involved by threatening to reveal the truth."

"This is just speculation," interrupted Kratusov.

"All theories are to some extent speculative," returned Holmes. "The advantage of my view is that it provides a sound explanation for the banknote found in Drachkov's hand. I think the meeting here had been arranged between Drachkov and his victim for the latest payment to be made, but the man that Drachkov was blackmailing had decided that he could bear it no longer and intended to put an end to it once and for all. He was here before Drachkov, removed the knife from its box and secreted it in his clothing. When Drachkov arrived, he handed over some banknotes, and then, no doubt pretending to feel for some more money in his pocket, pulled out the knife and thrust it into Drachkov's chest before he could react."

"But Vorovny was seen here by several witnesses," protested Major Kratusov. "Your supposed murderer was seen by no one at all."

"There are good reasons for that. In the first place, he was already in this building before the painters returned to their work. In the second place, he left the building by that back window over there, and escaped through the wood. I know this as well as if I had seen it with my own eyes. You will have observed," Holmes continued, as Kratusov made to interrupt him again, "that flowers have been planted in a narrow bed all around the outside wall of this building. Immediately below that window, however, there are no flowers, but simply bare earth. The reason is that when the murderer dropped from the windowsill, having pushed the window shut from the outside, he landed on some of the flowers and broke them. Realizing that the crushed flowers would betray his escape route, he pulled them out of the ground altogether, smoothed the earth with his foot and carried the broken flowers away with him into the wood. When he judged he was far enough away, he dropped his bundle of flowers behind a tree, believing that no one would ever notice them there. Unfortunately for him, my colleague and I found these remains where he had left them."

At this point, Holmes indicated the bundle of brown leaves in my hand, and I held them out for everyone to see.

"These leaves and stems," my friend continued, "are of the same type as the other flowers planted by this building. There are no flowers of this sort growing in the wood. My colleague will vouch for where we found them, and I have also left some of the leaves there to help you identify the spot."

"That is certainly suggestive," said Major Kratusov. "But there is something you have overlooked, a simple fact that renders your whole theory valueless. The window over there was found by one of my men to be fastened shut on the inside. The supposed murderer who you claim jumped down from the window could not possibly have closed the catch."

"I have not overlooked that fact," returned Holmes in a measured tone. "Indeed, that is one of the last pieces of evidence which enables us to solve this little riddle. The catch was fastened later."

"Later? That is impossible. When? By whom?"

"There is only one man who could have any reason to fasten the catch on the window, and that man is the murderer. There is only one time it could have been done, and that was when Vorovny had been sent to get a policeman, and the other men had been sent to get a stretcher. It was you, Major Grigoriev," said Holmes, turning to the medical officer, "when you were left alone here with the dying Drachkov, the man you murdered."

Grigoriev burst out with a stream of heated language. "He says that is nonsense," said Plyanki to us.

Holmes shook his head. "You claim you stayed at the infirmary at dinner-time in order to do some work, but it was really because you had arranged to meet Drachkov here. When Vorovny came to fetch you, you say that in your haste you dashed out with him in your shirtsleeves, but why were you not fully dressed in the first place? According to your own account, you had not been engaged in medical work of any kind, but simply in clerical work. Of course, the true reason you did not have your tunic on was because you had just hurriedly taken it off when you realized it was splattered with the blood of your victim. You did not intend to sever the aorta, for you knew how the blood would surge out from such a wound. You meant to stab Drachkov in the heart and kill him instantly, but your aim was not true. Where is that bloodstained tunic now, Major Grigoriev?"

For a long moment, Grigoriev stood in silence, swaying slightly from side to side. His face was pale, and his manner was far removed from the composed figure who had entered the tower just a short time before.

"Drachkov was a swine," he said abruptly. "I wish I had killed him years ago. During the time we were posted to the Caucasus, I foolishly allowed myself to become involved in the illicit sale of Army medical supplies. Drachkov discovered this, and had the evidence to prove it in some records he had taken from the supplies office. He threatened me with exposure unless I paid him off. I had no choice but to do as he demanded, or it would have been the end of my Army career and a possible prison sentence. But he was never satisfied and always demanded more, until he has practically bled me dry. The filthy swine even tried to make love to my wife, knowing that I dare not oppose him.

"So, yes, I killed him, and would happily do so again. I had no intention of placing the blame on young Vorovny, but just as I thrust in the knife and snatched the money back from Drachkov's hand, I heard voices outside and saw through the window that Vorovny was about to enter the building. I quickly climbed out of that back window, dropped onto the flowerbed below, and ran as fast as I could through the wood, back to the infirmary. Shortly afterwards, when I returned here with Vorovny, I closed the catch on the window when I was left alone for a few moments, as this gentleman has surmised."

Later that afternoon, Count Vorovny called at our hotel, as we were taking tea in the garden.

"Michael is being released," he informed us. "Major Kratusov is just completing all the necessary forms. I have sent an encrypted telegram to his Imperial Majesty at St Petersburg, describing the outcome of your investigations. He sends his warmest congratulations and says he will communicate with you again after your return to England with a suitable token of his appreciation. He expresses astonishment at the speed with which you conducted your investigation, Mr Holmes. He says he had expected you would be looking into the matter for a week, but you completed it in half a day!"

"It was not so difficult," returned Holmes in a depreciatory tone. "I had the great advantage of having before me all the information that Major Kratusov and others had already gathered. Under such circumstances, it often becomes a matter of simply sifting the evidence to separate what is significant from what is not. Sometimes it is the one item that does not fit very readily into the official theory which turns out to be the most significant clue. So it was with the torn corner of the banknote found in the dead man's hand. Major Kratusov's explanation for that was undoubtedly the weakest part of his whole case, but it became one of the foundation stones of my own explanation."

That evening, after we had dined, we took a stroll in the park and sat smoking our pipes and listening to the Kursakov Regimental Band playing a succession of melodious airs. The daylight had almost gone by then, and a series of lamps had been lit along the pathways in the park, giving it a gay, almost magical appearance. As we sat there, we were joined by Lieutenant Plyanki, Count Vorovny and the latter's son, Michael, a pleasant-looking dark-haired young man who wrung our hands warmly and expressed his profound gratitude to us in a mixture of Russian and English which was difficult to follow but clear in its intent. Moments later a carriage arrived which Plyanki informed us was that of Colonel Korniev and his family. As they alighted, the Colonel's daughter at once sought us out and the hand-wringing performance was repeated, with the addition this time of a flood of tears. Holmes patted Miss Kornieva's hand, but that only seemed to make her cry more, until, at last, she went to sit next to Michael Vorovny and wring his hand instead.

"Young ladies!" said Holmes to me with a chuckle. "Have you ever noticed, Watson, that they cry when they are sad and cry, too, when they are happy. That is surely a mystery which no detective will ever solve!"

# The Mystery of the Red City

## Alison Littlewood

In all my years of recording these sketches of my friend Sherlock Holmes's remarkable capacity for observation and deduction, there have been several cases of which I have found it pertinent not to speak. Some of those, through the passage of time, have since become possible to recount, but there remain some that may only be committed to the memory and not the page. Some concern matters of state too momentous to impart; others, the reputation of illustrious families; while others still have remained the secret only of those directly involved because of the bidding of Sherlock Holmes himself, increasingly so, because of his growing disdain for popular notoriety.

And yet there is another case of which I have never yet spoken for quite another reason; that being my own troubled mind. In truth, it can barely be called a "case" at all. It was less an investigation than an odd incident that surely left too great an impression upon me; an effect that can only be caused by my own credulity and a singular lapse in judgement. No: it was an odd incident to be sure, and yet I have determined to lay it before the interested reader, not for any purpose of enlightenment but for mere amusement, and perhaps some insight into the mind of my brilliant colleague. Perhaps too, my motive is in part a selfish one, for despite the cast it lays upon my own character, I must confess that I find it lingering in my thoughts on these, the darkest of evenings; and as meaningless as the incident may be, I find I cannot rid myself of the memory of it in any other fashion.

It was several years ago that Sherlock Holmes made a some-what dramatic entrance at the door of 221b Baker Street. It was a grey afternoon somewhere on the verge of autumn, yet the air was warm and a little humid, interspersed with colder draughts that gave every expectation of rain. My companion had been gone for some months, having been called to the Continent to assist the French *gendarmerie* on an entirely different matter, one that he had telegrammed to inform me that he had solved almost at once. The note of triumph was followed by the news that he was on the trail of a new mystery, one that would take him down through Spain to the southern-most coast of the Continent, and from thence on a steamer to the north of Africa.

I felt no little consternation at the news, for life had seemed a trifle dull without my dazzling companion to enliven it with some new puzzle at every turn, and this case seemed likely to take him away for some time yet. Holmes did not travel for pleasure but for intellectual and professional stimulation, and I fancied that the lure of a mystery in such lands must have been of a most intriguing nature. Thus it came as a great surprise, if not a shock, to look out of the window that evening at the sound of a hansom cab and to see the familiar tall figure, yet sadly emaciated, if not gaunt, being helped from it by the driver. He glanced up at the window, just once, and upon catching sight of the deathly paleness of his face, I hurried down the stair to assist him.

"Quite unnecessary, Watson," were the first words to pass his lips, and yet at close quarters, my thought was that he appeared more stricken than ever. His skin, though pale, had an unhealthy grey tinge, most unlike the tanned complexion which should have been expected from someone who had travelled so far to the south, and he seemed quite weak as he stepped towards the door. He did not object, moreover, when I took his bag and escorted him inside. Twice he stopped for breath upon the stair, though he waved away my hand when I went to support him.

Once inside, he did not pause to remove his warm grey travel-ling cloak but settled back into his chair, rested his feet upon the bearskin rug with a sigh, and proceeded to look about the room.

His gaze rested upon his old accoutrements: the pipe rack on the corner of the mantelpiece; the Persian slipper in which he was wont to keep a supply of tobacco; and the jackknife with which he transfixed as yet unanswered correspondence. There was his violin in the corner; on an acid-scarred table, his chemical paraphernalia; there, on a shelf, the books with which he expanded his knowledge of matters which pertained to his chosen course of career. He looked over them all, as if taking a catalogue, or ensuring that nothing had been removed during his absence.

I reminded him that I was a doctor as well as a friend, offered him assistance and indeed sustenance, but he waved away all of my questions and endeavours as if they were circling flies.

"All in good time, Watson," he interjected. "I will take nothing, if you please; but I should like to tell you of my rather peculiar journey."

"Anything," was of necessity my answer; for I knew that when Holmes's mind was engaged on some fixed course, he often refused all repast until the fervour of his will had carried him through to its conclusion. Now he turned his eyes upon me, and I saw that, despite his pallor, they shone as brightly as ever.

"I had not meant," he began, "to travel so far, and into such unfamiliar lands. However, following the conclusion of the case of the missing hatpin, and leaving its repercussions in the hands of the *gendarmerie*, I was approached by no lesser a personage than Lord P—, who pressed for my assistance in a matter concerning his recently widowed cousin, a Mrs Mary Stanier, who was currently residing in Morocco. The situation offered most interesting possibilities as well as the promise of many varied sights along the road, and Lord P— seemed able to provide the hospitality and company of a not unintelligent travelling companion. And so I was drawn ever onward, towards a case that promised to be one of the most odious and distasteful I had yet experienced.

"By his account, Mrs Mary Stanier was a steady, sensible woman of seven and twenty, who nevertheless appeared to have become prone to certain fancies since her widowhood. Still, there remained some oddities about the case that aroused my interest.

"Mrs Stanier was a much devoted wife, who had followed her husband's interests as far as the heights of the Atlas Mountains and to Marrakech, known for the colour of its ancient walls as the Red City. The late Mr Stanier, a man of private fortune, was a naturalist who had of late become fascinated by palaeontology. The mountains of Morocco, now cast high, once lay beneath the ocean, and their richness in trilobites and ammonites, some of remarkable size and quality, is renowned in such circles. Her journey must have been one of extremes, for the heat of the city would soon have given way to the coolness of the heights, which at certain times of year are capped with snow, even while, far below, the deserts burn. Her constitution, while never particularly strong, bore such tribulation admirably. Mr Stanier, unfortunately, despite previous rude health, showed no such fortitude. It was only a few months since his arrival in the country that he sickened and died.

"It was Mrs Stanier's wish that his body be returned to the cool verdure and calming air of the country of his birth, but because of some difficulty over their travel arrangements and her inability to gather her wits following his sudden death, together with the unfortunate effects upon a cadaver of such persistent heat, matters were settled in a rather hurried fashion; namely, that the gentleman was buried, far from his home and connections, in a foreign grave.

"One can only imagine his wife's distress, and such, indeed, was the reason she herself had lingered in the country. It is a sorrow that she did, according to Lord P—. If she had only left sooner, perhaps the following events would never have occurred.

"But she did not leave and, soon after, awful news reached the lady. The grave, so recently closed, had been ransacked; her husband's remains terribly mutilated, indeed, rendered unrecognizable; and the whole left open to the burning heat of the Moroccan sun. One can only imagine, Watson, the putridity of what remained in that open grave. Perhaps, indeed, it would be a mercy that much would have remained hidden by the swarms of flies that must have descended upon it."

Holmes leaned back in his chair at this, his eyes taking on a faraway expression. Well could I imagine that he saw, not the room in which he sat, but the red walls of some desert city. I could not suppress a recollection, too, of his penchant for any case that offered anything out of the common way, and did not fail to see how such astonishing particulars would have captured his attention. Little wonder, then, that he had followed it headlong, even to his current state of health.

"If that were not enough for her to bear," he continued, "the very next evening, she was subjected to further distress – that caused by a rather odd theft.

"That evening she retired rather late, as had become her wont since her bereavement. The nights were rather warm even for the time of year, and her disturbed condition of mind had made her restless. That night she awoke to a sound in the room below her own, the one that her husband had used as a study. She knew it to be full of fossils, the traces of creatures long dead. The room had been left unchanged since the demise of its owner, and none had disturbed it.

"Noises were not unknown throughout the night in the heart of Marrakech. Often she would awake to the sound of some strange industry or the coarse bray of a donkey or mule, or the pre-dawn wail of the muezzin calling the faithful of that land to prayer. The home they had made for themselves was in one of the more ancient structures in the city, namely, a riad. In that nation, Watson, they do not wear their wealth on the outside. The plainest wall can hide wonders, as I was soon to discover.

"In the lady's case, a bare wooden door in a simple ochre wall, coated with the dust of the passage of foot and hoof, was the only clue to her residence. The rooms of a riad are all outer; their windows and doors look inward. And at the centre of the dwelling is its heart, a magnificent courtyard garden, open to the sky yet shaded from its worst excesses of heat, with cool arbours and gently rushing fountains to soothe the mind. And unlike the snub face the riad turns to the world, every surface within bears the most splendid decoration: mosaics of every hue and pattern, the tile-work named *zellij*, the secret and pride of the city's master craftsmen. Intricate forms confuse and delight at every turn. The radiance of their plan almost exhausts the eye in its detail and yet, when seen as a whole, it becomes a most harmonious achievement, a reflection, perhaps, of the glories of nature. And yet here is science too; the geometric shapes are the embodiment of logic and reason. And here is art and religion, for great words are woven around the walls, their curving forms a mystery to the foreign eye and yet redolent of the spheres of thought to which man should aspire.

"I digress, dear Watson. Mr Stanier's study was similarly lined on every wall and indeed the floor with such work, and its surface was the cause of the sound which had disturbed his widow that night. For it was footsteps that she heard, quite plainly, ringing out against the tile and amplified by their cold, hard surface.

"Surprised that one of the servants must be about at this unaccustomed hour, she rose and went to seek the reason why. The lady's feet were clad in soft slippers, and so she was able to make her approach quite silently. Once outside the room, however, her courage failed her, and though she reached out a hand to push open the door, she did not immediately enter.

"What she saw, Watson, was this: a dark figure standing at the opposite side of the room, by her husband's desk. The room was lit only by a lamp left burning in the corridor, but by their height and form, she ascertained the intruder to be a man. He was holding something in his hand, staring down at it, quite lost in thought. She knew at once what it was, however, by the flickers of light that caught its edge. It was a photograph of her. Mr Stanier had kept it ever by his work. It had been taken on the occasion of their wedding, and was housed in a small yet rather valuable silver frame.

"At that point, the lady let out a gasp, and the intruder responded at once. He leapt across the room and brushed by her in the doorway, the picture still held in one hand while he endeavoured to cover his face with the other. He failed, Watson."

Here my companion, ever with a sense of the dramatic, paused for effect. I waited.

"The man turned as he passed, and the light coming from the corridor, for a moment, lay full in his face. The lady swears that the features revealed to her were those of her husband."

"Goodness."

"Goodness indeed, Watson. Here he was, the man with whom she had spent her life – he was before her just as if he had never left – and he was standing close by, so as to convince her that no room for doubt remained.

"She called to him, but he did not answer. He sprang away with the most unaccustomed speed, and hurried from her. Sure-footedly, he aimed straight through the inner rooms and into the courtyard, and to the outer door, through which he made his escape, taking with him only one thing: her likeness. Now, what do you think of that, Watson?"

"Why – that the man wasn't dead; that perhaps he wished to leave and had somehow convinced everyone he had died."

"Such was my thought. It seemed straightforward enough, and yet . . . intriguing."

"Indeed."

"But our mystery goes deeper. The next day, the photograph was discovered, abandoned, in the very place where Mr Stanier had been buried. It was not by his memorial, however; it was found next to another disordered grave, this one belonging to a local man, a purveyor of perfumed oils in the souk, who had been interred there the day before."

"Good heavens."

"Odd, is it not, Watson? Though it was fortunate that, in this case, the grave was merely disturbed, and not desecrated. The body had not been exposed as had that of Mr Stanier – or at least the body that had been buried in his place, for the vehemence of the attack was such that none had been able to recognize his features."

"Then my theory is even more certain." Even as I said the words, I knew my friend must have seen more in it. His eyes flashed in triumphant confirmation. However, he was not yet ready to reveal his conclusion.

"Observation, my dear Watson. Observation and deduction are the key, not theories."

He had said as such a thousand times. I bowed my head in acknowledgement. "And yet you requested I proceed from incomplete information," I said with a smile.

"I did! Then let me tell you, Watson, of my arrival in that place, and of the things I found there."

"I am all attention." I noted that there seemed to be no tiring him. Though his countenance remained pallid, his eyes shone more brightly than ever. I am not sure, even now, if there was not a sparkle of mischief about them.

"I found Mrs Stanier just as she had been described to me: a sober, sensible-seeming lady who could have been called a beauty, if one were to take an interest in such matters. She was accompanied by a maid, a silly-looking creature with a mass of curls protruding from her cap. Also with her: a cook, a Moroccan housekeeper and his thirteen-year-old son, who ran errands, cleaned boots and such like. Her recounting of the tale was much as I have told you thus far; I shall not repeat it. I shall tell a little of the locality, however.

"The morning after my arrival I called upon the housekeeper's son, Hamza, and required that he should show me about a little, for the streets of Marrakech are a labyrinth to those unaccustomed to its ways. I also surmised that the youngest of eyes sometimes see more than those of their elders, and was curious to question him without seeming to do so. He led me down through the medina, deeper into the city, and into the souk. The souk of Marrakech is one of the world's wonders, Watson. Or rather, it is many souks, all joined into one; its narrow alleyways actually have a pattern, concealed to the unfamiliar eye, and it has a logic and districts all of its own. There is the souk *chouari*, that of the carpenters, the air redolent with the scent of cedar; the souk *des bijoutiers*, a narrow lane gleaming with jewels of all kinds; the souk *el attarine*, heady with perfumes, spices and oils; and others with used items, leather-working, copper goods, basket-weaving, silver teapots and rather splendid intricate lamps.

The mean alleyways confound the eye, not just with their meandering, but with the ever-changing colours, scents and noise; the crowds pressing everywhere, men in hooded djella-bas, women covered head to toe in black; cries in Darija, French and Berber, calls to try wares, or just to look, look, *look*; and, every so often, a yell of command meaning that one must move immediately or be trampled by a passing donkey.

"It is an assault upon the eyes, ears and olfactory senses, Watson, and yet it has a certain beauty all its own, the sense of a half-glimpsed pattern that, should one care to make a study of it, would resolve into some hitherto unsuspected meaning. And yet I had to suspend my interest and listen to more wonderments from the lips of my guide, for he told the most fantastical stories as we went, local fairy tales, I suppose, about those who went into the souk and never emerged again. In truth, Watson, I could not find that a strange idea in itself. It seemed to me not at all unlikely that a person may be lost in the souk, without the need to imagine any supernatural occurrence.

"And yet he recounted another tale, one that, in the local eye at least, had rather more relevance to our case.

"We emerged from the souk, quite suddenly, into a wide, paved area of dust and brilliant sunlight, dotted with yet more traders. This was the square of Djemaa el Fna, quite famous, and quite foreign. Women sat on stools concealed beneath their abayas, in the full heat of the day, holding out their hands painted with henna, offering to carry out similar daubings to the women passing by. Hawkers sold the most remarkable assortment of goods: apricots, figs, tobacco, tinctures of argan oil, side by side with street dentists plying their trade, sitting before blankets covered with old and yellowed teeth. And a cacophony of sound raged over it all – harsh, discordant squeals emerging from the most fabulous of instruments, each virtuoso vying with the next to make the ears ring. I had been led to expect snake charmers, and there they were, in abundance, flutes at their lips. Besides all this, there were the apes."

Here he paused.

"Barbary apes," he continued, "are not strictly apes but monkeys; namely, the only macaques to be found outside of Asia, as Mr Stanier, as a naturalist, would no doubt have been able to tell. I steered well clear of the brutish creatures, I can tell you, Watson, though one scoundrel tried to throw one onto my shoulders, afterwards demanding some small coin in return for his 'service'. The thing's mouth gaped wide as I passed, in some sort of challenge or grimace. It was possessed of long, yellow teeth, some appearing quite the length of a man's fingers, and they protruded like fangs.

"Most unpleasant creatures, and ones which, I understand, in certain quarters, some pains had been taken to drive from the city, rather than make them the point of their entertainments." Holmes sat back with a sigh, passing a hand across his face before continuing.

"And then we found the storyteller's tent, and my young guide pulled on my sleeve and bade me stop. That was when he told of the superstition I aforementioned, which also happened to be the subject of the storyteller's art. The boy told me of a terrible and most shocking creature, namely, the ghul."

He grinned. No: he bared his teeth.

"I must tell you, Watson, the Moroccans are most spiritual people, who see the workings of the ineffable all around them. As an example, they believe that spirits, the djinn, are every-where. Men set charms over their doors to ward them away. They remove their shoes before entering the temples, lest djinn should cling to them and steal their way inside. In every turn of the wheel of fate, they see their hand. They say they are made of the desert's hot breath; unsurprising, perhaps, in a climate where one can feel the Saharan air blasting through the streets." He pulled his cloak more tightly about him, as if he were not yet re-accustomed to the cooler climes in which he found himself.

"The ghul, though, is a different creature, and of a peculiarly godless and wicked temperament. It hungers, always, for the taste of human flesh, though not that of the living. No: the ghul consumes only the dead. And once it has tasted such foul meat, the ghul in some way takes on a little of the deceased person's essence. It assumes their outward form, the aspect of their eye, their nose, their lip, every detail being exactly alike. Some even believe it assumes a little of their temperament.

"One can only imagine the effect of such a tale, when applied to the case of the late Mr Stanier."

"Indeed! So the locals must have believed him eaten: his grave opened, his body consumed, and this seeming appearance of him at his home, after his burial – that was the ghul, outwardly like him in form . . ."

"Exactly, my dear Watson. Such was their surmise."

"And yet it is impossible. You no doubt eliminated it from your inquiry at once."

"I eliminated it, but I did not forget it. For one cannot tell how such a chimera of the mind may influence the actions of living men. Still, I could not help but smile at the seriousness of the young fellow's telling. After that he became most taciturn, and shortly afterwards we returned to the riad. We made only a brief visit to the graveyard where Mr Stanier had been buried, which was unenlightening, and besides which, most unpleasant; on such a hot day, the stink coming from the leather tanneries situated just beyond the place was something to be endured.

"And now we have all the clues before us, Watson. Whatever do you make of them?"

I laughed. "Surely not all, Holmes."

He bowed.

"Well . . ." I thought a little. "Perhaps, if Mr Stanier had been poisoned in some way – perhaps by the venom of a snake – he may have been taken for dead when he was merely rendered insensible. Such cases have been known. Later, he could have been revived, but kept isolated, either by his own confusion or the malevolent intent of some third party. You said the body in the grave was rendered unidentifiable, which may have been a deliberate ploy, against the event that Mrs Stanier had carried her wish to have her husband's remains removed to England."

Now it was Holmes's turn to laugh. "You delight me, as ever, dear fellow," he said. "And such had, briefly, entered my mind, before being dismissed as nonsense. But before my case could be concluded, my investigation was curtailed. I was taken by some foreign illness into the arms of such a fever that I was confined to my bed."

I ran my eyes once more over Holmes's wasted visage. I knew him to be capable of the highest exertions when in the midst of an especially interesting case, and it was quite disturbing to think of him laid low in such a fashion.

"Indeed, I do not exaggerate when I say that, on one particular night about a week after the preceding events, I lay in my room as near to death as any man may be without entering its door," said Holmes. "And yet, despite my fever, I often found myself to be extraordinarily cold." He suddenly looked off into nothing, his eyes unfocused and blank; I thought I saw him shudder.

"One night, I had lain awake, listening to the peaceful sound of water trickling into the courtyard fountain, feeling its cooling air drift in through the open door, and I found myself dwelling on my diminutive guide's lurid tales. At some time I must have slept, for hours later I woke again, and my fever must have reached its height, for I fancied, Watson, that Mr Stanier, now long passed away, was standing at the foot of my bed."

I did not know what to say; I made some murmur of consternation.

"The next day, Watson, I began to recover, and yet with new travails; because during the preceding hours of darkness, I had gained on my forearm a most ferocious bite."

"What? Why, Holmes, I should examine you!"

"Nonsense, Watson. It is by now quite healed. You have surmised, of course, what must be the cause of such an injury."

"Some kind of ape, I imagine?"

"Exactly. One of the macaques must have crept across the roof of the riad, down the inner wall and onto the walkway, and from thence into my room. It is obvious, is it not? And yet Hamza, the house boy of whom we spoke, would never be in the same room as me again."

"Why ever not?"

"Why? Because he thought I had been bitten by the very creature of his superstition – the ghul." Holmes smiled. "It is a nice idea, is it not? From it one sees how man can leap from fact to wonderment in the merest moment." He sighed. "It is hard, however, to imagine the boy's terror. His father recounted his nightmares to me, Watson. For the ghul's repast is dead flesh, and the poor lad could not put from his mind the horrors of what may result from a ghul mistakenly taking a bite from a living man.

"He had the idea that a ghul could steal a person's visage, but not wholly his mind or his feelings. Those things, in such a creature, would be nothing but a shadow, a reflection in some dull mirror. Such was the remnant of affection that drew back the ghul which had feasted on Mr Stanier, compelling it to steal the photograph of his wife. But if a ghul was to partake of living flesh – ah, what torments must it suffer!"

"Torments, Holmes?"

"Of course! Imagine how terrible it must be to crave such foul repast, while possessing all of the faculties and sensibilities of a man! To long for the human life and the human world, and everything it offers, whilst exiled from it forever! And to be subject to enduring sickness, perhaps, from taking such unnatural sustenance – why, all these would be fitting punishment for its filthy appetites."

I made to laugh, but at that moment Holmes turned his face to look out of the window, and he appeared so uncharacteristically affected that I found I could not.

He did not speak again for a while. Instead, he reached for his violin and, adjusting it under his chin, as if growing accustomed to the weight of something almost forgotten, he commenced to play the most exotic and melancholy air I have ever heard before or since. The cadence and rhythm were strange to me, and yet I could not doubt that every note of it was perfect, such was the effect of the whole upon the listener. I was nonplussed at how he had contrived to learn it in so short a time, and marvelled again at his most extraordinary powers of mind. Yet, as he manipulated the bow, he had such emotion written across his features so as to brook no word from myself.

At last, he stopped and, with a sigh of regret, replaced the instrument. "I recovered, Watson," he said, as if he had never paused. "I recovered, and found that Lord P— had kindly awaited such an event. Mrs Stanier, however, had taken her leave of the country, and departed for England but two days before. Lord P— himself was keen to follow after her, and I admit I was anxious to once more be among the cool, sweet breezes and soft green hills of home. And so we left."

He sat back and set his black clay pipe between his lips. He patted his pockets, eyeing the mantelpiece, where sat the Persian slipper filled with tobacco.

"But, Holmes!"

"Yes, dear fellow?"

"What of the case?"

"Ah! That. Well, it was obvious."

"How so?"

"You forget, Watson, that the most strange and remarkable facts can veil the most undistinguished of causes. Stanier was a man of means, engaged in a pursuit that fascinated him, and with a marriage that to all appearances was characterized by mutual devotion. What need had such a man to disappear? No, it is impossible.

"Place against this a wife in a condition of distress, left alone in a strange land full of stranger stories, and we begin to see what must have happened. Our solution is that of simple robbery. That of the grave was no doubt carried out by the very apes who bit me in my fever. Driven out from their previous sources of food, they must have smelled the recently buried man, discovered the soft, newly turned ground, and—well, there is no need to embellish that aspect of our tale with further detail.

"The inhabitants of the riad, as I have mentioned, were in the habit of leaving their inner doors open. One night, some vagabond crept inside, and found a photograph of a beautiful lady, which I have already stated to be in a rather valuable frame.

"There, he was discovered. In a state of distress and in the midst of a disturbance, Mrs Stanier naturally panicked; ordinarily a sensible woman, it remains probable that she merely imagined her visitor to bear the face of the man she had loved. It must be so: particularly if one takes into account the lateness of the hour, the darkness of the room and the possibility that she had heard Hamza's wild tale – a story as contagious, perhaps, as a desert fever.

"The thief made his escape. He proceeded to the graveyard, which lay in the direction of a poor part of the city – the foulness of the tanneries. There lie huge vats full of corrosive dyes that strip the hair from the workers' arms; others, full of reeking camel urine, are used to turn hides into leather. There men stomp the skins, submerged up to their thighs in the dreadful stuff. The stench, as I have said, is quite unimaginable.

"There, Watson, is where a poor man, such as one forced to stoop to robbery by some desperate situation, may have fled. In the darkness, however, and coming across another grave disturbed by starving beasts, he must have stumbled, thus losing the fruit of his night's work – the photograph.

"And the ghul, wearing the guise of Mr Stanier, was never in actuality seen again, because it never existed."

Holmes sank back in his chair, finally exhausted by the telling. And what a tale it was – yet with such a dull conclusion to such a colourful adventure. I could not help feeling a little disappointed, but still, I was a doctor as well as a friend, and I could no longer delay; his complexion was now quite ashen. I moved to ring the bell for tea and such nourishment as Holmes might be pressed to take, when, suddenly, he leapt to his feet.

"I hear something!" he cried. "I hear it, Watson!" and with a wild light shining in his eyes, he rushed from the room and was gone!

I hurried after him, only to see my friend walking away down the street, into the greyness and the bustle of London, and I was making to follow him when the most singular part of my tale thus far brought me to a halt. For while I stood at the door, looking after my departed friend, a hansom drew up outside, and who should step out of it but – Sherlock Holmes!

My astonishment may only be imagined. He was a little pale, though his skin was sallow in tone, and lacking the greyish tinge I had noted previously. His movements spoke of fatigue and yet were possessed of more vitality than heretofore, as he stepped down and halloed, and bade me help him inside with his things, for his journey had been long. I stood there but a moment longer, quite lost as to how he had performed such a trick, and then I hastened to do exactly that.

Afterwards, Holmes sat in the same chair, a pipe once more in his hand, puffing out clouds of blue smoke, and eyeing me, as if waiting for me to challenge him on what had taken place.

Now, it may seem surprising that I had not yet done so, but I confess that many are the times I had given some hasty theory for strange-seeming events, only for Holmes to show at once how wrong-headed were my ideas. This time, I was determined to have all before me prior to speaking.

I thought of my friend's skill in disguises. In all the time I had known him I had seen Holmes play the part of a parson, a groom and a veritable assortment of common loafers and vagabonds. How much simpler would it be, then, should he for some unknown reason have call to disguise himself as himself!

Also, I knew that it was not beyond the capacities of Sherlock Holmes, when his own mind was not occupied with some seemingly impenetrable puzzle, to devise one, in order to play a little game with his old friend. Ennui ever lay heavily upon him, and he was ever in possession of a sense for the dramatic; I could certainly imagine him spending his faculties in inventing some challenge of the mind for me to solve, if only in his constant efforts to escape the commonplaces of life. It may seem difficult to believe that any man would go to such extraordinary lengths in order to test any of their acquaintance, but if there ever were a fellow capable of doing it, that man was Sherlock Holmes.

He sat back now, eyeing me, as if he knew what was passing through my thoughts. I was half inclined not to rise to his bait, even tending towards some irritation at his foolery, and minded not to mention his previous entrance at all; and yet I could not help biting.

At first, at my words, his look was surprised; then, when I pressed it as really having happened, incredulous; then curiosity and bewilderment had equal mastery of his features before amusement took their place. Finally, his old piercing gaze succeeded to all. He looked at me that way for some time without speaking. Then he drew a sharp breath, reaching for his pipe once more.

"My dear Watson," he said, and I realized that amusement hadn't quite fled; for though his countenance remained steady, his shoulders were fairly shaking with mirth. And then he stood and began to pace the room. "Our present mystery has a most ready conclusion." He pointed at the fire, which I noticed was burning low. Then he pointed at my chair, my shirt, an empty glass by my side, and finally at my cheek. "Sitting in a warm room so long, without any engagement to keep the mind alert, so long as to let the fire gutter – just poke it a little, would you, dear fellow – in the most comfortable chair, having consumed a glass of brandy, slumped so as to let one's shirt pull quite awry, resting one's cheek on one's hand so as to redden it most comically and, from all observations, one must carry out a rough and hasty deduction, that, in short, our dear Doctor Watson has been asleep." He smiled and gave a slight bow. "You dreamed I came in and left again. Not realizing you were dreaming, you hurried from the room, to see someone wearing a travelling cloak a little like mine rushing down the street. You leapt to the conclusion that it was I, just at the very moment that I arrived." He shook with laughter once more before a dry chuckle burst from his lips. "Eliminate the impossible, Watson," he fairly gasped through his merriment, "and what remains?"

He could not finish the sentence, and so I had to carry it for him, though I did not speak it aloud. *What remained, no matter how improbable, was the truth*; and in this case I had to admit that the outcome wasn't at all improbable; it wasn't even unlikely. Still, I could not help feeling quite sure that I had never closed my eyes at all.

But Holmes must have seen everything as clearly as ever, while I had been carried away by strange dreams and notions. Now any thought of such nonsense dissolved from my mind, chased away in an instant by the keen eye of Sherlock Holmes.

It was a humorous incident to be sure, but it was one that nevertheless, upon remembering, leaves one feeling a little melancholic. Sometimes, on dark and lonesome evenings, I find myself dwelling on it still. Many cases have found their way to our door, as I made mention, of which it is impossible to write, though they have still provided a source of discussion for Holmes and I. The case of the ghul, however, is one that neither Holmes nor I have ever felt the occasion to mention again, much less discuss. I little meant to write of it, and yet this evening, with the night drawing in humid and warm and pressing in close, it seems I can think of nothing else.

What lingers in my mind the most, in truth, is the same thing that troubled a boy, little more than a child, lacking in education and a thousand miles away: what if a ghul *was* to partake of living flesh? How much of the person would it assume inwardly, as well as outwardly? If the thing that had returned first from Morocco was such a creature, having taken Holmes's fevered body for dead, having bitten his arm and assumed his visage, his speech, even his memories and personality – what then? Imagine a creature of such great and terrible hunger, but with the sensibilities and, yes, the honour of Mr Sherlock Holmes. And when I think of that, I remember the sadness in his eyes as he looked from the window, as I saw him in my dream that day.

But the ghul would eat again, would it not? If such a thing existed – which, of course, it cannot – it would soon assume another guise. And yet a part of me likes to think of the simulacrum of my good friend, out in the world, continuing in some way his battle against injustice; his image in men's thoughts forever, as if glimpsed from the corner of the eye at odd moments, his quixotic temperament and his peculiar genius, not lost to time, but kept and treasured by mankind forever. What need of all my memoirs then? But perhaps that, after all, is my object in writing them. Perhaps the idea of this ghul refuses to leave me because of its sympathy, in some way, with my own intentions. As Holmes pointed out, a story can be contagious; a seed, that once reaches a man's ear, can take root and grow. And isn't that my hope? For what a tragedy it would be, if Holmes's talents should be forever lost to the world.

Now all that remains in my mind's eye is my last view of my friend after his fantastical and certainly dream-like story, hurrying away into the grey streets, the busyness and bustle, and indeed the graveyards of London, without turning or once glancing back over his shoulder.

And now I must shake my head in wry amusement at my own wild imaginings. I will turn from these preoccupying fictions and – yes, chimaeras of the mind, as Holmes put it – and turn to matters of fact. I am, as is Sherlock Holmes, a man of science, and as such must not allow my mind to wander in the lands of fancy; I shall chuckle at my own credulity, and put these papers away, and possibly even burn them on some lighter and more rational evening. Thus I shall no doubt prevent what must be the sternest lecture I have yet had cause to elicit from Holmes upon the subject of my literary shortcomings. For, as I write, I hear him in the passage, and the eagerness of his step speaks of more promising beginnings. No doubt my thoughts shall soon be occupied in some more profitable direction, and these little flights of fancy will be banished from my mind forever.

# The Doll Who Talked to the Dead

Nev Fountain

'So please grip this fact with your cerebral tentacle,
The doll and its maker are never identical.'
Sir Arthur Conan Doyle, *London Opinion*,
12 December 1912

## JOURNEY TO THE NEW WORLD

In case this document is unearthed long after I have passed into obscurity, I suppose I should tell you about myself. Truthfully, I don't know quite where to begin; I confess I have had an eclectic life, so to précis is difficult, whether I should emphasize my role as ship's surgeon, army doctor, sportsman, political activist, spiritualist or author – who is to say how I will be remembered?

Logic would dictate I say "author" as I am best known for my fictional detective, but let us put that notoriety to one side for a moment; his stories have been described and picked over in tiresome detail.

But, as far as this story is concerned, I will describe myself as a Christian spiritualist, for it was in my capacity as representative of the Marylebone Spiritualist Association, that once again I set my foot upon American shores; a new world, and a new frontier. I had already searched for knowledge, happiness, justice and friendship in my life, and more or less found them all. Now, I fill my days with the greatest expedition of all; the search to find out what lies beyond the veil. An "undiscovered country" in more ways than one.

It all started last year, at my home in Crowborough. The headline of my newspaper read:

### *HOUDINI DEAD*

The headline hit me like a cricket ball in the solar plexus, and robbed me of breath for several seconds. It was true that Houdini and I had been at loggerheads for several years, but when you get to my age, even the demise of a bitter enemy is a cause for shock and remorse. But shock soon subsides, and when there is no grief to replace it, then life continues apace. I am not ashamed to admit that my thoughts about the doll remained with me long after the thoughts of the doll maker faded like a photograph in the sun.

Then, two months later, we were seated at breakfast, my wife and I, when the maid brought in a telegram.

YOU MAY PURCHASE DOLL IF YOU MEET ME ON FINAL DAY OF OCTOBER. I LOOK FORWARD TO MAKING YOUR AQUAINTANCE. REGARDS MILO DEVERE

"What do you say, dear?' said Lady Doyle, looking across at me. "Will you go?"

"I don't see how I can do anything else," I said. "That doll will be of invaluable help to our cause. Probably more than anything else in this world."

"And that is all the doll means to you, my dearest heart?" she asked, buttering her toast warily. "Truly?"

"Of course. Isn't that enough?'

She did not answer, and I was glad of her silence. As far as I was concerned, that was the end of the matter.

## THE ARRIVAL AT THE DEVERE ESTATE

Two months later, I took an ocean liner to America, a train to Utah, and then finally a carriage to the home of Milo DeVere. The house was white and gleaming, nestling in the middle of its own well-tended gardens. I must admit I regretted allowing my cab to drop me at the gates, as despite the autumn chill I found it a long, hot walk to the front door.

I pressed the bell, and was immediately confronted by a stocky man with a grey moustache, thick eyeglasses and unruly hair.

"Sir Arthur Conan Doyle?" the man enquired, with a sly expression.

"I am indeed."

"Sir Arthur *Ignatius* Conan Doyle?' the man persisted.

"That is so."

The grey-moustached man gave a conspiratorial smile, as if I had supplied a password, and he ushered me inside. "Mr DeVere is expecting you. I am Frank, Mr DeVere's butler. Should you need anything during your stay here, then call me on the telephone in your room."

I was asked to wait in an oak-panelled room. There were chairs of English teak around carved chess pieces, set upon an occasional table made of oak. An eclectic mix of paintings covered the walls. A Holbein horse was above the mantelpiece, running into the arms of a Gustav Klimt nude. The whole ensemble radiated money, but little taste, or artistic judgement.

## MR HOLMES AND DR WATSON

It was a full minute before I realized I was not alone. There was a man sitting in a high-backed chair facing the fire, his long tapered fingers tapping on the arm.

I cleared my throat. "Mr DeVere, I am delighted to finally make your acquaintance, sir."

The fingers stopped drumming and a languid voice floated from the chair. "I am afraid that your presumption is incorrect. I am not Milo DeVere."

"My apologies, sir, I mean no offence."

"None taken, Sir Arthur."

"You seem to have the advantage of me, sir."

"My dear Sir Arthur. I always have the advantage of everybody." The voice continued in a patronizing air designed, I'm certain, to set my teeth on edge: "I'm sure your fictional detective Dr Bell would immediately deduce that I am not Mr Milo DeVere; even if he saw the merest glimpse of my right hand. He would deduce that my gnarled appendage belongs to a much older man. Moreover, it is not adorned with a wedding ring, a memento from a long and happy marriage to Nancy, who passed away five years ago. Neither is this hand encircling a glass of bourbon, which the *Tatler* salaciously informs us is his tipple of choice."

I could now see the man was thin, with grey hair swept back from a high forehead, and a slender, aquiline nose. His profile was unmistakable, and even though his visage was much older than his caricature in the pages of *The Strand*, of course I recognized him instantly. It was Sherlock Holmes.

I knew him, of course. How could I not? Feted by barons, kings and emperors, his fame was second to none. It was churlish of me not to join in the worship of such a man, but I must confess I found him a singularly irritating fellow. Since my conversion to Christian spiritualism he was ever more prepared to bait me in public in the name of his own narrow philosophy, including one notorious incident at the Athenaeum Club. For several years, to my shame, I sincerely wished him dead. Nevertheless, I have always been nothing less than a gentleman, and I had no wish to provoke an argument.

"Mr Holmes, what a pleasant surprise. I did not expect to find you in this corner of the world. I thought you had retired from public life to tend your bees."

"That is true. But when I am called upon by old friends to act on their behalf, it would be churlish of me not to spring into action – as much as my aged frame allows me to spring anywhere."

"So . . . What brings you here?"

"The same thing as you, I imagine. I assume you are here for the doll."

"I am indeed. How did you know that?"

He chuckled. "The moment I mentioned to Mr DeVere that he should not speak about the doll to you or your spiritualist brethren, I should have predicted he would do that very thing. I think the more pertinent question is 'How could Sherlock Holmes *not* have deduced that Sir Arthur Conan Doyle was going to turn up here seeking the doll, before he arrived in this very room?'" He sighed and looked into the flames. "Age is a curse for a man of my abilities. The reactions grow dull, the mind grinds ever slower . . . I sometimes wonder if I am afflicted with an ague."

"Perhaps you would like me to examine you. I am a doctor."

"Fortunately, Sir Arthur, I have brought my own physician."

As if on cue, a stocky man with a tidy moustache arrived into the room. He spied me, and almost rocked back on his heels.

"Sir Arthur? How wonderful to see you!" He surged forward and shook my hand. "You haven't changed a bit. Not since the regimental reunion in Redhill in '21."

"Well, a little greyer perhaps." I patted my stomach. "And I have a little more ballast around my waist."

John Watson patted his own middle in solidarity. "In my case, that is certainly true. I think I might prescribe myself a diet."

Then, behind us, a voice with a Midwestern twang said: "Welcome to my home, gentlemen."

## ENTER MILO DEVERE

Milo DeVere was much like his house: large and pale and square. He was a vision in monochrome: white hair, a white beard and clad in a white suit. The only hint of colour resided in two pink spots on both of his cheeks – a sure sign that Mr Holmes and the *Tatler* were both correct, DeVere did indeed have a predilection for hard liquor.

"Sir Conan Doyle! And Mr Holmes! This is an incredible honour, gentlemen! To have both such . . . such . . . luminaries of the age under my roof! I can scarcely believe I'm not dreaming!" He shook both of us by the hand; a firm, vigorous handshake. "I trust Frank has shown you to your rooms and offered you refreshments? I do hope you both will be comfortable here."

"Comfort is not why we are here, sir," said Holmes briskly. "Can we get to the matter in hand? Dr Watson and I have come a very long way . . ."

DeVere became aware that Dr Watson was standing patiently by the mantelpiece, and remembered his manners.

"And Dr Watson too! How could I have not noticed you there! I am an avid reader of *The Strand*, Doctor. Your recounting of Mr Holmes's exploits has made an impact on even this side of the Pond. You have an amazing knack for making his stories come alive."

Watson blushed as scarlet as a side of beef from Billingsgate. "Well, I can't take all the credit. I just transcribe events as I see them; it's Sherlock who provides the narrative . . . I do owe a debt to Sir Arthur Doyle, here, for without his own stories of his police pathologist, Dr Bell, I would never have had the courage to . . . well, to write my own."

"Why, thank you, Dr Watson," I said. "I am honoured to think I would take some small role in the legend of Mr Holmes."

I said it warmly, but I did not feel so honoured. Sherlock Holmes's exploits had eclipsed my own stories. If he wasn't such a tiresome individual, perhaps I would have felt some pride in Watson's hero worship, but in truth I resented this languid character seated before me.

"Watson has long been a devotee of Sir Arthur's tales in *The Idler*," said Holmes, sniffily. "Hence his lurid prose. Pray, let us get on with this venture, so the good Doctor can serialize this one in his usual sensationalist style."

"Of course, of course." DeVere nodded and, despite his bulk, settled himself quite gracefully into a chair and beamed at Holmes like a child who had unwrapped his biggest present on Christmas morning.

"I must admit, Mr Holmes, I did expect to be approached by the Houdini estate on the occasion of Harry's death, but to be contacted by none other than your good self . . . that I did not foresee."

"I am here at the behest of his family. Mr Houdini and I were long-standing friends, ever since I uncovered a plot by his rivals to secrete sulphuric acid in his escape apparatus. The family has charged me to bring back the doll in accordance with Houdini's final wishes. So, Mr DeVere, if you can pack up the doll, we can take it with us."

DeVere's smile didn't flicker. "I'm not sure why you are asking me to do this, Mr Holmes. The doll is mine. In 1904, Houdini made a wager with me about whether he had the courage to catch a bullet in his teeth, and the prize was the doll."

"I take it that Houdini lost the wager?" I asked.

"Correct, Sir Arthur. He changed his mind and chickened out, much to the relief of his family and friends, and much to my joy, as I won the doll for my collection."

Sherlock Holmes said: "Mr DeVere, all that you say is true – up to one vital point. He did indeed make the wager, but as you know he had the foresight to request the doll be kept intact and returned to his family in the event of his death. Is that not so?"

DeVere smiled, not unkindly. "I recall no such condition."

"Houdini certainly did. He told me so himself."

"What he told you and what is the truth of the matter might be completely different."

Holmes flapped open a large notebook and examined the contents. "I believe there was a witness. The wager was made in the presence of a Mr W. T. Stead, and a document was drawn up."

"A fine journalist," said I, "and a fellow spiritualist. Alas, he is no longer with us."

"Precisely, Sir Arthur," said DeVere. "He passed away over a decade ago, one of the tragic souls taken by the *Titanic* disaster. I believe all his personal effects are currently lying at the bottom of the North Atlantic Ocean." He waved his hand airily. "So in the absence of this alleged 'document', we only have Mr Houdini's account, which is contrary to mine. And I'm afraid that the word of a dead man cannot outweigh the word of the living."

"That was Houdini's last wish, DeVere." Holmes's reproving voice echoed around the gloom. "It is not wise to ignore a dead man's wishes. There could be grave repercussions."

"I'm afraid I cannot accommodate you, Mr Holmes. I recall no such condition. As far as I'm concerned the doll is mine to do with as I please." DeVere's fat fingers meshed together, and he perched his hands on his bulging waistcoat. "Perhaps I could, if persuaded, sell you the doll, if the price is right. But as you can see, Sir Arthur's presence complicates the situation."

"I can see you have gone against my wishes and put the doll up for auction," Holmes said, with some asperity. "Sir Arthur's presence here makes the situation perfectly plain. He is obviously here on behalf of some organization; I gather he has fallen out with the Society for Physical Research, or 'Ghost Squad', so I imagine he is representing the Marylebone Spiritualist Association."

"Correct again, Mr Holmes," I said. "Your powers are almost unnatural."

"Are they indeed." Mr Holmes fixed me with a mocking glare. "I am not the first person whose natural abilities you have attributed to the power of the occult. Over the years you have made no secret of your belief that Mr Houdini's trickery disguised a deeper power. You are, are you not, gripped by the delusion that Houdini used spiritual forces to aid in his showmanship, and masked the influence of the supernatural by calling it trickery? Do you deny this, Sir Arthur?"

I could feel colour creeping into my face. "I do not deny anything, only that I suffer under no delusion."

Holmes snorted with barely concealed contempt.

I continued. "Just as you do not deny your delusion there is nothing more in heaven and earth than your philosophy. You, sir, are content to stand flat-footed on the Earth, and are afraid to look up at the clouds."

Holmes barked with laughter. "Why would I want to stare at puddles of evaporated water, when there is much more of interest in the dirt beneath my feet? The world is big enough for me, sir. No ghosts need apply."

We glared at each other, and Dr Watson smoothly interposed himself between us. "Well, Sir Arthur, Holmes and I have come a long way and, using my monstrously inferior powers of deduction, I'm guessing you have, too. I'm sure we are keen to get this business settled."

Remembering my manners, I smiled. "Yes, of course, Doctor."

Holmes nodded, too, and smiled at his friend. "Excellent point, Watson. You are, as always, the most practical one here."

Watson turned to Mr DeVere, who was observing proceedings with a slight smile on his face. "Mr DeVere. If you have enticed us here using Houdini's doll, the least you can do is satisfy our curiosity."

"Good point, Doctor. I will get Molly to unlock my personal museum."

He rang the bell and a maidservant, a middle-aged woman with curly blonde hair and sharp bright eyes, scuttled into the room.

"Yes, Mr DeVere?"

"Molly, will you open the museum for us? My guests would like to see the doll."

Was it my imagination, or did she give a little shiver when the doll was mentioned?

## INSIDE THE MUSEUM

Molly left the room and, after a few minutes, returned and informed Milo DeVere that the museum was open. DeVere escorted us along corridors until we were standing in his "museum".

The room was a shrine to magic and mesmerism; posters, props and trinkets lined the walls.

DeVere proudly pointed to a mangled piece of metal in a box. "See that, gentlemen?" said he. "That was the bullet which killed Chung Lin Soo. The one he tried to catch in his teeth. He had the courage to try the trick when Houdini did not. Unfortunately for him. He paid the price of failure with his life. Me? I paid fifteen thousand dollars for it."

Sherlock Holmes uttered "charming" under his breath and, for once, I was in full agreement with him. The whole collection felt rather distasteful. There were also artefacts pertaining to Houdini; large glass boxes contained trinkets of the magician's life. There was a straitjacket, with the long sleeves draped on stands so it looked like a dog-eared ghost.

There was also a framed copy of *A Magician Among the Spirits*, Houdini's "magnum opus". It was a book that, more than any other, had done its best to ridicule and degrade the science of spiritualism. For me that book, and the public insult to my wife, was the chisel that finally chipped away the keystone of my friendship with Harry, and all of a sudden I felt very sad and lonely in this dark room, surrounded by faded memories of happier times.

Dr Watson looked around the room with naked awe. "This is quite a collection, Mr DeVere."

"This used to be the finest collection of Houdini arcana next to the Houdini family's own collection. Given their inexplicable tendency to destroy his secrets, it is now *the* finest. Come, gentlemen, the doll is over here behind this curtain."

He pulled a string, the curtains glided back and there it was.

The doll who talked to the dead.

## THE DOLL

I had seen photos, of course, but nothing prepared me for witnessing it in all its glory.

The doll was a wicked-looking thing, dressed formally in an undertaker's greatcoat and top hat. The face was a grinning skull. One of its bony hands held a sharp stylus, about the length of a knitting needle. Its black sockets looked deep into my eyes and I felt chilled to the very soul. Every instinct told me that those sockets held hidden secrets of the occult.

It was sitting at a desk, upon which an Ouija board was inscribed into the wood. A lectern protruded from the corner of the base, upon which was perched what looked like the carcass of a typewriter.

"Oh my prophetic soul," said a voice, and to my surprise I realized the owner of the voice was me.

"There you have it, gentlemen," said DeVere proudly. "The doll who talks to the dead. Houdini's greatest creation. I'm sure I do not need to give an account of its history. I am willing to wager that you all know everything there is to know about it."

I nodded, and so did Holmes.

"Sorry, but I don't," said Watson, stoutly. "Read a couple of articles here and there, but, as usual, Holmes was less than forthcoming on our voyage."

Sherlock Holmes circled the doll and I did too, carefully keeping our equidistance.

"I apologize, Watson," said he. "Let me enlighten you. Houdini constructed it some fifteen years ago, when he started to sour on the notion that we could talk to the dead. He wanted to prove how easily the illusion of channelling spirits could be synthesized."

"That is another assumption, Holmes," I said coldly. "I believe he actually constructed the doll when he realized his mother was becoming frail, and he wanted to ensure that he would maintain contact with her when she departed. He only claimed later that it was a trick because he was influenced by the Catholic Church to deny evidence of occult phenomena."

"Really," muttered Holmes. "Well, you believe what you want to believe, Sir Arthur. I gather you've had a lot of practice on that score."

"Gruesome-looking chap," muttered Watson, as he walked around it.

"Oh, but this device is a thing of beauty," countered Holmes. "Every cog and wheel and valve arranged with such an eye for planning and detail that one could call it a work of art."

"If you say so, Holmes," grunted Watson. "But I wouldn't hang this monstrosity on my wall. Or have it in the house." He peered into the cavernous eye sockets of the skull. "So how does it work? How does it . . . um . . ."

Mr DeVere smiled and supplied the correct phrasing. "How does it channel the spirits, Doctor?"

"Exactly. Um, quite so."

Mr DeVere guided Watson to the typewriter on the pedestal. "One types in a question, pulls this lever and the doll answers it."

"What, any question? Anything at all?"

"Within reason, Dr Watson. The spirits are very temperamental. They like to be treated with respect. Any attempt to ask fatuous questions, or ones that are designed to catch them out, and the machine will not respond."

Sherlock Holmes allowed a "Ha!" to escape his lips. "I'm sorry, but a temperamental machine that will not deign to answer any 'difficult' questions? How very convenient!"

I could stay silent no longer. "Really, Mr Holmes. Would it cost you anything to entertain the fact that there might be something elemental about this doll? To retain some sense of an open mind?"

"It would cost me a great deal, Sir Arthur," retorted Holmes. "I consider that a man's brain is like an empty attic. A fool takes in all the furniture of every sort that he comes across, so that the knowledge which might be useful to him gets crowded out." He pulled a sour grin. "I choose not to clutter my brain with useless furniture."

## A QUESTION ANSWERED

Milo DeVere spread his hands like Houdini himself after a feat of daring. "I'm happy to provide a demonstration. Why not ask the doll a question, Mr Holmes? What harm could it do?"

"No harm at all."

"Well . . ." said Mr DeVere. "What shall we ask it?"

Holmes cocked an eyebrow and smiled. "Perhaps we should ask this device if its current owner is an honourable man?"

Mr DeVere smiled, too. "Hardly worth bothering the doll with such an . . . esoteric question. Perhaps a better question would be, how many people are present in the room here, at this moment?"

The three of us looked at each other, and then, one by one, we shrugged and nodded our assent. The question seemed as good as any. Mr DeVere strolled to the plinth, and his stubby fingers played over the typewriter keyboard. The air was filled with the dry clacking of keys.

"There," he said at last.

He pulled the lever and, after about five seconds, the doll juddered into life, twitching and convulsing on its pedestal like it had Saint Vitus's dance. The wicked-looking stylus glided over to the Ouija board – and it settled on the number five.

"Five?" uttered Watson. He looked around for Molly but she had departed. "Five? But there are only four of us."

A silence settled on the room, as we puzzled at the answer.

"Perhaps . . ." I began at last. "Perhaps the doll counts itself as the fifth presence."

"You may have a point there, Sir Arthur," said Watson, with a wary look at Holmes.

"That makes sense, Sir Arthur," added DeVere. "I have often felt that the doll is imbued with its own sense of self."

"Maybe the doll is . . . well, perhaps the doll *is* Houdini himself," said Watson with hushed awe.

"It is funny you should say that, Dr Watson. Ever since Houdini's death I have often fancied that he is present in my house."

Was it my imagination, or had the room got colder?

"He was always tempting his own fate," I said, nodding at the framed copy of his book. "Perhaps he should have known better than to have called his book *A Magician Among the Spirits*."

"Really, gentlemen!" Holmes erupted with scorn. "This strikes to the heart of this nonsense. A performance falls short of what is expected, and the credulous mind immediately fills in the gaps. The doll gives the wrong answer and you conjure up reasons as to *why* the doll gave the wrong answer, rather than come to the simple and obvious conclusion that the doll has no powers whatsoever." Holmes patted the pedestal. "This is a device, nothing more, like one of Babbage's calculating machines. The mechanism detects the frequency of letters in the typed question, vowels and consonants, and can determine from that what kind of question is asked; whether to give a specific 'yes' or 'no' answer, or a more general one. I suggest it would find it more difficult, if, for example, I asked the doll for the address of our old lodgings in London."

Amazingly, without waiting for input from the typewriter, the doll jerked back into life, circling back to the desk. Its bony hand reached out once more, pointing its stylus to the Ouija board, specifically the letter "b". The stylus then glided to the "a", and then the "k", and so on.

We watched with fascinated horror, as the doll, slowly, and with remorseless deliberation, spelled two words: "baker" and "street". Once it had finished and had glided back into place and the cogs stopped turning, there was a profound quiet. We were stunned into silence.

Watson broke the quiet. "Good Lord," he muttered.

I stared at the doll. We all did. Propelled by the movement of the mechanism, its head was bouncing gently on a concealed spring tucked under its collar. It seemed to nod with malignant satisfaction at our apprehension.

Holmes suddenly laughed. "Only 'Baker Street'? If it was any kind of truly magical device, surely it could have also given us the number of the street and the letter of our rooms."

I could see Holmes was discomfited, his face stretched into a position of mild incredulity, but that was nothing to the look on his face as he witnessed what happened next.

Barely were the words out of Sherlock Holmes's mouth and the stylus moved again, gliding to the numbers. It pointed at the "2" and then the "2" again, then the "1", and, with a final flourish, the bony arm hopped from the numbers to the letters, where it positioned the stylus against the "b".

## WATSON DEFIANT!

"My stars. I've never seen it do *that* before," said Milo DeVere. His statement, coming after such a profound moment, was almost absurd.

Holmes scrutinized the homunculus on the stand. He peered closely into its face, and it struck me how similar Sherlock

Holmes's profile resembled the doll's. Holmes had always possessed a skull-like countenance, but now in old age, his very flesh seemed to be peeling slowly from his body. All that was left of the man was his piercing eyes and a collection of increasingly exaggerated affectations.

"Oh well done, sir," he laughed, addressing the air. "A conjuring trick from beyond the grave? How very characteristic of your good self. Well done. I salute you, the great Houdini, wherever you may be."

"Holmes," muttered Watson, fearing for his friend's sanity, "it could not have been pre-prepared. It answered your question, the very moment you asked it."

"It reacted to my presence," said Holmes dismissively. "Perhaps when I entered the room I triggered something. I am taller than the average man, perhaps a wire suspended in the air?"

"That's impossible, Holmes."

"No, Watson. The *impossible* is the soul of a dead man making sport with us. The *possible* is trickery. I lean to the latter."

DeVere bristled. "I assure you, Holmes, there is no such wire in this room."

"Well, you would say that, sir. As you are the one who prepared this demonstration."

"Believe me. I have done nothing but place the doll in my collection. Why would I tamper with it to produce such an incredible result?"

"To convince Sir Arthur of the doll's significance, of course. To increase the value of the thing and encourage him and his colleagues to open their pocketbooks."

"I'm already aware of its value and significance," I retorted. "That is why this doll should return with me to the Spiritualist Association as proof that Houdini covered up his real powers."

DeVere protested further. "But I haven't manipulated this thing! Even if I wanted to, I haven't the faintest inkling of how I could achieve it!"

Holmes sniffed with distain. "I think we are being played by a common huckster, hoping to get a good price for his snake oil. I refuse to be the audience for his performance. Good day to you. Come, Watson." Holmes started to walk away, but Watson remained in the same place. "Watson, come along."

"I refuse, Holmes. And I do not think you should leave, either."

Holmes stood at the door, surprised. "Really, Watson? Give me one reason why we should not leave?"

Dr Watson took a long time to speak. It seemed the words appearing on the Oijja board had left an impression on him too. "There is a mystery here, Holmes."

"Our host is the culprit. There is no mystery."

"It seems to me," the good doctor said slowly, "that it is obvious that Mr DeVere does not intend to sell the doll to either you or Sir Arthur."

"And what makes you say that?"

"He is not in the business of selling. Only collecting. This artefact is the prize of his collection. It would go against every fibre in his being to part with it."

"Good, Watson. Very good," said Holmes. 'And therefore?"

"Therefore, he has no motive in making us think the doll is possessed. Unless the intention is to send Sir Arthur away with wondrous tales of the doll to his society."

"Well done, Watson," said the detective. "I knew you'd get there in the end. Well, Mr DeVere, is Watson's deduction correct?"

DeVere's face fell. "I apologize to you all. I must confess. I did not have any intention of parting with the doll under any circumstance. But when the great Sherlock Holmes contacted me, and mentioned that Sir Arthur Conan Doyle would also be interested in the doll, how could I resist having you both here, under my roof? I thought to have a little sport with you both, watch you use your wits to compete for the doll before, after some deliberation on my part, I would reluctantly decide not to part with the doll after all."

I felt my face grow hot. "This grotesque performance is beneath you, sir," I said. "Despite what some say, I am not a Quixote, a credulous buffoon rushing and embracing every charlatan."

"But I swear, Sir Arthur. I had no part in this doll's performance. I barely know how the contraption works."

Our altercation was torn into shreds by an ear-splitting shriek. The maid had returned to lock up the room, but now she was clutching her mouth and pointing at a section of the wall hitherto hidden by the open door. As the door had been pushed to, it had revealed letters – approximately two inches high – scratched in the varnish.

## THE MESSAGE FROM THE DEAD

It formed two words:

*ROSABELLE BELIEVE*

"Holmes . . . You look pale," said Watson.

I would have thought it impossible for Holmes to look any whiter than his usual blood-drained countenance, but he had succeeded. He also sagged and clutched a chair for support.

Watson continued, "I think you know what that means, Holmes. Tell us."

Still, Holmes did not respond.

"Holmes," Mr DeVere said in great agitation. "I have read enough about you to know you worship facts above all other. Have the good grace to tell us what these words mean."

Holmes looked wildly at all of us, to DeVere, Watson, and finally into my eyes. "These are code words," he said. "A secret phrase that Houdini agreed with his wife. On the event of his death, he would impart these two words, should he ever try to make contact with her from the other side. This phrase 'Rosabelle Believe' was to separate out the genuine fraudsters and cranks."

## EXIT MR HOLMES

Over the next half an hour Holmes darted around the room like a mad thing, trying to find the trick of it. Or perhaps there was no "like" about it. He seemed genuinely deranged, pacing like a tiger unused to being caged.

This message changed things for me; the irrefutable truth of the doll had emerged, but Holmes, it seemed, refused to see it.

I tried to placate the clearly agitated detective. "Mr Holmes. Calm down. Just believe the evidence of your own eyes, as I have done."

Holmes snorted. "A message from beyond the grave? Anyone could have found out the phrase."

"Did you not say the intention was to keep the phrase as secret as possible? In order, as you say, to 'separate out the genuine fraudsters and cranks'? How many knew of this phrase?"

Holmes answered reluctantly, "Only Bess his wife, his immediate family . . . and myself."

"So look at the evidence!" I swung my arms wide and gestured to all corners of the room. "Even if this . . . phrase . . . was leaked to some mischief maker, we are standing in a room lined with solid walls, and the room was locked. The maid swears there were no scratches on the door on her last visit this morning. There is nothing in this room that could have possibly made those marks."

"Except the doll." Watson allowed the words to tumble from his lips.

Holmes shot him a look of pure scorn. "Really, Watson, I expected better of you."

Watson's cheeks coloured, but he stood his ground. "I'm merely exploring all the possibilities, Holmes. You should, too."

Sherlock Holmes fixed Watson with another stare, but he broke his gaze and abruptly turned and walked to the doll. He knocked hard on the doll's head, producing a dry, hollow sound.

"Not the doll, Watson," he retorted. "This is a hollow wooden carving. If you were thinking that there was some kind of substitution for a person in a costume, *as I dearly hope you were*, then I can confirm that no such substitution occurred."

"Perhaps . . ." I began.

"If, Sir Arthur, you are going to suggest that the doll was somehow possessed with the soul of Houdini and it waddled off its stand, stylus aloft, with its dread message from the spirit world—" Holmes knelt down and tugged at the doll's legs, and the doll lurched sickeningly on its springs "—the phrase is scrawled on the far wall, too far for the automaton to reach, and the doll is fastened to the desk with nails and screws."

"I am well aware that it is fixed into place," I snapped. "My eyesight has not failed me yet. What I was going to say was that the doll did not have to do this. It is known for spirits to assume corporeal form, for at least a short time. They have been known to throw crockery, books, even suspend whole pianos in the air."

"All disproved by Houdini himself."

"A smokescreen he created, to disguise his real powers."

Holmes shook his head disbelievingly. "You really are still convinced that Houdini was more than a simple conjurer?"

"I am, sir."

"Then I will apologize in advance, as I tear your beliefs from you." He paced the room with long strides, coming to a halt before Milo DeVere, who had remained silent for a long time. He looked more shaken than the rest of us and, by the smell of his breath, I suspected he had slipped out of the room for some "medicinal support".

"This is a sealed room?"

"Yes, Mr Holmes."

"Always sealed?"

"Of course. The artefacts in this room are priceless."

"And there is only one key?"

"Yes."

"In your possession?"

"The maid has the key. She opens the room to dust the artefacts. That's why I called her to unlock the room."

"So you did. We decided to visit the doll, you called for the maid, she opened the door. When she arrived to lock up she pulled the doors ajar, saw the scratches, screamed, and so here we are."

"Yes, Holmes," I said. "Here we are."

Then, without warning, he walked out of the room.

"What the devil is he playing at?" muttered DeVere.

"Don't worry, Mr DeVere," said Watson. "He often does this."

We waited for a long while, but he didn't return. We eyed each other – and the doll – nervously. DeVere called for Frank.

"Frank, do you have an idea as to the whereabouts of Mr Holmes?"

"Yes, sir. He left the house about a half-hour ago."

DeVere's mouth dropped open. "He's . . . left?"

"Yes, sir. He didn't say where he was going. I arranged for a carriage."

"Well, I'll be jiggered," said DeVere. "The fellow really is the Devil."

## HOLMES TESTS A THEORY

We had little choice but to wait for Holmes's return, and stayed up until the small hours, smoking and talking. We had all been gravely spooked by the doll, and none of us seemed willing to retire to bed. But fatigue finally conquered us, and I bid Watson and DeVere goodnight.

I slept uneasily that night. My dreams were plagued with disturbing, profound images. I was in my garden, picking flowers for my first wife Louisa, and suddenly fairies surged out of the flowerbeds to greet me – but they were wearing top hats, and their faces were grinning skulls.

They danced around my head leering at me, and I ran and ran, but my legs felt so heavy and lifeless. I ran to the bottom of the garden, and I fell down, down, down, into a trench, and the fairies buzzing around my head became bullets buzzing in my ears, and the air was clouded with smoke and poison gas and the screams of dying horses and dying men.

Hands emerged, groping for life, followed by arms, a body. And my eldest son Kingsley erupted from the noxious clouds. I knew it was my son, even though his face was also a grinning skull, and then he vanished into smoke. Then I saw someone struggling to free himself from barbed wire. It was Houdini himself. He was calling for help.

I rushed to assist, but when I reached him he just walked out from the tangle, dusting his hands smugly.

"You weren't trapped at all," I said accusingly.

"Of course I wasn't. Sir Arthur, you are the most gullible person I've ever met. You'll believe anything."

"You tricked me."

"Well, you tried to trick me, with that show you put on for me, Lady Doyle contacting my mother using automatic writing? Automatic my eye! What a load of baloney."

"How dare you call my wife a fraud!"

"If the cap fits . . . She wrote her messages in *English*, Arthur. Mother never spoke a word of English in her life! Let me give you a bit of advice, sir. Never hustle a hustler!" Houdini laughed, and kept on laughing until his mirth was drowned by gunfire.

I awoke to a noise outside my door, and I screamed, thinking I was still in the dream. Then I recovered myself. I opened the door and looked up and down the corridor, only to see Milo DeVere, wide-eyed and fearful, at the door of his own bedroom.

"Sir Arthur, did you hear some kind of noise?" he asked.

"Why yes, I did," I replied. "Tiny footsteps past my door. Like a monkey. Or a midget."

"They were outside mine as well," he said. "I heard scratching on my door, and a scuttling, but I took so long to get to my door the cause had long since vanished."

"Well, there is nothing here now."

"Yes." His eyes flicked back to the bottle on his dresser. "Well, perhaps this is another mystery for Sherlock Holmes to solve."

"Perhaps," I said. "Perhaps."

Sherlock Holmes was sitting waiting for us when we went down to breakfast, reading the *New York Times*. He greeted us warmly, and asked us if we'd slept well. He made no mention of where he'd been.

He turned to Molly, who had been waiting patiently with serving tongs in hand. "Molly, may I have a fresh pot of tea?"

"Of course, sir," said she, and off she went.

The moment the door clicked shut, Holmes spoke. "I expect you will have been wondering where I have been. I will tell you right away, as I have no interest in generating a gratuitous sense of mystery."

"There's a first time for everything," muttered Watson.

"As there is enough manufactured mystery occurring within these walls to last a lifetime."

My cutlery clattered on my plate as I threw up my hands in despair. "There is no mystery here. The evidence before us points clearly to a spiritual event. It is only the close-minded who keep searching until they find an answer that suits them."

Holmes continued, "I went to Phoenix, where I conducted research into a certain individual in this house."

"Which individual?" cried DeVere. "Do you mean me?"

Holmes shook his head, put his fingers to his lips, and his eyes flicked to the door.

"The maid?' DeVere uttered, incredulously. "My maid?'

"Yes, DeVere. Your maid. Molly Hopkins. It is true, is it not, that she has come into your employ quite recently?"

"Yes, within the past few months. But she is of impeccable character and splendid at her work."

"I am not interested in her efficiency in making beds, DeVere. I have discovered, through talking to her friends and family, that Molly Hopkins regularly attends seances and is a firm believer of the powers of the occult."

I sighed. "I hardly think that's unusual, Holmes, a great deal of people are. It is just a matter of time that doubters such as yourself become the minority."

Holmes ignored me. "I think the maid was already privy to your intention not to sell, and she is working with spiritualists. She is manipulating us, or more specifically you, Mr DeVere, so you will be so disturbed by the doll's behaviour that you would allow it to leave here in the hands of Sir Arthur. I believe she fixed the doll, and made the scratches on the wall in the few minutes between her entering the room, and us following."

"The maid? Some kind of secret agent?" spluttered DeVere. "That sounds a bit far-fetched."

"I agree," I said. "She is nothing to me. I know nothing of any plan. Molly, fixing the doll? Knowing Houdini's secret message? It's incredible to the point of absurdity. When will you allow yourself to face up to the simplest solution?"

He looked at me sharply. "I think it is reasonable that we exhaust all the improbable solutions before we look at the impossible one, don't you agree? Even if you are not privy to a plan, Sir Arthur, we cannot therefore conclude that no such plan exists. I am going to conduct a little experiment, to try to get her to show her hand. Once she returns, you, DeVere, shall look like you are willing to sell the doll now, and acquiesce to everything I say. It would help if you, Sir Arthur, and you, Watson, also go along with what I say."

We all nodded.

As soon as Molly returned with the tea, Holmes raised his voice. "It seems, gentlemen, that we have two competing and conflicting views on what the doll is. Either it is merely a piece of mechanical trickery, manufactured by an expert conjurer, or it is an agent of spiritual forces."

"Agreed," said Watson, a little too emphatically.

"So it seems to me that whatever the doll truly is, whether science or magic, should have a direct bearing on who it should ultimately belong to." He paused for effect. "So I think we should ask the doll who it wants to belong to."

"I . . . I beg your pardon?" stuttered DeVere.

"If it is simply a mechanical machine constructed by Houdini, then it is bound to reflect his wishes and request to return to his family. If it is a thing powered by preternatural forces, then would it not demand to be set among a group like the Spiritualist Association?"

His reasoning sounded utterly ridiculous and, not for the first time, I wondered about Holmes's deteriorating wits. Why would a doll possessed by Houdini have any interest in leaving with me? Nevertheless, I played along. "Possibly."

"Then it's settled," Holmes declared. "We ask the doll."

For a moment, DeVere appeared as if he had forgotten we were play-acting, and looked like he was going to refuse. Then he steadied himself, smiled and said: "What a good idea. Whoever the doll wants to belong to, I will sell it to them. Molly, would you open the museum for us, please?"

"Of course, sir."

Once she had gone, Holmes leaned in conspiratorially. "There. The trap has been baited. If I'm right, then she will manipulate the doll's response to go with Sir Arthur."

## A FAILED EXPERIMENT

We waited for a very long time for Molly to return, but she did not appear. We looked at each other in confusion.

"Perhaps she has lost the key?" Watson suggested.

"No, she always has it with her, at all times," replied DeVere.

"Perhaps the key has stuck in the lock?"

"Perhaps. I think we should go and see what the problem is."

DeVere rose to leave and we followed. As we neared the museum we could see the doors were standing ajar.

"She must have unlocked the museum, but neglected to tell us," I said.

"That is most unlike her, I have a strict protocol. She is to inform me at once when the museum is—" As we entered, the words died in DeVere's throat.

The maid was lying on the floor, a crumpled heap in the middle of the room.

I ran towards her, but Doctor Watson was ahead of me. He knelt down and felt the woman's pulse, and his face was grim.

"She's dead," he said, in a hollow voice. He raised his hand to show us that it was coated with a sticky red substance. "She's been stabbed through the heart."

"Holmes," breathed Milo DeVere, pointing with a rigid finger. "Look at the doll! Look at the stylus!"

The doll was in its place, grinning savagely, and everything was as it was . . . But the stylus in its hand was bright red, and dripping.

"Oh my stars!" shrieked DeVere.

"Look at the wall!" cried Watson.

On the wall, next to the last message, was another. Again, it comprised of two words:

*RELEASE ME*

Holmes looked wildly around him. "This is impossible!" he shouted. "Impossible! I am never wrong! I have to find the trick of this!"

"The trick of this?" I cried. "The trick of this? Listen to your own words! You have dabbled in forces you do not understand, and now a woman is dead. In the name of all that is decent, have some humility, sir!"

"Humility? Am I supposed to put this death down to super-natural forces?"

"In a nutshell, yes!"

"Are you suggesting that Houdini has escaped death as easily as he escaped a set of handcuffs, and has somehow trapped himself in the doll?"

"There is no suggestion about it, sir! It is a fact! Look at what has happened?"

"Arrant nonsense. Perhaps we should check the man's coffin to see if he's still in there!"

"Gentlemen!" Doctor Watson's voice was loud and angry. "Have some respect for goodness sake! There is a dead woman at your feet! Take your philosophical arguments elsewhere and allow me to make her decent!"

Milo DeVere lurched forward. "Dr Watson. The resources of my house are at your disposal. What do you require?"

"I suggest that you ring for your butler. He can assist me in carrying this poor devil to a quiet room. Then, if you have a telephone, I will ring for the police."

Frank was sent for, and together they manhandled the body of Molly into the parlour.

## TRAPPED

Watson telephoned for the police, and they came and took the body away. A gruff Irish officer questioned all of us, one by one, his voice becoming more incredulous with every word we said. He obviously thought that one of us was responsible for the murder. He told us all that he would leave a police officer outside the front door, "to protect us", and he and his men would be back to question us further presently. Under no circumstances were we to leave the house of Mr DeVere.

Milo DeVere was suffering. He now made no secret that he was drinking heavily. He slumped in his chair in the library, bottle in hand, watching Holmes. If anything, Holmes looked more affected out of the two of them. I could see that he had been unsettled by the experience. He retired to a chair in the other corner, and pulled out his pipe. He puffed furiously on it, staring into the middle distance. The smoke billowing from it didn't smell like pure tobacco.

He kept muttering the words "improbable" and "impossible" over and over again, alternating between the two. He looked like he had been faced with something so completely out of his frame of reference that he scarcely knew how to react.

"Will Mr Holmes be all right?" I whispered to Watson.

"Alas, Sir Arthur," he sighed. "I really couldn't say for sure. I'm afraid that his long-term habit of indulging in narcotics has taken its toll. I have become less of a colleague and more a doctor to Holmes over recent years. His mind has become so fragile that he has become a prisoner of his own ego, and anything that impacts on his infallibility leads to a morbid depression and hysteria."

We waited, but the officer didn't return. We questioned the policeman guarding the door but he could not say when we would be questioned, and when Milo DeVere tried to use his status to bully his way out, the officer's hand strayed to his revolver.

The house grew dark, as evening gripped the sky. Holmes and Watson retired to their rooms and DeVere, the worse for wear for drink, was escorted up the stairs by Frank.

I stayed in the library. Frank lit a fire and, despite the tension I was feeling, I could not prevent my eyelids from drooping.

I awoke to the sound of a gurgling scream. I crashed out of the library, and looked up and down the corridor.

"Mr DeVere!" I cried.

Milo DeVere was there, in his nightshirt, leaning against the wall. His pale face was now chalk white, and his pink eyes were wide with terror. In one hand, he limply held a pistol; his other hand pressed hard against his neck.

"The doll! It was . . . the . . . doll!" he croaked.

I ran over to him. He was obviously deep in shock, stiff as a board and drooling. When I unpeeled his fingers – not without some effort on my part – there were long red marks upon his skin. My imagination could not prevent me from seeing them as the imprints of bony fingers.

"The . . . doll! It was . . . in my room . . . Hands around my . . . neck!" DeVere gasped. He pointed along the corridor and, in the shadows at the far end, I thought I saw the shape of a ghastly skull-like head, grinning at us, shrouded by the brim of a top hat.

"Stay here," I said, but DeVere clutched at my sleeve like a child afraid of the dark.

"No, Sir Arthur. Don't leave me! Please!"

"I have to pursue that thing. That . . . that abomination has already murdered one person and attacked another. Whatever spirit inhabits that doll, Houdini or no, it must be stopped."

As I turned to face the corridor, the *thing* was truly immersed in darkness. I ran towards it, and the figure darted around the corner.

I gave chase. I must concede, I am not a nimble man; I do come across to strangers as an ungainly figure, somewhat akin to a walrus in a greatcoat, but I have been an active sportsman all my life, so I can put on a good turn of speed when required.

I hurtled along the corridors, but every time I turned a corner the doll was just ahead of me.

I ran around a corner, collided with another figure, and was sent sprawling. I tried to struggle to my feet, but suddenly I was looking down at the barrel of a revolver. It was pointing right between my eyes.

## HOLMES HAS A THEORY

"Good Lord!" exclaimed Dr Watson, putting up his revolver. "Sir Arthur! What are you doing running around the place like a mad thing?"

"I was pursuing the doll."

"You, too?" he said grimly. "I'm almost glad you said that, because when I saw the thing scurrying across the hallway, I feared I was going mad."

"There is no mistake, I assure you. I'm afraid Holmes will have to give up his accusations of delusion."

"Not yet, I'm afraid. Holmes has a theory. The butler may have done it."

"Frank?" I gasped.

"Who else? He is the only one left in this house who could be responsible for what has occurred in the last few hours."

We ran down to the servants' quarters, reading the signs on the doors, until we found the door marked "BUTLER". It was already ajar, and Holmes could be seen within, sitting by Frank's bed. The bed was occupied, and it looked like there was someone huddled deep under the covers.

Holmes glanced at us when we entered, but he did not say anything. A tear trickled down his cheek. He held up his hand. It was soaked with a deep red substance.

"Oh, dear Lord," Watson breathed. "Him, too?"

"Him, too," Holmes sobbed. "Stabbed, just like the maid. It seems everything I have deduced about this case is wrong. Everything is a mystery, and this decrepit old detective is finally at a loss." Holmes looked quite sick, but it was not the queasiness of a man facing death, it was the look of a man whose very world was crumbling around him. "If you eliminate the impossible," he muttered to himself, clutching his forehead and allowing his thin hair to protrude in alarming tufts from the side of his head, "then whatever remains, no matter how improbable, must be the case. The maid was improbable. And she has been eliminated. The butler was improbable. And he has been eliminated, too. There is no one else but the doll. Don't you see,

Watson? Everything has been eliminated. Everything!" He
giggled like a child. "I must concede that everything has been
eliminated and the only solution ... is the impossible one!
Houdini has come among us, to punish us for doubting his
abilities!"

"Holmes!" snapped Watson. "Pull yourself together, man! We
must find the police officer and report this!"

Milo DeVere blundered in, just as Holmes's eyes widened as
he looked over my shoulder.

Holmes's bony finger extended, much like the doll's, as he
pointed at empty air. "He is here! He is here, DeVere! Houdini,
the Prince of the Air, has come among us!"

"Holmes, there is nothing there! There is nothing!"

"Yes, there is! Holmes is correct! Houdini's spirit is in this
house!" shrieked DeVere.

There, above us, at the top of the flight of stairs, the doll
looked down at us with pure malevolence. Then it shrank back
into the shadows.

Holmes grabbed DeVere by the shoulder. "Come, my good
friend! We must seek out this embodiment of evil and destroy
it!"

DeVere nodded, and spittle flew from his lips.

"Do you have your trusty revolver, Watson?"

Again DeVere nodded, even though Holmes had used the
name "Watson", rather than "DeVere". This perplexed me, to
say the least.

"Good. Come, Watson, the game's afoot!"

Holmes ran up the stairs and dragged DeVere with him.
Watson and I looked at each other in horror, and we bounded
after them.

## THE CHASE IS JOINED

Holmes ran at full speed and, despite his inebriation, Milo
DeVere kept up with him. It was all Watson and I could do to
keep them in sight.

"There he is, Watson! He is over there!" yelled Holmes.

"Yes! I see it!" Milo DeVere shouted.

Shots were fired in the darkness, and we instinctively threw ourselves to the floor.

"DeVere has a gun," muttered Watson. "We must be careful. We can't get too close. The fellow is so thoroughly intoxicated he's likely to take a potshot at us by mistake."

We followed the sound of their voices. It gradually dawned on us that we were heading back into the centre of the house, and the museum. Holmes and DeVere were standing outside the door.

Holmes grabbed DeVere by his nightshirt collar and shouted into his face, "We have tracked this creature to its lair. Are you ready, my good friend, Dr Watson?"

"I surely am, Holmes!" said DeVere.

"Then . . . onward!"

Milo DeVere pulled out his revolver and ran screaming into the museum.

The doors were open and we saw the doll, once more at its stand. It was moving again, the stylus gliding towards the Ouija board. Milo DeVere never gave the doll a chance to relate another message from beyond; he aimed and shot the doll. The head exploded like an overripe fruit, and the top hat hurtled into the air.

Before the doll's hat had even settled on the ground, DeVere sent two more bullets into its torso. The impact flung it off its stand and threw it against the wall. Tiny cogs and wheels rolled and rattled across the floor.

The doll lay there crumpled in the corner, but not for long, because Milo DeVere ran to it screaming and smashed it furiously and repeatedly with the butt of his revolver. Down and down went the gun, but still he continued to pound on the doll, wrenching limbs from the torso with the sheer force of his fury.

## THE TRUTH EMERGES

There is little more to say about the events of that evening. The whole episode still feels like a dream to me. We left Milo DeVere crying and screaming in the wreckage of his prized possession, and searched for the policeman, who was nowhere to be found. Watson sedated Holmes and, once he was fast asleep, arranged for a carriage to go into town where he could alert the authorities.

Watson returned with policemen, who looked around them in frank disbelief. I offered to give them my account of events, but they seemed disinterested in what I had to say, and assured me I was free to leave whenever I liked (Watson claimed that they were impressed with my title of "Sir Arthur". They considered me English royalty, and did not wish to bother me with any unpleasantness).

Watson showed me to the door, shook my hand warmly and promised me that he would "sort Milo and Holmes out". Already Milo DeVere was sobering up, and coming to terms with what he had done.

I booked my ticket to Phoenix, and stayed in a hostelry for a few days to wait. Long-distance express trains in America are infrequent, to say the least. I didn't mind, as I was glad of the time to gather my wits. At last, however, the shout went up that the locomotive had arrived, and I hurried to the station, where I clambered into a carriage, placed my bag on the rack and settled down for the journey. I allowed my eyes to close as my mind scrambled over the events of the last two days.

The doll. Houdini. I didn't know quite what to feel about what happened. I had been elated that I had seen proof, at last – such proof would have shook the world. But now I felt shattered and utterly despondent, because that proof had been turned to dust.

After a few minutes I realized I was not alone in the carriage. I opened my eyes and saw that someone was watching me intently.

"Mr Holmes!"

Sherlock Holmes was a very different man from when I saw him last. He was more his old self, calm, composed and impeccably dressed. There was no preamble or pleasantry.

He merely said: "I would like to offer you an apology, Sir Arthur."

"Oh really?" I said. "In what regard?"

"I have done you a great injustice."

"I understand. We cannot be right all the time. I accept your apology for doubting me."

"That is not quite the apology I had in mind." Holmes took out his pipe, smelled it, and tapped the contents out in disgust. "Smoking lavender is not the most pleasant of experiences." He refilled his pipe, and puffed on it thoughtfully. "How do I begin? In these last few years, Houdini had, like myself, become aware that he was not as young as he was. He experienced reoccurring health problems, and was increasingly aware that he had a finite number of days left to him."

"As we all are. Mr Houdini is not unique in that regard."

Holmes allowed himself a thin smile. "That is true. But he was unique in so many other ways, and when an extraordinary man decides to put his affairs in order, it is only natural he would do it in an extraordinary way." His intelligent grey eyes bored into my face, and I suddenly felt quite unnerved. Holmes continued, "Houdini had become agitated about the fate of the doll. He did not trust DeVere, and had severe doubts that upon his death the man would not keep his promise and return the doll to the Houdini family, especially since all documentation was lost and the witness was dead."

"That makes sense."

"He employed me to test this hypothesis. And, in the event of DeVere's reluctance to part with the doll, I was to synthesize a scenario where he did part with it. Much of what you have seen in that house over the past two days has been nothing more than a fairy tale."

"I beg your pardon? Are you saying that everything that I have endured has been a . . . performance?"

"Yes," said Holmes, resting a hand, not unkindly, on my shoulder. "And that, my dear sir, is why I am here to apologize to you personally. Nothing less than the mental breakdown of the great Sherlock Holmes would have convinced DeVere that the doll was a product of dark forces."

He produced a series of brass keys punched with square holes, which he fanned out like a magician performing a card trick. "Unbeknown to Milo DeVere, the doll operated using a series of punch cards, just like a nickelodeon, which I slotted into the mechanism unseen by all of you. I cued the doll into divining my Baker Street address just seconds before I challenged it to do so. Yes, sir, all done by sleight of hand – my hand. The maid did indeed scratch 'Rosabelle Believe' on the wall, which I convincingly deduced, only to have my chief suspect spirited away by her apparent death. To my obvious 'distress'."

My mind was racing through the implications of what he was saying. "So . . . the deaths . . .?"

"If you look at out of the window, Sir Arthur . . ."

I looked out of the window and through the clouds of steam I saw two figures. I saw Frank, the butler, and Molly, the maid, standing happily on the platform, miraculously risen from the dead.

They were waving at me. Absurdly, I waved back.

Holmes continued, "They were your doll, sir. They took it in turns to dress up as the doll to create the impression it moved about. The real doll never moved from its pedestal. And of course there was no reason for you or Mr DeVere to suspect their part in this subterfuge, as they were already dead. That is why I conscripted my good friend Dr Watson for this escapade. He was needed to convincingly pronounce them deceased and remove the suspects from the story. And the police you saw were also actors, paid to add credence to the fiction of their demise."

"They – and you – acted it very well, Mr Holmes," I said, flabbergasted.

"It was all a show, all for the benefit of Mr DeVere. But you were the most important element of all, Sir Arthur. An impassioned advocate for spiritualism, who would convince DeVere there were supernatural forces at work. Your performance was the most convincing of all. That's why I planted the suggestion in DeVere's mind to contact you about the doll."

"But, Holmes, your scheme was all for naught." Even though the layers of revelation shocked me to the core, as a logical man I was duty bound to point out the flaw in Holmes's plan. "You did not get the doll after all. It was completely destroyed."

"And destroying it is exactly what the Houdini estate intended to do, once they had it in their possession. You see, Houdini wanted the secrets of his tricks and his illusions to go with him to the grave. Perhaps some of them will survive. But the doll was his greatest secret of all, and he had no intention of allowing the truth of how it worked to be uncovered."

"Well, of course Houdini would want this. He had no wish to admit to being allied with the spirits."

Holmes sighed, a very world-weary sigh.

"But you cannot explain how you knew the secret message 'Rosabelle Believe', or how to operate the doll. As you say, Houdini didn't pass on his secrets lightly."

"You are an intelligent man, Sir Arthur. The solution has just stared you in the face. Look out of the window again. Do you not recognize Frank and Molly?"

I looked again. Perhaps it was because Holmes prompted me, but I suddenly found them very familiar. Beneath the moustache and the eyeglasses, the old butler suddenly took on the likeness of Houdini himself. And the maid, shorn of her blonde curls, could have been the spitting image of Houdini's wife, Bess.

But then the train hooted, the steam devoured the figures on the platform, just like the smoke of war shrouded the figures in my dream, and then we were moving. I turned back to Holmes, but he too had gone.

It was only much later, back in England, that I mused on Sherlock Holmes's story. It had suddenly dawned on me how fantastic it sounded; and the hoops he and his accomplices would have gone through to create this fantastic plan.

Houdini faking his own death? Taking the absurd risk that I, an old friend, would see through his disguise? It sounded completely impossible, as impossible as my own fictional detective, Dr Bell, suddenly coming to life before my eyes.

Upon further consideration, I came to the conclusion that it *was* impossible, and I would settle on the nearest improbable alternative: that Holmes, faced with the incontrovertible fact of the occult, constructed a typically far-fetched explanation of

events, as detectives are wont to do, and had boarded the
carriage to try to convince me of its veracity.

Perhaps, like Houdini himself, Sherlock Holmes had been
persuaded by the Catholic Church to deny all evidence of what
we had all seen in the house of Milo DeVere – the house that
contained the doll who talked to the dead.

I have written this account, but I choose not to publish. The
existence of spirits, ghosts and fairies is now fast becoming
immutable fact, and the acceptance of spiritualism as a branch
of the sciences is only a matter of time. I do not wish to embar-
rass the great detective in his lifetime. His desperate attempts to
disavow the evidence of his own eyes will only diminish his
legacy.

I only hope that when this account is finally unearthed, people
will understand and sympathize that Sherlock Holmes was very
much a man of his age, and his quaint beliefs were very much a
product of the time he lived in.

Sir Arthur Conan Doyle, Crowborough, 1928

# A Concurrence of Coincidences

## David Moody

One never appreciates the true comforts of home more than
when one is far and forcibly removed from such welcome familiarity. Indeed, as I found to my cost in the February of 1899, the
effects of such painful detachments inevitably become
compounded the longer the return trip home is delayed. On this
particular occasion I had been quite prepared to spend a long
and enforced period of time away from London – for despite
the advances of the day, a short visit to Quebec remains both a
physical and technological impossibility – and yet as circumstances conspired to defer mine and Holmes's return home, my
unease steadily increased, almost by the hour. In fact – and I
took great care to keep my feelings on this point to myself – the
emotions I experienced many thousands of miles from London
were not unlike the childish homesickness I experienced during
my first few days at school: trapped in an unfamiliar place
surrounded by unfamiliar faces, quite unable to leave.

But, of course, despite the distance and detachment, whilst in
Canada I felt none of the lonely isolation I had suffered at
school, for I was not alone, and my friend Holmes's companion-
ship was eminently welcome. Our familiar late-night conversations and reminiscences of old adventures in steamer cabins and
hotel lounges over a glass or two of sherry did, at least, provide
some temporary illusion of normality.

Our business in Quebec having been satisfactorily resolved (a
frightful inconvenience involving three bodies, a tenor alto, a
bassoon and more than a trace of thallium), Holmes and I

boarded the half-empty steamer which, we presumed, would transport us directly back to Liverpool. My temperament improved the moment we set sail, for even though thousands of miles of ocean still separated us from home, that distance was decreasing by the hour. I had assumed we had reached the end of our North Atlantic sojourn, and yet, within little more than a day of leaving port, we were quite literally all at sea again.

I had intended to spend as much of the return journey as possible below decks in the reasonably well-appointed cabin Holmes and I shared. I planned to occupy my time with sleep and books, but a recurrence of mild seasickness soon put paid to that idea.

"You must remain on deck with me, Watson," Holmes announced. "It will inevitably be better for your disposition to be in plain view of the ocean to physically witness each new swell and roll of the waves. A mild shift will feel as an uncontrolled churn without such visual reference."

Holmes was right, of course, but had I remained below decks, I would have been spared the terrifying panic and confusion which quickly seized the crew and our fellow passengers without but a moment's warning. I later remarked to Holmes that it was the most unfortunate concurrence of coincidences: a fog bank that materialized most unexpectedly, a dense patch of floating sea ice and a sudden mechanical failure all conspired to render our vessel helpless and to send us drifting wildly off course. And by the time sufficient emergency repairs had been completed and control regained, our captain (a normally stalwart and occasionally egregious gentleman whose usual red face had become blanched white in the panic of the moment) advised that our deviation after such a prolonged period of drifting was such that we found ourselves far closer to Greenland than anywhere else. He informed all aboard that we would alight there temporarily in order that the ship be thoroughly inspected and restored. He anticipated a delay of three days at least, possibly longer.

I am sorry to admit that my frustrations got the better of me, and I vented my anger at a luckless steward who, truth be told, had as much (or, more accurately, as little) influence over our situation as I, and who could only proffer empty apologies and endless cups of tea. Sherlock Holmes, by comparison, appeared uncharacteristically enthused by our unexpected stranding. He accepted the inevitability of our enforced stay on that strange snow- and ice-covered rock with far greater alacrity than I.

"Why, Watson," he remarked, "with so few inhabitants, the chance of my ever being called here to Greenland on business is as remote as this island itself. You really do limit yourself unnecessarily. Desist from your endless grumbling and we will take in our surroundings while the opportunity presents itself."

For a short while longer I maintained a dogged resistance to leaving the ship, electing to remain in our cabin with a few choice volumes from the ill-stocked library, but it was not long before curiosity overtook me and I stepped out with my companion to at last survey the alien landscape upon which we had become stranded. Truth be told, it was less Holmes's words of encouragement that forced me to leave the cabin, and more the continual wayward rolling of our under-repair vessel. The bitter cold outside gradually became less of a concern than my infernal nausea, which steadfastly refused to pass.

"I believe there are some magnificent vistas to be witnessed here, Holmes," said I as we alighted from the ship, wearing appropriate boots and various other layers and overcoats purloined from the crew. I had busied myself with an atlas in the hours preceding, but I need not have bothered. We had barely walked three hundred yards before the entire world appeared to open up ahead of us: a view so vast it was difficult to fully appreciate the enormity of it all. To the north, a mountain known locally as Sermitsiaq – a name I could barely bring myself to write correctly, let alone pronounce – which I knew to be some three-quarters of a mile in height, appeared no larger than a snow-dusted molehill in the distance.

Despite the bitter cold, I found myself beginning to slowly warm to our remarkable surroundings. Between the port and the mountain lay Nuuk – the largest settlement on the island, by all accounts. Before we had taken more than another few steps forward we were accosted by a most unusual-looking fellow: a native Inuit, his distinctive face was partially hidden by a circle of fur around the rim of the hood of his heavy over-jacket. I noticed one of the ship's crew running after him, unable to match his speed along the icy walkway, seeming to take two steps sideways for every single step forward. Eventually, he reached us.

"This here fellow is a local guide," the crewman explained. "He will find you accommodation in the town."

"Town!" said I, looking again at the motley collection of wooden roofs peeking out through the snow. "It's hardly a town!"

The native man appeared to take exception to my tone, and assaulted me with a volley in his unintelligible language, a mix of Inuit and Danish I presumed, none of which was even slightly familiar to my ears.

Holmes sidled closer to me. "Languages may differ, Watson, but faces and expressions are often the same. You'd do well to remember that."

Suitably admonished, I nodded an apology in the direction of our guide.

As we neared Nuuk, the numerous peaked wooden roofs appeared not unlike the beach huts at Brighton in winter and my mind wandered back home again. "I say, Holmes, could you imagine taking a dip in the sea here?"

"I can certainly imagine the after-effects," he replied. "It would not take long for a man to lose his life in such waters. We would both do well to remember the inherent dangers of this country. The temperature, the geography, the wildlife ... we really could be no further removed from home."

"Indeed. There seems to be so little here that I wonder, perhaps, if we might at last conclude an expedition without having to resolve a crime or mystery of some sort?"

When the captain of our ship had spoken of Nuuk as a town, I had immediately anticipated the familiar bustle of towns at home, and whilst I clearly did not envisage there being anything like the hurly-burly of the streets of London, what we found was more akin to a ghost town; a settlement abandoned.

"Do you suppose there is actually anyone here, Holmes?" I asked, for I had barely seen a soul.

"No doubt they are all indoors, as should we be."

But the end of our brisk walk through the snow appeared still to be a long way off, and the temperature was dropping steadily. I was beginning to lag behind both Holmes and our guide, or was it that their pace had quickened, keen, as we all were, to find shelter. The glare of the slowly sinking sun on the ice and snow was intense and disorientating, and for a while the two figures just ahead of me remained my only point of visible reference. With much effort and cursing, I adjusted my speed, barely managing to remain upright in the wind and fresh-falling snow, until I had at last drawn level. Our Inuit guide turned to look at us both and broke into a broad, toothy grin, just visible under layers of sealskin and fur.

"What is it?" I asked, panting with ungentlemanly exertion.

"It seems this fellow fancies himself as something of a match-maker," Holmes announced, sounding as fresh as if he'd just returned from a brisk walk along Baker Street, nothing more.

"I don't understand."

"I wager you'd struggle to pick our friend here out from a line of his countrymen, Watson."

"And why would I want to, Holmes?"

"No reason. But to you or I, one Inuit male looks remarkably similar to another, wouldn't you agree?"

"I do not believe I have yet laid eyes on enough individual Inuit males to possibly be able to comment," I answered, increasingly confused.

"To this gentleman, one man from London might look all but identical to another."

"Please, Holmes, I'm desperately tired – is there a point to all of this?"

"I believe our guide has taken it upon himself to try to pair like with like."

And then all became clear. We were most definitely being taken towards a particular abode now: a reasonably sized wooden dwelling of basic yet sturdy construction, surrounded by a number of outhouses and stores, all set a short distance beyond the outskirts of Nuuk. As we neared, I was able to discern a number of gentlemen busying themselves with sleds and tools and the like. Though as well covered up and insulated as our native guide, from the way they carried themselves I could see that they were somewhat less adept to the conditions than he. It did not seem too wild a stretch of the imagination to assume these characters might be as British as Holmes and I.

I stared in surprise. "Why, could these fellows be from our neck of the woods?"

"From Oxford, actually," Holmes replied, and the geographical precision of his comment caused me to stop in my snowy tracks.

"From Oxford? Holmes, how could you possibly know that?"

"Watson, I'm in no doubt you've already observed the manner in which these gentlemen move is more akin to you and I rather than indigenous inhabitants of Greenland, but I'm less convinced you have noticed they are all wearing similar variations on the same winter garments and boots. Unless I am very much mistaken – and I am not – those are designs exclusive to Pinkerton and Jarvis, extreme outdoor tailors and bootmakers of some repute, established in High Wycombe."

"And yet you surmise Oxford?"

"When one considers the remoteness of our present location, Watson, yes. One must ask oneself why such an unexpected brigade might be found here? Given the delicacy with which some of their equipment is clearly being handled – indicating, perhaps, that it is scientific in origin – it would appear they are here to explore rather than to sightsee."

"I remain unable to see how these observations lead you to deduce Oxford."

"Professor Stanley Darrington," Holmes announced. "Do you actually read *The Times*, Watson, or merely use its pages to hide behind? Darrington, an eminent geologist, and his party set out from Oxford this past April to carry out a scientific survey of these particular shores."

Holmes walked on and I followed. Our guide had already reached the building and appeared to be attempting to announce our arrival quite excitedly. He came back towards us with another man in tow who introduced himself as Mortimer Jennings, a student of Professor Darrington. He welcomed us both most effusively and led us into the building.

"Why, it is as if a direct passage between Greenland and London has been uncovered here," I remarked to Holmes as I shook myself dry of snow. The building was a veritable home from home. Simple in decoration, as expected, and yet extremely welcoming and warm. A young and handsome woman sat warming her hands by a blazing fire while, all around her, the few men we had seen working outside continued now to busy themselves.

Mortimer Jennings disappeared into an anteroom then returned, just moments later, behind another, much smaller man. He had the air of a well-educated fellow who did not much care for having been disturbed. He peered inquisitively at Holmes and I through wire-framed spectacles perched on the end of his nose as if looking out over a classroom full of unruly students.

I took it upon myself to make our introductions. "Forgive the intrusion, sir," said I. "My name is Dr John Watson, and this is my colleague, Sherlock Holmes. I am afraid we have become somewhat stranded on this peculiar little island whilst the steamer charged with taking us back to England undergoes repairs. May we impose on you while—?"

"Holmes, you say?" he interrupted, quite rudely. "Sherlock Holmes? Sherlock Holmes of Baker Street?"

"Indeed," Holmes replied, extending his hand. "And you, sir, must be Professor Stanley Darrington."

"I am. And, sir, what an honour it would be to have you stay here. Why, you are just in time to join us for dinner."

And so, before long, we found ourselves seated around a rough-hewn table with the professor's entire party, which numbered five in total. Our meal, prepared by a local Inuit woman who worked feverishly and chattered unintelligibly, was very welcome and most filling, if a little salty for my usual tastes. I chose not to ask too much about what we were eating, for I had already heard mention of seals and whales and all manner of other beasts indigenous to the seas surrounding this remote outpost. Indeed, it was not just the species of animal we consumed that concerned me, but also the cut. Whilst in the ship's library prior to leaving I had glanced at an article that detailed how, as food supplies in this vicinity are so clearly sparse and hard to come by, not a scrap of any hunted kill would be wasted. What could not be eaten was used to make clothing or tools, or burned as fuel. Why, it occurred to me we could have been dining on absolutely *anything*! But it was warm and filling, and I was suitably cold and empty, and I politely chewed and swallowed for as long as I felt able, certainly long enough so as not to cause any offence to our gracious host.

As we ate, the professor introduced us to his small crew. His daughter, Clara, was seated to Holmes's right. I – whether because of my girth or position, I could not be sure – was seated at one head of the table, the professor at the other. Three more men were crammed elbow to elbow opposite Holmes and Miss Darrington. We had already met Mortimer Jennings. Next to him sat a large, quiet man named Alvis Matheson, and next to him, furthest from me, was a gentleman by the name of George Eyre, who engaged Miss Darrington in conversation almost continually. I could already detect from his demeanour that Matheson was tiring of the volume coming from his left.

"Do you ever desist, Eyre?" he asked most abruptly. "Why, your noise tonight is more constant than the wind through the rafters of this building."

Miss Darrington sniggered. Eyre, however, did not. He turned to face Matheson. "You would do well to keep your opinions to yourself," he retorted. "Good conversation is a fine art, wouldn't you agree, Clara?"

"And you think yourself some kind of artist?" Matheson goaded.

"I have a keener eye than you, sir."

Thankfully the uncomfortable conversation ended quickly. It appeared that Matheson was ready to prolong matters, but Miss Darrington immediately drew a veil over proceedings with a word, leaving him to stare into his stew, suitably admonished. Eyre, however, continued to chatter aimlessly.

"When we return to Britain, Clara, I will show you true natural art. There are cliffs on our ancient coastline with beautiful strata running through them as you would not believe. I will show you the fossils of creatures which lived millions of years ago . . ."

"You forget my father's influence, George. After Mother died Father took me on many holidays to the coast. It never ceased to amaze me how there always seemed to be *something* of geological interest to be found wherever we happened to be holidaying. Why, I lost count of the times my bucket and spade were snatched from me in the interests of science."

There was much laughter at Miss Darrington's gentle jibe at the expense of her father.

"So is that your intent here, Professor?" asked Holmes, somewhat impertinently. "You intend to plunder this isle for its natural resources?"

"I hardly think 'plunder'," the professor replied, indignant. "The purpose of this expedition is purely scientific."

The incessant George Eyre seized the opportunity to take over the conversation again. "You are right, Mr Holmes, in that we believe there are considerable geological riches to be found here in Greenland."

"And I am sure the island's Danish governors will be extremely interested in your findings," Holmes retorted.

"No doubt the locals too," I added.

Eyre continued, his enthusiasm unabated. "Whilst you are perfectly correct in that this is a Danish territory, there are few in the world today who possess the geological acumen of the professor."

"And your good self?" enquired Holmes.

"It is true, I have studied under the professor for a number of years, as has Jennings here, but neither of us can claim even a fraction of his understanding of the complexities and properties of this immense spinning ball of rock upon which we all live."

"Though often you do claim as much," I heard Matheson mumble into his stew, and then he reacted as if he had been kicked quiet under the table.

"You do yourself a disservice, George," the professor announced. "Mr Eyre here has long been a prized pupil of mine. And he possesses a business acumen which far surpasses my own."

Eyre smiled with some satisfaction. He struck me as a peculiarly forthright fellow. I glanced across at Holmes to try to gauge his opinion, but my friend remained as resolutely imperceptible as ever. His ego suitably inflated, Eyre continued to lecture us: "The possibilities here are almost limitless. Silver, nickel, platinum, molybdenum, iron, niobium, tantalum, uranium, not to mention coal and oil . . . we are certain there are a wealth of valuable minerals to be uncovered here. And though you are quite right, Holmes, that the Danes will stake their rightful claim, such claims will be valueless without the assistance of this expedition to locate and advise."

"So yours will be a purely advisory role?" Holmes asked.

"In essence, yes. Whilst we have limited physical strength in our number," he continued, glancing pointedly at Matheson, "the Danes and the natives will carry out the bulk of the physical work."

"And is that all you think me good for?" Matheson demanded, offended. "Do you think me a packhorse?"

"Please, Alvis," Miss Darrington said, appearing to sense trouble was again afoot. "George, you should apologize."

"I'll do no such thing. My dear Clara, you must keep things in perspective here. Remember that muscle and brawn are easy enough to come by on this island, as sparsely populated as it may be. Without your father, Jennings and I, however, this expedition will achieve nothing."

"That's as maybe, but there is no call for such rudeness."

"Let it go," Matheson said, appearing to wipe away an unwanted tear of frustration. "I'm used to his tireless goading."

Jennings, who had remained quiet throughout the meal, excused himself and got up from the table. He went out to another room, only to return a few moments later to make an announcement. "The door to the smaller of the outside storerooms has been left open again, Matheson. Go out and secure it, will you?"

"I thought you were supposed to have secured that door?"

"I did secure it, but it seems there is a fault with the lock you installed. Matheson, the responsibility for the overall security of the camp is yours. You heard Mr Eyre just now . . . muscle and brawn are easy enough to come by. Would you rather we relieved you of your duties and employed a simple labourer from Nuuk? It really is not that difficult a challenge."

Matheson's temper immediately got the better of him, and it was all I could do to push my chair back out of the way to avoid being caught up in the sudden explosion of violence myself. He ran across the room and grabbed Jennings by the collar of his padded jacket, then threw him to the floor and stood over him, fist raised ready to strike.

"Matheson, stand down," the professor ordered.

"Alvis, please," Miss Darrington exclaimed.

If anything, Matheson pulled his fist further back. The professor threw down his napkin and stood. "Matheson, I said STAND DOWN!"

This time, Matheson did as he was instructed. He dropped the other man then snatched up his own outdoor jacket, quite furious, and made for the door.

"Will he be all right out there?" I asked, once some semblance of normality had been restored.

"He has a violent temper, that one," Eyre remarked.

"Only when provoked," Miss Darrington said quickly.

"He is fast becoming a loose cannon," Jennings said, sitting down at the table having readjusted his clothing and calmed himself down somewhat. "He is a liability, and we would do well to be rid of him."

"What of the door you mentioned?" the professor asked.

"Sir, you know how I struggle with such menial tasks on occasion," said Jennings, "particularly in these conditions. Are such situations not why we tolerate having Matheson here at all?"

The atmosphere that followed dinner was awkward and uncomfortable to say the very least, particularly when a snow-covered Matheson returned an hour or so later. I remarked to Holmes that had it not been for the blizzard-like conditions outside, and the fact it was pitch-black and ice-cold out there, I might well have suggested taking a late-evening stroll back to our ship and returning to the security of our cabin: nausea or no nausea. As it was, however, we were effectively trapped, prisoners of the inclement Greenland conditions. Home had never felt quite so very far away as during that long, dark night.

We were shown to a small guest room for the evening, and what it lacked in space it more than made up for in warmth. Our beds were firm and, after a period of acclimatization, reassuringly comfortable under layers of furs and sealskins.

"Well, Holmes, what do you make of our host and his party?" I asked across the darkness. I had been waiting to hear his thoughts all evening.

"When one considers their few numbers," he answered, "there appears to be a tangled web of connections between them. They have been here several months without respite; little wonder tempers are becoming frayed. Now, Watson, if you don't mind, I should very much like to get some sleep."

And with that our conversation, and our first day in Greenland, ended.

We were awoken next morning by Alvis Matheson, and I must confess to having being more than a little unsure as to what to make of the fellow. His behaviour at the dinner table last evening would not have been out of place in the roughest of public bars in the darkest backstreets of London. He had, however, been instructed by the professor to apologize and to offer to show us some of the sights of the island by way of recompence. Holmes declined, but insisted I took Matheson up on his offer. Once we had dressed (though neither Holmes nor I had particularly *undressed*, given the conditions) and had partaken of a particularly salty, fish-based breakfast (throughout which Holmes grumbled continually for eggs, bacon and muffins), I set out with Matheson. After the chaotic weather of last evening, it was now a brilliantly sunny day. The sky overhead was as deep and blue as the best days of British summer.

And I was soon glad that I had agreed to go, for Matheson proved to be surprisingly good company once free from the confines of the camp, generous both with his time and his humour. He provided me with suitable attire: crampons, sturdy boots and outer garments, and even permitted me to use one of his prized ice picks to help me with the journey – a particularly brutal-looking implement with an exquisitely carved bone handle. Indeed, my companion was so accommodating I began to wonder whether it was the same man. He appeared to be a sensitive soul at heart, albeit with a fiery temper, and he anticipated my reservations from yesterday evening.

"Dr Watson, please allow me to apologize for the scene you witnessed at dinner last night. I am most ashamed of my actions."

"Think nothing of it," I told him.

We climbed to the top of a snowy peak. Although not particularly steep or high, the layer of fresh snow beneath our boots made the climb feel that much more tiring. But the view that greeted us at the summit was breathtaking, and allowed me to cast aside all thoughts of being cold and of missing home temporarily. We were gazing down over the wooden roofs of Nuuk, nestled as they were between vast crags and snow-covered mountains.

"And tell me," asked I, "how did you come to find yourself here in Greenland?"

He paused before answering, appearing to still be taking in the full enormity of the view as if he were witnessing it for the first time. "I've known Clara – Miss Darrington – since we were children. My late father worked for the professor."

"Doing what, may I ask?"

"Groundskeeper, sir."

"And your role here?"

"My official title is Chief of Camp, not that it seems to carry much weight around these parts."

"I detected that last evening."

"And again I apologize. But, sir, believe me, you saw nothing last night. In years to come I feel sure someone will invent a phrase to describe how fellows begin to feel about one another after spending so long in such close confines. Some kind of snow fever, I shouldn't wonder. It really is the most frustrating malady, and I fear that it is why Jennings, Eyre and myself clash so frequently. I believe there is no treatment for the condition other than to leave."

"And is that what you wish to do?"

"Some days, yes," answered he, "but there is more for me here than anywhere else. I am more of a man than they give me credit for, Dr Watson, and . . ."

"And what?"

"And I fear the professor, Jennings and Eyre are too focused on the task. They strive to reach their goals at the expense of everything and everyone else."

Alvis Matheson struck me as a man of principle and character. Physically strong, and whilst not particularly academic, it was clear that he was no idiot. I remarked to myself that of all those I'd met since arriving in Greenland, here was, perhaps, one of the more capable.

"You see," he continued as we stood together and took in the wonder of the endless snow-covered vista which stretched out for ever before us, "there remains a fundamental difference between the others and I."

"And what is that?" I enquired, intrigued.

"Quite simply, they look at this wondrous place and see only profit, mere fame and fortune."

"And you?"

"I see nothing more than a vast, unspoilt and impossibly beautiful landscape, barely touched by the hand of man. I would rather remain a pauper and leave this wilderness untouched, wouldn't you, Doctor? There are things in life far more valuable than money and reputation."

I very much enjoyed the rest of my unexpected excursion with Matheson. I found him an agreeable and disarming fellow whose depth of character took me quite by surprise. The events of the remainder of the day, however, left me seriously doubting my own ability to judge a man.

Around lunchtime, Holmes and I were left at base camp with Professor Darrington and his daughter while the rest of the professor's staff went about their daily tasks and routines. Matheson had several repairs to make good, buildings and stores having become damaged in the previous night's snow, whilst Jennings and Eyre took a group of Inuits each to carry out surveys – Jennings to the north, and Eyre to the south of Nuuk near a particularly craggy stretch of coastline. Outside, the bitter weather of last evening had returned.

The professor sang his protégés' virtues almost incessantly. "They are such good fellows," said he. "George in particular. You know, when I see the way he conducts himself, the way he goes about his work with such vigour and enthusiasm . . . why, I'm put in mind of a younger version of myself. A *much* younger version of myself, of course."

"Oh, Father, please," Miss Darrington said to herself as she gazed into the fireplace.

"Clara, my dear, do you really find me so wearisome?"

"Not you, Father, the topic of conversation."

"But you should be pleased I am so taken with your intended."

"Your intended?" Holmes asked.

"George and Clara recently became engaged," the professor explained, with more than a little pride evident in his tone.

"Congratulations to both of you," I ventured.

"There will be some delay before the wedding, of course," the professor continued to enthuse. "Our work here must be completed, then there is the not insignificant matter of returning to England. I do not think that—"

The conversation was abruptly interrupted. The door to the building flew open, letting in a blast of icy air, which chilled me to the core, a savage, biting wind that immediately negated the effects of the roaring fire we had been gathered around.

A figure blundered inside. At first it was impossible to see who it was, but when they removed their fur-lined hood I saw it was an older Inuit man. There was no mistaking the look of abject horror on his face. He frantically beckoned us to follow him.

There was an inevitable delay as Holmes, the professor and I struggled to dress appropriately, then a further bottleneck as we each tried to exit the building, our girths bolstered, as they were, by many additional layers. For the first time since arriving in Greenland, I felt uncomfortably warm as we followed the Inuit across the snow. He moved with a remarkable fluidity. For all his advancing years, the professor was not far behind, and neither was Holmes. I brought up the rear with an unfortunate lack of grace, and when I reached the grisly sight I found before me, I began to wish I had walked slower still.

Mortimer Jennings was dead. There was no need for Holmes's keen skills of detection, or my medical knowledge, for the truth of the matter was plain to see in this most grim situation. Why, Jennings lay flat on his back in the blood-drenched snow with an Inuit harpoon protruding from his chest, his hands wrapped around its shaft. The tip of the harpoon had all but disappeared into his torso, leaving the long wooden shaft extending out at a right angle to the corpse. He had a puncture wound to his left temple also.

"Holmes," said I, "whoever could have done something as awful as this?"

Holmes was given no time at all to answer, for George Eyre was ready at hand with an explanation. "I saw it all," he announced, shouting to make himself heard over the gusts of the chill Greenland wind. "I saw everything."

"And pray tell us more," Holmes said.

"It was Matheson. He's gone quite mad, I tell you. My Inuits and I were returning from the morning's surveying, carrying my samples and instruments between us. We had reached the track back there," he explained, turning back and pointing south, "when I saw Matheson and Jennings. At first I thought little of it

– after all, we have been becoming used to Matheson's flashes of temper and their altercations – and yet when I saw Jennings drop and Matheson run, I immediately feared the worst. My fears were quickly confirmed."

"And to where did he run?" the professor asked.

"I have little idea, sir. He seemed in such a confused state, I'll wager he did not know either."

"The Lord above," the professor wailed. "This is terrible."

In the excitement of the moment, it seemed those present had temporarily overlooked the visitor in their midst.

It was Eyre who realized the significance first. "It is an astonishingly fortunate coincidence, Professor, but with the world's greatest detective stranded here in Greenland with us, would it not be prudent to allow him to investigate this awful crime."

The professor appeared as flabbergasted as the rest of us, and it was some moments before he had composed himself enough to speak. "From what you have already told us, George, there is little to investigate."

"Quite so, but Holmes can put the matter beyond doubt, can't you, sir? And perhaps he will also be able to help us locate the elusive Matheson and bring him to justice?"

"Well?" asked the professor.

"I will do everything within my power to help, though the evidence appears quite incontrovertible," Holmes replied. "There are boot marks here alongside those belonging to the victim, and they clearly match Matheson's for I noticed earlier that he has a quite distinctive gait and hits the ground with his left foot heavier than his right. There is no question of him being involved here."

At that moment one of the Inuits – who had remained close at hand but still a short distance away – became quite animated, pointing at the ground nearby. Eyre ran through the snow and dropped to his knees to investigate. He stood upright again moments later, holding a distinctive-looking ice pick in his gloved hand. I recognized it immediately.

"That belongs to Matheson," I explained to Holmes. "He loaned one to me – if not that very same implement – just this morning when we were out walking together."

"Quite so," Holmes said. "And I'll wager the blood staining the tip of the tool belongs to Jennings here."

"Then there is little more to be said," the professor announced. "Matheson has gone quite mad and killed Jennings in a fit of temper. George and the Inuits witnessed the whole sorry incident, and incontrovertible evidence has been discovered close at hand. I should have anticipated this."

"Do not punish yourself, Professor. How could you possibly have done so?" Eyre exclaimed.

"You are right, George, I suppose. I'm afraid Matheson's desperate disappearance has somewhat sealed his fate."

"We must search for him," I ventured, and I was ready to set out when the professor held me back.

"Not today, Doctor," said he, raising his voice above the wind. "The conditions are taking a turn for the worst. We must retire indoors for the night."

With reluctance we each followed the professor's lead, knowing that if Matheson did not soon return to the camp or take shelter elsewhere, the oncoming night would surely finish him off.

Indoors, we found Miss Darrington to be disconsolate at the day's events. Both her father and her fiancé did what they could to try to comfort her, but to no avail. Their kind, well-meaning attentions seemed, actually, to have the reverse effect to that which they intended, appearing almost to increase her distress. Whilst the three of them busied themselves with each other, I took the opportunity to talk privately to Holmes.

"Whatever is going on here, Holmes?" asked I. "Why, just this morning Matheson was talking about being gripped by a kind of mania ... a claustrophobic snow- and cabin-bound malady, if you like. Do you think one or more of these men has gone quite mad?"

"No, Watson, I do not."

The abruptness of his answer rather took me by surprise. "Then what do you suggest?"

"I suggest you might cast your mind back to several of our previous investigations and look for similarities."

"Black Peter?" I ventured, quickly recalling a case some four years previously concerning the murder – by harpoon – of a drunken and, by all accounts, most unpleasant seaman.

"No, Watson, that is not the case to which I refer: the only similarity there is the murder weapon. No, do you remember our investigations in Boscombe Valley . . . it was 1888 – I am sure you can cast your mind back that far?"

"Of course I can," I replied, indignant.

"Then what do you remember about the case?"

"My overriding memory, Holmes, is of a gentleman's son who, it was believed, had killed his father by beating him with a shotgun. All the evidence initially seemed to point to that summation, as I recall."

"You recall correctly. You will, of course, also recall that the truth we uncovered was wildly different."

"I do. Holmes, do you suggest that something similar has occurred here?"

"I am not in the business of suggesting, Watson. In cases such as these, we must be careful to consider all positions and all perspectives. Tell me, do you think Matheson is guilty of the murder of Jennings?"

It pained me to give my honest answer. "Well . . . yes. I fail at present to see that there can be any alternative explanation, or any ulterior motive. And our cast of characters here is so limited that it can be no one other than Matheson who struck the fatal blow."

"And that, my friend, is exactly right."

"So *you* believe Matheson is guilty?"

"No, I do not," he answered abruptly, surprising me.

"Then who? George Eyre? The professor or his daughter? An Inuit? A spear-wielding seal?"

I had overstepped the mark, and the withering look I rightfully received from Holmes put me firmly in my place.

"I have my suspicions," he told me. "While the others are distracted, you and I shall brave the elements again to uncover the truth."

"But, Holmes, it is rapidly darkening out there and you can plainly feel the temperature falling by the minute. Is it safe to go outside?"

"My dear Watson, I fear this may be our only opportunity. I'll wager the body will be gone by morning, courtesy of the ravenous local wildlife."

And so, barely half an hour later and unbeknownst to the others, we found ourselves outside again, examining Jennings's frozen corpse. He had become quite hideous. A hellish expression had frozen across his pallid and lifeless face: a foul, rictus grin. His twisted hands continued to grip the shaft of the harpoon, refusing to let go, even in death.

Holmes had with him the ice pick the Inuit had discovered near to the body: a clear match for the puncture wound in Jennings's right temple. He then proceeded to use the pick to dig down into the fresh snow beside the man's head. "Whatever are you doing, Holmes?" I asked over the howling wind. Though the light was poor, I saw that he had uncovered a patch of darkness deep below the covering of white. "What is it?"

"Blood, of course," he answered as he continued to scrape the ground clear. "And plenty of it, too."

"That is only to be expected, given the injury this poor soul has suffered."

"Damn unfortunate, though, to have been set-to around the head like this despite having already been speared through the chest."

"What?"

"Allow me to explain."

Holmes then stood and turned his attention to the harpoon itself, still standing rigidly like a flagpole, marking Jennings's location. "What are you inferring, Holmes?"

"Look at the footprints around here," he continued without answering, as he was wont to do. "There's no doubt Matheson and Jennings had some kind of coming together here, but there are other prints too, their relative depth under the fresh snow indicating how long they have been here. This is just as I surmised."

"But what does it mean?"

"It means, Watson, that I have an urgent errand to run and you have an important job to do. Return to the dwelling immediately and keep the professor, Miss Darrington and George Eyre suitably occupied. Tell them I have become unwell and retired to bed for the evening to recover. Use additional sheets and furs to give the illusion of my sleeping."

"And where will this foolhardy errand take you, Holmes? Can it not wait until morning? It is too cold and treacherous to be out here at this hour, even more so if you are alone."

"Alone?" said he. "Who said anything about being alone?"

And with that he was gone, disappeared into the snowy wilderness of the night. I must confess to having thought that might be the last time I saw Sherlock Holmes, and I immediately felt a sense of sudden loss as the darkness swallowed him whole.

Such was their continuing preoccupation with each other, I was able to slip back into the building unnoticed by the professor and his companions. I made Holmes's excuses for him as requested, then took my place alongside the others by the fire. Although the warmth was initially comforting, the longer the evening progressed, the more my fears for Holmes grew. It became increasingly difficult to maintain my silence and so I took myself to bed at the earliest opportunity. I lay awake all evening, staring at my friend's empty bed.

It was next morning, as I sat down to breakfast and readied myself to try to explain Holmes's unannounced disappearance, that he unexpectedly returned. It had been snowing heavily outside since before daybreak, and he appeared in the doorway, appearing to be more snow than man.

"Good heavens, Holmes, where the devil have you been?" I could not help but exclaim.

"Did you not sleep?" the professor enquired.

"I slept perfectly comfortably, thank you."

"You have been examining Jennings's body?" Eyre supposed.

"I did, sir, last evening."

"And this morning?"

"Why, I have been out hunting," he answered, his teeth chattering wildly.

"Hunting what, exactly?"

"Innocent men, unfairly blamed for crimes they had no part in committing."

Eyre shifted in his seat and put down his napkin and spoon. "I'm afraid none of us have the slightest idea what you are talking about."

"I rather think you do. You, sir, in particular."

"Then pray, please explain."

"I shall do exactly that," he said, peeling off his sodden overcoat and moving closer to the fire. "It seems we have all been the victim of, as my dear friend Watson would call it, a concurrence of coincidences."

"I'm afraid you've lost me already," I admitted.

"Miss Darrington," said Holmes, "please excuse my impertinence, and I apologize in advance for the question I am about to ask in public, but are you in love with Alvis Matheson?"

She withdrew her hand from Eyre's grip. He made a faint attempt to hold on to her for a few moments longer, before letting go. "I am," she admitted, though her answer was almost completely lost amongst her suddenly free-flowing tears. All at once there was a tremendous outburst of bluster and noise from her father.

"What is the meaning of this, Clara? You are engaged to be married to George."

Miss Darrington stood and moved close to the fire. Closer to Holmes, also, whose clothing was dripping water onto the floorboards.

"Father, please do not think too badly of me. I agreed to marry George at your insistence, and yet my heart belongs completely to Alvis. It always has."

"But he's just a manual labourer . . . he would never be able to keep you in the manner to which you are accustomed. George, on the other hand, is my heir apparent. Please, Clara, take time to fully consider the implications of what you are saying."

"Believe me, Father, I've thought of nothing else since we arrived in Greenland."

"And now an equally uncomfortable question for you, Mr Eyre," Holmes announced. "Are you aware that your intended has feelings for another, and that she intends to continue a relationship with this other person at the expense of your own proposed marriage?"

Eyre refused to answer. He simply stared into the flames of the fire. There was at once an unexpected silence throughout the building, the stillness indoors seeming to emphasize the echoing emptiness outside. I must confess, in all my years, I had never felt quite so isolated.

The silence did not last indefinitely. The anger on the professor's face was plain to see. He looked like a kettle left to boil too long, and yet I sensed that Holmes was deliberately prolonging the awkwardness of the moment.

"Explain yourself, man," the wizened academic yelled in a voice disproportionately loud for such a diminutive fellow. Holmes nodded curtly, unimpressed by the professor's less than dignified conduct.

"I shall, sir," he began, and at once the attention of everyone became fixed singularly upon my esteemed friend. "Alvis Matheson did not kill Mortimer Jennings. The unfortunate Mr Jennings, whom you, Professor, knew was not particularly practical with his hands, having been unable to properly secure an outbuilding the other evening and having a reputation for such menial inadequacies, was the victim of a most bizarre accident. Having studied the body and the scene of death, I have deduced that rather than being stabbed, Jennings instead stumbled in the snow, dislodged the harpoon from the rack where it had been stored, and fell onto its point. As I said, a freak accident."

"Preposterous," Eyre interrupted, but Holmes was having none of it and continued regardless.

"The position of Jennings's hands still wrapped tightly around the shaft of the harpoon and the height of the bloodstains on the exposed shaft of the weapon – a kind of tidemark, if you will – indicate that he managed to pull the harpoon out by several inches before his untimely death. And the other end of the harpoon itself became embedded in a wall of ice and snow opposite, meaning that the poor fellow died standing up, then froze solid in that position."

"This is balderdash," came another protest from Eyre, yet Holmes was still not finished.

"Had Jennings been attacked by an assailant, Matheson or otherwise, I'll wager the weapon would have been buried as deep as possible inside him, not withdrawn at all."

Miss Darrington visibly winced at the level of detail with which Holmes illustrated his gruesome detection. And still Eyre was not done. "But, Holmes, you neglect to mention the wound to his temple caused by Matheson's hand."

"Caused by Matheson's ice pick, yes, but not by his hand."

"How can that possibly be the case?"

"Because the ice pick injury was inflicted some time after Jennings was already dead, perhaps in a vain attempt to distract a passing detective from the truth of the matter."

"The truth of the matter? Sir, it seems you are further from the truth than any of us."

"Allow me to surmise," said Holmes. "You did not witness Matheson fighting with Jennings, rather you saw him trying to help. He discovered the dead man, frozen upright, and laid him down so that he might remove the offending harpoon. You disturbed him and, fearing you would blame him for Jennings's death – as you clearly now have – he ran, dropping his ice pick in the process. It was you, Eyre, who saw an opportunity both to hopelessly discredit your love rival and also to take advantage of my presence on this island to fabricate a crime which was, in fact, a tragic and wholly coincidental accident. You delivered the blow to the already dead man's skull with the pick, therefore implicating Matheson as the perpetrator of a crime that had never actually occurred."

Eyre was, for once, speechless. As was I.

"But Matheson was becoming deranged," said the professor. "You saw his conduct on your first evening here."

"You are, of course, right," Holmes said. "But rather than some form of cabin claustrophobia, he was suffering from a broken heart. And whereas back home in England he might have simply chosen to take his leave and go elsewhere, such actions are a physical and practical impossibility here. He was forced to watch Mr Eyre fawn all over Miss Darrington with your blessing every day.

"You strike me, sir," he continued, turning slightly to directly address Eyre now, "as a man who is clearly more attuned to rocks and minerals and their value in pounds, shillings and pence than you are the finer details of crime scenes and human emotions. After making his grim discovery, Alvis Matheson felt he had no choice but to run, presuming, as he did, that your inevitable accusations would go unchallenged. Given the weight of circumstantial evidence, you wagered that I would not look for any alternative explanation as to Jennings's death."

"What do you say to these accusations, George?" the professor demanded of Eyre. His mouth opened and closed continually like a fish out of water, starved of breath. Before he could speak or summon any answer, Miss Darrington interjected.

"Where is Alvis?"

"I'm here, my love," came a voice from the other end of the large cabin. I looked around – as did we all – and saw that Matheson had slipped into the building unnoticed. The two lovers ran to each other and embraced, no longer any need to keep their feelings for each other secret.

"But where did you find him?" I asked Holmes.

"Our steamer had gained a stowaway," explained he. "No real detection was required: there really was nowhere else for him to go. Given the extraordinary accusations Matheson suspected would be levelled against him, and the suppressed feelings he felt for Miss Darrington, I assumed he would see no option but to try to get away from Greenland. The arrival of our crippled ship – another remarkable coincidence – provided him with a means of leaving here and returning home to England."

"Quite incredible, Holmes," I remarked as I watched Miss Darrington and Matheson talk excitedly about a life together which would, had it not been for my distinguished friend Holmes, have been impossible to countenance.

We left the camp later that afternoon, having summoned an Inuit guide and several native labourers from Nuuk. We returned to the steamer, leaving the professor and George Eyre to continue with their work. I couldn't help but remark that all the riches they might find buried under the snow and ice which covered Greenland would be but mere pennies when compared to the wealth Miss Darrington and Matheson had gained.

We set sail for Liverpool the following morning, Holmes and I, along with the newly engaged couple.

# The Strange Death of Sherlock Holmes

## Andrew Darlington

*The lamplighter is moving down Baker Street, igniting a series of trapped fireflies as he goes. I watch him from the broad windows, as a purposeful distraction from more productive pursuits, until he moves out of sight. I draw the curtain back and return to my desk. This is a tale unlike all other tales I have chronicled. A story for which the world is not yet prepared, although place it on record I must, even though none may read it, for this singular episode will never grace the pages of* The Strand Magazine. *It begins, as our other exploits begin, with the street door creaking on its hinges, Mrs Hudson's voice in brief conversation, and a visitor's heavy footfall shaking the seventeen steps as he ascends the wooden staircase ...*

He entered the sitting room, a prospective new client, a fawning little man, to whom I took an instinctive dislike. He was, as his card announced, "Mr Tom Norman: Showman". He had a proposition. But first, he delved into the inside breast pocket of his velvet jacket, with braids and epaulettes, and extracted a tooled leather case. With a flourish, he produced a bulbous Havana cigar from it, snapped the end away with gold pincers linked by a fine gold chain to the case, and then ignited the cigar from a gold-cased lighter set with a single sapphire. He strolled the length of the room in an unpleasantly proprietary way, vomiting acrid smoke from between his large, bristling moustache and his trim goatee beard.

"I seek your help, Mr Holmes, and your discretion," he began at length. "A youth has been abducted. A youth held in trust on behalf of myself."

"What exactly is the nature of your claims upon this boy, Mr Norman?"

"Fully legal claims, Mr Holmes. Legitimately binding. I advanced a small fortune to Mr Cavor, considerable sums to fund what he terms his 'research'. In return I was to receive exhibition rights to the monkey-boy. Only he reneged on our arrangement. Claimed my venture to be cruel and unnatural. Said I was placing undue stress upon the boy." His eyes glinted unpleasantly behind the fog of cigar smoke that hung in the air, part-concealing his face.

Between his words I interpreted that Mr Norman's protestation to showmanship meant no more than that he owned a penny gaff shop off Whitechapel Road. A "Freaks of Nature" exhibition, a distasteful attraction designed to prey upon the prurience of the gullible.

"I take it you feel such charges to be unjustified?" asked Holmes.

"Justification is not the issue here, sir. Everyone everywhere is embarked on some kind of enterprise. Everybody worth a damn. Everyone has something he wants. All must pay their way in society, Mr Holmes, or else they starve. I rescue these unfortunate individuals from penury, and give them a career as living exhibits in my show. If I do not, pray tell me, who will? So you tend to your business, and I'll manage mine."

"Quite so. Forgive the impertinence of my curiosity."

Naturally my own role was merely to observe. But in that capacity I was nonetheless well positioned to draw certain conclusions of my own. I resented this man's intrusion into our otherwise ordered lives. To "like" or "dislike" are irrational responses, I concede. Logic, analysis, the process of deductive reasoning must be the prerequisites of detection. Yet I persist in considering intuition as something of no small value. But I could tell that "the great detective" was already intrigued, and that as from this moment a new venture was afoot. As always, I take no keener pleasure than in following my friend in his professional investigations into this, another scandal of bohemians.

Once the usual formalities were completed, our inquiries took us to the property of the aforesaid Mr Cavor, at which the youth was last known to have lodged as ward in trust. A swift hansom cab conveyed us. It was a fine tree-darkened house standing in its own grounds, the long drive thick with fallen leaves. It at first appeared deserted, until a manservant responded to our persistent knocking, and grudgingly admitted us. A tall sombre man with a deeply lined face, he explained that he was the only member of the household staff remaining. Retained to maintain the property in good order until its occupant should return. But no, he had no certain knowledge of their present location. There seemed no reason to suspect he was telling anything other than the truth. He offered no objection to our further exploration; indeed, he seemed particularly anxious to return to whatever activity had been occupying him prior to our arrival. From which we had distracted him.

My companion stalked in a state of some preoccupation through darkened rooms where furniture was shrouded with sheets into menacing shapes of indeterminate dimensions, tasting the stale air, pausing here and there to examine whatever attracted his attention, an aspidistra, a chandelier, or cluttered *objects d'art*. Through a study lined with stuffed animals in glass cases, their amber-bead eyes tracking our progress sightlessly. Past a display case containing meteorites and fossils, each carefully labelled. Fused-black tektites, aggregated chondrites, glittering mesosiderites, spiral trilobites, fan-rippled stromatolites and some meteorites that appeared to be embedded with fossils. Surely that couldn't be correct. The result, instead, of some blatant charlatanism?

As usual, I followed, perplexed by the complicated deductive process his thought patterns assumed. Picture, if you will, this tall, slender sketch of a gentleman I am pleased to call my friend, Sherlock Holmes. His proboscis, as long and thin as a sharp knife, yet no sharper than his keenest of intellects. I sometimes suspect he uses that distinctive nose to detect the various odours of criminality, but such speculation must be regarded as baseless calumny. He prefers to use so noble a nose for cocaine powder, and that in no small measure!

Down a dark, curving stairwell we discovered a workshop crammed with bronze scientific apparatus. From there our perambulations took us into the library. Holmes uncovered a chair, carefully folding its shroud once, twice, three times and placing it precisely on an adjacent writing desk. He sat down contemplatively, indicating me to silence. His eyes traced rows of bound volumes in their ordered cases. I noted a preponderance of scientific, technical and anthropological books. An even layer of dust stippled the books, as there was dust everywhere. At length he stood and selected a number of specific books.

"You will observe, my dear Doctor, that amongst all of the works here, these are consistent in that the dust accumulated upon them is of a lesser density than their fellows. Hence these must be the final volumes consulted by our absent friend immediately prior to his abrupt and unexplained departure. Taking with him the missing youth." He returned to the chair, placing the books upon the bureau adjacent to the folded shroud. Examining the titles in turn by flattening them open upon his knee, he carried economy of movement to the point of avarice.

"Observe. All we seek to learn of the quarry is here," he said sardonically. "The history and antiquities of the Venetian Republic. The art and architecture of Paris. The geography of the Italian lakes. I feel certain that, as he was reading these books, he was researching the journey he was planning to undertake. The journey we must now replicate . . ."

*When scientific deduction has spoken*, I told myself wryly, *it behoves us to be silent.*

Suffice to say, that following the leads Holmes deduced in various ways, we charted our travels across Europe. We made inquiries at ticket offices. Departure points. Railway stations. We identified hotels where the fleeing party had stayed for a weekend, for a week, seldom longer. We sought three individuals, which comprised that fleeing party: a distinguished gentleman of middle-aged appearance; a tow-headed, quiet youth who avoided attention; and a bustling, maternal maidservant. We traced their presence to a Left-Bank rooming house overlooking the Seine, strolled the same *arrondissements* as they had, and imitated their leaving from the Gare de l'Est, and travelled to a white hotel on the shores of Lake Garda. And, ultimately, to Venice. A haunted city of beautiful ghosts.

It was about four in the afternoon when we disembarked at the Piazza San Marco. Clouds passed slowly on a day neither too mellow nor too tart, neither too hot nor too cool; the air seeming keener for our presence. Once booked into the faded grandeur of a hotel, opening out onto a view of the Ponte de Rialto, we resumed our investigations in the hope of discovering information that would take us to the three individuals that we pursued – alas, we discovered nothing that would help us. But upon returning that same evening, the desk clerk made himself known to us and revealed that an envelope had been deposited for us to collect. Thanking him, we hastened the bulky package to the privacy of our suite where the Great Detective sat, drew his calabash pipe and commenced to smoke, while instructing me to read the contents. He had his back to the windows leading out onto the balcony. In an agreeable gloom, thrown into sharp contrast by being framed against the deep blood of the setting sun, I extracted sheets of closely written manuscript, coughed to clear my throat, and commenced to read . . .

Sherlock Holmes is dead. I don't recognize the prose style of the words I'm writing. It resembles the raving of delirium madness. A drugged nightmare provoked by narcotic excess, infiltrated by the themes of cheap fantasy fiction. Nothing London can offer can provide consolation to the gnawing restlessness that devours my waking hours.

The great Palace of Westminster breasts the city as a liner does a sullen sea. A beacon of democracy illuminating this benighted world. Yet even this must be seen as transitory. All of this must fall, clarified by the strange and disturbing ideas first propounded by Herbert George Wells in his *The New Review* serial of January to May of 1895. Across unfathomable depths of future time this empire, its gifts and benefits to the lesser nations, will be an annihilated place, left as less than a faint memory to a thousand generations as yet unborn. As Shelley wrote "look on my works, ye mighty, and despair". There are mysteries of time and space about which even the keenest and most analytical intelligence can ascertain nothing.

Sherlock Holmes is dead. Suddenly, I am the only planet in my own solar system. My mind turns upon these silences. There is no cure. I know this to be true, yet knowing can only be a small part of understanding. As I walk terrified through an evil, fog-thick night, I envisage his corpse laid out upon the bed within his rooms at Baker Street. The door locked from the outside. I see echoes of his face. What is left of it after the single bullet removed the upper-right side of his temple. His head resting on the goose-feather pillow upon which I'd laid it. The image of his dark eyes before I close them, and even though I scrutinize as hard as I can, the soul has gone. There's an ancient tradition that coins should be placed upon the eyes of the dead, a toll with which to pay the ferryman. Despite all evidence to the contrary, I cannot bring myself to perform these last rites.

With a towel and tepid water I gently clean his fatal head wound, sponging runnels of blood from skin that is already chalk white and rigid as marble, the enamel basin of water soon rich red with his lifeblood. I see brain matter spattered on the wall. All that remains of that great penetrating intellect is smeared across the dark chocolate wall-pattern. I stare fixedly, concentrating my attention on the wallpaper, until its pattern takes on a diseased edge, as though the house itself is leaching the sickness from the air.

Pacing breathless through twisting, torturous alleys, where shapeless masses sprawl, acrawl with scuttling, watchful bugs. I slip, feet juddering on rain-slick pavement. My frantic eyes strain through the black and diffused grey of the night, avoiding with a shudder the yellow cones of light spilling from the gas-lamps to reflect from the wet, slimy cobblestones. Yet it is better to be out here than remain within the madness of this opium den my imagination must inhabit. There are nefarious slinkers and lurkers in the stinking streets of Whitechapel, the murderers of mutilated whores who must be tracked down and snared. A naked corpse dragged from the Thames at Richmond, hands and feet missing. An investment banker crucified upside down, his throat cut as in a ritual killing. Anything, but this nightmare thing ensorcelled by deliriums of drugged dream.

"Conjurers and music hall magicians utilize a technique called 'misdirection' to distract the attention of the audience while more important sleight-of-hand is being done elsewhere." So he had lectured me.

"Yes, Holmes, so I understand. Yet I fail to understand."

"What if the exercise of crime detection through logic and reason is, itself, a personal misdirection from other, more profound questions?"

"I fear to enquire as to what questions you mean. You refer to those of life and death itself? If so, I'm content to leave such issues to the Creator."

"I put it to you that a Creator that imbued its creations with curiosity would hardly expect anything other than for its animal-cules to be curious. Yet here, investigative skill has limits. It is dependent upon clues on which to base deduction. Unless the clues are indeed here, embedded around us by those gods who play such ill-defined roles in human affairs. If only we can inter-pret the clues correctly. Such as, for example, frogs and dragon-flies. We observe that frogspawn becomes tadpoles, which, in turn, becomes frogs. There are grubs that enter a pupae state and emerge dragonflies. Are they metaphors? Clues strewn by your Creator? It is incumbent upon us to find out. To discover if death is not an end, more a change of state from one evolving form to another."

"But we can never know."

"Every thesis can be tested. And now, my trusted friend, the means to that end has been provided. I intend to die, Watson. I intend to kill myself . . ."

\*      \*      \*

I read from the sheets of Cavor's closely written manuscript.

"H. G. Wells was wrong. Unless he deliberately misunderstood for the purposes of political allegory. The future does not exist until by our actions or inactions we create it. He was a draper at the Southsea Drapery Emporium. A draper with socialist views. It was there in Southsea, at an unruly Fabian meeting, that we met, briefly, and we got into pleasant conversation lubricated by an unaccustomed measure of liquor. I told Mr Wells of my device, a thing of bronze cogwheels synched into a cascade of ticking gears, energized by a pellet of material opaque to time. He pressed me for details. Against my better instincts, I found myself telling him more than was in my interest to divulge.

"Perhaps Mr Wells misconstrued my words, or simply took my idea as the basis for his fanciful political fable of the far future? But he was wrong.

"I set and spun the planet backwards, not forwards, in my quest for meaning. And I found a meaning more terrible than I could have envisaged. Stepping into a place tinted with swirls of opalescence so vivid it hurts the eyes. This antediluvian world, fetid with the aroma of rotting vegetation, a place and time where I can scarcely bear the touch of earth underfoot, or see the sky beyond the dense mesh of rippling foliage. Yet Earth it was. And then I found the dead child of those dawn days. My heart touched by the pity of it. His body shrouded by a storm of flies, bluebottles fat with feasting. His shattered legs mangled where he'd fallen. Where gangrene had ravaged him in fevers of excruciating pain. His people had gone. They could do nothing.

"Yet I could. If there is such a thing as destiny, this must surely be the reason for my presence here. If there is a divine spirit who watches o'er us and controls our actions, this is where it has brought me. I reset my device by five days. Just five days. That is all that was required. And stepped out again. This time the child's tribe was creating an unholy noise. Like beaters on a Scottish moor, they moved through the forest, their line driving their prey before them. Elk, or some kind of giant caribou. The boy should not have been where he was. Perhaps through curiosity, or a very humanlike sense of mischief, he'd wandered to where he should not have. I could see it all. The animals fleeing in helpless confusion before the encircling hunters. The boy in their path, just seconds from being fatally trampled by those stampeding beasts. All I had to do was lift him to safety into my machine. So, I did so. An action entirely governed by instinct. Thought did not enter the equation. He had been dead and, in a moment, his life was mine.

"The future does not exist until by our actions or inactions we create it. Yet by this action I had created a new present. My thoughtless pity might have impossible repercussions. If I returned the boy to his tribe, and he lived when he should have died, what results would that action set in chain across the intervening millennia? He would grow to maturity and have children of his own. Of course, he might yet die childless. His is a brutal age, even more so than our brutal age. But there's a chance his progeny could persist, to alter the world's precarious balance. That the Neanderthal would survive in stronghold Europe, so our great civilization might never happen. That the benefits of European civilization would never arise to spread their munificence across the less-fortunate nations of the globe.

"Was it right that I should gamble on such an outcome? No. I could take no such chance with history. It was imperative the Neanderthal boy, whom I had saved, be removed from his time, and brought to our own."

After a large tea, followed by thick chunks of Madeira cake, we met Cavor in his hotel room overlooking the Ponte de Rialto. Its faint taint an irritant at the back of my throat. Cavor was a small, compact middle-aged man of absent-minded charm, with pebble eyes magnified by gold-rim spectacles. The plump maidservant hovered behind him, engaged in fussy activities that betrayed a certain nervousness. Despite the heat, she drew a shawl around her scrawny neck and about her shoulders.

The eyes of that Chronic Argonaut glittered as if harbouring a hidden joke, shards of some secret knowledge, which he kept to himself. "You have read my story, Mr Holmes. You have evaluated the moral conundrum it embodies. We can flee no more. I throw myself at your mercy. The decision is yours to make. What are your intentions now?" A tone of suitable earnestness ran through his voice.

"Are we to believe that your account of these incredible events is true?"

"All the evidence you need is here." Cavor smiled enigmatically.

The squat, ugly boy crouched protectively close by Cavor's side on bowed legs. His mouthful of wedge-teeth more prominent than his wide flattened nose, above no real chin; instead, the jawbone ran smoothly off the curves of his face. This crouching child is what the disreputable Tom Norman callously dubbed the "monkey-boy". The designation he'd painted in a flourish of gilt lettering above the cage in which the boy was to be exhibited for the frivolous titillation of the public. Despite my concerns about the illegality of this abduction, my sympathies lay with Cavor. I gazed at the boy, seeking more anatomical traits of primitive brutishness.

"Does it talk?" I blustered, staring at the robust figure that returned my stare from beneath a forehead retreating flatly under a mop of untidy russet hair. My medical knowledge of physiognomy detected the bony formations that ridged the skin above those eyes. The back of the misshapen cranium bulged in such a manner that it caused the head to seem over-heavy, as if, by sagging forward, it forced the stumpy torso into a stoop. Those characteristics could conceivably be the result of tragic deformity, a variety of genetic throwback. But something intimates that no, this is a child of humanity's dawn-ages.

"Of course *he* talks," responded Cavor indignantly. "The fossilized skulls excavated in the Neander Valley near Düsseldorf indicate a cranial capacity of sixteen hundred cubic centimetres, compared to *homo sapiens* fourteen hundred cubic centimetres. They had language, Dr Watson. Already, day by day, he is learning to converse. The only difference between us and the Neanderthal species is the legacy of our accumulation of cultural history. Do not underestimate this child's potential. And you, Mr Holmes, do you have a question?"

"In the light of such assurance, no, I have no question. Instead I offer a proposition," he said, ignoring our digression. The almost audible wheels of speculation rotated within his head. There was no hesitation. That's the way his life is arranged. Neat and scientific. Everything balances. Nothing wasted.

"Then I must insist on a counter-proposal," Cavor declared. "My device must be destroyed, you understand? My one condition is that it is not allowed to infect the world with instabilities beyond human comprehension. In my naivety, I pursued research without thought of consequences. Yet what I achieved is so terrible a thing that it would render every certainty a phantasm, everything we know and value a spectral shade of what is and what is not."

Once the agreements had been finalized, we took our farewells on the Piazza San Marco, wishing Cavor and his ward well. We would not betray his location to the predatory Mr Tom Norman: Showman. In this way, Holmes was breaking the cardinal rule of his profession. He was deliberately deceiving our client. For myself, such a result was a moral choice: weighing the natural rights of the boy against the legal obligations to which he is subject. For Holmes it is different. Morality is less a consideration. For him, there is a new impetus to metaphysical enquiry enabled by Cavor's unique science.

Back in Baker Street, Holmes generously allowed Mrs Hudson two weeks' leave to visit her sister in Broadstairs. Then later, five days after the dread thing was done, a hansom cab conveyed me back to the darkened house standing in its own grounds. As I paced the long drive, thick with an accumulation of fallen leaves, the loom of surrounding trees creaked in the slight breeze, adding to its somewhat sinister aspect.

The manservant grudgingly responded to my persistent knocking. He spoke even more truculently than before: "I am providing a service. I expect to be paid," he grumbled.

So I paid him. He examined the coins critically, and admitted me.

An unreasoning disturbance stirred within me as I passed through the study of taxidermy exhibits. A chill sense of supernatural apprehension, as though they are watching me with evil intent. The fox with bared needle teeth. The pheasant with wings raised in stilled fear. They accused me with their insolent gaze. I am an educated professional with a respected medical practice. I should be making diagnoses and dispensing pills, potions, liniments and soothing unguents. Lancing boils. Making house calls, clutching my black bag and stethoscope. *So why am I chasing around on these hare-brained escapades? Is this my own form of escapism misdirection? No more. No more.*

Below stairs, the gloomy workshop awaited me, crammed with bronze scientific equipment. Mechanisms shrouded into menacing shapes of indeterminate dimensions. Beneath a covering dust sheet, as Cavor had described, I located his apparatus. *This is his device?* I asked myself. *This flimsy construction?*

This thing of cogwheels synched into a cascade of ticking gears, energized by what Cavor had described as "a pellet of material opaque to time". An unearthly element deposited into our terrestrial realm by a Perseid meteorite, as fantastic as a fragment of Martian alchemy, or a Ganymede dream-diamond. My resolve almost failed. My mind and heart equally uneasy. At that moment, I believed that I was incapable of fulfilling this task with which I'd been charged. Yet the luxury of choice had surely been removed. I had no other option than to follow the detailed step-by-step instructions Cavor entrusted to me.

I crossed the stone slabs of the workshop floor, brushed a centipede from the seat positioned adjacent to a set of handle-bars, and placed myself warily upon its contoured cushion. Other than for the large shoulder-high bronze disc behind me, the machine was suggestive of a bicycle, complete with pedals. A machine that would, seemingly, do nothing more hazardous than take me on a peregrination around Hyde Park. However, the similarity to a bicycle was only approximate, because its pedals connected to an electromagnetic induction system using some armature arrangement. There were also carbon-zinc cells resembling those devised by Leclanché. A T-shaped lever protruded from beneath the handlebars. And, directly in front of me, dials adapted from naval surplus. I adjusted the dials, this one and that one, following Cavor's detailed instructions. The pedals grated as I began a cycling motion, building up an electrical charge. I attempted to ease the lever down, but it refused to budge, so I applied increasing pressure while still pedalling, until it abruptly slammed down, accompanied by a constellation of magnesium-bright sparks from the surrounding wires. Followed by an even louder grating sound, the disc positioned immediately behind me stuttered, once, twice. It gained purchase and began to spin. Slowly, then faster.

From the corner of my eye I could see that the cascade of sparks had ignited the shrouds of cast-aside sheeting. Flames flickered greedily across the dust, crackling and exploding in brilliant bursts. It was too late for me to intervene. Too late for me to dismount and attempt to extinguish the blaze. For the temporal process has already begun. I gripped so tightly my knuckles went bone white. So tightly, in fact, that I feared the imprint of my fingers would be forever etched into the handlebars. The laboratory became an inferno. But I was seeing the flames as though through an insubstantial veil, a permeable membrane. It became less real, less solid.

I've never been so afraid. During all our adventuring together, Holmes and I, we have never faced such a terror as I felt now. I tried to watch what was happening. To record the sensations surging through my body, so I could accurately document them later. But it was impossible. The compulsion to clam my eyes firmly shut fell strong upon me. I cringed within myself, caught in the grip of novel and unknown forces. In a curious state where both fear and courage have become words without meaning.

When I opened my eyes the fire had gone. The disc spun slower, spiralling down to a halt. The handlebars were faintly warm to my touch. There was silence and gloom. I glanced around warily. The workshop was as it had always been. As it was the first day Sherlock Holmes and I had crossed its threshold. Nothing had changed. The insane delirium that consumed me had passed. I had achieved nothing. I stepped from the device on unsteady legs, mopping perspiration from my forehead with a red-and-white spotted kerchief. The breathless chemistry of fear provoked heart palpitations that took me close to fainting. I should have rested, but feared to do so. I climbed the steps up into the house. There was no sign of the manservant. That no longer struck me as strange. He'd always seemed anxious to return to whatever activity our arrival had distracted him from. Perhaps other projects Cavor had initiated and entrusted to his care? Anti-gravity? Invisibility? A New Accelerator? The front door was locked. But its heavy key was suspended from a row of hooks adjacent to the kitchen entrance.

It was a full moon. A flitter of bats criss-crossed its silver orb. Surely it was daylight when I entered the house, less than an hour ago? Had I miscalculated? Was I too late? There was no hansom cab. The gravel crunched beneath my feet as I hurried along the drive, emerging at last into the avenue beyond, shivering a little in the chill air. It was necessary for me to walk for half an hour before being able to attract the attention of some passing mode of transport. But eventually, after what seemed an interminable period of time, I safely returned to Baker Street where the lamplighter had ignited a series of trapped fireflies along its familiar length – the glass boxes atop their poles leaking a pale, yellow light. There was the different glow of an illuminated window above me.

Scarcely daring to believe what my senses told me, I let myself in. My footfall creaked on each of the seventeen steps as I ascended the wooden staircase. Sherlock Holmes looked up briefly as I entered. On the writing desk before him, an empty glass. He had drunk the shot of whisky it contained. He held a pistol in his hand. Its barrel pressed to his upper right temple.

"No, Holmes." I crossed the room in three great strides. Seized his wrist and prised the gun away. He was a stronger man than I, but my strength was powered by desperation. "No, Holmes, it is done."

His eyes met mine with stubborn defiance. For a moment, our intentions were in fierce conflict. Our struggles forced him backwards until the chair tipped and we both sprawled in a confusion of flailing limbs. The gun tumbled sideways across the floor. When it came to a stop it was safely beyond his reach.

There was a sharp retort above us. A gunshot, yet as though strangely muffled, a distanced echo. At first I feared that I had failed. Yet Holmes sat where he always sat. At the writing desk. The empty whisky glass to one side. The pistol held to the bloody ruin of his upper right temple. White brain matter spattered across the wall. All that remained of that great penetrating intellect, smeared across the *fleur-de-lys* motif of the flock wallpaper. He slumped forward, and lay still. The glass toppled to the floor and shattered. There was a drip-drip-drip of pulsing blood.

I stood gradually, straightening my back up against the wall, watching anxiously. Aware that we were standing side by side, stunned into the same kind of awful stupefaction. Transfixed in supernatural fear we watched. After a pause, the door opened. I watched myself enter, and saw the shock and horror on my face that stilled my tread. There were tears in my eyes – me, the other Watson, who stood there before the other Sherlock Holmes, the dead Holmes. We watched as I struggled to drag the corpse across to the bed. Draping and arranging the lifeless limbs, resting his shattered head on the goose-feather pillow. Then tenderly sponging the blood away from the fatal cranial wounds. Until the water in the enamel basin was rich red with his blood.

But already, even as we watched, the bizarre scenario we had witnessed was becoming less true. The figures imperceptibly faded into translucent ghosts, grey and palsied, as existence itself adjusted to my temporal interference. Cavor had travelled back five days in time to rescue the Neanderthal child. The boy was dead. Then he was alive. I have performed the same service for my friend, Sherlock Holmes.

"Do you remember death, Holmes? Does the memory remain within you?" My voice was hushed, as if wary of our phantom selves overhearing.

"I remember it all. I fear I will never rid myself of that knowledge."

"And what did you see, beyond the veil of death? Was it glorious?"

His eyes were dark. He met my curious gaze unflinchingly. "I saw blackness, my dear Watson. Nothing but blackness . . ."

# The Climbing Man

## Simon Clark

"Holmes! Take cover!"

The searing heat beat our faces with the savagery of a fist.

"Holmes, for pity's sake, keep your head down!" I cried those words as another salvo of bullets struck our boat.

Sherlock Holmes stood upright, his razor-sharp eyes scanning the riverbank as our enemy took aim.

"How many riflemen do you see, Watson? Seven? Eight?"

"Holmes! In the name of mercy, take cover."

"Information is essential, Watson. Know thine enemy! Know how many! Identify the weapons they carry."

A bullet punched a hole through the white sail, not twenty inches from that striking profile of a man I knew so well. What's more, I knew absolutely, that a bullet travelling at five hundred miles an hour would destroy the detective's remarkable brain in a heartbeat. That exquisitely sophisticated machine of observation, analysis and consummate deduction would be horribly reduced to bloody ruin. My friend would be no more, and I would be bereft. I, John Watson, understood that fact only too well as men on the far bank of the Euphrates River aimed their rifles.

"Holmes! If you do not lie down behind these crates then I, myself, will put a bullet in your leg. That way you'll damn well stop parading there in plain view of those devils.'

"Ha! Nine men," Holmes exclaimed as if not hearing me. "Armed with single-shot Snider-Enfield rifles. They're not the swiftest when it comes to reloading. That's to our advantage, I'd wager."

Clearly Holmes would not accept my advice – my plea! – that he take cover on the deck of our little sailing boat. Instead of calling to him again, I, sheltering behind the crates stacked on-deck, cried out to the man operating the tiller at the stern. His Arab clothing shone whitely in that all-powerful midday sun.

"Make for the opposite bank! Get us away from the gunmen – as fast as you can; do you understand?"

The dhow's helmsman was so immersed in terror that he froze. He held the same course in the Euphrates, leaving us exposed to gunfire. His brown eyes were vast in that sun-blasted face. Meanwhile, the phrase "sitting duck" thundered inside my head.

Yet more bullets struck the boat. One tore a shard of timber from the packing case close by.

Holmes's voice gave a snap of triumph. "Those scoundrels can't keep up with us. We'll outrun them."

A bullet clipped the dhow's rigging before continuing on its way, with a piercing shriek. For once, I'd left my old service revolver behind in London. Thank providence, however, I'd purchased a German Mauser pistol. This formidable weapon contained ten extremely powerful rounds that could, if need be, stop a charging bull.

So, beneath vast Mesopotamian skies of the most dazzling blue, while riding downstream on a shimmering river, flanked by seemingly endless desert, I rose from behind my little timber fortress of packing cases, aimed the Mauser at the men who strove to murder us, and I fired. My finger squeezed the trigger, discharging one bullet after another, until all ten bullets smashed through the hot air in the direction of the gunmen. A figure on the riverbank, clad in grey, clutched its forehead, and tumbled back into the reeds. I confess that my humble revolver of old wouldn't have had the range to claim the gunman. My choice of the Mauser pistol had been a fortuitous one.

"Good shot, Watson. One down, eight left. Also, you've spoiled the aim of the others, by Jove!"

And that became a rare occasion when events proved my friend wrong. The remaining eight men returned fire. A grunt of pain to my right prompted me to spin round. I was just in time to see our helmsman, and sole crew member of the dhow, clutch at his stomach as a red stain spread across his white robes. He lost his balance and fell over the side of the boat into the Euphrates. He vanished beneath its surface in a moment.

Holmes shouted, "Watson, I'll take the helm! See if you can make them keep their heads—"

*Heads down.* That's the phrase Holmes would have used. However, a rifle bullet exploded against the boat's mast, sending out splinters of wood that flashed in the sunlight. Holmes flung out his arms as that tall, thin body of his toppled like a falling telegraph pole. His head struck the deck with a loud thump. That was a hard blow. I confess that the sound of bone slamming against wood was so dreadful that bile rose up through my throat.

The man lay still. He didn't respond when I shouted his name. My emotions of shock and despair did not overwhelm me, I am gratified to say – at least, not at that moment. I am a doctor. My medical training came to the fore and I did what I could, tearing pieces from my shirt and pressing the cloth against his wounds to stem the bleeding. There was, however, little I could do about the bruise on that high forehead of his that he'd suffered due to the fall. Gathering Holmes into my arms, I hauled him behind the packing cases. The dhow was small; there was no cabin, so no other place of refuge from the gunmen. All I could do was cling to my friend and endeavour to make us as small a target as possible, hoping that the wooden boxes would be stout enough to block rifle bullets from penetrating and reaching us, the softer, living targets beyond.

The boat, with no one manning the helm, floated downstream. And yet, as I write these words three years later, I begin to wonder if there was, indeed, another hand on the tiller. A hand, unseen, and all together more mysterious: one that guided the vessel, and its two passengers, towards one of most the most baffling mysteries I have ever encountered.

## 2

Mesopotamia is the most extraordinary place on Earth. This land, lying between the two rivers of the Euphrates and the Tigris, is where civilization was born. Here, 6,000 years ago, human beings built the splendid cites that would become known as Baghdad, Ur and Babylon. Massive temples called ziggurats rose high above the deserts. For centuries, Mesopotamian kings were laid to rest in tombs that were veritable treasure houses of jewels, and swords made out of solid gold. It must be said that wherever there is money, whether it be earned through labour or commercial enterprise, you will find industrious folk of honest nature – and you will also uncover the worst kind of scoundrel, one driven by naked greed that is bereft of all moral scruples. It was the latter sort, in the shape of plunderers of ancient sites, that Sherlock Holmes was called upon to hunt down by the authorities. Holmes didn't search for the native peasant who'd uncovered a few ancient pots by chance while searching for a lost lamb in the hills. No, my friend Sherlock Holmes, the world's most famous detective, had been tasked with investigating the activities of nothing less than a vipers' nest of Europeans who had made it their quest to loot Mesopotamia of its ancient riches.

Holmes and I had made off with a dhow laden with stolen artefacts, which by rights belonged to the people of that nation, not the scoundrels who'd illegally acquired them. This criminal gang employed riflemen clad in grey, who pretended they provided legitimate protection for travellers and archaeologists. We soon discovered that the troops in grey had no legitimacy whatsoever: they were thugs, robbers, murderers. It was these grey-shirts that pursued Holmes and I as we sailed upon the Euphrates. The packing cases on deck were crammed with ceremonial helmets and swords made of gold. These had come from a royal tomb that had been raided by the Grey Guards, as they had come to be known. Those Grey Guards had fired upon us from the riverbank. Their intention: to retrieve the treasure for their masters and, more importantly for them, to silence us so that we could not report their criminal enterprise. Our aim was to sail to a fort manned by bona fide government soldiers where both we and the fortune in gold would be safe.

Alas, it was not to be. The Arab gentleman, who'd steered the craft, had been killed. Then a bullet had shattered against the mast, wounding Sherlock Holmes, my friend and companion in many an adventure. I cradled the unconscious man in my arms as the boat carried us away from the riflemen and down that vast body of water: one that flowed almost eighteen hundred miles from the snow-covered mountains of Turkey and then through Mesopotamia to the Persian Gulf.

The sun had begun to set, painting the sky in crimson fire. Holmes still hadn't stirred. I feared that the blow to his head, resulting from the fall, had inflicted an injury far more severe than the fragments of rifle bullet that had punctured the skin of his arm.

At last, the boat ran aground at the river's edge. There were no houses, only a scattering of palm trees and, beyond those, an ocean of pale sand. The desert seemingly stretched away forever and ever. Would these prove to be my final sad moments with Holmes? My life was tightly interwoven with his. We'd formed close bonds of friendship of the kind that can only be made by facing danger together. I had saved his life, and he had saved mine on many occasions. Those bonds of friendship had been transmuted into something golden and unbreakable by such experiences. Now this? Would I sit here with Holmes's head resting on my lap? With my hand placed on his chest, gauging the strength of his heart? Would I quietly, and with utter sorrow, remain thus, feeling such despair, as his life receded, and his heartbeat grew fainter and fainter until I could feel it no more?

The sun gradually vanished beneath the horizon. With the approaching gloom came utter silence, too. I couldn't even hear the lap of water against the boat's hull.

"Holmes, my dear Holmes," I murmured. "What am I to do? I cannot save you. Dear fellow, my heart is breaking."

I gazed at that pale face. Drops of blood had dried on the prominent nose and the broad forehead. His thin lips were almost white. Blood loss, together with shock, had robbed the man of his colour. At that moment, I began to utter a prayer in the hope that a miracle would save my friend. The first words of my plea to the Almighty had barely left my lips when I heard the sound of feet tramping down the riverbank. This was followed by shouts.

"*Sahib! Sahib!*"

I looked up to see an Arab youth of perhaps fourteen clad in European clothes, yet wearing the traditional *keffiyeh* headdress fashioned from a red and white scarf. He stared at Holmes and I in astonishment, then he cried out in English: "Master! Master! I see two ghosts! There are two ghosts on the river!"

He raced back up the slope, shouting in astonishment.

A hand rested on mine.

I looked down as Holmes opened his eyes. The expression in them was almost of amusement, and . . . dare I use the word? *Warmth?* Such heartening *warmth* as he recognized me.

"Watson. We aren't ghosts, are we? Because I doubt that there was ever a ghost with such an infernal headache as mine."

## 3

The boy had fled from the river and into the desert only to return moments later with a blond-haired man dressed in a suit of cream linen. By this time, night had fallen. The man didn't wear a hat; he appeared quite dishevelled as if he'd spent many hours working in the roughest of conditions, yet he had the air of an educated gentleman. He approached, holding a lantern above his head for darkness had engulfed the shore. I estimated his age to be around thirty years or so. He seemed to be weighed down by many worries; he glanced this way and that, his vivid blue eyes darting with a nervous agitation.

The Arab boy, meanwhile, urged him forward, pointing at us, while saying over and over, "The ghosts, master, these are the ghosts."

I managed to help Holmes to his feet. The detective steadied himself by holding on to the mast of the dhow.

"Ghosts," the boy cried in excited tones. "There on the boat!"

The man stepped forward; his lantern flooded the deck with light.

"Great Scott!" he exclaimed. "Are both of you hurt?"

"Only my friend here," I replied. "He's—"

"I am quite capable of answering on my own behalf, Watson, thank you. The habits of a doctor, hmm?" Holmes had recovered his composure somewhat. "Good evening, sir. We are travellers that received some unwanted attention from local bandits."

I glanced sharply at my friend, wondering why he hadn't revealed that we'd been hunted by armed thugs of European origin, rather than local rapscallions.

"Your arm, sir?" said the blond man. "How were you injured?"

"A bullet struck the mast; fragments peppered my flesh."

"Then you must have medical assistance at once."

"My friend here is a doctor," explained Holmes. "He's stemmed the blood flow."

"I wish to examine the wounds more closely," I said. "The pieces of bullet must be removed or there'll be blood poisoning." Then I gave Holmes the severest glance that I could muster. "I insist."

"As you wish, old friend."

The boy pointed at us. "They are ghosts such as you, master."

"We are ghosts?" Holmes raised the dark arch of an eyebrow in amusement.

The blond man clicked his tongue in exasperation. "All Europeans are regarded as ghosts by Sarim here. The paleness of our skin, you see."

"And yet, sir, your face is burned dark." Holmes spoke those words as he allowed me to help him from the boat onto the shore. "The skin has been exposed to strong sunlight for a considerable period of time. However, you have spent most of today working in a confined space without daylight."

"How the devil did you know that?" He seemed more suspicious of Holmes's observation than surprised.

"You have faint, yet telltale marks of soot around your nostrils. Those marks occur when someone uses an oil lamp in a confined space that is poorly ventilated, resulting in that individual repeatedly inhaling smoky fumes given off by the lamp. There are unusual areas of wear on the sleeves of your jacket. You, sir, repeatedly brush against walls that hem you in at both sides;

those self-same walls have had an abrasive effect on the material of your jacket sleeves."

"Ha." The man displayed little amusement, it must be said. Instead, he seemed deeply troubled. "I'm an archaeologist. I spend hour upon hour in underground tunnels that have no natural daylight, hence the lamp – and, yes, the tunnels are a snug fit to say the least, hence I brush against them." His eyes turned downward to gaze at the ground, which is the natural way when someone recalls a matter that worries them. "You are quite correct in your observations, sir. I wish I possessed your talent for seeing what many a man does not."

Holmes fixed him with that characteristic piercing gaze of his when something interested him. "Then why not tell me what troubles you, sir? Perhaps beginning with the theft of your ring from the small finger of your right hand. Ah . . ." He held up his own hand. "No, that was overly hasty of me to make that statement, which is quite incorrect. I should have asked what prompted you to wrench the ring from your own finger, causing you to graze the first joint?"

The blond man stared at Holmes in what could only be described as alarm. His expression suggested that Holmes had, perhaps, dramatically emerged from the waters of the Euphrates in a flash of supernatural light.

"Master," began the boy, "are the ghosts here to murder you? Like the men tried to do last week."

The air of tension grew. I sensed an air of mounting panic and terror in both the man and the boy.

"Believe me, we are here to murder no one," I said, in order to bring some calm to the proceedings. "My friend here is hurt. I need to convey him to the nearest town."

"Impossible," said the man.

"I must examine his wounds in a strong light, remove the bullet fragments and cleanse his injuries with iodine."

"The pair of you can't travel through the desert. You'd be attacked by bandits for sure. These are the men that Sarim alluded to just now. Just a few days ago, they fired shots at me as I walked in the hills."

"Then where do you suggest we go?" I asked.

"Return to the camp with me. We have armed guards. There are medical supplies, too."

Holmes smiled politely. "Then we shall accompany you. Thank you, sir."

"Ah . . ." I remembered the crates stacked on the boat. "We have a rather valuable cargo."

The gentleman nodded. "Don't worry. I'll ensure that it's brought to the compound where it will be safely guarded. We employ former military men to protect us. A necessary evil, I'm afraid, because thieves have been targeting archaeological sites such as ours." He gave a grim smile. "Gold attracts people in the flash of an eye."

"You are capable of walking?" I asked Holmes.

"Indeed, I am."

The blond stranger appeared to recall his manners, which must have faded somewhat through lack of use out here in the desert wilderness. "My name is Edward Priestly. My work here involves the search for the lost libraries of the Sumerians. Last week, I found something that I was not searching for." He grimaced. "My brother." He rubbed his eyes as if hoping to erase images burned into the optic nerve. "How he got there I . . . I can't begin to imagine."

"Master." Sarim showed great concern at the way his employer suddenly became unsteady on his feet. "Master. The shock has made you ill. You should have medicine."

"I'm all right, Sarim."

"But yesterday you were shouting so loud I was afraid you'd die of grief."

Priestly managed a weak smile. "Sarim has grown up in the company of English scholars. He speaks like an Oxford don, doesn't he?"

"Your brother?" began Holmes. "The circumstances of his discovery shocked you. Why were they so extraordinary?"

"I must not concern you with personal matters. That would be impolite of me. This way, please. I'll take you to the camp."

"Perhaps we can be of assistance?" Holmes's face became

eager. He had scented a mystery. And mysteries to this singular individual are as tempting as delicious food to a hungry man.

Priestly spoke with dignity. "I shall not trouble you with such matters. After all, despite these unusual circumstances, you are my guests."

Holmes's sharp eyes studied the man's face as if he read a fascinating page in a book. "Thank you for your hospitality, Mr Priestly."

"I beg your pardon. I don't think I caught your names, and your purpose here in Mesopotamia."

"My name is John Watson."

"And I am Sherlock Holmes."

"Those names . . ." He tapped the tip of his nose with his finger as he dredged through his memory. "They ring a bell with me." Once again, he swayed; clearly the man wasn't well. "We should return to the camp. Mr Holmes, Mr Watson, please step this way"

And so we did walk alongside Mr Edward Priestly. Priestly had handed the lantern to the boy, and we followed Sarim into the desert, which had become invisible in the darkness. Above us, stars burned with such breathtaking intensity.

Priestly attempted to speak in conversational tones about the animals he'd glimpsed in this ocean of sand that flanked the river – wild camels, ibex, jackals, the vultures that glided through such perfect blue skies in search of carrion. Abruptly, he turned on us with such savagery I truly believed he would attack us.

He lunged forward to within inches of Holmes. "Sir, I must tell you this because I need reassurance that I'm not mad! My brother! My brother is dead!"

"I'm sorry to hear that, Mr Priestly," said Holmes as soothingly as he could.

"That's not the worst of it, Mr Holmes. I found his body inside an underground chamber that can't possibly have been opened in thousands of years!" His eyes bulged. "How can that be, gentlemen? How can Benjamin have died inside a vault that has no entrance, or exit. How? How!"

I caught hold of Edward Priestly as he toppled forward in a dead faint.

**4**

The archaeology team, of which the troubled Edward Priestly was a member, had based itself in a compound beside a small oasis ringed with thorn trees. In the lead, walked the Arab boy, Sarim, holding the lamp to light our way. Cicadas chirped in bushes that dripped resin onto the ground; from that resin came a heavy, sweet scent. The strength of that perfume made my head spin.

Priestly muttered, "Forgive me. That's the first time I have fainted in my life."

"It's understandable," Holmes said quite gently. "I gather you have suffered a considerable nervous shock."

"Yes, but I am rather embarrassed. Men don't faint as a rule, do they?"

"I am a medical doctor," I reminded him. "It is more common than you might think."

"Nevertheless—" he spoke stiffly "—I am ashamed of myself. Quite unmanly."

I intended to reassure him on the matter of men passing out in such a fashion; however, before I could speak he tapped the boy on the shoulder.

"Sarim, go on ahead. Let the sentry know that we're coming. I don't want him mistaking us for thieves and shooting us."

Sarim loped the remaining hundred or so paces to the compound. By now, my eyes had adjusted somewhat to the gloom. I could make out that this settlement appeared to be comprised of a small number of two-storey buildings surrounded by a wall, standing a good ten feet in height. A partly enclosed platform above the gate housed a silhouette of a figure. I could see nothing of him other than the tip of a cigarette that glowed yellow when he inhaled. Sarim ran up to the gate; he briefly conversed with the silhouetted guard.

Holmes cradled his injured right arm in his left hand, thus improvising a sling. "Your settlement is as secure as a fortress."

"It needs to be, Mr Holmes." Priestly cast a nervous glance out at the desert, lying in darkness. "If we dropped our guard for a moment the compound would be overrun with bandits. They know we have excavated ancient sites hereabouts and store all manner of precious artefacts within those buildings. I confess it was foolhardy of me tonight to take a walk to try to clear my head of troubling thoughts."

My professional concerns rose to the surface. "Mr Priestly. Perhaps you would permit me to conduct a medical examination on you?"

"Goodness. Whatever for?"

"You did lose consciousness for a while back there."

"Of which I am most embarrassed."

"There may be an underlying medical cause. A disturbed rhythm of the heart, perhaps, or a fever."

"No, Doctor. I've been overtired, that's all, due to certain recent events that I'd prefer not to discuss. You understand?"

"Of course. Nevertheless, if you should change your mind?"

"Ah, here we are," said Priestly before calling out, "Mousaf, you may open the gate now."

An elderly Arab, with a magnificent beard – a veritable waterfall of silver cascading down his chest – shuffled from a doorway at the other side of the gate. With a key that was as big as a man's hand, he unlocked the gate, opened it and stood back so that we could enter. Looking upwards, I glimpsed the silhouette of the watchman once more against the starry night. I saw nothing of his face, and he did not speak. Within seconds, we were ushered into the compound, and thenceforth into a building, which contained a large room lined with shelves on which clay tablets sat. These tablets were covered with cuneiform, that ancient type of Sumerian writing that is formed from symbols that appear to consist largely of triangles, squares and arrowhead shapes. A large oil lamp hung from the ceiling.

Priestly explained: "This is where we work on our finds when we require bright light." He pointed at a wooden cabinet fixed to the wall. "Doctor, you will find medical supplies in there. There is also a bottle of brandy. Please use whatever you need to take care of your companion."

"Thank you."

"You have been so kind," Holmes added. "Perhaps we could trouble you for one more favour?"

"If it's within my power, I shall only be too willing to help."

"I should like to place a telephone call to Baghdad."

"Ah, alas that is beyond my power, sir. We have no telephone."

"I see."

"Indeed, the nearest building equipped with telegram apparatus is half a day's ride from here."

Holmes swayed a little as he stood by the table. I quickly pulled out a chair. He immediately allowed that tall frame of his to drop quite sharply onto the seat. The man clearly suffered from the wounds, which I wished to urgently examine.

Priestly noted my friend's condition. "I shall have rooms prepared. Both of you must rest here tonight, at the very least. I'll have food sent to you. Although, at this time, all our kitchen can to offer is bread and soup."

"That will be admirable." Holmes managed a weak smile. "I shall indulge in a little tobacco, if I may?"

"Of course." Priestly nodded with due courtesy. "If you will excuse me, gentlemen, I shall make the necessary preparations for your stay."

Once he'd withdrawn from the room, I immediately pulled the lamp lower, as it hung from the ceiling by means of a line and pulley. The light fell with an intense brilliance on Holmes.

Opening the door to the medicine cabinet, I asked, "Will you be capable of removing your jacket?"

"Yes," said he.

"Bandages, gauze, tweezers, laudanum, iodine. They are well equipped. Excellent."

"Well guarded, too."

"I noticed the sentry above the gate. Rather reassures one, doesn't it, Holmes?"

"Not so much reassuring, my dear Watson, as alarming."

"By Jove. What makes you say that?"

"Perhaps the precise detail escaped you. When the man inhaled on his cigarette it produced enough light to reveal the colour of his uniform." Holmes unbuttoned his jacket. "Grey. The uniform was quite grey."

"Good God, you're telling me that the Grey Guards are already here?"

"Yes. That's why I asked Priestly if I could make a telephone call." With a grimace of pain, he eased his arm from the blood-stained jacket.

"But there is no telephone."

"No, and we must thank the mercies for that. For if there was, and the other Grey Guards, who delighted in taking potshots at us from the riverbank, were to telephone here to ask if two Englishmen had suddenly arrived from nowhere, then our lives wouldn't be worth that." He clicked his fingers. "Without a shadow of doubt, our bodies would be left in the desert to feed the vultures."

"Good gracious, Holmes, then we're in danger."

"Yes, we are."

"We must leave immediately."

"We can hardly do that at this hour." He rolled back his shirtsleeve to reveal a peppering of shrapnel wounds in the deathly white skin of his forearm. "Besides, I'd like to hear more about Mr Edward Priestly's brother – all those delicious clues are making my curiosity sing such sweet and beguiling songs."

"Holmes, the blow to your head must have muddled your reason."

"Nonsense, my dear Watson."

"Remember, you yourself told me that the Grey Guards are in this compound: they will be colleagues of the very men that tried to murder us not half a day ago."

"Pish-posh! I have the scent of a case in my nostrils. One that will be exquisitely satisfying to unravel.

"Holmes! You are impossible."

"Be so good as to light a cigar for me. I'd do so myself, but my fingers are quite stiff and useless. Perhaps I suffered a modicum of nerve damage. Ah, thank you, Watson. I shall smoke and examine my thoughts while you busy yourself with tweezers and these funny little holes in my arm."

"You don't need a surgeon, Holmes. You need a psychiatrist."

This amused Sherlock Holmes. He was still laughing when I dug the tips of the tweezers into a bloody wound in his forearm, in search of the first fragment of bullet.

## 5

I sat to a table with Sherlock Holmes. The elderly man, by the name of Mousaf, he of the magnificent silver beard, served us with bowls of onion soup, together with that flat, unleavened bread favoured by the people of this vast desert land. I'd cleaned the wounds that Holmes had suffered just hours ago when the bullet had shattered upon striking the mast. Splinters of that bullet had peppered Holmes's right forearm. Now Holmes occupied the chair opposite mine. Although his right arm rested in a sling, he appeared to have no difficulty in spooning the thick, flavoursome soup into his mouth. I engaged him in conversation, because, in truth, the blow to his head when he fell on the boat concerned me more than the small puncture wounds caused by the bullet fragments. A few moments ago, he'd appeared quite unconcerned about the presence of Grey Guards here at the compound. Those men would be comrades of the ones that tried to assassinate us earlier on the river. Thankfully, the men here could not possibly know that their brethren had been pursuing us, otherwise we'd now be held at gunpoint, or, quite conceivably, been on the receiving end of bullets fired at point-blank range.

Holmes appeared to be quite blasé about the danger we might face in the very near future. In fact, a short while ago he had uttered "pish-posh" in such a light-hearted way when I voiced my fears. That injury to his skull, I mused, has it led to swelling of the brain? Has concussion muddled his instincts? Does he delude himself that he is quite safe from the Grey Guards? And so I talked, endeavouring to discover clues that might reveal damage to that remarkable brain of his.

"Holmes," I began conversationally, "when I removed fragments of bullet from the wounds I had to pull apart the skin where it had begun to heal."

"Indeed so, Watson. This is delicious soup, don't you think? Thickened with milk from a camel, no doubt."

I didn't comment on the meal. Instead, I probed for signs of mental dysfunction. "The operation I performed on you, without anaesthetic, must have been incredibly painful.'

"Ha! Pain, Watson. The clamouring alarm bell of the nervous system."

"You appeared to feel no pain. In fact, you chatted and, at times, laughed quite merrily as I drove those pincers deep into your muscle tissue."

"I have developed a theory that the human mind has developed to such an extent that its power can override certain functions of the body." He pointed at me with the spoon. "We can, at will, hold our breath, can we not? Holy men of the Hindu faith can, by the power of thought, slow their heartbeats to levels where other men would lose consciousness. We know that if we are interested in our work we do not notice hunger, or physical discomfort. It occurs to me that if we fix our minds with such acute intensity on a subject that fascinates us to the exclusion of anything else, including physical sensation, then we can exclude pain from our mind. While you picked, snipped and probed those holes in my arm I spoke to you about the distinctive fibres of garments, which, if correctly identified, can be used to help trace a suspect in a criminal case. I focused my mind on the experiments that I have conducted and disregarded everything else."

"Are you saying, Holmes, that you felt no pain when I cut away your flesh?"

"Nothing, my dear fellow, not one jot of hurt. Merely the sensation of you fiddling away with your tweezers. More bread?"

"I'm quite full. How's your headache?"

"Ha! Over and done with."

"You appear in good spirits?"

"The prospect of a fine mystery elevates my mood, Watson."

"You do recall that Grey Guards infest this compound, and—"

"And that they are our enemy?"

"Yes," I said firmly.

"The men in this little fortress aren't the same ones that attempted to shoot us earlier. Moreover, we left our would-be assassins behind fifty miles or so upriver. We can take comfort knowing that the guards here are happily ignorant of events today."

"For the time being – that state of affairs might change quite quickly."

"Communication is poor in this part of the world, Watson. Rest assured, the men guarding this compound are ignorant of our mission here in Mesopotamia."

"Isn't it time we made our report to the authorities, to ensure that the guards are arrested forthwith?"

"All in good time, Watson. After all, we cannot grow wings and fly across the desert to the nearest town. We must be patient."

"And we should hope to high Heaven that the men that attacked us don't visit their colleagues here, or—"

"Good Lord, what is happening out there? What on earth are they chanting?"

Holmes leapt to his feet. In the blink of an eye, he'd bounded through a door at the back of the house and entered a yard that formed a private area within the walled compound. Here there were potted plants that stood fully six feet tall. The lush greenery partly screened off a number of people who chanted a chorus. I heard deep male voices and the lighter tones of a woman.

Three spoke as one: "*Hear my plea. Please let me see him in my dreams tonight. Please show me how he died so that I might regain a peaceful heart. Please reveal how he entered the chamber. I ask whatever gods, spirits or angels whom do so shape my dreams to grant this wish.*"

I whispered, "Holmes, we shouldn't eavesdrop. People are at prayer."

"Prayer? I think not. This is a séance."

A light flared from behind the line of plants. A well-made gentleman of seventy years or so stood there dressed in a suit of cream linen so favoured by the British in a hot climate. His face had been scorched and darkened by the sun, which enhanced the vivid, electric blue of his eyes. His receding hair was white, and quite long, and gave the uncanny impression that the man's head was haloed by a white glow in the lamplight. His intelligent eyes fixed on Sherlock Holmes.

"Mr Holmes," he rumbled in tones that held an equal measure of gentleness and force. "Edward told me that chance has bestowed upon us guests who, I realize, are extremely famous. I've read many a report in newspapers, concerning your tenacious pursuit of criminals." He dipped his head in greeting. "And this is your colleague, Doctor Watson. Do forgive Edward for not recognizing such illustrious individuals. Recent days have been most trying for him."

Three figures stepped out from behind the plants that sectioned the yard into two parts. I recognized Edward Priestly, the nervous young gentleman who'd brought us here. He, too, wore cream linen like the older man. The third figure, a young woman, dazzled the eye in her confection of white muslin. Her long dress was as bright as a flame in the lamplight. Her blue eyes were as distinctive as those of the older gentleman. She'd protected her skin from the fierce sun – it was pale, possessing a freshness that reminded me of a newly unfurled rose petal. One glance at her hands, though, revealed that they'd felt the transforming heat of the sun and were golden brown.

Priestly's expression remained one of unease; in fact, he was so ill at ease that he stammered as he made the introductions. "Mr . . . Mr Holmes, Doctor Watson, allow me to introduce you to Professor Hendrik. He is the senior archaeologist in charge of the excavations here."

We shook hands. The professor's grip had undeniable strength.

Priestley continued, "And Miss Eden Hendrik, the Professor's granddaughter."

"Gentlemen," she said in pure, silvery tones, "a pleasure to meet you."

Professor Hendrik's blue eyes locked onto my face and then onto the face of Holmes, assessing us no doubt: appraising us, judging whether we were to be trusted with what he would tell us next, for clearly he appeared to be reaching a decision.

"I overheard you, Mr Holmes. You claimed we were conducting a séance."

"You beseeched gods, spirits and angels for information to be revealed in a dream."

"You are familiar of the practice in ancient times where priests of a certain religion would match the gods and goddesses of their faith with another?"

"Indeed so." Holmes nodded. "Did not the Romans believe that their god of war, Mars, was the one and the same as the Norse god Tiw? The pagan god that gives us the word 'Tuesday'."

"Forgive me." I rubbed my forehead utterly perplexed. "How does this talk of gods resembling other gods equate with your . . . *utterances* just moments ago?"

Professor Hendrik looked me in the eye as if challenging me to laugh at him. "I have studied the religions of the Ancient Greeks, Romans, Sumerians and Hindus. Those people readily accepted the notion that the world's gods, though they might have a stunning multitude of different names and wear different faces were, in fact, members of the same small group of deities. Yet another example would be the Celtic goddess Sulis being equated with Rome's goddess of wisdom Minerva."

I shook my head. "I still don't see what that has to do with . . ." I concluded my sentence with a helpless gesture of my hands, rather than verbally reiterating my bewilderment.

Eden Hendrik's voice rang out: "I shall tell the gentlemen in plain terms, Grandfather. We believe the ancient Sumerian gods of Mesopotamia are still alive in our hearts, just as Roman and Greek gods still live on. They change their names and their external appearance, but the many – apparently – different gods of the world are manifestations of the same universal deities."

"My dear," Professor Hendrik rumbled in gentle tones. "These gentlemen are weary. Explanations should wait until tomorrow."

"I will not have them leave this yard believing we are deluded fools, Grandfather. We gathered here to speak to gods that have many different names. We implored them to grant us dreams tonight that would explain the death of a man that was very dear to us."

"Mr Edward Priestly's brother?" ventured Holmes.

"Yes."

"His death is inexplicable." Priestly shuddered with unpleasant memories. "Indeed, how the body came to be in its present location is inexplicable, too."

Eden spoke so fiercely that nobody attempted to interrupt. "For thousands of years, human beings have believed that gods and goddesses have visited them in dreams, often with a message that is vital to their understanding of an existing state of affairs or predictions of what is to come. We stand on sacred ground, gentlemen. The dividing line between this world and the next is exceedingly delicate here. We ask the deities for dreams tonight that will answer important questions."

Priestly murmured, "I do need to know what happened to my brother, gentlemen. I fear that madness will consume me if I do not. Already, such fits come upon me . . . absolutely wretched fits that are beyond my power to control."

Holmes's sharp eyes fixed on the man's troubled face. "You were engaged to Miss Hendrik. And you have now ended that engagement."

"Yes. We must not marry until I can be sure of my sanity."

Tears sprang to the young woman's eyes. She quickly turned away, raising her hand to her mouth as she did so, the universal expression of distress.

"You broke off the engagement in the last two or three days," continued Holmes.

"That is correct. How can you possibly know that?"

"Ah, the most simple of deductions, Mr Priestly. You will recall I told you earlier that I noticed the graze on your little finger. You'd clearly wrenched a ring from your hand in the grip of such a powerful emotion that you grazed the skin in the process. Miss Hendrik's finger, specifically the third finger of her left hand, bears a pale mark where a ring has recently occupied it. The sun hasn't had time to darken the skin in keeping with the rest of the hand. Therefore, an engagement has ended suddenly and quite recently. I may have speculated that a marriage had ended, but the young lady was introduced to me as Miss Hendrik without any hesitation on your part."

"You are right, sir. What would benefit me greatly is . . . oh no . . . here it comes again . . . much stronger, too."

Professor Hendrik's blue eyes flashed in triumph. "Omens, Edward. Omens! The gods are stirring!"

Holmes and I exchanged glances of surprise. The ground on which we stood rose and fell smoothly without clamour or noise. For all the world, the sensation was the same as standing on a boat that floats on a hitherto calm lake, and suddenly the waters are stirred into a series of slow ripples that gently lift the boat a few inches before just as gently lowering it. Far off in the nighttime desert, wild dogs began to howl; a ghostly sound to be sure.

"The gods have sent us a sign," Priestly marvelled.

Eden's eyes shone with joy. "I shall dream of Benjamin tonight. I know I shall, Grandfather."

Holmes frowned at the three people. "Geology is the cause of the yard shaking, not a pantheon of waking gods. Does this phenomenon occur frequently?"

"Yes," said Eden. "Stronger and more marvellously every time."

I confess that the lady's peculiar statement caused me some surprise, and I pointed out, "Earth tremors. That's what they are, as you yourselves must know. Earth tremors and nothing more."

## 6

The next morning, Holmes breezed into my room after a rapid tap on the door.

"Awake, Watson?"

"I am now."

"Then I should be grateful if you would dress and join me in the same room where we ate supper last night."

"Confound it. The Grey Guards? Do they know we're in this compound?"

"Nothing of the sort, Watson. But Priestly is here. He now knows that I am a detective. He's in an excitable state and demanding that I listen to what, he claims, is a remarkable and interesting story concerning the death of his brother."

"You wish me to be present?"

"I do, Watson. I know that you love to hear of bizarre events and strange occurrences – these are what cause the ink in your pen to flow. Here: shirt, tie, jacket. Hurry up, Watson. I sense a mystery coming up to the boil – I want to taste it while it's hot. Ha!"

He whirled from the room, leaving me to dress in a rush. Yes, yes, I admit it: I felt the blood race in my veins, too – for I anticipated that the next hour would be an interesting one indeed.

## 7

Mr Edward Priestly sat at the table, knitting his fingers together, while his tense facial expression radiated nothing less than anxiety. *A man on the verge of a breakdown*, I told myself. *He's trembling from head to toe*. I sat opposite him. Holmes slowly paced back and forth, still supporting his injured arm in a sling. Through the open window, I glimpsed a road of no more than a hundred feet in length that ran through the walled compound. Native workers carried baskets, picks and shovels as they filed through a gateway in the wall, no doubt to commence their day's labours on the archaeological excavation nearby.

Holmes paused to gaze out of the window, his sharp face in profile; the nose that reminded me of a curving hawk's beak was an especially striking feature. The man showed no sign of being weakened by the injuries he sustained yesterday. On the contrary: his mental energies were more abundant than before; his concentration ever more sharply focused; the detective's intelligence shone so brightly that the very air seemed to glow around him.

Holmes turned to our visitor. "Mr Priestly, commence your story at what you consider to be the beginning. I shall let you speak without interruption. Please endeavour to include every detail, no matter how small or apparently insignificant."

"Yes, Mr Holmes." Priestly's voice was whispery – the voice of a man who'd been hollowed to a mere husk by worry. "I shall do my best to describe this . . . this gruesome and horrific night-mare." He stared in dread at his hands as if snakes had begun to slither out from beneath his fingernails.

"Pray continue, sir. There is coffee, should you need it."

Priestly inhaled, striving to muster his self-control. At that moment, I felt true sympathy for the young fellow. The blue eyes that shone from that handsome, suntanned face struck me as ones that belonged to an honest, caring soul who'd performed good deeds throughout his life. And yet now he found himself in the grip of terrifying events that had turned his peaceful life upside down.

Edward Priestly began his story: "Fifty years ago, my grandfa-ther, Harold Priestly and Professor Hendrik were young archae-ologists who set out to explore this part of Mesopotamia in search of ancient towns that had been buried by desert. They discovered Tirrash, which is often referred to as the Bibliopolis – the name means the City of Libraries. Tirrash was destroyed by an invading army three thousand years ago. You will see noth-ing of it above ground. Its mud-brick houses and temples decayed into dust long ago. Sand has blown in from the desert to bury every last sign of this legendary City of Libraries. What is remarkable, however, is that its basements and subterranean storage vaults still remain intact. It's the marvellous things that have been found there that cause scholars today so much excite-ment. You see, before the barbarians destroyed the city, its people emptied the libraries of the clay tablets, on which they had writ-ten their scriptures, prayers and records of their lives – these clay tablets were then carefully stored in the basements beneath the houses and sealed shut. Yes, the barbarians conquered the city. What they did not find, however, were the precious contents of the libraries. There are hundreds of underground vaults still to be found here.

"My grandfather and Professor Hendrik decided to devote their lives to excavating this site, and left Cambridge to make their homes here. They raised their families in this compound. I have lived here in Mesopotamia for most of my thirty-two years. I consider this world of sand, sun and sky my homeland. My grandfather and grandmother are now dead. My own parents retired to Dorset five years ago. Yet work continues. If I, myself, am blessed with children and grandchildren, I dare say they will continue this excavation. There is still much of historic importance to be discovered. The ancient documents found here are of incalculable value to linguists and historians alike."

Licking his dry lips, he poured himself coffee from the silver jug. After taking a sip he resumed thus: "We have a workforce of thirty local men. The only Europeans here, apart from the guards, are Professor Hendrik, his granddaughter, Eden, and myself. Now, I come to the strangest part of my story. What happened has shocked me to such an extent I now doubt my own sanity. I am a changed man. I suffer such outbursts of impetuous anger. I was once a quiet fellow who wished nothing more than to get on with his work, but the terrible end that my brother suffered has left me emotionally shattered." With shaking hands, he took a gulp of coffee. "Mr Holmes, I must have my brother's death explained to me, and I must understand the nature of the grotesque transformation that affected his body after he died."

Holmes formed a steeple from his fingers, closed his eyes, and listened carefully as Edward Priestly told one of the strangest stories I've ever heard.

"My brother, Benjamin, was thirty-five when he disappeared from this compound. He vanished without trace one night. Benjamin never gave so much as a hint that he was dissatisfied with his work here, which might have suggested that he intended to leave. Quite simply, on the evening of third September he retired to his bedroom. The next morning the room was empty. His suitcase, clothes, passport and money had gone. We concluded that he'd packed his belongings and slipped quietly

away in the night. Maybe he wished to start life afresh elsewhere. That's what we believed. Three years went by. Work
continued here. Then ... oh, my good Lord ... we made a
shocking discovery – one that is an absolute nightmare. I still
wonder if what we found was real, or whether I'm suffering a
ghastly hallucination." His eyes flashed with alarm as he recalled
shocking events. "Am I making myself clear, gentlemen? Do
you understand what I'm telling you?"

Holmes spoke gently. "We understand perfectly. Please
continue."

"Eight days ago we were exploring a passageway that branches
off the main arterial tunnel that runs beneath where the city of
Tirrash once stood. There we discovered what had once been the
basement of a house. The vault lies a dozen feet beneath the
ground's surface; it has not been disturbed in three thousand
years. Its doorway had been closed off by stone blocks, presumably just before the barbarians conquered the city. We did not
immediately break into the vault, because our investigations are
conducted in a meticulous, scientific manner and are never rushed.
What we did was cut a small aperture into the vault's wall to enable
us to look inside." His eyes grew round with terror. "I held a lamp
close to the aperture. Do you know what I saw, gentlemen? I saw
Benjamin's face ... his dead face ... shrivelled and dry." He took
a deep breath. After that, he spoke with absolute clarity. "I had
found my missing brother. His body is contained within a sealed
underground chamber that has not been opened in three thousand years. I do not use the word 'lies', because Benjamin does not
lie in the chamber. Even though he is dead ... *quite dead* ... my
brother is still in the process of climbing up the basement's inner
wall." Priestly covered his face with his hands. "My brother is
dead, yet he is still trying to escape from his grave."

# 8

After making that remarkable statement: *My brother is dead, yet
he is still trying to escape from his grave*, Edward Priestly sat with
his head in his hands. He did recover somewhat to stammer

some words about not yet attempting to report the discovery of the body to the police in Baghdad. Evidently, Professor Hendrik and Priestly regarded the Ottoman-controlled officials in this country with suspicion, verging on complete distrust. I suspected that Hendrik and Priestly were so isolated from civilization that they didn't know what to do for the best. Therefore, they had done nothing – neither reporting the death, nor recovering the corpse from the chamber. Holmes and I withdrew from the room for a few moments to leave the evidently horror-struck Edward Priestly alone to gather his composure.

Holmes ascended the steps that led to the roof of the house. He paced about the flat roof, while smoking a cigarette. Already, the blazing sun felt like a red-hot sheet of metal pressed to one's face. Scents from a kitchen of roasting meat flavoured with spices and garlic flooded my nostrils. Mesopotamia launches nothing less than a ferocious attack on the senses – the pungent odours of sun-baked dirt and exotic cuisine. Even the sounds are so outlandish to one's ears: local people cry out at the tops of their voices, whether calling to friends or howling commands at their donkeys and camels. Above all, there is the brilliance of the sun that transmutes the desert into an ocean of molten gold, or so it seems to me.

"What do you intend now?" I asked.

"My intention," said Holmes "is to enter the underworld."

"You plan to visit the subterranean vault?"

"Of course."

"Is that wise?"

"It is essential, my dear fellow."

"Last night there was an earth tremor. If there should be a full-blooded quake when you are beneath ground then the tunnels might collapse on you."

"Do you wish to deny yourself the unique opportunity of witnessing a dead man climbing up a wall?"

"That must be a delusion on the part of Edward Priestly. Dead men do not climb."

"Then it's high time that we unravel this particular conundrum, Watson." He paused as he watched two men in grey uniforms ride out through the gates. "Kindly ask Mr Priestly if he feels strong enough to accompany us."

"Holmes, those two men on horseback are Grey Guards."

"Indeed they are."

"Dare we suppose that they are merely patrolling the immediate neighbourhood?"

"Alas, we dare suppose nothing of the sort. See? They're well provisioned. The jars fixed to their saddles must contain a gallon of water apiece. They intend to embark on a journey of some considerable length." Dropping the cigarette, Holmes scrunched it beneath his boot. "Those gentlemen in grey don't know that their colleagues elsewhere in the country have been pursuing us; they are, however, intelligent enough to ask themselves why Sherlock Holmes, the detective, and his companion, Doctor Watson, have mysteriously fetched up at a remote archaeological excavation."

"Then we must presume that they have set out for the nearest telegraph office."

"Which is half a day's ride away, meaning the guards will be back here by tonight." His hooded eyes sought out mine. "By then, my dear fellow, they will have orders from their commander to silence us forever with a well-aimed bullet or two."

"We must escape from this place."

"Indeed we must, Watson. By this afternoon at the latest." Holmes led the way to the flight of stone steps that descended from the roof of the house to the courtyard below. "First of all, I want to view this mysterious cadaver that has such an interesting talent for scaling walls. After you, Watson, take care with the steps; they're very steep. And avoid venturing too close to that trelliswork. There are some rather lively scorpions performing a merry dance behind there."

## 9

Edward Priestly led the way across a stretch of desert, a short journey of five minutes or so. Soon we came to a ladder that descended into a pit in the earth. At either side of the shaft's opening, spoil heaps stood at least thirty feet in height. Those spoil heaps consisted of a talcum-fine dust that had evidently been removed from the tunnels.

Priestly explained. "Many tons of dirt accumulated naturally down there, sifting through cracks in the ground over the centuries. Our research strongly suggests, as I've already mentioned, that the men and women who lived here in Tirrash, three thousand years ago, decided to hide the contents of their municipal libraries when the city was besieged. During the last five decades, tens of thousands of ancient documents have been recovered from the basements of homes that once stood here. Of course, there is now no sign of the buildings above ground. The entire city was destroyed by the invaders."

I gazed at the wasteland surrounding me with shivers of awe. "But the basements are still intact?"

"Yes. We can imagine the awful scene. As barbarians fired arrows into Tirrash, and tried to shatter its walls with battering rams, the defenders hurled spears back at their enemy. During this pandemonium, the citizens carried the books they loved so much from the libraries to carefully prepared hiding places beneath the houses. Even as the barbarians tore down the city gates, men and women preferred to continue the hard work of concealing the tunnels that linked the basements, rather than flee. Their books were precious to them. They valued their literature and sacred writings more than their lives."

Holmes nodded. "You paint a vivid picture of self-sacrifice."

"And sacrifice themselves they did, Mr Holmes. We found human skeletons when we excavated the debris layer formed by what remained of the houses."

"You say that the books were written on clay tablets?"

"Yes."

"Are those the only ancient items you and your colleagues found in the basements?"

"The people who lived here also stored their valuables underground in the hope they wouldn't be found by the invaders. We've uncovered jewellery and gold."

"Then there is treasure to be found in these vaults?"

"Indeed so, Mr Holmes, but it's the clay tablets that are of real value to historians. The information recorded there opens a window onto the lost world of Mesopotamia."

Edward Priestly had regained his self-composure. He'd spoken enthusiastically about the ancient city and its buried treasures. Clearly, being in the company of the world's greatest detective had given the man a renewed air of confidence.

He said, "Please follow me, gentlemen. Hold on tight to the ladder. It's quite a long climb."

Holmes ably managed the descent, even though he still supported his injured arm in a sling. When we had all reached the bottom of the ladder Priestly lit three oil lamps, handing us one each; thereafter, he led us through a maze of tunnels. The subterranean complex was cold after exposure to the blazing sun. Very cold indeed. After walking several minutes along a tunnel so narrow that its walls brushed our elbows, we reached a section with a low roof that required Holmes, a man of rare height, to lower his head a great deal.

Clouds of white vapour blossomed from our lips.

I shivered in the cold. "Good grief, it's as chilly as a Scottish winter down here."

"And very dry," said Priestly. "See these wooden timbers that form a doorway? They were installed more than thirty centuries ago. Not only do they remain un-decayed, they are so dry that they have become as hard as iron. You would require a hammer and chisel to put so much as a dent in that woodwork."

Holmes and I inspected the timbers and found that they were, indeed, as resilient as metal. Holmes glanced at the openings to tomb-like chambers that led off from the passage.

"Mr Priestly, have you discovered many of these chambers?"

"There are almost a thousand that have been uncovered during the excavation, begun by my grandfather and Professor Hendrik when they were young men."

"That is remarkable," I marvelled. "A lifetime's work."

"The work of many, many lifetimes, Doctor Watson." Priestly rapped on the side of the tunnel. The sound his knuckles made suggested an empty void lay behind the rock. "We have discovered thirty-eight vaults in this tunnel alone."

"Simply by tapping the walls?"

"A remarkably effective method, Doctor. We catalogue the location of each hidden vault. When time allows, we carefully take down the blockwork that conceals the entrance. All such work is done very slowly and with meticulous care. After all, archaeology is a science; it is not an excuse for looting valuables. The vaults must be shored up with timber supports before we enter, as the rock is often unstable here. There is always a danger of sudden collapse."

I nodded, appreciating the difficulties faced by the archaeologists. "Time-consuming work."

"Opening all thirty-eight chambers will take at least ten years. And it's likely there are many more secret chambers to be found in this tunnel alone."

I ran my fingers over the wall where Priestly's tapping had produced the hollow sound. "If there is a concealed opening here then it is hidden well."

Priestly said, "The openings were sealed with stone blocks. After that, the city's craftsmen made up a plaster, which is identical in colour to the surrounding natural bedrock that surrounds the opening. The plaster was applied with such artistry that it is almost impossible to identify the position of the concealed entrance, even though we are probably staring at the very spot."

Holmes approved. "Such precise attention to detail appeals to me greatly. However, Mr Priestly, where is the vault that contains your late brother?"

"This way, gentlemen."

A walk of a dozen seconds delivered the three of us to another section of tunnel. Here, plaster had fallen from the wall, exposing a doorway that still remained sealed by neatly hewn cubes of pale stone.

"The vault in question," whispered Priestly, shivering with dread. "It lies on the other side of this stonework."

Holmes regarded the doorway that had been sealed shut

*Simon Clark*

before the birth of Christ. "You say that you haven't entered the vault yet?"

"No."

"Is there another way in?"

"This doorway is the only entrance. It hasn't been breached since it was closed off during the siege in ancient times."

Meanwhile, Holmes's razor-sharp eyes studied the floor of the tunnel, its ceiling, its walls, then he turned his attention to an aperture of around eight inches wide and three inches high; this was perhaps eighteen inches or so above the floor.

"You discovered the vault eight days ago?"

"Yes, Mr Holmes."

"And you cut this opening to allow you to look inside?"

"Indeed. We expected to see what had once been a domestic basement containing clay tablets."

"What did you see?"

"A face – just inches from mine."

"The face of your brother?"

Priestly gave a grim nod.

Holmes crouched in order to peer through the aperture. My skin shrivelled and puckered with chills. Shivers ran down my backbone. For even the habitually cool and unemotional Holmes flinched with shock when he set eyes on what was on the other side of the wall.

"Take a look, Watson," he invited. "Brace yourself. What you will see isn't pleasant."

I put my eyes to the slot. Instantly, the light from my oil lamp illuminated a face. And, dear Heaven, what a face! The dryness of the vault had sucked moisture from the flesh, causing the face to shrink, drawing back its lips to expose a line of teeth that formed such a grotesque picture of savagery. The eyes had shrivelled to nothing, leaving eyelids that partly covered the empty sockets. The cadaver's hair had been turned yellow by a coating of dust.

Holmes spoke briskly: "How do you know that the corpse climbs the wall?"

"This passage turns to the left, and left again, before running parallel to another wall on the outside of the same vault. We have made a small opening there, enabling us to see my brother from the back."

"Is the opening large enough for a man to enter the chamber?"

"No, sir."

We followed the corridor, making two left turns. After a few paces we reached another slot that had recently been cut into the stonework by the archaeologists. Once again, Holmes put his face to the aperture (this at shoulder height), while holding the lamp in such a way that the basement's interior was illuminated.

Holmes described what he saw: "Ah. The door to this vault, which was sealed shut by the unfortunate people when the city was besieged, is a good ten feet above what I should say is the level of the floor."

"Indeed so," agreed Priestly. "Access to the basement floor will have been by ladder. The ladder's missing now, suggesting it will have been removed before the entrance was closed off three thousand years ago. The floor appears to be covered by dust to a depth of around four feet. The thickness of the layer means that the clay tablets and any other items placed inside there are completely submerged. Dust has trickled in through cracks in the rock that forms the ceiling. This has occurred before in other subterranean cavities hereabouts."

"This chamber has been hollowed out of bedrock?"

"Yes."

"Have you been able to examine the cracks in the ceiling?"

"They are no more than half an inch wide," Priestly answered, "so if you're considering the likelihood that my brother could have lowered himself down through one of the cracks in the rock then that, clearly, is impossible. There is no entrance to the vault other than the doorway, which was sealed by stone blocks. Those blocks were plastered over. They haven't been disturbed in centuries."

Holmes stated, "Men cannot dissolve themselves to atoms and pass through solid stone."

"Nevertheless—"

"Nevertheless, sir, we must be governed by facts, evidence and logic, and not fall prey to fantasies of magical transportation."

"Holmes," I began, "do you see the climbing figure?"

"I see the figure of a man somehow fixed to a vertical section of rock. Benjamin Priestly's body faces the wall. His arms are stretched up above his head as if he does climb in the direction of the ceiling. The body is well preserved; it will have been naturally mummified by the dry air."

"Do you see any sign of injury?"

"Ah, the doctor in you seeks a cause of death." Holmes continued to stare hard into the gloom of what had become Priestly's grave beyond the peephole. "No. No sign of injury." Suddenly, he leaned forward with a gasp of astonishment. "This is a remarkable scene, Watson. Most remarkable!"

"Then will you allow me to look for myself?" I could barely restrain the urge to shoulder the detective aside in order to feast my eyes on what must be a bizarre spectacle.

"Of course, Watson."

He relinquished his peephole with evident reluctance.

Eagerly, I stepped forward, positioning the lamp so that the light fell into the vault. I gazed upon that macabre display. The mummified body of a young man clung to the wall, facing the stonework. Of course, a hole had been cut into the wall from the tunnel at the other side just eight days ago. By sheer chance, the stonework had been chiselled away directly in front of the dead man's face. The corpse was dressed in a linen suit. On its back, a large leather bag, or satchel. The feet of the corpse were four feet, or thereabouts, above the layer of dust that engulfed the chamber.

Holmes touched my elbow to attract my attention. "He's not attempting to climb from the grave, is he, Watson?"

"Although the way the arms stretch above the head do give a strong impression of climbing. However, I very much agree with you, Holmes, the body is fixed there."

Priestly shuddered. "How does my brother defy gravity? Why are his arms stretched upward above his head, as if he reaches up to find hand-holes?

Holmes recalled what he'd observed before yielding the spyhole to my eager gaze: "The chamber is perhaps thirty feet long by fifteen feet high. Wooden pegs have been driven into the walls."

"The people who used this cellar in everyday life long ago would have done that," Priestly said. "They embedded wooden pegs into the rock in order to hang domestic items, such as ropes and tools there. They'd also suspend bags of food high above the floor, beyond the reach of rats."

Holmes nodded. "A simple yet elegant solution to protecting foodstuffs from vermin."

"I haven't counted the wooden pegs. However, typically there would be dozens embedded into the walls of a cellar like this one. After so many years in this arid environment the pegs will be as hard as iron."

"Your brother wears a satchel. Leather straps secure it to his body. I am confident that one of the leather straps has caught on a protruding shaft of wood, and he hangs from one of the pegs."

"But his arms . . ." Priestly shuddered again. "How does a dead man keep his arms stretched out above his head?"

"I need more facts before I begin voicing conclusions." Holmes gestured for me to move aside. I surrendered that fascinating window, of sorts, into the house of the dead.

Priestly sounded even more baffled than before. "Are you suggesting that someone killed my brother, hoisted him high up the wall, and hung him there from one of the straps of the satchel? How did the killer leave a room that has been sealed for three thousand years? Good God, how did my brother even enter it in the first place?"

"I need more clues, sir, just as a house-builder needs bricks and mortar. If either of us are deprived of what we need, then the master builder does not construct his house, and I cannot build my theory."

The intensity of Holmes's gaze into that chamber made my heart pound faster with excitement. What was he seeing? What evidence did that magnificent brain feed upon?

The detective's words came in forceful spurts. "There is a dark patch above the aperture – the one that your workers cut into the wall. I am certain that patch is the dried residue of a liquid, which has adhered there. That dark patch is approximately four feet above the cadaver's head. My certainty extends to it being Benjamin Priestly's blood."

"But so high on the wall," I exclaimed. "How on earth did the man's blood stain the wall more than a dozen feet above the floor?"

"Splashed?" hazarded Priestly.

"No." Holmes shook his head. "It's almost as if it has been daubed there quite thickly. Wait here." He left the aperture at this side of the chamber, darted back along the tunnel, and returned a moment later.

"Hah! We're getting closer to the truth! A little of the blood has seeped through the cracks in the blockwork four feet above the aperture. I can see how the blood beaded from narrow gaps between the blocks before it dried. The marks are minute and barely discernible to the naked eye. They are there, nonetheless."

Priestly gulped. "What devilish force could hold a man against a wall at such a great height, and then release his blood so it daubs the stonework?"

"I shall not make a fool of myself by jumping to conclusions. This requires a modicum of tobacco and plenty of thought. Firstly, however, I require a closer examination of the area where I first looked through the aperture."

We followed Holmes back to the other section of tunnel. There he minutely examined the stonework that separated the corpse's chamber from us – three living men – on the other side of the barrier. This had been erected long ago to seal the entrance to what had been a domestic basement. After that, the ancient craftsmen had smoothly covered the stones in plaster, which was the same colour as the surrounding rock – their intention being to conceal the entrance from the barbarians that would steal the precious items and spitefully destroy the clay tablets that bore the sacred writings. He paid especially close attention to the area around the aperture, which opened up directly onto the face of the deceased. Priestly explained that his workmen had cut hundreds of similar slots in order to peer into the basements that they discovered. By chance, one such hole had revealed his brother's dead face. Holmes listened to Priestly, and asked several more questions. The detective then drew our attention to the very narrow gaps between the stone blocks. He pointed out miniscule beads of blood that had trickled from the other side before drying to form black speckles on the wall. My friend softly hummed with pleasure as he removed a glittering item from the narrowest of gaps between the stone blocks and slipped it into an envelope. He picked up an object from the dusty floor – an object so small that I failed to see what it was.

"Mr Priestly." Holmes folded the envelope carefully before slipping it into his pocket. "Who had access to this tunnel before you discovered this particular vault?"

"Professor Hendrik, Eden, myself and the native workers."

"Not the Grey Guards?"

"No, we forbid them from entering the excavations. A misplaced step could destroy a priceless artefact."

"Is the entrance to this complex locked at night?"

"Yes. Only the Professor, Eden and I have access to the key to the gate that seals the entrance to the shaft."

"Four years ago, when your brother disappeared, there were only the three of you working here, along with the local men?"

"To be accurate there was another. Professor Hendrik's wife lived at the compound. Mrs Prudence Hendrik was, alas, dying of consumption. She could barely sleep at night, the pain was so great."

"Consumption is a vile illness."

"Alas, I believe the shock of Benjamin's disappearance hastened her death. Mrs Hendrik died a few days after he vanished."

"I see."

"Can you explain how my brother died, and how he came to be in a sealed vault with no entrance?"

I couldn't restrain my curiosity. "And how the devil was he glued so high up on the wall like ... like a gigantic spider?" I noticed Edward Priestly flinch at my choice of words. "I beg your pardon," said I. "A rather unfortunate description."

He gave a humourless laugh. "I found myself making precisely the same comparison. Is that how you see him, Mr Holmes? A human spider, forever stuck to the wall, hands reaching upwards?"

Holmes didn't answer. Instead he fired back another question. "How long were you engaged to Miss Hendrik?"

"Is that relevant?"

"I shall decide when you answer."

"Three years."

"You've lived in the same compound for much longer than that?"

"Yes."

"She is older than you."

"That is an impertinent observation."

"Supply me with facts, sir. I am building my case. Miss Hendrik is older than you?"

"Yes, in fact she was born in the same year as my brother."

"Ah."

"Not that age matters in affairs of the heart, surely?"

"Agreed. Yet, perhaps, we approach a shining nugget of truth."

"I don't see what—"

"You became engaged to Miss Hendrik three years ago?"

"Yes, I've already said—"

"And before?"

"What do you mean, sir?"

"Tell me to whom she was engaged before you."

"Dash it all, sir. Do you need to pry?"

"I must, sir, I must – if I am to solve this mystery."

"Eden was engaged to my brother, Mr Holmes. Yes, sir, Eden was set to become Benjamin's wife."

And, as if the man's inflamed emotions had the power to disturb the Earth, the ground began to tremble. I touched the wall and felt vibration there.

"Another tremor, gentlemen," Holmes announced. "It's time we left before we find ourselves confined here forever."

Dust trickled from cracks in the rock above our heads as we quickly made our way back to the surface, and into that deluge of burning sunlight.

## 10

Holmes took himself up to the flat roof of the house again. There he sat on a bench in the shade of a tall palm tree that grew from the courtyard, his injured arm in its sling. With what must have been a headful of restless thoughts, ideas, possibilities and theories, he gazed into a teacup, which he lightly tapped with a pencil.

The *chink* . . . *chink* . . . *chink* did nothing to quell my searing urge to demand that he explain what had happened in that subterranean room, and why Benjamin Priestly had, for the last three years, been left fixed tight to the wall, with his arms stretched out above his head. The mystery worked on me like a devil of an itch that I could not reach to scratch.

"Watson," murmured Holmes deep in thought, "I should like a bowl of dust."

I glanced at his bruised forehead, something he sustained when he fell on the boat. I wondered if he suffered from concussion, which was causing him to make strange comments.

"Watson. Some dust, please, from the yard."

Mindful that this request might not be an aberration after all, I descended the steps, borrowed a soup bowl from the kitchen, collected some dust, and returned with my powdery cargo.

"Thank you." He set the bowl down upon the bench beside him. Languidly, eyes dreamy, he resumed tapping the pencil against the teacup.

I could not repress the question any more. "Do you yet know what happened to Benjamin Priestly?"

"A sequence of events does indeed present itself in my mind's eye, although I require another hour of meditation."

"There is the matter of the Grey Guards. If the pair we saw leaving earlier on horseback are indeed making their way to the telegram office in order to contact their commanding officer?"

"Then they will discover that Holmes and Watson intend to expose the Grey Guards as a criminal gang – one that has conspired to commit theft on a grand scale. They will hasten back here to silence us before we reveal their secret to the police. Yes, I am aware of the danger, Watson."

"Given the distances involved, the soonest they can return here will be this evening."

"So that gives me ten hours to solve the mystery of the climbing corpse." He smiled. "If you will permit me such a lurid and inaccurate phrase?"

"Perhaps we should go now and return on a later day?"

"And leave this excellent mystery to grow stale? Come, come, Watson. Cases such as these are the stones on which I sharpen the blades of my mind."

"Even so, the Grey Guards here will put an end to us."

"Watson, Rome became a great civilization, because it had mighty Carthage as an enemy. Rome needed a powerful foe to compete against, just as a weightlifter needs heavy dumb-bells in order to build muscle."

"Will you solve the mystery soon?"

"I have worked out the mechanics that created the remarkable scene we saw in the vault. What I must do now is decide which individual murdered Priestly. I beg you, Watson, kindly leave me to my bowl of dust."

I did as he asked. I strolled around the walled compound – that little fort in the vast Mesopotamian desert. Sarim, the Arab youth, sat upon the earth, grinding corn into flour with millstones. A green locust alighted on the white sleeve of his shirt. He didn't brush it away, merely contenting himself to gaze down as he rotated the millstones, turning yellow corn into glistening, white flour. Did he not see the green insect on his sleeve? I realized that Sarim did not pay any attention to the locust, even though it was in plain view, such was his deep contemplation of some other subject – a sweetheart, perhaps. At that moment, a revelation struck me, because I understood that even though the dead man in the vault had been in plain view to me, and I had gazed upon the dried blood, smearing the inner wall, I did not have an inkling of what had happened. Holmes, however, had set his clear eyes upon the same scene. Certain clues had presented themselves to him, which had put the millstones of his mind to work, grinding raw facts into refined deductions. The harder I tried to puzzle out the mystifying scene in the vault, the more muddled I became until my head throbbed. In comparison to the man high on the roof, I felt infuriatingly stupid. Then was there ever a smarter fellow than my friend, Sherlock Holmes?

What eventually distracted me from a stern examination of my own lack of intelligence was the sound of gunshots. I rushed back to the roof occupied by Holmes. He slowly stirred the bowl of dust with his finger. So entrenched in thought was he, that he barely glanced up when tribesmen in flowing clothes, their faces masked by black scarves, fired rifles in the direction of the compound from a distance of some two hundred yards. Immediately, the guards on the walls fired back. The gun battle ended abruptly with neither side suffering any apparent injury. The tribesmen vanished back into the thorn trees.

"Good grief, Holmes," I gasped. "How could you remain so calm when we were under attack?"

"Hmm?" He gazed at the dust, fascinated by those swirling grains. "Those gunshots . . . most revealing, weren't they?"

"How so?"

"You were in the Army. You know that a bullet should leave the muzzle of a modern rifle with a sharp *crack*."

"Indeed."

"We heard loud bangs. The crack of the speeding bullet was absent. Therefore: the tribesmen attacking the compound were firing blanks. The guards retaliated with blanks. Not a single genuine bullet has been fired."

"Then what on earth was the purpose of that charade?"

"A pretence, Watson, for the benefit of the guards' employer, namely Professor Hendrik."

"Why on earth should the guards orchestrate a false attack?"

"If you built an all-metal house that could never burn, you wouldn't purchase fire insurance, would you? From time to time, it seems to me, the guards pay tribesmen to fire blank rounds to remind the professor why armed protection is essential."

"Ah, you believe that the Grey Guards plan to steal artefacts from the excavations here, as they've been doing throughout the country?"

"They are probably biding their time until Professor Hendrik discovers an exceptionally valuable hoard of treasure. After that, the guards will restage a sham attack. On that occasion the guards, themselves, will murder the professor, his granddaughter and Edward Priestly. They will steal the treasure, and then claim that local bandits committed the murders and the theft."

"Then we must act."

"All in good time, Watson. Now, pray, give me another hour of introspection."

## 11

One hour later, Sherlock Holmes swept down from the sunlit heights of the flat roof to find me cleaning my Mauser pistol.

"Please load that weapon, Watson."

I clicked a metal strip, holding the bullets, into the pistol. "There, loaded."

"I fear that you might need the gun soon."

"It's midday. We have around eight hours before the two guards return."

"Then there is no time to spare. Will you accompany me?"

I followed him to a house where the professor, his granddaughter and Edward Priestly were about to partake of sandwiches.

Holmes didn't hesitate. "This is an abrupt intrusion on my part. I have questions to ask. I cannot delay for one more second."

Professor Hendrik's blue eyes widened – they held a trace of alarm as well as surprise. "Sit yourself down, Mr Holmes, ask away."

"You know that Mr Priestly showed us his brother's body in the vault?"

"Yes, he told us that you'd made a thorough examination there."

"I take it that the workers and your guards are aware that a body has been found."

"Indeed so."

"Forgive me if my questions appear insensitive, Miss Hendrik. However, time is running out; soon you will face great danger."

Priestly reacted with shock. "What kind of danger?"

"Edward." The woman spoke firmly. "Let the detective ask his questions. We should not distract him."

"Thank you, Miss Hendrik. I will explain the threat we all face shortly, but first I wish to clear up the matter of your former fiancé."

"Of course."

"Professor, you say the body was discovered eight days ago when you cut an aperture into the outer wall of the basement to allow you to see inside?"

"Yes."

"Why has there been no attempt to extract the body?"

"Ground tremors make this entire area unstable. As the basement lies beneath a dozen feet of fractured bedrock we must install timber supports before we break through the sealed doorway. That work will take ten days or more."

"When you realized that there was a hidden vault there, did you notice footprints? I ask this because the tunnel's floor is covered with fine dust."

"The tunnel, itself, was discovered over three years ago. Since then, we, and our workers, have walked back and forth along it hundreds of times."

"Then there is little point in me trying to identify Benjamin Priestly's murderer from any footprints that might have left behind."

Miss Hendrik's eyes blazed with astonishment. "You believe that my fiancé – my former fiancé – was murdered?"

"I do."

"How?"

"I'll explain shortly."

Priestly ran his hands through his hair, a nervous gesture to be sure. "I shall be eternally grateful to you, sir, if you can do that. Not knowing how my brother died is torture."

The man's fiancée rested her hand on his "We will know, Edward," she murmured gently. "Then Benjamin will be laid to rest."

Holmes continued briskly: "Are there any excavations, or deep holes, that are no longer subject to your scrutiny?"

Professor Hendrik shook his head. "The entire subterranean complex is still in the process of excavation. We constantly discover basements and municipal storage chambers near or below vaults that we found years ago. The ancient people who lived in this city were like moles, relentlessly burrowing to construct man-made caverns. Most of the entrances to these were blocked off when the city was besieged. The sealed entrances were disguised in such a cunning way that they exactly look like the walls of the tunnel in order to prevent the invaders from finding them. One way we discover the position of hidden vaults is by methodically tapping the tunnel's sides and listening for a hollow sound, which is indicative of a void. That's how we found the vault containing poor Benjamin."

Holmes wasn't satisfied by the answer. "You're certain that there are no pits nearby that are neglected by your diggers?"

"No. None."

Eden sat up straight. "Grandfather, the scorpion wells! They're just a hundred paces from the compound."

"Ah, indeed, my dear. Forgetful old soul, aren't I? Hmm?" He smiled fondly at her. "Eden is quite correct, Mr Holmes. There are three wells close by. They are very deep, quite dry, and of no scientific value. All we found at the bottom, when we investigated the wells twenty years ago, were relatively modern food cans, broken bottles and scorpions galore, which gave the wells their name."

"Is it possible to gain access to the wells?"

"I had them covered with boards to ensure that nobody fell down. Other than that they are just as we left them."

"Holmes," I began, "when you were examining the outer wall of the vault you found certain objects which you placed in an envelope. Are they significant to this case?"

"Absolutely significant. I shall reveal what they were. A strand of hair, and one piece of gold chain the length of my little finger."

Eden asked, "Do these items speak to you?"

"They speak most powerfully."

"Do you have any more questions?" Priestly asked.

"Two, only. Question one: will you all come with me now to the Priestly vault? I wish to reveal my deductions at the scene of the crime."

All three nodded.

"Question two: Professor, are your labourers completely loyal?"

"Yes, I would trust them with my dear granddaughter's life."

"Good. Because, today, you will have to put that trust to the test." He walked swiftly to the door. "Please come at once – the clock ticks down to zero hour!"

## 12

Sherlock Holmes explained to the three the danger that they faced as they approached the tunnels' entrance. He told them that he and I had been employed by the Ottoman government, which rules Mesopotamia, to investigate the systematic pilfering of ancient treasures from archaeological sites. Holmes discovered that the hitherto unsuspected culprits were none other than the Grey Guards. This company of mercenaries had been formed by Captain Grey, a much-respected naval officer, in order to protect Europeans working in this remote part of the world. Naturally, the Grey Guards provided this protection service for a fee. In recent years, however, the Grey Guards had been infiltrated by a sophisticated team of criminals: they had corrupted many of Captain Grey's men, who then stole precious items that had been dug from the ground by honest and unsuspecting archaeologists. The thefts occurred in such a way that blame always attached to local peasants. The villains, who'd infiltrated the Grey Guards, formulated the elegant philosophy that it is much easier to steal treasure if you are the ones guarding it in the first place. Holmes had, at last, the evidence he needed. This would ensure wholesale arrests among the private army in grey that was corrupt to its core.

As we walked along the desert path towards the archaeological site, I noticed the way the Grey Guards stationed on the compound wall watched us with interest, even suspicion. They knew that the detective, Sherlock Holmes, had arrived yesterday, which had, we believed, prompted a pair of guards to make the half-day journey to the nearest telegram office in order to contact their commanding officer. The commander would know by now that Sherlock Holmes intended to expose the crimes of the Grey Guards. Undoubtedly, an order would fly along hundreds of miles of telegram wire: "KILL SHERLOCK HOLMES. KILL DOCTOR WATSON. THEY MUST NOT BE ALLOWED TO REVEAL WHAT THEY KNOW."

Our little party stopped at the pit that yawned darkly in front of us. An entrance to the underworld: the land of the dead. I confess, I shivered. Yes, death saturated the ground here, for the people of Tirrash were slaughtered by their enemy long ago – and the promise of more deaths to come seemed to pulsate in the hot desert air. Just hours from now, a pair of criminals, masquerading as our protectors, would return. They would have a bloody task to perform.

Nearby, a dozen labourers shovelled sand onto a mound. Holmes spoke to Professor Hendrik, explaining what the man must do. The professor gravely nodded and went to speak to his workers.

"Watson," said Holmes, "considering that my arm is still confined to this sling, would you be so good as to help me with an experiment?"

"Of course."

"Do you see that tin bowl there on the table?"

"Yes."

"Please bring the bowl with you. The experiment I have in mind will demonstrate quite vividly what occurred in the vault four years ago."

With that, we descended into a world of darkness and flesh-tingling air that oozed through the ancient tunnels. Holmes managed to descend the ladder; the injured arm didn't handicap his movements unduly. When we stood at the bottom of the shaft I noticed that Eden Hendrik took Edward Priestly's hand in hers. A gesture of both love and reassurance, and I sincerely hoped they would both live to see their wedding day.

## 13

Holmes and I, and Mr Priestly and Miss Hendrik, lit our lamps, which we held aloft as we walked through the tunnels. Dust trickled from narrow cracks in the ceiling. The grains of dust were so light that they hung in the air, creating a yellow mist that made this labyrinth a mysterious, unearthly place: it was as if we trespassed in a forbidding realm. Eden Hendrik shivered in the morbidly cold passageway, her breath producing ghostly clouds of white vapour.

Presently, we reached the vault that had become Benjamin Priestley's tomb.

Holmes indicated the tin bowl that I carried in my hands. "Watson, please scoop dust from the floor into the bowl."

I complied. Eden and Priestly watched with astonishment, clearly baffled by Holmes's request.

Eden asked, "Is a bowl containing dust from this tunnel significant?"

"Absolutely significant. I shall explain when your grandfather arrives."

My pocket watch ticked – a loud sound in that confined space. The respiration of my companions formed whispery echoes. I glanced at the aperture, recently cut into the wall, which allowed a view of the vault's interior. Dipping my head a little afforded me a glimpse of Benjamin's dead and gruesomely withered face.

Ten minutes later, Professor Hendrik arrived, puffing out his cheeks with the exertion of hurrying.

"All is done?" Holmes asked. "You have spoken to your workers?"

"I have, sir."

"They know what is expected of them?"

"Yes."

Holmes set down his lamp upon the floor. "At this moment, you do not know how Benjamin Priestly entered the sealed vault, how he died there, and how he became fixed to the wall. Five minutes from now you will know everything. It's been an interesting problem, and now I have the bones of the truth."

Eden spoke softly. "Do not omit any detail, Mr Holmes. The time has passed for us to be shocked by Benjamin's death. I, myself, have seen his face through the aperture. I have steeled myself to the horror of it all. We need to know what befell the man I loved so much."

Holmes gave a single, sharp nod. "Benjamin Priestly was a thief."

Professor Hendrik cried out, "Confound it, sir! How dare you make such a vile accusation?"

"Grandfather," Eden said calmly. "Please let Mr Holmes speak."

And my brilliant friend did begin to speak – in masterful tones that made his words echo from the tunnel walls. "For reasons I have yet to discover, Benjamin stole valuable items from this vault, which he'd found. I've been told that there are many such chambers down here that have yet to be opened by your good selves, so it's not unreasonable to suppose that he'd soon locate one, if he set his mind on doing just that. In my mind's eye, I see him secretly venturing back here at night, when the place is deserted, to break into the vault."

"There is no opening that we can see," remarked Priestly.

"That is because there is a layer of dust in the chamber that is at least four feet deep. The hole in the wall that Benjamin cut must be just above the vault's floor level. Over the years, dust has drifted into the chamber, so burying the entrance that Benjamin made. You will undoubtedly find a tunnel, currently unknown to you, running beside the vault, and at a much lower level than this one in which we stand. When you break in to recover the body you will discover that there are valuables in the leather bag that Benjamin carries on his back. No doubt he made a deal with the Grey Guards to supply them with jewels, gold and so on, in return for hard cash."

Priestly's eyes glistened. "Did the guards kill him? Did they think that he'd cheated them, or planned to report them?"

"If the guards had decided to end his life they would, in all likelihood, simply have lured him away from the compound before cutting his throat and burying him in the desert. No, sir. Someone else planned Benjamin's death using great cunning and intelligence. In one stroke, they would murder him, and conceal his body, while making you conclude that he'd packed his bags and left like a thief in the night."

Priestly squirmed with discomfort. "Who would do this?"

Holmes produced an envelope that he'd concealed in his sling. "The evidence that identifies the killer lies in here. First, however, you should understand the sequence of events that resulted in that grim scene inside the vault – one where Benjamin appears to cling high up on the wall with his feet nowhere near solid ground." Slipping the envelope into his sling once more, he said, "I ask you to picture this. Benjamin has secretly chiselled his way into the vault at the dead of night. He discovers that it is waist deep in dust, meaning that the precious objects he wishes to find there and to steal are buried. Imagine: he cannot risk discovery by removing the dust and leaving it on the surface. A mound that has grown larger overnight would be noticed. However, he has the perfect solution. All he need do is bring his spade, dig down into the dust, and leave it piled against the chamber wall. We might well picture him digging by night, the lamp burning, perspiration and dust streaking his face. He is young and strong, and he is also very desperate. Eventually, he piles the dust high on the other side of this wall." Holmes tapped the stonework with his finger.

"Night after night, Benjamin digs. We can picture him discovering clay tablets that were hidden down here during that dreadful siege long ago, but he is not interested in those. No, he searches for treasure concealed here at the same time. The man does indeed find precious artefacts, which he places in his bag, and carries back to the compound before you or your employees wake in the morning. Of course, the guards are aware of his labours and hide the loot in their own quarters. They cannot help him with the excavation itself, because suspicion would be aroused if they were found to be missing from their posts on the compound wall."

Holmes gazed into space for a moment. "Then, one fateful night, Benjamin is at work. The bag is on his back. He's already tucked away a silver chalice that he's found, or something of the like. However, at some point he notices the glint of gold in the lamplight. Only this is high up on the wall. Almost up near the ceiling, more than a dozen feet above him. The gold will be easy to reach – for has he not laboured so mightily to pile tons of that fine dust up against the wall? Accordingly, he puts down his spade, and proceeds to climb the mound; it is steep, and almost the powdery consistency of flour. He must use his hands to claw himself upwards. At the top of the mound, on the other side of this very wall, which we now stand beside, he sees a gold chain. Strangely, it hangs from a narrow gap. Nevertheless, he wants it. Gold is readily converted to cash. He leans in close to the wall to see where the gold chain leads. He wonders if it will guide him to another vault full of treasure. Closer and closer he leans, in order to peer through the half-inch gap in the stones from where the gold links snake. Then!" Holmes slapped the wall so hard that everyone flinched. "There's a gunshot. At that range the murderer doesn't have to be a marksman. They are firing from a distance of five inches into a narrow gap, which will guide the bullet as surely as a gun barrel. The bullet strikes Benjamin. Where? I don't know the point of impact yet – maybe the throat or upper chest. It's still not possible to see a gunshot wound. In any event, Benjamin dies in an instant. His blood runs down the wall on the other side. A stain we've seen with our own eyes. A little of the blood dribbles through cracks between the stone blocks to this side of the wall where we stand now. You can just make out black specks where blood beaded from the joints in the stonework before drying in this supremely arid air. The corpse lay with its face pressed to the basement wall, many feet above the floor. We can visualize the body lying on the steep mound of dust that Benjamin had laboured so hard to pile up."

"You claim he was shot?" asked Priestly, dazed by Holmes's revelation.

"If you carefully look through the narrow gap – that one there shaped like a letter L –

you will see smudge marks left on the stone by a gun when it discharged the bullet; such residue is quite distinctive. I have, myself, written an article on the subject for the *Police Gazette*."

Professor Hendrik shook his head in bewilderment. "There is no mound in the chamber now. The dust lies as flat and as smooth as a pond. Yet Benjamin is suspended upon the wall. How the dickens did that happen?"

"Watson, the bowl, please."

I handed him the bowl, which was perhaps half full of dust. Holmes slipped his arm from the sling. With the bowl in one hand, he used the fingers of the other to mound the powdery stuff so that it sloped steeply up one side of the bowl, leaving the bottom almost clean of dust.

Holmes said, "You have told me that ground tremors occur frequently here. They vibrate the bedrock to quite a substantial degree. Now, if you will observe." Without tipping the bowl this way or that, and keeping it absolutely level, he began to lightly tap the bowl's rim. The dust began to flow, disturbed by the vibration. Soon the mound had gone – the dust covered the bottom of the bowl again and was quite smooth. "This is what happened during the four years since Benjamin's death. Earth tremors gently shook the vault until the mound adopted some of the characteristics of a liquid. After a while, this powdery material covered the floor again to a depth of at least four feet, erasing all trace of digging."

Priestly still seemed dazed. "But the body . . . why was it left hanging?"

"Surely, that is easy to envisage. The tremors caused the millions of grains, which formed the mound, to flow downward. All this happened slowly over many months. For a while, Benjamin's corpse descended as the mound began to diminish in size. The lowering of the corpse revealed the bloodstain on the wall. Then, at some point, a little further down, one of the protruding wooden pegs, which had been inserted all those centuries ago, caught one of the bag's leather shoulder straps. The dust continued to level itself out until the mound had vanished. However, it left the body literally high and dry. The corpse hangs there because the mound simply vanished from beneath it."

Eden said, "Yet Benjamin's arms stretch upward, above his head, as if he is frozen in the act of climbing. Why is that?"

Holmes turned to me. "I am certain that my friend, Doctor Watson, will most ably supply an answer that relates to human anatomy."

I nodded. "When Benjamin Priestly suffered the fatal wound he must have slumped face down on the mound, and no doubt the body slid down by a foot or so, which was enough to leave the arms extended above the head as it lay on the bed of dust. This underground complex is so arid that all moisture is drawn from organic matter. The woodwork down here dries out, becoming as hard as iron. The muscles in Benjamin's body, including the arms, will have dried out, too – over time that muscle will have become inflexible and hardened. When the dust gradually fell away from beneath the body, leaving it hanging by the leather strap, the arms will have remained stretched out stiffly upwards."

Holmes said, "Thank you, Watson. That is absolutely correct. The cadaver has been mummified by these supremely dry conditions. The limbs will be rigid. Hence they give the appearance of a dead man climbing."

Eden digested this rather gruesome explanation in the blink of an eye; she asked quickly, "Then who is the murderer?"

Holmes passed the bowl to me, took the envelope from where he'd placed it in the sling, and opened it. From the envelope, he removed a fragment of gold chain, no more than five links. He also removed a single hair. "I found the hair on the floor here. The fragment of gold chain had been lodged in the crack between the blockwork. After the killer had used the chain as bait to lure Benjamin up here to their level, they tried to pull the chain free. However, the end link snagged. The killer broke the chain, trying to withdraw it, and left this small fragment behind. The killer must have been confident that the trapped links would never be found, as they were out of sight – and nor would they, if I hadn't carefully searched the gaps between the stones. Usually, this would be the moment for me to name the killer . . . however, that isn't necessary, is it, Professor?"

The professor's eyes bulged with shock. "What are you trying to say?"

"That you know the identity of the killer."

"Good grief! How can I possibly know?"

"Your late wife had long red hair. Did she not?"

"I refuse to continue with this preposterous conversation."

"Miss Hendrik, here, has long chestnut brown hair," said Holmes calmly. "No other European woman has, supposedly, ever been in this tunnel, other than Miss Hendrik, and yet this morning I found a single, long hair that is quite clearly red. A bright copper red."

The professor stared at the gold links and strand of hair with an expression mingling astonishment with utter shock. At last, he sighed, and nodded as if understanding he must accept what would be the inevitable truth of the matter. "The gold chain belonged to my wife, Prudence. I discovered the broken chain in her jewellery box after she died. I thought nothing of it." He swallowed. "And she had such beautiful red hair. You, sir, hold one of her red hairs in your hand."

Eden gasped. "Why would my grandmother kill my fiancé?"

"We now enter the realm of conjecture." Holmes fixed his deep-set eyes on the wall in front of him, as if his gaze could penetrate the rock and view the vault beyond. "Your grand-mother must have decided it was necessary to dispose of Benjamin. Her reasons would have been compelling. I believe she devised this plot to not only kill him, and cause the body to vanish, but also to make you believe that he had cruelly deserted you so that you would not grieve."

"But why? What had Benjamin done that was so terrible?"

"He had begun stealing from this underground complex, because he had a desperate need for money. If he was prepared to break the law doing this, then where would it have ended? When a person routinely commits criminal acts, they often escalate from petty theft, to acts of robbery, and then to the most savage crimes of all."

Edward Priestly gave a long, unhappy sigh. "My brother loved to gamble. I did fear that the compulsion had become his master. He'd often borrowed money from his friends to repay gambling debts. If they hadn't given him such loans, the scandal would have ruined him, and brought shame to my family."

Holmes remarked, "Then we might suppose that the gambling vice led to Benjamin becoming even more indebted to his card-playing acquaintances. Once more, we're in the realm of theories, yet one can suppose, also, that Mrs Prudence Hendrik discovered that he had financial troubles. Perhaps he'd shamelessly begged her for money to avoid the scandal of an unpaid debt. Mrs Hendrik knew only too well this fact: that when Benjamin married Eden she was likely to suffer shame and become an outcast from society, if he failed to cover the costs of his gambling habit. Therefore, Mrs Hendrik devised a beautifully intricate plan.

"Even though she was desperately ill at the time, she followed Benjamin at night. She discovered that he stole from a vault that nobody else knew existed. With every atom of her remaining strength, coupled with indomitable willpower, she followed him one night. And while he burrowed into the dust for precious objects, she fed the gold chain through a narrow gap in the wall here. Then she inserted the muzzle of a pistol into the same aperture. When she saw Benjamin's face on the other side she fired. We can imagine that she waited for quite a while after firing the gun, listening for movement, wondering if he still lived. Many times she will have called his name. There was no reply. And then she will have seen tiny drops of his blood seeping through the blockwork. Confident that she had killed him, she removed the chain, or most of it, for she left some links behind when the end snagged in the gap. She was gravely ill and, I dare say, her hair was falling from her head. One strand dropped to the floor here. With iron determination, and summoning the last of her strength, that dying woman returned to the compound, packed up Benjamin's belongings into his case before disposing of it. Why she wasn't noticed by the guards I cannot say, but I suspect they literally dozed on the job. Mrs Hendrik couldn't muster the energy to drag the luggage far, so she will have dropped it down one of the old wells near the compound."

Holmes turned to Eden who clutched Edward Priestly's hand. "I say it once more, miss, and with all my heart. Your grandmother killed Benjamin because she loved you so much. She didn't want you to suffer the misery and shame that would inevitably result from becoming the wife of a man who could not pay his gambling debts. Many a woman has committed suicide to avoid the consequences of such a scandal."

Professor Hendrik took a deep breath. "What now, Mr Holmes?"

"I should like to tidy up the last details of this case. Then we must prepare to fight for our lives. The men who intend to murder us will reach here before nightfall."

## 14

Events moved quickly. Within minutes of Sherlock Holmes explaining how Benjamin Priestly had been killed, and why, we arrived at the Scorpion Wells. The youth, Sarim, was lowered by rope into the first well. He found nothing but discarded beer bottles. The second well yielded something else entirely. The professor's native labourers hauled Sarim up, carrying a leather suitcase coated in grime. Its initials confirmed the owner.

"B. G. P.," murmured Eden. "Benjamin Gordon Priestly."

"Mrs Hendrik consigned the case to the well," Holmes said. "She executed the perfect crime."

"Hardly," I remarked. "You discovered how the victim was killed and the identity of his murderer."

"Perfect in the sense that Mrs Hendrik achieved the result she desired. She saved her granddaughter from the misery of financial ruin, and a scandal that would have destroyed her life."

"Mr Holmes," cried the professor. "Over there in the distance! I can see the guards returning. They'll be here within minutes. Just look at how they're whipping their horses to a gallop!"

"The time has come to act." Holmes strode towards the compound gates.

The Grey Guards, who had remained behind, opened the gates for us. They glanced at one another; their questions were clearly present in their glances. What had the detective been doing in the tunnel complex? Why were the native workers returning to the compound earlier than usual? The profound change to the customary routines of the day aroused an obvious suspicion in the guards.

Holmes had decided to show hand. He spoke to the guards in a forceful way. "The game is up, gentlemen. My name is Sherlock Holmes, and I arrest you for the crimes of conspiracy and theft."

One of the guards reached for a pistol in his belt whereupon I fired my gun into the air. The man quickly raised his hands in surrender. Meanwhile, the professor's native diggers eagerly surged forwards to catch hold of the grey-clad figures before they could deploy their rifles. Soon they were deprived of their weapons.

The voice of Sherlock Holmes rang out: "You will be held under lock and key until government troops arrive. You will then be sent to Baghdad to face trial in a court of law."

One of the men spoke up. He was red-faced and wore a monocle in his right eye. "Although I will submit to a trial, I shall not be treated like a common scoundrel. These other guards are of the lower orders; therefore, I refuse to share a cell with them. I demand an officer's quarters."

"Sir," began Holmes, "you conspired with your colleagues here, you stole together, and so you shall occupy a cell together."

The labourers bundled the shouting red-faced man away to be incarcerated in a stockroom with his colleagues. When the two horsemen arrived with orders to kill Holmes and myself (we learned of this later), they, to their surprise, received such a welcome party they will never forget. The professor's labourers pounced, seized their rifles, and in no time at all the pair joined the other Grey Guards in the cell for a jolly reunion.

Later, Sherlock Holmes smiled at me as we sat on the flat roof in the cool of the evening, with a whisky and soda, and enjoying vast cigars of the finest Arabian tobacco.

He said, "Today's adventure filled me with nothing less than a crescendo of excitement. I solved an intriguing mystery, and we cheated death. But do you know what frightens me to the bone, my friend?"

"The arrival of more Grey Guards?"

"Ha! That would be a delicious escapade, wouldn't it?" He blew smoke up towards a shining moon. "But, sadly, no . . . the Grey Guards throughout Mesopotamia will be receiving word that their schemes for theft on a grand scale have been exposed. Some will flee, but many will be arrested. Trust me: the reign of that particular criminal gang is all but over."

"Then, pray, what does frighten you?"

"What absolutely terrifies me, my dear Watson, is that nothing of interest will come my way tomorrow. Then I shall be horribly bored."

"I am certain that you could chivvy adventure from the dullest of places."

"Ha! I know just the thing. Shall we take a midnight stroll through the site of that long-vanished city, stamping on the ground, and seeing if any of the ancient skeletons comes out to play?" With that, Holmes threw back his head, and he laughed so loudly that the sound disturbed the wild dogs in the desert, and they howled at the moon like an entire legion of demons.

# The Curse of Guangxu

## Sam Stone

The envelope was on the dresser when Sherlock Holmes returned to his room.

The year was 1897 and Holmes was on the last leg of what had been a most satisfying and fascinating tour of China. Having visited several less civilized, even archaic villages, he had planned to round off his trip taking in the delights of Beijing. Once there, Holmes had been amazed at the forward-thinking and somewhat modern city, which was so far removed from the small shanties he had so far seen, that it made him aware of the poverty suffered by the people who were not fortunate enough to live in the capital. It was something he observed the world over and, on many warm nights, had pondered upon whilst smoking his favourite pipe.

He was much like his old self because of the travel. Slowly his cognitive functions were returning to normal. The torments of Moriarty were ended and the death of his arch-enemy, and his own subsequent faked demise – a somewhat knee-jerk reaction – was starting to feel like a distant, insane memory – or worse: an overly dramatized play. In the last week, he had begun to consider the possibility of going home again but, when surrounded by the exotic, London seemed to be nothing more than a place that he had once dreamed. He thought of Doctor John Watson sometimes too. His old friend was probably happy with Mary. Married life would suit him, Holmes was certain, but he also believed that Watson would have missed the excitement that their investigative days had brought them. But, perhaps, he would soon respond to the urge to brave the now seemingly alien London streets once more.

Holmes sat down on the edge of the bed and slipped out of his shoes, replacing them with comfortable slippers. Then he removed his overcoat, hung it casually over the back of a chair and pulled on a blue velvet smoking jacket. He picked up his pipe from the bedside table and then his eyes fell on the dresser.

The envelope was an obvious intrusion in the room. He had noticed it immediately but he had not been in the right state of mind to acknowledge its presence. Now Holmes eyed it for a moment, checking for obvious traps, and then picked it up, observing the telegram markings before opening. The envelope bore his name as well as specific and carefully penned Chinese lettering – 紅雙喜的酒店 – which he recognized as the name of the inn where he was staying: the Inn of Double Happiness.

"Fascinating," he murmured.

No one knew that Holmes was in Beijing. No one even knew that he was still alive – or so he thought.

He glanced around the room, eyes scanning the bamboo furniture; the ornate dressing screen that sheltered a tin bath from the rest of the room; the bed that was covered in decadent cushions (which promised more comfort than he had seen throughout his entire journey); and, of course, his trunk stood in the far corner near the balcony window.

He raised the envelope to his nose and sniffed. The scents of ink and bamboo paper filled his nostrils with the subtle fragrance of jasmine. Holmes focused on the perfume, which would have been foreign anywhere else but here in this fascinating world. The smell jarred even so. It felt wrong, inappropriate, though the mystery of why was still a long way from unfolding.

He didn't have an envelope knife and so Holmes picked up the tiny paring knife that had been left beside the full basket of fruit he had requested earlier, and he opened the envelope.

Inside, as expected, was a telegram.

TO: SHERLOCK HOLMES, 紅雙喜的酒店
FROM: SAMUEL JAMES DANBY, 故宮

MY DEAR CHAP HOLMES x HEARD YOU WERE IN
THE CAPITAL x IN URGENT NEED OF YOUR HELP
x I WORK FOR EMPEROR GUANGXU x HAVE HIS
PERMISSION TO CONTACT YOU x A GRAVE
ILLNESS HAS STRICKEN HIS BELOVED CONSORT
x I AM AT A LOSS x DOES NOT CONFORM TO
ANYTHING I HAVE SEEN BEFORE x POOR GIRL
SIMPLY FADING AWAY AS THOUGH SOME EVIL
FORCE IS DRAINING HER LIFE x COME TO THE
PALACE YOU WILL BE WELCOMED x YOUR
FRIEND x DR SAMUEL DANBY x

Holmes read the words carefully; the message was rushed, unlike Henry's usually careful and often more detailed notes, but this was the nature of telegrams. They held such impersonal information and required the sender to write with brevity. Holmes always felt you could not gauge the mood of the sender without the swirl of pen and ink. It was strange that Danby had sent the message this way. If he was working for the Emperor, why had he not merely sent a handwritten note around from the palace?

He pondered over the last time he had heard from his old university friend. Danby had been a dedicated man of medicine even then. He recalled how he had chosen to leave England some years ago. Holmes hadn't heard from him since, but had been told that Danby had taken a missionary post. The picture of Danby's life since then began to shape in Holmes's mind. He saw the man, shiny-faced with raw enthusiasm, boarding a ship, doctor's bag in hand.

So, it was to China the man had gone, and he had, it seemed, endeared himself to the Emperor. Maybe Danby wasn't naive after all.

Holmes pulled the bell cord beside the window and sat down at the bamboo writing desk to pen a reply to Danby. He chose to send the letter direct, and not via the telegram office. When the bellboy arrived at his room, Holmes had already sealed his note ready to send.

A few hours later, Holmes opened his door to find a small, thin Chinese man with a long droopy moustache; he was dressed in ornate robes of regal blue and silver, holding a scroll tied with red ribbon.

"Misser Sherlock Holmes?"

"Yes," said Holmes. "I am Holmes."

"I am envoy from Imperial Palace. I come to take you to Emperor Guangxu. My name is Chang Li."

"The Emperor? I was expecting to hear from my friend, the Emperor's physician," Holmes said. "Samuel Danby."

The man nodded, but Holmes noted a slight twitch around the eyes. Holmes narrowed his own gaze to study the man, but the stillness and formality was back in place and his body language was difficult to read. Even so, Holmes knew something was wrong. A tightness around the mouth, an aversion of his gaze.

"Emperor will give you audience now. You come with me," Chang Li said.

Holmes didn't enjoy being given an imperative and he considered asking Chang Li more questions, but thought it better to hold all of his concerns in check. He still doubted himself, not having fully recovered the usual self-confidence that had driven him for most of his life.

"Very well. Take me to the palace."

Holmes removed his smoking jacket and drew on his coat and deerstalker. Then he followed Chang Li out into the street. Two sedan chairs, each with four men to carry them, waited outside the inn. Chang Li nodded to the first, and Holmes took his cue, stepping inside. The runners picked him and the sedan up as though he were of no weight at all and both he and Chang Li were conveyed at speed through the bustling streets of Beijing to the Imperial Palace.

During the journey, Holmes made no attempt to converse with the man in the other chair, even though they were ferried side by side most of the way. Instead, he took the opportunity to examine the city, and observed the change in opulence as they neared the palace. The houses on the streets were bigger, grander, some had expansive gardens surrounding them.

As they arrived at the palace, the large entry gates opened and Holmes and Chang Li were carried inside without hesitation: it was obvious that he was expected. The sedans were placed down at the bottom of an impressive flight of steps and one of the servants who had conveyed him opened the shallow door beside him. Holmes stepped out.

"This way, Misser Holmes," Chang Li said. "The Emperor is waiting."

"Will Doctor Danby be there also?" Holmes asked.

Chang Li made no comment; instead he walked towards the steps and began his ascent into the Imperial Palace.

Holmes took his time climbing the steps and noted the many guards that lined the walls. At the top he glanced around. He was so high up he could see beyond the wall and observed that on one side of the palace was a magnificent moat, which was both functional and beautiful. The splendour of the palace, juxtaposed with the obvious paranoia of the Imperial guard, made the hairs on the back of Holmes's neck stand up. He straightened his hat, then walked briskly after Chang Li who had paused to wait for him.

The room was large, tall-ceilinged and adorned with flowing, colourful tapestries that hung from the walls. A long carpet led up the centre of the throne room to the focal point: Emperor Guangxu. The Emperor wore a long robe of brilliant red high-lighted with gold and he was seated at the far end of the magnificent chamber atop a throne that was placed on a platform. There were eight steps leading up to the throne, and the red carpet flowed upwards to end at the Emperor's feet. Guangxu sat with all of the royal presence one might expect. Beside him was a smaller throne – currently empty – which Holmes knew would sometimes be occupied by the Empress. Other than these two seats, this striking room was devoid of furniture. Those brought before the Emperor were not permitted to sit or indeed to expect any comfort whatsoever.

A row of guards stood either side of the room as still as statues, and Chang Li and the Emperor treated them as such. They were meant to be invisible and would only move if they suspected any threat towards the Emperor.

"Misser Holmes," Chang Li said. "I present his Royal Highness, Aixin Jueluo Zaitian, eleventh Qing Emperor of China: Emperor Guangxu. Please to bow to Emperor."

Holmes bowed politely.

"Step forward, Mr Holmes," Guangxu said. "I have heard much about you. You have travelled a great deal in my country?"

"I have, Your Highness," Holmes said.

Holmes was impressed by Guangxu's command of the English language. It was flawless and well studied, impeccable even, not at all the pigeon-speak that his envoy, Chang Li, used.

"I would like you to share your observations with me and tell me what you have seen if you will."

"Gladly."

Holmes had heard that Guangxu was extremely well educated. His English was perfect and Holmes told him so.

"An English governess was brought here to work with me. She came originally as a missionary," Guangxu explained. "We spoke in nothing but English every day for many years. She taught me a lot about your ways too. It is as much a part of me as my own language."

They exchanged pleasantries and Holmes was beginning to wonder whether he had been brought here more for Guangxu's intellectual interest than for the serious illness that had been indicated in Danby's letter when Guangxu changed the subject.

"Tell me of my villages," Guangxu said.

"What would Your Highness like to hear?"

"How you found my people?"

"There is much poverty. Many suffer in the smaller towns; hunger and thirst are daily torments," Holmes said with frank openness.

"Thank you, Mr Holmes. You have told me the truth, when none of my subjects will. Walk with me. I need to show you something." The Emperor stood, and his attendants bowed, and the guards looked at the floor. "Come."

The formality of the throne room fell away as Guangxu led Holmes through a screen doorway behind the throne.

"I will speak now in private to Mr Holmes," Guangxu said when Chang Li began to follow them.

Chang Li's eyes twitched, but he bowed his head as Guangxu and Holmes walked away. Holmes had the feeling that Chang Li did not appreciate being left out of the conversation or perhaps he was just concerned about the Emperor being alone with a foreigner. It was even conceivable that he, too, was curious about what Holmes knew of China's poor.

"I could see from your letter that you know something of my plight," Guangxu said, as ahead of them two guards opened an expansive door which was sumptuously decorated with colourful birds and flowers in blue and yellow.

They stepped out into a stunning garden. Holmes paused to take in the two ponds covered with water lilies and separated by a small red bridge. The garden was filled with pink peonies, pale purple Chinese roses and white lotuses. Never had he felt the quixotic more exaggerated than here, where poverty appeared to be another experience that Holmes had only imagined.

A woman walked slowly towards them across the bridge. She was wearing a pale blue *cheongsam* with silver birds woven into the fabric. Her jet-black hair was piled on top of her head and an ornate headdress was woven into it. Silver and blue beads dangled from the front, over her face.

As she approached, Holmes could see that she was only young, perhaps in her early twenties. She was not beautiful in the sense that some of the women he had seen here were, but her eyes and lips were accentuated by kohl and rouge, and her skin was powdered to look an unearthly white; qualities that were admired in this world for reasons he did not entirely understand.

She bowed to Emperor Guangxu.

"Mr Holmes, may I present to you Imperial Noble Consort Jin."

"Your Highness," Holmes said bowing.

Consort Jin did not answer and she kept her gaze averted downward as she walked away with tiny, precise steps, which Holmes knew were due to the bindings on her feet.

"You understand that she is my . . . wife . . . of sorts?"

Holmes nodded. He understood the situation perfectly. He had already established that Guangxu had a wife and a mistress. It did not shock him, as he had learnt much about the culture of China on his travels. Guangxu had been a mere child when he came in line for the throne and had not been permitted to rule until he had reached a certain maturity. Even then, he had been refused the privilege of choosing his wife and consort for himself. Holmes noted all of this, compartmentalizing it all as possibly relevant information for later, but also made no judgement.

"Consort Jin appears to be in perfect health," he noted.

"She is. It is not her that I need you to see."

Guangxu walked on and Holmes followed, even more intrigued.

They re-entered the house through another small garden.

"I now take you where no man other than myself, Doctor Danby and my own physician have ever been. This is the chamber of Consort Zhen."

Two eunuchs stood before the door of Zhen's chamber. Holmes made no comment about them being "men". In Guangxu's eyes the eunuchs were less than human.

"We have been keeping watch over her, day and night, but nothing we do seems to help the condition," Guangxu said.

The eunuchs opened the door, then bowed as the Emperor and Holmes entered.

The room was filled with beautiful, vibrant furniture. A dresser with a large, gold-framed oval mirror stood before a window, which had red and gold silk drapes pulled across to keep out the bright sunlight. On the opposite side of the room was a two-seater sofa, again covered with silk. This was red, with gold fire-breathing dragons woven into the complex design. A huge tapestry hung from the wall behind the sofa; it depicted two lovers, standing on a bridge in a garden not dissimilar to the one they had just walked through. There was a silk screen, and a further doorway that concealed the sleeping area.

The screen parted and a young girl in a bright blue *cheongsam* bowed to Quangxu and then stepped back. There were other girls in the room, quietly attending the person in the bed. One of the eunuchs clapped his hands and all of the women bowed to the Emperor and left without him having to say a word.

Holmes could now see a frail young girl in the bed. Her face was whiter than bleached flour. As he approached, Holmes realized that the powdering was an attempt to hide the terrible deterioration of the woman's face. But, even ravaged by sickness, he could tell that Consort Zhen was the most beautiful woman he had ever seen.

"This . . . is Consort Zhen . . ." Guangxu said, though his explanation was unnecessary as Holmes already knew, but the detective noted the genuine emotion that was evident in the Emperor's voice.

Zhen lay with her eyes wide open, staring at the canopy above her. She didn't acknowledge their presence.

"In my culture, an emperor may neither choose his wife nor his concubines. These are chosen on suitability. I was given Consort Jin and Consort Zhen, as well as Empress Xiaodingjing. I do not love my wife, or Consort Jin. Consort Zhen means more to me than life itself."

Holmes nodded to show he understood the sentiment, even though the words of love that Guangxu spoke were as alien to him as the Chinese culture that he had encountered on his travels through this vast land.

"How long has she been like this?" Holmes asked.

"One week. We do not know what to do. This affliction struck almost overnight. She became at first lethargic. Then after a day or two of barely eating or drinking she lapsed into this state."

"May I examine her?"

"Yes," Guangxu said.

Holmes looked into Zhen's unusually pale eyes: the whites were yellowing, the blue irises – rare though they were in China – were turning white, like the cataract-covered gaze of the old. He bent his head to listen to the shallow breathing that rasped through her lips. The vile odour of impending death wafted from her skin. He pressed his fingers to the pulse at her wrist and felt the slow and irregular beat of a labouring heart. Then he lifted the covers to gaze down at her legs. They appeared to be thin, wasted: already the lack of sustenance was having its toll. Holmes noted the bare feet, though, and glanced at Guangxu.

"This is most unusual for one of your culture," Holmes said.

"Zhen wanted to remove the restrictive bindings. She believes we can make a better future for our country. I agreed with her. Her feet had been bound since infancy. Releasing them gave Zhen much pain, but she was determined to set an example for other women of China."

"I'm impressed with your forward thinking," Holmes said. "Now, I must speak to Doctor Danby and hear his diagnosis."

"*Speak* to Danby? But surely Chang Li told you?" Quangxu said.

"Told me what?"

"Doctor Danby is dead . . ."

Danby lay with his arms crossed over his chest. Two gold yuan coins were placed on his eyes. He was wearing his formal dinner suit and black leather shoes, which were polished to a fine sheen.

"When did this happen?" asked Holmes.

Having left the Emperor in Consort Zhen's chamber, Holmes was once again in the company of Chang Li. He was grateful for the placing of Danby in the cold tomb. The body appeared fresh with little or no rigor mortis and the heat outside had been unable to speed up decomposition.

"We did not know if he have any family, Misser Holmes," Chang Li explained. "Emperor feel that Doctor try very hard to help. He like Doctor. He like we inter him in traditional English manner as far as possible in our culture."

Holmes nodded, but he was impatient for answers. "I see. So when? A few hours ago I assume?"

"No, Misser Holmes, Doctor die five days ago. He has been here ever since then."

"*Five days, you say?*" Holmes did not point out that the telegram he had received had been sent only that day. "Does your physician know what Danby died of?"

Chang Li shook his head. "It mystery. Like affliction of favourite concubine."

"But different," Holmes observed.

He glanced over Danby's body. There was no sign of the ravages that plagued Consort Zhen. Danby's skin appeared strangely healthy. Holmes lifted Danby's arm – the joint bent, the skin felt soft as though the blood still flowed around the body. Danby seemed to be merely asleep. But then, the softening of the limbs was also consistent with a body that was several days' dead.

"Fetch me a small mirror," Holmes said.

Chang Li was confused for a moment, but then he sent one of the guards to obtain what the detective required. When the guard returned with a small hand mirror, Holmes placed the glass near to Danby's lips. He waited several minutes but the mirror did not mist.

"If only Watson were here . . ." But to send for the good doctor would take too long. Besides, Watson, like the rest of the world, still believed that Holmes was dead. For the first time Holmes felt truly alone.

Holmes pressed his head against Danby's chest. A faint odour wafted up from the body. But it wasn't the smell of death that he detected, it was the faint aroma of jasmine.

"Tell me how you found him," Holmes demanded. "Omit nothing."

"There are some strange circumstances here. The most peculiar of all is that Samuel Danby apparently sent me a telegram from his grave," Holmes observed. "Do you know anything of this?"

They were drinking jasmine tea outside in the garden. The smell reminded Holmes of the telegram he had received, and the scent on Danby's body. Consort Jin had poured the tea into the two cups and then she bowed to the Emperor and quietly backed away.

"I assumed he had written to you a week ago and that was why you were in Beijing," Guangxu said.

"I need to get back to my hotel. There are some items there that may help with my investigation."

"But you must stay here," Guangxu said. "We will take care of you and you may have Chang Li to help you with your inquiries."

"I really would prefer to stay at my hotel at this time."

"Mr Holmes, I am concerned that these things that have happened . . . these afflictions . . . have a sinister origin. I would feel happier if you were under palace protection. Doctor Danby did not live in the palace, then . . . this terrible thing occurred. My physician is even now concocting a medicine to ward off evil. It is a concern that a curse has been placed on the house of Guangxu."

"I don't believe in witchcraft," Holmes said. "It is my experience that anything unexplained, which may appear supernatural, is usually down to the machinations of man. That is to say: Evil comes from men."

"I have been raised with Western understanding," Quangxu said. "But there are many unexplainable things that happen here."

"Sometimes we must eliminate the unexplainable in order to find the truth. Is it possible that Consort Zhen has been poisoned?"

"No. Like me, she has a food-tester. The eunuch in question has never shown any signs of illness."

"Her symptoms do not conform with any poison that I'm aware of, either," Holmes said. "Arsenic would show in the fingernails. But small doses, such as a food-tester may absorb, are unlikely to affect the tester at first, especially if the tester is physically larger. This could be the same with any other slow-working poison."

"So it is possible?"

"Yes."

Guangxu was quiet and thoughtful. "But who would poison Zhen?"

"The question you have to ask is, who does it hurt to make Zhen ill? And who will gain from her death?"

By the time Holmes was escorted to a room in the palace, all of his possessions had been transferred from the inn.

The room he was allocated was less ornate than other parts of the palace and lacked any personal touches at all. The room held a bed, a writing desk and an upright chair with a curved back. There was a small dresser made of bamboo but stained red. The room, though sparse, was still far more vivid than anything Holmes would find in London. Behind a parchment screen, which was decorated with birds that resembled peacocks but were painted orange with gaudy plumage, was a ceramic bathtub.

Holmes saw that his trunk had been placed at the foot of the bed, and on top of it was his carpet bag, which contained all he needed to make his ablutions. The carpet bag also featured a secret compartment in which he hid the tools he used for his investigations.

The room was clean. It appeared to have been freshly prepared with bedding that smelt of the fragrant flowers that filled the private gardens. Perhaps his final agreement to stay had been anticipated?

Holmes opened another screen door to find that he had his own balcony, facing the royal gardens. It was warm but a breeze blew gently into the room.

He sat down to write at the bureau. There was bamboo paper and a sharpened quill, with a small pot of ink. Holmes rarely wrote down his thoughts during an investigation, preferring to mull over all problems first, but he wanted to make a list of the strange details he was already observing.

Soon he was lost in his thoughts. Thinking of the tale that Chang Li had told him of how Danby had been found.

Danby had stayed in the same inn that Holmes had occupied and Danby's body had been found on the floor of his room by the hotel owner. His death appeared to be of natural causes, if the sudden demise of a relatively vital man could ever be called natural.

"The room was tidy, all of Doctor's possessions untouched," Chang Li had explained. "Inn owner not know what to do, but know Doctor was working with Emperor and he call us. I come and I see nothing wrong in room."

"No upturned furniture? No windows open?" Holmes had prompted.

"No. Window locked. Door on inside locked. Innkeeper have to use own key to open. Royal physician come and he look at Doctor. He say Doctor dead. He not understand why."

Holmes considered the possibility of giving Danby's body a thorough examination. Though it would be difficult without the help of Watson.

As he began to write some notes on the bamboo paper there was a knock at the door.

"Come in," Holmes called and a man entered.

He was wearing a simple black long *chang pao*, made of silk, with silver thread sewn around the collarless neckline.

"I am Hui Sen, physician of Emperor Guangxu," he said.

Holmes observed that Hui Sen was above average height, and his very slender physique made him appear even taller. He, like Chang Li, wore a long moustache that tapered down almost to his chest. He carried with him a leather bag, not dissimilar to the doctor's case that Watson owned.

"Emperor Guangxu request I take you to my room, show you Chinese medicine."

Holmes stood, and then something small caught his eye. It glittered in the sunlight that came from the balcony and had fallen under the foot of the bed. He placed the quill he was using down on the table.

"I must first get something from my bag," Holmes said.

He crossed the room and began to rummage in the bag, pulling free a magnifying glass and a small glass phial. He dropped the phial as though by accident. It bounced lightly on the bed and then rolled off the edge. Holmes caught the phial seconds before it hit the floor, in the process he also scooped up the glittering thing he had spotted across the room. He quickly placed both the phial and the item in his pocket. Then he followed Hui Sen out of the room.

A myriad of opulently patterned jars covered a wide centre table in the doctor's room. The room served as both laboratory and sleeping quarters with an area cordoned off with screens.

"You live in the palace?" Holmes asked.

"Sometimes I sleep here when Emperor need me. House is just outside palace walls," Hui Sen explained.

"What is in the jars?"

"Old medicine from ancient Chinese recipes."

Holmes lifted the lid of one of the jars. A waft of damp earth met his nostrils. Another jar yielded the smell of liquorice root. There was an array of herbs and spices and unfamiliar substances. One of the jars contained opium, an aroma that Holmes was familiar with, but he made no comment. Then he opened a jar that exuded a strong perfume   it smelt of jasmine.

"Tea?" asked Holmes.

"A herb to calm the nerves," Hui Sen said. "It contain jasmine and is dispensed in tea. Favourite with Consort Jin."

Hui Sen was helpful on the surface, but Holmes felt as though he were hiding something. The man was full of superstition and it made the detective wary of the medicinal content of the potions, which seemed little more than old wives' tale medicine. Yet, he had heard from other sources that Chinese medicine had made advances that Western doctors could only dream of. There was no evidence of this in Hui Sen's chamber, however. All Holmes saw were the makings of quackery. He was no doctor of course, but Danby was, and Holmes felt certain that Danby would have seen through Hui Sen far faster than he did himself.

The Chinese physician knew nothing of how to cure Consort Zhen: how could he with only herbs and teas to help soothe any symptoms? This explained why Danby had been brought in to help and why Guangxu had insisted that Holmes see Hui Sen's medicine. Guangxu knew that his physician was incompetent, but he obviously did not know what to do about it.

Back in his room and finally alone, Holmes removed the phial and the glittering object he had found earlier on the floor by the bed. Just by the feel of the item he had known it was a ring. Now on close inspection he recognized the gold piece, with a miniature shield, as an alumni award which was given only to the highest achievers at his former university. He had never received one, not expressing much interest in the place after his studies had ended. However, Samuel Danby had been the top in his class. Holmes recalled him wearing the ring. The fact that it was here in this room gave Holmes every reason to feel suspicious of Guangxu himself. Hadn't the Emperor declared that Danby had not stayed within the walls of the palace? Had he not used this as a reason to justify Holmes's stay, for his own safety?

Holmes examined the ring carefully. He found a purple-black stain – a dry powdered substance that was not unlike dried blood in colour and consistency – ingrained in the grooves of the shield. He took a pair of tweezers from his carpet bag, then he scraped off the substance onto the paper he had written upon earlier. An overwhelming aroma of jasmine wafted up from the powder, together with a strong and potent metallic smell that set Holmes's teeth on edge.

Jasmine was the one common element that brought some of the pieces of this mystery together, but Holmes refused to make any deductions. He knew from experience that this would not be the last clue he would find and he never made a habit of drawing conclusions based on first findings.

He sent for Chang Li.

"I wish to talk to the Emperor," he said.

"You have discovered something?"

"If I have then it is for Guangxu's ears only."

"Emperor is busy," Chang Li said. "He in meeting with Empress Dowager Cixi. Cannot be disturbed."

"Then I will be here when he is free," Holmes replied.

Chang Li bowed politely and left. After a few moments, Holmes decided that he would ask Hui Sen more questions. He left his apartment and walked down the hallway, turned right and paused. He could hear raised voices. By then he had learnt enough Chinese to recognize a few words.

"Holmes is a problem . . ." he translated. He wasn't sure, but he believed this was the voice of Hui Sen.

Then he heard Chang Li's nasally tones as he responded in rapid Mandarin. It was too fast for him to be positive, but he heard Danby's name and a reference to a medicine that would "confuse" the detective if he "interfered". Holmes backed away and hid behind one of the large marble pillars. A few moments later, Chang Li hurried past, confirming Holmes's suspicion that he was one of the men in the room. Fortunately, Chang Li did not see the detective hiding in the corner.

Hui Sen's door was left open. Holmes moved quietly and peered in through the gap in the hinges. He saw the physician opening a secret panel in the table that held all of his medicines. He extracted a jar from inside, then, with great care, took out a rusty looking powder. Another jar was removed from the panel; this one contained dried berries. They were familiar to Holmes, as he had seen them on his tour of western Asia and knew them to be highly toxic. These were the berries taken from an *Atropa belladonna* plant. Also known as deadly nightshade.

Holmes watched as Hui Sen mixed a potion together in a mortar. He used a pestle to grind the powder and the berry together. Then he extracted some of the tea-like leaves from the jar in which Holmes had smelt jasmine. Hui Sen boiled water over a small tray, under which candles burnt; he added the hot liquid to the solution and poured the contents into a teapot. Then he placed the jars back into the secret panel. A few moments later, he took the pot, slipped out of his room via a screen door on the opposite side to the door where Holmes hid, and disappeared into some part of the palace that detective did not know.

Holmes was concerned. Who was the potion for and what was the rust-like powder that he had seen added to it? Surely it had resembled the substance that Holmes had found in Danby's ring. One *Atropa belladonna* berry was not enough to kill, but it could induce sickness in the person who ate it. Holmes was sure of that at least. He had to find out who the drink was destined for and what Hui Sen was really up to.

He entered the room and opened the panel. He took out the jar that contained the powder and peered inside. He then extracted the phial from his jacket pocket once more, and tipped a small quantity of the red dust into it. He pondered as the metallic smell hit his nostrils once more. Why would it be used in the tea? Was the compound somehow poisonous?

He hurried across to the back of the room and opened the screen gently. He found himself in a back corridor with two directions to go in. He glanced left, then right. His eyes fell on a small splash of liquid spilt on the floor and so he turned right and followed the corridor down. There, he found another screen, which he opened and walked through. This was an empty antechamber of sorts. Holmes looked around. There was yet another screen door. He moved forward and slid this one open also.

He found the physician standing next to a Chinese rose bush in a small walled garden. Hui Sen poured the tea solution into the roots of a plant next to the roses.

"Hui Sen?" said Holmes.

Hui Sen turned to look at Holmes, his eyes widening in surprise. "What are you doing here, Misser Holmes?"

"I followed you. Can I ask what you are doing?"

"Please you must leave. No one is permitted in Empress Dowager Cixi's garden."

"I will leave when you explain that concoction."

As Holmes spoke the plant began to wither. "Interesting," he murmured.

Whatever the solution was, it proved highly toxic to the plant. The stem shrivelled up and wilted down to the ground, at which point, Hui Sen pulled the plant out. The roots looked burnt and black.

"This is poison for plant that Empress Dowager does not like," said Hui Sen.

Holmes could not help but wonder what the Empress would use on a person she didn't like, yet he made no further comment until they were back in Hui Sen's room.

Hui Sen openly removed the jars from the secret compartment.

"This cadmium oxide. In its metallic state it similar to zinc or mercury," Hui Sen explained. "I use this to kill weed."

"You mixed it with tea . . ."

"Easy to dissolve and get in soil. And herbs in tea keep good the soil," Hui Sen said.

Holmes listened but there was still a nagging doubt in the back of his head. This concoction was highly dangerous. What would it do to a human who drank it? His mind was still not working as efficiently as it had done in years gone by. He was beginning to wonder if he would ever regain his faculties. He knew he had heard of cadmium oxide before, somewhere on his travels in Europe . . . It was highly poisonous, but for the time being he couldn't quite access the memory of what its effects were on the body, or if there was indeed any cure.

"This is dangerous to humans also . . ." he said.

"I only use for plant," Hui Sen insisted.

Holmes questioned the physician further, but when the physician's story never wavered, he gave up and took his leave to think over everything he had learnt.

"You wished to see me, Mr Holmes," said the Emperor. "I am sorry I was unavailable earlier, but Chang Li told me as soon as I was free. I am, you see, in the middle of much dispute with the Empress Dowager Cixi. She and I do not always see things in the same light."

A guard had been waiting to escort him back to Emperor Guangxu when he reached his own rooms. Now Holmes was in the throne room once more. This time he was completely alone with Guangxu. Not even the guards that had formerly lined the walls were present. It was becoming apparent that Guangxu did not know whom he could trust.

"If Your Highness would like to explain, I would be interested in hearing the nature of the dispute. It may have some bearing on things," Holmes said.

"Alas, the older generation does not see a need to improve. They resent all things Western. I, however, know that we will not survive the future if changes do not occur. The Empress Dowager Cixi has never been quite willing to yield her reign to me. I would like to improve the lives of my people and I have been working on ways to make reforms. And, I believe I will never be a great ruler if I do not take responsibility for the health of my subjects."

"Consort Zhen's unbound feet . . ." Holmes observed.

"Yes. This is one of the many changes I wish to make. This barbaric ritual of binding must be stopped. Women, I believe, should not be treated as mere pleasure objects. They have minds, and feelings, and a great deal to offer, if only we allow them the freedom to grow."

"Your Highness is indeed very forward thinking. How hard will the Dowager Empress fight to keep things the same?"

Guangxu turned sad eyes to Holmes. "I fear she may try very hard. But this is not your concern, or anything to do with the matter that you are investigating. Though I do appreciate having someone impartial to discuss this with. But back to the matter at hand. Consort Zhen has become worse. Her breathing has taken to labouring. Hui Sen thinks she does not have long on this earth. I still fight with the idea that some sorcery is the cause. If there is anything you can tell me to help, now would be a good time."

Holmes was not ready to tell. There was still too much fog in his mind that wouldn't clear. His battle with Moriarty, even though it was now quite some time ago, had left Holmes, as he knew full well, a changed man – a diminished man. His mind wasn't the precise engine it once was.

"I'm sorry," Holmes began. "I'm still not sure I can give you any clear information at this time. I do, however, wish to see Doctor Danby's body once more, if I may? I have new information that will help guide me in the right direction in my search at least."

"Very well, Mr Holmes, Chang Li will take you there once more. But I do hope you can give me some news soon. I am fast losing hope for Zhen. She has been ... my only ally. My only friend. You understand?"

"If we were in a position to follow the methods devised by Rudolf Carl Virchow for performing an autopsy," Holmes said, as he stood before the table on which the cadaver lay, "I believe we would be able to determine that Doctor Danby died because his kidneys suddenly failed."

"Failed? But how?" asked Guangxu.

"Witchcraft," said Chang Li.

"Poison," said Holmes.

"How?" asked Guangxu again.

"See here ..."

On Holmes's instruction two guards had stripped Samuel Danby's body of his funeral vestments, then Holmes had examined the hands, arms, feet, chest and neck of the man.

Now he pointed to a small swelling at the ball of Danby's foot. A tiny pinprick. He then examined the corpse's stomach and abdomen. There was a darkening of the skin and a significant amount of bloating in this area. Holmes inspected Danby's arms and torso. Previously, he had taken the change of Danby's normally pale complexion as being nothing more than a small amount of sunburn caused by the exotic heat, but now he realized – and cursed himself for his poor concentration on the first examination – that this was no sunburn. The colour change was all over the body.

It was then that he had requested the presence of the Emperor, Chang Li and Hui Sen.

He removed the phial that contained the cadmium oxide that he had taken from Hui Sen's room. The physician was startled by the sight of the chemical in Holmes's hands, however, he said nothing as the detective held the phial up to the lamplight.

"This is a highly poisonous compound," Holmes explained. "A highly concentrated form of this could easily be transferred into a victim through a pinprick. You can see that Danby has such a mark. He also had the signs of severe renal failure. Darkening of the skin, a bloating around the abdomen, and sudden death, would indicate poisoning. Cadmium oxide could do this."

"Who?" asked Guangxu.

"Your physician is the man who holds a supply of this chemical," Holmes said.

He watched as the guards seized the doctor.

"I did not . . ." denied Hui Sen.

"What about Zhen?" asked Guangxu.

"Her condition is different and I will need to think on this further. Perhaps a night's sleep will clear my head."

"This is no game, Misser Holmes," Chang Li said. "Emperor Guangxu need to know what wrong with Consort Zhen."

"I never play games," Holmes replied sternly. "A mystery can only be solved when all the facts are present. There is still some information that I need. This requires my full concentration. And a required amount of peace in which to do that."

"Of course, Mr Holmes must be tired," said Guangxu. "The hour is late. We will talk again in the morning."

Back in his room, Holmes removed Danby's ring from his carpet bag and stared at the red substance in the grooves. He placed it on the dresser and lit his pipe, then he walked around the room, allowing his shadow to fall on the screen that looked out to the garden. He then lay down on the bed, placing his pipe on a stand beside the oil lamp. After a few moments he extinguished the lamp by blowing on its wick.

He heard a strange hissing noise. The room filled with a familiar aroma and, as Holmes lay there, he could smell the beguiling odour of opium. He took a breath of air and held it as he slipped quietly from the room, leaving a strategically placed bulk of pillow and sheets on his bed. He hoped that whoever had piped the drug's intoxicating fumes into the room had been watching his shadow move and would, therefore, be completely fooled into thinking that the detective was still in his bed.

He headed back to the physician's rooms, which now should be empty. There, however, he saw what he had hoped he would find. As he hid quietly in the doorway, a small, slender figure moved through the dark room. He waited while the person opened another hidden panel in the doctor's desk.

After observing what they did with the chemical inside, Holmes slipped away. He did not, however, return to his room until dawn, when the overdose of opium in gaseous form, which Danby's killer had tried to administer to him, had cleared sufficiently. The one inhalation had been enough to sharpen his focus, though, and Holmes, a long-term user of the drug for just this purpose, was grateful for the way it had cleared his mind. He now saw the answer to the mystery unfolding before him.

He walked into the room at first light. There he saw that his bed had been disturbed. On the pillow where his head would have rested if he hadn't left the room secretly, was a small thorn. The thorn pierced the silk pillowcase and a rust-red stain besmirched the pale cream. Pulling his tweezers from his bag he picked up the thorn and placed it in another phial where it could do little damage. Then he scrutinized it carefully. The pieces of the puzzle were coming together; this final piece of evidence told him who the killer was, but not all the requisite details of their motivation. Having found the thorn, and having seen the perpetrator the night before, Holmes had a very good idea who was involved, but not what could be done about it.

In the light of day, he returned to Hui Sen's room, opened the other secret panel and removed the jar he found there. He opened the lid. A strong smell of *Prunus dulcis*, otherwise known as almond, assaulted his nose. He was now sure what was afflicting Consort Zhen.

Consort Zhen was sitting up in bed and tentatively eating a thin soup when Emperor Guangxu came into the room. Holmes sat beside her bed, a small smile on his face.

"Zhen!" Guangxu exclaimed. "You are better. What has happened here? Mr Holmes – do you care to explain?"

"Soon. I think we must wait for Consort Jin, Chang Li and Hui Sen."

"Hui Sen will be executed," Guangxu said.

"But of course he won't," Holmes laughed. "All the man is guilty of is a little incompetence. Plus he did help me catch our killer."

"Killer? But I thought . . ."

Two eunuchs entered the room and glared at Holmes; they were followed by Chang Li and Hui Sen, who were in the company of two of the royal guard. A few moments later, Consort Jin was also brought in by another eunuch. She was accompanied by Dowager Empress Cixi. As Jin was timid, Cixi was formidable. Holmes could see the strength of will in the dowager's stern face and knew that his revelation that day may possibly drive a further wedge between Guangxu and Cixi. Even so, he had to tell the Emperor all he knew.

The eunuchs brought in chairs, where Jin and Cixi sat down. The Emperor went over to the bed; Zhen smiled at him.

Holmes took the bowl from Zhen's fingers and watched as the girl, still very sick, slid back under the covers. The mere exertion of sitting and eating had quite exhausted her, but the pallor in her cheeks was far less than it had been. Even her pale blue eyes, which, just the day before had appeared so peculiar, were now looking much more normal in appearance.

"There has been a conspiracy," Holmes began. "This conspiracy was to silence those closest to you. I can give you the perpetrator, Your Highness, but not the person behind the conspiracy."

"Give me whatever you have, Holmes. Whatever you say this day, I will guarantee you safe passage from Beijing. You have restored Zhen; this is all that matters to me."

"Zhen is your consort and, as you have indicated, has been your closest ally," Holmes said.

"Zhen has always spoken up in my support." Guangxu took the concubine's frail hand in his. "She believes in the changes I wish to make. She believes this will make China great."

Cixi shuffled in her seat. She glared at Holmes, but he was back in full swing now and could not be intimidated into silence, even by such a redoubtable presence.

"My Emperor is good man," said Zhen timidly. "He speak of many things for future of China. Things that I think will make us better people."

"Quite so," said Holmes, "and we will come back to this, my dear girl. You must rest, but I want you to hear what has happened to you first." Holmes stood up from the bed for dramatic effect. "This poor girl was not bewitched, but poisoned. It was something I suspected all along, but there were some peculiar anomalies that masked the diagnosis. You see, I don't believe that the perpetrator planned to kill Consort Zhen, they merely wanted her out of the way for a while."

"Poison, but *not* to kill her?" Guangxu said.

"Yes. And that was easily done with a small dose of arsenic, every day. Resulting in some of the symptoms that she had, but not causing all. You see, Your Highness, small doses of arsenic can make someone sick, but not kill them. A person suffering from a mild form of arsenic poisoning is also quite easy to cure. Especially for someone with ancient knowledge of Chinese medicines."

"Hui Sen!" Consort Jin said.

All turned to her because the outburst was out of character for the plainer, more timid concubine.

"No, Consort Jin. Not Hui Sen. I refer to someone with knowledge. Hui Sen does not possess this knowledge. You see, he was merely a gardener's son, who was offered a bribe to pose as a physician in the palace, and was promised the knowledge to become what he pretended to be. Hui Sen is only guilty of ambition, and a lot of naivety."

"What are you saying?" Cixi demanded. "You Englishmen talk in riddles."

"If I may speak, Emperor?" said Hui Sen and Guangxu nodded his permission. "What Misser Holmes say is true. I was once a gardener; I love plants and do still cherish them. I take care of beautiful garden for Empress Dowager Cixi . . . I . . ."

At that moment, Hui Sen doubled up and would have fallen prostrate on the floor if it had not been for the two guards that flanked him.

"Take him into the other room," Holmes commented. "Our poisoner has struck again."

"No one has had access to him since he came in room," Chang Li pointed out.

"Precisely," said Holmes. "Hui Sen was most likely poisoned this morning when given his food in the prison."

"So many traitors among us!" Guangxu thundered "I will have these murderers executed."

"There is only one traitor, Your Highness," Holmes said. "Even though I am sure they acted as a marionette for a far more powerful puppet master."

"I have heard enough of this nonsense," Cixi said. She stood and left the room. Holmes made no effort to delay her.

"Which leaves us with the puppet," said Holmes.

Guangxu dropped Zhen's hand and stood up, stepping forward in amazement. "Are you saying . . .? Cixi . . . is the . . .? But how?"

"I cannot prove that she is unfortunately, I can only help you remove those that your enemies control, and help those who are your faithful servants."

"Mr Holmes, please say. Who has betrayed me?"

"Last night someone tried to see to it that I shared the same fate as Doctor Danby. I had, fortunately, anticipated this attempt on my life and took appropriate steps to avoid becoming the next victim of cadmium oxide poisoning. I did not expect that the assassin would at first try to confuse me with vapours of opium. I am no stranger to its effects, Your Highness; and, therefore, I was able to escape my room long before my potential killer entered it. The singular quality I find with opium is that in small and sensible doses it can be used to sharpen one's mind, not confuse it. Your enemy inadvertently aided my quest. After that I went to Hui Sen's room. I had a feeling that the killer would need to obtain his supply of poison from the physician's stock. Fortunately, my theory proved correct. I saw our killer, even in the dark. There was no mistaking that it was Chang Li."

The guards seized Chang Li, but Guangxu was too shocked to issue the order for him to be removed. This gave the Emperor's envoy a chance to object.

"Misser Holmes is grasping straws. When would I have access to favourite concubine? How could I poison her? No man allowed in here until today."

"But of course you didn't. The only person who could have done that was Consort Jin. Who has been jealous of the love that her sister inspires in Emperor Guangxu," Holmes explained.

Dealing with this issue first, Holmes explained how Jin had used a beauty remedy given to her by the doctor, a solution containing arsenic, designed to bleach her face and hands. Knowing the effect the poison would have, Jin had been gradually adding this to Zhen's food.

"What Consort Jin didn't realize, of course, was that Hui Sen was experimenting also with deadly nightshade as a beauty aid. Women in Europe already use drops of the plant in liquid form to dilate their pupils: something that is considered seductive I believe. The amount in the solution was small, but it was enough to induce the coma state that Consort Zhen had suffered. And it had also affected her breathing. I suspect that Consort Jin grew afraid once the doctor declared that Zhen was likely to die. She then stopped feeding the potion to her. Am I correct on this?"

Consort Jin was in tears before Holmes finished.

She sobbed, "I only want to make Emperor spend more time with me. I hope he then learn to like me more."

Guangxu put his head in his hands. No doubt at a loss as to what to do with the girl. Her motives had been jealousy, a state that his love for Zhen had encouraged. He must have realized that he had not spent time with her recently, especially after Zhen became ill.

Consort Jin threw herself onto her knees before him. "I never mean to hurt, just make sick enough for you to notice me. I would never have wished her death. Please can you and Zhen forgive me?"

Guangxu placed his hand on the girl's prone head. The weight of his position and his responsibility to all in his household gave him reason to forgive, but it would take a long time for Jin to be trusted again. He seemed incapable of speech and so he nodded to Jin's eunuch and the girl was led away.

"Obviously, all it took was a few days of recovery for Consort Zhen's body to start ridding itself of the poison. So, what you see this morning is not a miracle that I created, but a natural recovery now that she is no longer being poisoned."

"This is all well and good but how did Hui Sen, a common gardener, even know about these potions?" Guangxu asked.

"Chang Li is the man with the knowledge. He was secretly guiding Hui Sen. But he only imparted the very basic of understanding of the compounds to Hui Sen. It became obvious to me when I spent time with your physician that he had no knowledge of real Chinese medicine. He also could not explain to me what effects the compounds he was using had on human or plant life. You see, he did little more than dispense on the advice of Chang Li. This did not stop Hui Sen from believing he understood more than he did. His use of some of these potions has been reckless, but I don't believe he intended anything but good."

Holmes took a seat in the chair formerly occupied by Cixi. There was a strong smell of jasmine left behind from the perfume of the Empress Dowager.

"I deny all charges," said Chang Li. "What proof does foreigner have to support words?"

"The proof of my own eyes, Chang Li. I saw you mixing the cadmium oxide last night. You daubed it on a plant you were carrying. A rose bush."

Holmes reached into his pocket and retrieved the phial containing the thorn. "This was on my pillow this morning and you shot it there through a reed of bamboo in the manner of a blowpipe. I suggest you search him."

The guards searched Chang Li and found a small reed secreted in a pocket of his robe.

"And as you see, Your Highness," Holmes said, pointing to the end of the reed, "there is a small red stain. This is the same substance that you will find on my pillow."

Chang Li was taken away by the guards then. He could no longer deny his part in the death of Danby and the attempted murder of Holmes.

"But why has he done this? Other than Zhen, I trusted no one above Chang Li," Guangxu said.

"I think that is something that you and Empress Dowager Cixi will have to discuss. But I suspect that this is linked to your plans to reform your country."

"We will torture this information from him," Guangxu said.

"There is still one mystery that has not been solved," Holmes said. "Who sent me the telegram after Danby's death? I have been given many red herrings on this score. I even briefly considered the Empress Dowager Cixi as being the sender."

Guangxu smiled, and then Holmes knew: Guangxu had used his presence to help thwart Cixi's potential coup. It had been the Emperor himself who had arranged the telegram. It explained the stilted and abrupt tone that the detective had always been suspicious of. He should have realized all along that only Guangxu had the appropriate knowledge of the English language in order to execute such a ruse.

"Doctor Danby talked of you many times," Guangxu said, confirming in the only way he could that Holmes's hypothesis was correct even though neither of them voiced what that assumption was.

Nevertheless, the glance that Holmes gave the Emperor and the glint in the eye that Holmes received in return revealed that a secret understanding had passed between them.

With the mystery solved, Holmes took his leave of Beijing, taking with him Samuel Danby's ring with the intention of returning it to his family, if – and this was a possibility that crept in even closer to his thoughts now – he should ever return to London.

\*    \*    \*

Some months later, Holmes heard of Guangxu's plans for a "One hundred day reform" but the Emperor's ideals were never achieved. It seemed that by the time Chang Li reached the dungeon he had already swallowed enough arsenic to silence him forever. It was never proven who had killed him, but for the sake of preventing further unrest, Guangxu declared it suicide. Thus, Empress Dowager Cixi remained free to lead a coup, which ended the efforts of the Qing Dynasty's eleventh emperor. Holmes later heard of Guangxu's death at the hands of his own guard and the unfortunate demise of the outspoken concubine, Consort Zhen.

# The Case of the Revenant

## Johnny Mains

How then, to pick up my pen and write about this last case? I do not know if it is possible. *Unsolved.* The very word makes me bristle. The person I believe to have murdered the family ... well, it matters not to the Austrian police who had me leave under such a black cloud.

I was in Salzburg when the request to travel to the small town of Huben was made. The ability that people have to find me outside of England is a little disconcerting, but as far as I am aware most of my known enemies are dead, and as the "celebrated" Sherlock Holmes ... well.

I am carried away. Watson, how I wish you were here. My constant biographer, my friend. Even Mycroft, oh brother, even your soft brain and barely tolerable company would have been welcome on this strange adventure ...

The journey to Huben was treacherous. The scene of the crime, I was told, required another two days of arduous travel, deep into the unforgiving countryside.

My body ached. My bones sang weary songs. On more than one occasion, I nearly forced the driver to return, but I was again promised that the case was so very unusual and of such a grim quality that I would never see its like in England.

There came a place where we could go no further with the carriage and horses. So, transferring our bags to a pack donkey we walked through drifts of snow for what seemed longer than half an hour; each footstep was as hard and unrelenting as the last. The snow was compact under foot; and, looking out at the bleak landscape, it seemed to stretch on forever.

It took very little time to surmise that at the pace taken to cover the distance so far, by foot, there was, at least, another three hours walk ahead. I therefore decided to battle the exhaustion I felt in my body, by firing up my mind.

"You say that the alarm was raised by a farmer. How far away are the farmsteads and why would the farmer have cause to go there this deep into winter?"

"The farmsteads are almost three miles apart. The farmer had animals gone astray; that is why he approached the property of his neighbours'. The house to which we are travelling is at the bottom of a valley. He noticed no smoke from the chimney. The absence of smoke from dwellings is not seen here during winter months. There must be a fire burning all of the time on account of the cold."

"Astute. Do we know when the farmer saw the family last?"

"About one month ago, just before this last snowstorm. We have not endured the like of it for a generation at least. There had been a little snowfall when Nichola, the owner, told the farmer she had seen some strange footprints in the snow and that the footprints were in the attic also. She thought it must be one of the children running around in an old pair of shoes."

"The reason it wasn't reported to the police, perhaps?"

"That and, as you know, it is a day's journey to raise a policeman . . . and the journey is even longer with snow."

"Illness? Then what happens if someone is taken ill and you have need for a doctor?"

"Doctor? A doctor is a luxury item, Herr Holmes. Your leg must be black and half falling from you before you would consider calling one."

"Tell me about the maids." The ache I was feeling was almost gone. My brain was molten now, discovering channels into which I could pour myself, expand, crack the case before arrived at our destination, then I could retire to the comfort of a roaring fire.

"A fortnight before the storm, the previous maid left the homestead, saying it was haunted. She became hysterical at milking time. She claimed that the goats felt it also. She said that there were noises coming up from the ground, like a slow wail from a newborn! She left then, and Caziel, the eldest of the sons, drove her to Huben. He returned with another maid, a girl of sixteen, the daughter of a shoe smith. She is amongst the dead."

"Hauntings, mysterious footprints. Is there anything you can give me that isn't tied with superstition and paranoia? Honestly, Herr Holzer, if you hadn't insisted because one of the victims had an old connection with you, I would have enjoyed other delights than these treacherous ones!"

We halted by a huge blown down tree, and rested. I was breathing heavily, relishing the feel of the hard wood pressed against my back.

Abfel Holzer, Chief of Police of Umhausen, who had been answering my questions in near impeccable English, which he had learned, he said, when he studied at Cambridge, reached into the folds of his cloak and brought out a silver hipflask, with an etching on it. From this distance, I could not quite make out what the image was and was loath to put on my spectacles in case they froze to my face. Holzer twisted the lid, took a swig and proffered the hipflask to me. I accepted, sniffing the bottle: a cherry liqueur; German. I looked at the etching. The Austrian national emblem, a black eagle, with a mural crown holding a sickle and hammer. I took a liberal taste: my throat, then stomach burned pleasingly. I passed the flask to our guide and owner of the pack donkey. The man had only spoken once, when he introduced himself as Stephan. Stephan smiled and reached for the hipflask, but Holzer grabbed it back and looked indignantly at me as he secreted it away back into the folds of his cloak.

"Too good to waste on the help," was all he said.

I met Stephan's gaze. He looked thankfully at me and fingered a scar on his neck, then glared coldly at Abfel, the most murderous of glances. There was no love lost there.

The farmhouse was nestled at the bottom of the Billundam Valley – the house surrounded by a protective circle of trees – protective in the sense that they saved the house from the worst of the winds that whipped through the valley. Without the trees, it would have been near covered in the last storm. Two of Holzer's police officers were already present. They stamped their feet and blew into their cupped hands in a vain attempt to keep the cold at bay.

The main house was flanked by two long buildings to one side, both stables, the other building on the opposite side of the house held machinery. There was an outhouse a little further away from the main house and two sheds which stored smaller tools. Three windblown trees stood at either side of the house. The air was grainy. The winters would be aphotic, impenetrable.

"When will the bodies be moved?" I asked, as we arrived at the point where figures lay. They were at the entrance to the barn on the left, the place where the majority of the bodies had been discovered. The snow was a good seven inches in depth. There had been several falls since the murders. I bent down, my back protesting, as I pushed the snow away, getting down to ground level. Here the earth consisted of crushed, compacted, rough brown stone. On first inspection it seemed that there were no footprints, although there were several faint impressions if one looked closely enough.

Holzer had not replied. Perhaps even this seasoned police officer had been momentarily overwhelmed by the awfulness of the scene of so many deaths.

I repeated my question: "Herr Holzer. When will the bodies be removed?"

"Not until the spring, when the snow melts back. A horse and trap will not get through the snowdrifts until then. However, the temperature is such that they will remain frozen until the time comes to move them."

"They've not been moved at all?"

"No. They remain where they fell. We are considering removing the heads to take them back with us for examination – you will see, that is where the killing blows were made."

Inside, the barn was well lit; several torches and lamps lined the walls. They cast strange shadows. The ground was covered in bloodied straw. My attention was immediately drawn to the body at the furthest end of the barn. Its legs were sticking out of a collapsed hay bale.

I walked towards the bale, but was stopped by so pitiful a sight that I knelt down to take in the ghastly scene.

"No," was all I could utter.

Holzer said, "She died maybe hours, or even days after the murders. As you can see, she ripped out most of her hair with her own hands as she lay next to her family like that."

I felt my gorge rise. Her fists were clenched shut, tufts of hair gripped between locked fingers.

"Her name?"

"Liza. Only eight years old"

Her eyes were still open. Her face and eyelashes were covered in delicate frost crystals. The cold stopped the smell of death. There was nothing. There was no decay; the natural breakdown of the bodies in the barn and beyond would not come until the warmer weather arrived.

But I was seeking something else, something through the mustiness of the old straw, the now frozen mould that clung to the cold, stone walls – something alien that would link these crimes with an outside force.

I walked towards the body in the bale – the body of a man – and asked assistance of the officer standing by it. I grabbed one leg and he the other, we pulled with some heft and freed the body, its nose dragging a minute trench through the straw and dirt. I asked for light and was given it. My fingers ran through brittle hair until they found the deep hole in the skull, inflicted by whatever weapon had been used upon it.

"Has the weapon been found yet?"

"Yes, it is upstairs in the main house. Where the last body, the infant, was found. Although it wasn't used on the child." Holzer sighed a sad sigh.

I had no need to ask what that weapon was. We stared at each other; even the horrors of the War could not dull the horrors here, seen afresh time and again.

The body was turned over. "Caziel?" I asked.

"Yes."

"On first appearance, one would think that he was killed and dragged over to the bale, but as you can see, there is no continual dragging of the earth. So why was he running to the bale, and does that mean the killer was unaware what was under it?"

I started moving the hay, throwing it behind me in a way that might re-cover Caziel. Once the hay was moved, I took off my trench coat. The movement had worked warmth into my bones and a sweat prickled my brow. There was a small wooden door in the ground, too small for Caziel to get through. It was frozen solid, sealed.

I said: "Caziel wanted to hide the girl, only he never got the chance. He didn't even open the trapdoor to the cellar. Liza was hit first. I can only assume, at present, that the blow stunned her for a few moments; she didn't have time to react, or shout, which gave the killer ample enough time to bury his pickaxe straight into Caziel's head."

Holzer looked surprised at my knowledge of the weapon.

"What I don't understand," I told him, "is why the killer didn't pull Caziel out of the way first to see what he was heading towards. There could have been any number of things under the hay bale." I looked towards Liza. "It would have taken three steps to reach her; she would have been looking at her brother, not aware of who was coming in behind her. But why wouldn't she be right next to him, gripping onto his jacket, telling Caziel to hurry?"

I looked across at Holzer who simply shrugged his shoulders. His grey gaze was lost in the vastness of the darkened barn.

I let the thought go, not far, but far enough to let me take in the rest of the barn. There was nothing else of real importance, apart from the sad array of bodies, of course. These would remain frozen – as inflexible as marble statues until the arrival of warmer weather. No insects would burrow into that stone-hard flesh. Not even wild animals would attempt to gnaw on this icy carrion.

"I think we need to enter the main house," I said, thanking the officer and motioning for Holzer to come with me. "And can you give me some more of that liqueur, please?"

Back outside, I watched Stephan unhitch bags with ease from the pack mule. There would be no way of making our way to any hospitable town. Even if we could walk all those long miles back to where we'd dismounted from the horse and carriage they'd have gone by now. The driver, with his fare safely in his pocket, would have driven back to a cosy inn with a roaring fire. The thought of spending the night in a house of death was not appealing, despite the public's expectations that I lived and breathed the demise of others. And whilst that might indeed be the case, I invariably investigate homicide cases with a heavy heart and relentless scarring of my soul.

We walked slowly to the main house. I steeled myself for the rest of the bloodshed we were shortly to survey. The next body was just outside the house, and snow had been cleared away from her. It was the housekeeper, the shoe smith's daughter. Abfel Holzer told me quietly that they had only found her because her hand stuck out above the snow, nothing more.

Her skin was a deeper blue than the remains in the barn. There was some frozen blood streaking down her face, but most had been washed away by the snow. Her dress was set, up around her waist, revealing large bloomer-type underwear.

"Nobody has tried to preserve this girl's modesty?" I barked. I reached down and tried to manipulate the frozen fabric so as to give the shoe smith's daughter some dignity in death, which, of course, had been robbed of her as soon as the killer struck and left her there.

Holzer spoke to two officers who were waiting patiently by the door. "Move her into the barn now with the other bodies. She doesn't need to be out here any longer."

"How long has there been a presence here?" I asked, pointing at the policemen.

"They've been here for as long as the bodies have been found. Replacements came yesterday morning. After we leave, two officers will remain with the bodies until we move them in spring."

Holzer opened the front door of the house and we stepped inside.

The carnage revealed itself as we entered the house and turned left, through a small door into what was a tiny reception room. A table was overturned and against the far wall. An arc of blood had streaked up one wall and onto the ceiling.

"This is the body of the mother, Nichola." Holzer motioned, pointing at the carpet that had been kicked up under her foot. "As you can see she slipped, trying to get away from the killer, which made it easier to strike her."

There were several other wounds to the face, the split in the centre of the forehead. Her mouth was open and it looked like her jaw had been hacked off on one side. White bone gleamed through torn flesh and muscle.

I bent down and grabbed her head, lifting it to me; indeed, there was that massive hole in the centre of her forehead, that same killing strike . . . but then why spend more time destroying the face, unless that face had once taunted you?

"What other family members have been notified?" I asked, gently laying Nichola's head back where it lay. "Have we been able to ascertain if anything has been taken from the house?"

Holzer nodded, left the room and came back a few moments later. In his hand, he held several banknotes, including high-denomination fifty Krone notes. Hozler picked up the table and put it in its right place in the centre of the room, one of the legs gently sliding against the leg of Nichola as he set it down. He placed the banknotes on the table, left the room again and returned with a small bag. Opening it, he spilled semi-precious gems and gold coronæ coins across the wooden surface – such coins, I knew, were a sign of considerable wealth. The family that had been murdered had plenty of money.

"No robbery. It appears that nothing has been taken."

"One might think that this house had been taken over by the devil himself," I uttered. "I am thankful, however, that your officers appear to possess a healthy belief in reality. They have not been taken by supernatural fancies?"

Abfel Holzer chuckled, deep in his throat. "Let me tell you a story about the supernatural in these parts. You think that the War has destroyed any notion of the strange in this area? The occult? The magical? You would be very, very wrong! You have heard of Krampus?" The man looked at me quizzically before continuing. "There was a time, several years ago, when a man of the land, a farmer, had a taste for whatever charms he perceived children to possess. So he stole the children, in the middle of the summer. This did not stop the local folk proclaiming that the Krampus, from the Alpine countries, who punishes naughty children during the winter season, was taking them in the height of summer. This seven-foot creature with massive horns and the face of a demon! It was by chance that the farmer was caught and that the bodies of the children were found, but, be assured, confusion and fear has descended from our forefathers along with their kin. I think the War will do much to dispel these superstitions, but that is still for the future, Herr Holmes."

We left Nichola's cadaver and walked through a dark passageway to the kitchen where three more bodies lay; these were of Nichola's mother, father and eldest daughter, Mikka. There had been a struggle here, of that there was no doubt, the kitchen was entirely upended; shards of pottery and ceramic littered the floor. Bags of flour had covered the dead, dampening down the worst of the blood, like sawdust on a tavern floor.

Again, however, only a single entry wound to each head, and all in relatively the same place. To have the strength – and the accuracy! – to swing a weapon in such a tight place and be able to kill, once, twice, three times without having to do anything else to end as many lives was quite a feat, which against my better thinking I was starting to . . . not admire . . . but certainly appreciate. This was an assassin of some considerable skill.

I asked, "How have your officers been living, cooking, and so on?"

"We are in the second barn and have moved all foods and provisions out into the work barn. You see, the more that word gets out the more careful we will have to be that opportunistic raiders do not visit. You saw there is plenty of cash and jewels here. There is also valuable antique furniture and farm machinery that would tempt thieves. It is my duty as a policeman to protect property here, as well as preserving the crime scene until it can be properly recorded and investigated."

I nodded, telling the man that I admired his diligence. I rubbed my hands together for warmth and then asked Holzer to lead me to the final body. The child.

The stairs were old and rickety and I had to take care ascending them. The riser was low and I almost grazed my head against it as I climbed from the last stair and onto the landing. Directly above me was an opening in the ceiling. Placed against the wall, a ladder made out of sturdy tree branches.

"The loft where the footprints were discovered?"

Abfel Holzer nodded.

"Has anyone been up there?"

"None of my men have actually entered. They have climbed the ladder in order to look inside to make sure there is nothing amiss up there, or any more bodies. I don't know if anyone else has been up there in the time since the footprints were first discovered by Nichola."

We walked down the landing, passed the children's rooms and into the main bedroom. And another so pitiful a sight.

The cot stood by the double bed, its little mattress had been soaked red. The weapon, which had been used to kill the family, the pickaxe, was lying on the double bed itself. I peered into the cot. The child, only two years of age, lay face down. I gritted myself and took hold of the frozen infant, pulling it up and away from the bedding. The noises it made, as the child was torn away from the fabric was too much. I replaced the child, strode from the room and took leave of the liqueur from my stomach, a dismal, watery vomit. If only it was as easy to rid my mind of those grim images as it was to rid my gut of its contents. I knew the memories of what I'd seen today would haunt me forever. I would, I knew full well, revisit this tragic scene time and time again in my nightmares.

Breathing heavily, I walked back into the room, grabbed the child, tore it free from the bed and turned it over in my arms. Its throat had been slit.

I held the baby close to my heart and wept.

By dusk, all of the bodies had been removed to the first barn where Caziel and Liza lay. The infant was placed with its mother – in such a way that it appeared as if mother and child slept together in peace – and all were then covered with blankets. The policemen, it must be said, were tender and respectful towards the dead as they positioned the bodies.

A fire had been lit for me in one of the bedrooms unsullied by murder and I sat on the bed, smoking my pipe, thankful for the warmth. I wondered if Holzer knew that Caziel was the father of the infant. That we were looking at not only murder, but incest. Given the serviceable mind that Holzer had, after all he was an experienced policeman, I surmised that perhaps the thought had indeed crossed his mind, but that he had pushed it out, the abhorrence of the deed too great for his stomach to bear. Moreover, his family had some old connection to the family that had lived here.

During our trek to the farmstead, Holzer had told me that Horst, the husband of Nichola, and father to some of the dead family here, died three years previously, fighting for the Polish Legion somewhere along the Insonzo River. His body had been brought back and buried in the orchard a half a mile away from the homestead.

Caziel, Horst's son, would have taken it upon himself to become master of the house, but the leap from a woman being his mother to becoming his wife? Such unnatural practices weren't unusual in this remote part of Austria. Nevertheless, the curse of Oedipus . . . I shivered to the depths of my bones.

I put on my trench coat, tapped the ash from my pipe into the fire, and picked up my candle. I walked through to the home's master bedroom and sat on the bed, next to the pickaxe. My fingers trailed over the smooth handle, feeling the notches and nicks that had been taken out of it through the years.

"Yes! Ah ... such a slow mind you have, Holmes," I said, scolding myself for not realizing the truth earlier. "Of course!"

I hurried downstairs and out into the freezing night. My candle snuffed out three steps into the cold air. It was starting to snow again. I gingerly made my way to the barn where the bodies lay. Opening the door, I walked to mother and child, and removed the already stiff blanket.

I spoke, addressing the killer in my imagination: "You slit the child's throat not because it was easier than using the pickaxe: you did it because of the pain the truth was bringing you. That *your* wife had been lying in bed with *your* son! Holzer! Holzer!" I cried into the night. "I have discovered the identity of the killer!"

"The Great Sherlock Holmes?" Holzer said bitterly, staring at me from across the kitchen table. "This, I have to admit, is too far a stretch of the imagination ... You're saying that the killer is a dead man? You're saying that the killer is the dead husband and father of the slain, driven to revenge because he discovered that his own son had a ... a *relationship* with his wife? Too much, Herr Holmes!"

Abfel Holzer looked up beyond my shoulder and saw a bottle of schnapps alongside glasses on the shelf. He got up, reached for the bottle, gathered the glasses and poured out liberal measures of that potent liquor. He took his glass, which had flecks of blood on it, and drank, refilled and drank again.

Holzer said, "The man lying out in the orchard grave is Horst. He has been lying there for three years. I have been informed by others in the valley, and by several family members who came to visit, that they are certain the body buried is his. There is proof of identity. Horst's cadaver arrived here with letters from Nichola. There were photos of the family, also. Why would these letters and photographs be found on the body of another dead man?"

"Did anyone actually see the body?"

"Holmes! This is enough! In the morning, I will escort you back to town. We cannot have scandalous rumours flying around in the air like skittish birds."

I looked at Holzer coldly. "They are not rumours when they are the truth."

I took the bottle of schnapps and a glass and retired to the warmth of the room. Sleep did not come for a long time.

"Stephan. *Kannst du ihnen hilfen*?" I shook the help gently.

He was buried under several pelts and blankets, and lying on top of a heap of straw in the second barn. I had crept in, so as not to disturb the officers. His eyes snapped open, panicked, then he saw me and smiled wearily.

"*Was ist passiert*, Herr Holmes?"

I whispered to him that he didn't need to help me, if he chose not to, but no trouble would come to him if he did. He nodded silently, and got up, pushing away the thick woollen covers. The pack mule stared at us dolefully.

We left the stable, and I motioned him to follow me. I carried a bag, taking care not to allow its contents to "chink" as I walked. I didn't want to alert either Holzer or the policemen to my plan. Behind the work shed were several lit lamps; we both picked one up each and began to trudge through the snow into the darkness. There, in the distance, an orange glow, which became larger and larger the further into the night we walked.

The orchard where Horst was buried was ablaze: flames greedily devoured branches, which crackled and roared as they splintered, sap running into the fire. Stephan looked shocked as he approached the inferno, and turned to me, shook his head, *no*, and appeared to make some crude attempt at making the sign of the cross upon his chest.

I went to my bag, which I'd placed on the ground, and pulled out the bottle of schnapps, undoing the lid and proffering him it. He again shook his head and retreated away from me as if I were a madman.

"It's fine," I laughed, speaking to him in English. "They would not have buried him deep down in the ground to begin with; this land is too solid and yields very little! That is why I came here earlier to set the orchard alight. The intense heat will burn the earth. It will crumble under our pickaxes. I might be sixty-seven years of age and falling to pieces, but the ground will yield to this old man!"

Stephan looked at me, unable to understand what I was saying to him.

"*Hier bleiben,*" I said, raising my hand. "Stay here, the fire will soon burn down and we can begin digging."

I began moving the hot ash away from the grave, sending up large showers of sparks as I shovelled them off. That done, I tied a torn strip of linen around my head so that it covered my nose and mouth. I offered Stephan a strip of cloth, too, but he was standing a dozen paces from the grave, refusing to help, shaking his head. At times, I glanced at him and I couldn't decide whether he was genuinely scared of me or of what I was doing. I fully expected him to flee back to the farmstead.

As soon as I had cleared a sufficiently large enough area to dig, I picked up a mattock and started to attack the ground with it. Several times the iron head of the tool bounced off rock and sparked. I hadn't anticipated that the ground would be so rough, so unyielding. After a while, I started to make some headway, then all of a sudden I cried and grasped at my back, falling down to my knees.

Stephan's face came to me through the ghostly light of the kerosene lamps. He gripped my arm firmly and pulled me away from the site of the grave and sat me down next to an old tree stump.

He looked at the mattock, then to me, picked it up and started digging through the earth. Like he had been doing it all of his life.

"Horst," I said gently to him.

Stephan looked at me as if he had received a bayonet to his chest.

"*Entschuldigung?*" he started, his grip around the mattock tightening.

I reverted to the man's own tongue. "*Why did you kill your family, Horst? Why did you murder them? Couldn't you have left them to continue their lives as they were?*" I stood up, my ailing back a ploy, of course.

The killer spat, dropping the mattock to the ground. I was thankful for that at the very least.

I continued: *"And whatever it was you were looking for, you've not been able to find it. I'm presuming the gold and jewels belonging to Nichola's parents? Those were your footprints that had been seen in the loft all those weeks ago. You'd searched for the money and the gems, which, I take it, were once hidden there in the loft when you lived at the farm, but the money had been concealed elsewhere at some later point. In any event, you were frustrated – enraged – when you couldn't find that large sum of money. Such wealth as that would have been enough for you to start your life under any name you chose. I should have guessed straight away, the scar on your neck, the injury – received in whatever battlefield skirmish you became embroiled in – your dislike of Abfel Holst – ah, how the ravages of war can change a man's appearance, no? I suspect you also avoided people you knew in the past that would recognize you. In other less tragic circumstances, I would have complimented you on your talent to live in the area surrounding your old home in the guise of Stephan, the packhorse man. You must, at times, have walked past members of your family in the street and they never suspected that you were their own flesh and blood. Remarkable, quite remarkable."*

Horst, formerly known as Stephan, pulled a glinting knife from his belt.

*"What I don't understand, Horst, is why you left Liza to her misery, alone in the barn like that for days, slowly dying, tearing out her own hair."*

Horst started to cry. *"I wanted it to be quick for her. I didn't go back in after I hit them, if I had known . . ."*

*"And the infant?"*

*"Spawn. Spawn of the Devil. My* son, *sleeping with* his *mother? Pah! I should have burned that place to the ground!"*

Horst rushed at me, raising the knife, intending to drive its point through my heart. The blow never struck. He fell to the ground dead before the noise of the bullet whip-cracked through the valley.

\*       \*       \*

Since returning to England, I have kept my eye on the case as closely as possible, relying on month-old newspapers to keep me abreast of the situation. The heads of the deceased at the farmstead were, indeed, removed by a police doctor and taken out of Austria and to Munich; the cause of death for all of the victims, apart from the two-year-old, was a single blow to the head from a mattock.

One of the strangest and most repugnant aspects of the case was that they brought clairvoyants to Munich to see if they could extrapolate the secrets of the dead from the heads themselves. An experiment as grotesque as it was irrational, lacking any scientific credibility whatsoever. Alas, the twentieth century is not as enlightened as I'd hoped.

Abfel Holzer was an experienced policeman. He would have not liked to have ordered the heads removed and for there to be a faux investigation, involving so-called clairvoyants. However, he asserted to me that if the truth was to get out about the incestuous relationship between mother and son it would damage the reputations of surviving family members for many generations to come. In effect, they would continue to be punished for the crimes of others. And, in such a primitive backwater as that particular region of Austria, it would lead to financial hardship and social isolation. I kept quiet as to the possibility that the rumours might already be there. However, Holzer simply wasn't privy to them; either that or he had made up his mind to ignore any mutterings he overheard in beer halls and alleyways about that ungodly relationship between mother and son. But I kept my counsel and the case remains . . . unsolved. That dreadful word again that vexes me so, and keeps me awake at night. *Unsolved*.

I have written letters to Holzer, who is, at heart, a good man, and who will bear the burden of the two bodies buried in a single grave. One belongs to the tormented man who destroyed his own family and who Holzer, himself, shot, when my own life was in danger that night when I stood in the ashes of the orchard. And that was another mystery that made him despair so. Who was that soldier, if not Horst? Who was it that was buried in the orchard three years before the murders at the farmstead? My own feelings on the matter are that the solider was a friend, a comrade, who was fighting by Horst's side when he, Horst, was shot in the neck. Horst thought he was dying and passed his personal items to his friend for safekeeping. Horst survived, the soldier did not. I cannot guess at what happened to the unknown soldier's personal papers. Perhaps they were stitched into a secret pocket so as to be protected from the dirt of war. And are buried with him.

Ah . . . you see, even though the crime will remain officially unsolved, and there will never be a court verdict that names the man who slaughtered that Austrian family, I still feel compelled to return to this case and tie up every loose end. If my friend, Watson, had recorded events, he would have deftly brought the story to a close at his point. However, I believe it is vital to nail down every last feature of this case. I crave forensic detail. I long to discover the identity of the dead soldier that was laid to rest in the grave by a family who believed it was Horst. Unanswered questions are like itchy gnat bites upon my skin.

Yet, frustratingly, I do not have the information to give the unknown warrior a name. In closing, all I can say is this: Wars are stupendous generators of confusion. They spread entire plagues of errors. Who is to say how many disfigured corpses are not correctly identified and are consigned to the wrong grave?

What is certain is that the wrong man ended up in the grave intended for Horst. And as for Horst, himself? He exploited this mistake. Everyone believed Horst to be dead – yet he lived, and he brutally ended the lives of the people he once loved.

My letters to Abfel Holzer, Chief of Police in Umhausen, have gone unanswered.

# The Adventure of the Mummy's Curse

## Cavan Scott

"Great news," I exclaimed, as my dear wife enjoyed her breakfast one cold and blustery morning. She looked up from her toast and kedgeree to see her husband waving a letter as happily as if it were the Union flag itself.

"He has agreed to come, then?" Mrs Watson asked, giving me that polite, if ever so slightly cautious, smile she reserved only for conversations about Mr Sherlock Holmes.

"He has indeed, Alice," I replied, reading the dispatch from deepest, darkest Sussex.

She sighed and returned to her meal. "So, when do you leave?"

The year was 1905. In early January, I had received an invitation to visit my good friend Charles Sprotley in Luxor, Egypt. My wife had declined to travel with me; the prospect of five days traversing the waters between Naples and Alexandria too much to bear. Dear Alice was a formidable woman on dry land, but suffered greatly on water, so her decision came as no surprise.

"You should invite Mr Holmes," she suggested and I seized upon the idea, although I suspected that her reasoning was that if Holmes were safely ensconced in Africa, there would be little danger of enduring his company.

It is fair to say that the relationship between my wife and the great detective was strained at best.

Indeed, since his retirement to the south coast I had barely seen Holmes, save for his infrequent visits to the metropolis. This seemed too good an opportunity to miss. A expedition to a far-off land in the company of the finest man I had ever met. As I sent the telegram, I prayed that he would agree to accompany me, and was overjoyed when he replied in the affirmative.

*My dear Watson*, he wrote, *I can think of nothing better.*

As I waited patiently at St Pancras for my friend to arrive, not a month later, I had convinced myself that Holmes was eager to spend the next few weeks reminiscing about old times as we explored the ruins of the Ancient Egypt.

It was pure fancy on my part, of course. Whether he felt a pang of nostalgia for our time together or not, Holmes would never admit to such a thing.

"I must thank you for your invitation, Watson," said he, as we boarded our train for Folkestone on the first leg of our journey. "A man cannot ask for a finer friend."

"Holmes, really," I said, pleasantly embarrassed. "There's no need for that. It is good to see you too, old chap."

"How wonderful of you to remember that I have always wanted to make a thorough study of Egyptian tobacco in its native land."

"Tobacco?" I repeated, somewhat deflated.

"Yes, there's a paper in this, mark my words, Watson. Mark my words."

Any disgruntlement I felt as the train pulled away from the station soon dispersed as we lost ourselves in conversation. Even though he had recently celebrated his fifty-first birthday, Holmes was as alert as ever, his advancing years only betrayed by the slight increase of laughter lines upon that gaunt face and a smattering of grey in his slickly parted hair.

His enthusiasm and vigour as we crossed Europe was a tonic in himself, banishing the rather morbid thoughts that had plagued me of late. I had recently attended a spate of funerals and memorial services for fellows I had previously considered all but immortal. Fellow doctors and surgeons had gone the way of all flesh. Even that bloodhound of Scotland Yard, George Lestrade was no longer with us. An awareness of my own mortality had crept upon me, heightened by the sad fact that children had blessed neither of my marriages. Of course, I could not bring myself to discuss such a sensitive subject with Alice, or indeed, for that matter, Holmes, but his mere presence dispelled such shadows from my mind, turning back the clock as effectively as one of dear Herbert's fictitious time machines.

From Alexandria we travelled the one hundred and thirty miles to Cairo, making use of the Rosetta branch, the first stretch of railway to be laid in the Ottoman Empire. After a day admiring a mystery that even Holmes couldn't fathom – how the denizens of antiquity had constructed the great pyramids – we boarded the Luxor sleeper and spent the night speeding towards our final destination, some four hundred and twenty miles to the south. As we trundled along through the darkness, how I wished we could see the treasures dotted along the banks of the Nile. To be so near to history was intoxicating. This was the land of Moses and the Sphinx, of the wonders and miracles that had so entranced me during my otherwise dreary Sunday school years. That night, as I dozed in my bunk, I dreamt of ancient pharaohs and vengeful gods.

I awoke an hour from Luxor, eager to see the man who had invited us to this exhilarating land of discovery.

I had first made the acquaintance of Charles Sprotley on the deck of the SS *Orontes* some twenty years before, following the bout of enteric fever that cut short my military career. Charles was an officer in the 66th Berkshire Regiment and had been invalided out when a wound to his leg had gone bad. The man had only narrowly avoided having the limb amputated from the hip, although now walked with a limp.

The second son of the Earl of Ingleshire, Charles had built a hugely successful newspaper business on his return to England, which he subsequently sold for a small fortune – some say greater than his later inheritance.

For all his great wealth, Charles remained as grounded and pragmatic a man as ever you would meet, his only indulgence being a seemingly unquenchable love affair with all forms of motorized transportation.

Charles and I fell out of touch soon after my taking up with Holmes, but our paths crossed some time after the peculiar case of the Cricklewood Golem. Charles had been keen to meet Holmes, although the detective had already thrown himself into another investigation, keen to shun unwanted publicity whenever possible.

Following the sale of his newspaper empire, I knew that Charles had taken to travelling the world, but was none the less surprised to receive his letter, inviting me to visit Luxor of all places.

*I am currently in Egypt,* Charles wrote, *having become the patron of the illustrious archaeologist, Sir Benjamin Starkings, who I am sure you must have read about.*

I must confess that I had never heard of the man, but duly read up about the fellow who had persuaded Charles to commit a king's ransom to finance a dig near the ancient city of Thebes.

Charles signed off by saying that it would do him the greatest honour if I were to consider visiting him in his temporary home. *Egypt will speak to the poet in you, John,* he wrote. *It will be an experience neither you nor Mrs Watson will ever forget. Please say you will come. I will, of course, cover all travel expenses.*

"A generous man, your Mr Sprotley," Holmes commented as we approached Luxor. "He must think highly of you."

"Not jealous, are you, Holmes?" I laughed, noticing the slight flicker in the corner of my companion's right eye whenever Charles was mentioned by name.

"Jealous?" Holmes barked in outrage. "What makes you think I would be jealous?"

"The fact that you bristle every time you are forced to acknowledge that I enjoy a friendship with someone other than the former inhabitant of 221b Baker Street."

"Nonsense," snapped Holmes, dismissing the thought. "You are your own man, Watson, as your choice in wives aptly demonstrates."

I sought to infuriate him further by choosing to smile at the ribbing rather than rise to the bait.

"Besides," Holmes continued, "I am intrigued to meet the fabled Mr Sprotley, especially as you have conspired to keep us apart for so long. I was beginning to think that the news baron was a figment of your ever fertile imagination."

And so it continued, the incessant banter of two men who knew each other as well as they knew themselves. I often wonder if I have done Holmes a disservice in my stories. Reading them back, I fear I have lost much of the humour that so characterized my friend, leaving the impression that he was somewhat soulless and lacking in humour. In reality, nothing could be further from the truth.

Indeed, as we reached our destination, Holmes's thin face was the very picture of eagerness, even as we stepped out into the stifling heat of the platform.

Ignoring the trickle of sweat that already cascaded down my back, I looked around, searching for Charles, but my friend was nowhere to be seen.

Then a voice called my name.

"Doctor Watson. Doctor Watson, it must be you?"

I looked up to see a local boy rushing towards us. He wore a long white overshirt, with light trousers tucked beneath, and a felt tarbush on his head. He was clean shaven save for a light moustache and must have been no more than seventeen years of age, if he were a day. When I turned, his young face lit with an infectious smile.

"Doctor Watson, I am pleased to meet you," he said in perfect English, much to my relief. "My name is Tarik."

"That of a warrior," said Holmes, regarding the boy with interest.

"I'm sorry, sir?" the lad said, obviously as confused as I.

"Your name. It means warrior, does it not? Or perhaps the Morning Star."

Tarik's eyes flicked between us nervously, unsure what to say.

"Holmes, behave yourself," I said, jumping to the boy's aid and holding out my hand. "Please forgive my friend. He has a rare condition that means he finds it impossible to keep his considerable knowledge to himself."

The young man took my hand and grinned. "How dreadful. Does the affliction have a name?"

"I believe Watson has previously diagnosed it as 'ostentation'!" Holmes remarked, taking my joshing in good grace. "Sherlock Holmes and Doctor John Watson at your service. You have been sent to meet us by Mr Sprotley?"

Tarik nodded. "He apologizes for not being here in person."

"I do hope that Charles is quite well?" I enquired, as Tarik indicated that we should follow him.

"He will explain everything once we get to the campsite."

"Your English is truly remarkable," I commented, as we weaved in and out of the bustling crowd.

"Thank you, sir," the boy acknowledged. "Sir Benjamin is a fine teacher."

"The archaeologist?" Holmes enquired.

Tarik nodded. "He has been teaching me to read."

A smile played over Holmes's lips. "Tell me, Tarik, have you tackled any of the Doctor's contribution to world literature?"

"I have not yet had the pleasure, sir."

I should have guessed what was coming next.

"I would not worry yourself," Holmes continued dryly. "I doubt you will find them taxing."

"Touché," I muttered, as we were bustled out of the station to be greeted by a sight that caused the colour to drain from Holmes's face.

"Am I to assume that this is how we shall travel to the camp?" the detective asked, to which I clapped a hand on his shoulder.

"Well, we are in the desert, Holmes."

Of all the sights I witnessed in my travels, none have been more wonderful than Sherlock Holmes coming face to face with a large, masticating camel.

"This way, if you please, gentlemen," said Tarik, indicating what looked like two chairs lashed across the beast's back.

"There is really nothing to be afraid of, Holmes," I said, walking around the creature to clamber onto my seat.

"Of course not," Holmes said, immediately changing the subject to disguise his obvious discomfort. "An interesting timepiece," he observed, noticing a flash of brown leather on Tarik's wrist.

The lad's broad smile faltered for a moment. "Thank you, sir," he said, pulling his cotton sleeve back over the strap. "Now, if you will take your seat."

"It appears I have little choice."

Holmes eased himself into the chair while Tarik explained that our luggage would be sent on to the Imperial Hotel, where Charles had booked us suites for the night.

"I hope that our cases will be safe," I said, recalling a report in the previous day's paper. "Wasn't that the hotel the wife of the French Ambassador was staying?"

"When her jewellery was stolen last week, yes," Tarik confirmed. "An unfortunate incident. I can find you alternate accommodation if you prefer?"

"I am sure the Imperial will be more than adequate," Holmes insisted, gripping the arms of his chair tightly. "Now, if we are going to do this . . ."

I laughed, patting our steed and enjoying the feel of its coarse pelt beneath my fingers. "There is nothing to worry about, Holmes, trust me."

"I suppose you saw enough of these brutes back in Afghanistan," Holmes commented, only to fall uncharacteristically quiet as the camel rose at a command from the caravan leader. We lurched into the air and started the long trudge to the camp, Tarik riding a camel up front while similar beasts laboured beneath heaped supplies behind us.

Holmes looked decidedly uncomfortable as we swayed back and forth.

"I'm sure they could find you a donkey," I called across to my friend, only to be sharply informed that our current mode of transport was more than adequate.

It was a relieved Sherlock Holmes that dismounted the camel on our arrival at the dig, some two hours later.

The camp was bigger than expected, a dozen or so tents clustered around an imposing rock face.

I stretched, easing a knot out of my spine, and smiled as Holmes tried his best to hide the fact that his back was obviously as stiff as mine.

Satisfied that his charges had survived the journey, Tarik informed us that he would find Mr Sprotley.

"No n-n-need," came a voice I barely recognized. "I have f-found you."

We turned to see a tall man with handsome, angular features walking towards us. He wore a sand-coloured safari jacket and a pith helmet, looking every inch the intrepid explorer.

"John, how d-delightful to see you, old th-thing," Charles said, grasping my hand and pumping it gratefully. "You have n-no idea how m-much I mean th-at."

Before I could respond, Charles turned to Holmes, my two friends finally meeting. "And M-Mr Holmes, it is w-wonderful to m-make your acquaintance. J-John has told m-me s-so much ab-bout you."

Holmes returned the sentiments and Charles ushered us into a nearby tent, keen to get us out of the blazing sun.

As soon as we were in the shade, Charles sent Tarik off to fetch some tea, but I had concerns other than quenching our thirst.

"Charles, slow down for a moment, won't you?" I said, after the boy had been dispatched. "Whatever is the matter?"

In an instant, our host crumbled in front of us, his lively, almost manic, facade falling away.

"Is it t-that obvious?" Charles asked, all but collapsing into a folding chair.

"You are obviously under a great deal of pressure," I observed, drawing up a seat beside him.

"And recent pressure too," Holmes added, regarding Charles with an analytical eye. "You are a man who takes pride in his appearance, even in these rarefied conditions. Your shirt is spotless, the crease on your trouser leg sharp enough to cut glass." Holmes threw up a long-fingered hand to take in the contents of our surroundings. "Indeed, this tent is a veritable bastion of cleanliness and order; a place for everything and everything in its place, and yet your mind was not on the job when you dressed yourself this morning, and I fancy that you did not enjoy your breakfast."

Charles looked up in confusion. "I'm not s-sure what you m-m-m—"

Charles stumbled on the word, and before I could stop him, Holmes cut in.

"What I mean? It is simplicity itself, Mr Sprotley. Your belt has been fastened upside down, and there is a yellow stain on your cravat. I doubt you even realized that the egg yolk had dripped from your spoon – and then there is your affliction . . ."

"Holmes," I warned, embarrassed for Charles, but the former newspaperman raised a hand to ward off my concern.

"N-no, John. It is f-fine. I am aware how d-d-distracting my speech is this m-morning."

"Indeed," Holmes continued. "Doctor Watson has often talked about you, Mr Sprotley, always with fondness and often with the unnecessary detail characteristic of frustrated authors—"

"Frustrated?" I blustered.

"And yet never has Watson mentioned a speech impediment," Holmes informed our host. "I can only conclude that it is a condition that you usually control, but have lost the ability of late."

Holmes paused, waiting for Charles to answer. It was true, I had long been aware that Charles suffered with a stutter, but it was so minor as to be almost indistinct when he spoke. However, to mention such an affliction in such a direct manner? Such an act was unforgivable in my view. A man had his pride, after all.

My heart grieved to witness the effort that was required for Charles to string together even the simplest of sentences. For the sake of his dignity, and the legibility of this account, I will no longer replicate his laboured manner of speech.

"You are correct, Mr Holmes, of course," he replied. "This is why I was so glad to hear you were accompanying Doctor Watson. I am beside myself."

"Whatever has happened?" asked I, drawing up a seat and placing it opposite my friend.

Charles looked at me with tired eyes. "It is the curse, John. The curse of Itisen."

The dig, it transpired, had been going well. Starkings had discovered the tomb of an Ancient Egyptian by the name of Itisen. This was not a pharaoh or queen, but an architect of renown who, millennia ago, had built the final resting places of his royal masters. Itisen's tomb had been something of a hobby horse of Starkings' for many a year. The architect's name had first appeared on tablets found in the excavations of a chapel in Luxor, but his tomb itself had remained elusive. Convinced it was nearby, Starkings had searched long and hard. "If it is found," the archaeologist had told Charles, "then imagine what secrets we may learn? Maybe even how the pyramids were constructed all those years ago."

"Sir Benjamin's enthusiasm was contagious," Charles explained. "It all seemed so exciting, to come out here and witness a tomb being opened."

"The thrill of discovering what lay beneath the sand?" I ventured.

Charles agreed. "And it was, John. Oh, it was."

"Sir Benjamin knew the location of the tomb?" Holmes asked.

Charles shook his head. "Not at first. We had a false alarm when we uncovered another tomb, a few miles north of here, but it was empty, looted by tomb-robbers centuries ago. But Sir Benjamin never gave up hope. 'I can feel Itisen,' he told me, 'calling to me through the ages.'"

"Rather whimsical for a historian," Holmes commented.

"Sir Benjamin is a man with an eye for the theatrical, Mr Holmes," Charles admitted, "But he was right. Itisen was nearby. Here, in the very rocks outside this tent."

"The discovery itself must have been quite a moment," I said.

"It was. We had been working the site for about three weeks when Sir Benjamin finally found the entrance, hidden behind a pile of rocks so prosaic that you or I would have walked straight past them without a second thought. Not Sir Benjamin. He removed each stone by hand, until he found himself at the entrance of a low passageway that ran deep within the hillside. We ventured inside, and found a second heap of rocks, piled high to the ceiling. Again, these were removed, stone by stone, to reveal a scene that no living soul had laid eyes upon for nearly three thousand years."

"What was it?" I asked, leaning forward in my seat. Even Holmes had fallen quiet, absorbed in Charles's incredible narrative.

"A chamber, cut into the rock itself," came the reply, "its ceiling no more than six feet in height. Artefacts were scattered all around – ornate chairs pressed against the wall; a bed blocking our path and beyond that a pair of large wooden doors, intact and looking as if they had been hung yesterday. In fact, at first I believed we had been the victims of some kind of damnable prank; that these doors were no older than you or I, but Sir Benjamin was convinced. He examined the lock, and declared that it at least appeared genuine. What is more, there were no signs that anyone had tampered with the device. If he was correct, no one had come this way since the doors were sealed all those years ago.

"You can imagine how difficult it was not to break the doors down there and then – but these things take time. There are procedures to follow. The lock was removed using a fretsaw and carefully put aside. Then, by the light of our flickering torches, Sir Benjamin turned to me.

"'Charles,' he said. 'Will you open the door?'"

By this point in the tale I knew my eyes were as wild as a child's but I didn't care. "What did you do?" I asked, my voice catching in my throat.

Charles smiled. "I took a step back and, attempting to keep my voice as level as possible, told Sir Benjamin that the honour should be his."

I felt like applauding but restrained myself. "Good show, old boy. Jolly decent of you."

"Sir Benjamin's hand reached for the door. His fingers seemed only to brush the wood before it swung open, with barely a creak. 'I knew it,' he exclaimed, hardly daring to take another step."

Charles stood up and gestured for us to follow him towards a table at the centre of the tent. A series of photographs were laid out before us, the contents of the tomb captured exactly as they were found on that fateful day.

"This is what greeted us, gentlemen. The burial furniture was neatly arranged around the tomb, covered in thin linen dustsheets. Not that dust seemed to be a problem, you understand. The floor was immaculate, no doubt swept by Itisen's final attendant before the door was locked."

For the first time since we'd arrived, Charles's eyes glistened with something resembling their usual sparkle as he remembered the momentous day. He turned to me and grabbed my shoulder.

"John, would you believe there was still ash in the lampstands?"

"Good Lord!"

"Ash from flames that lit the room three thousand years ago."

There was one detail Charles had, as yet, failed to mention. "And the mummy?" I asked, my own mouth dry with anticipation.

Charles's face fell at my question, the boyish delight with which he had recounted his story fading in the instant.

"It was gone?" Holmes queried, as we waited for a response.

"No," Charles finally said, struggling to form the word. "Itisen was there, even if that is no longer the case."

I could make no sense of Charles's words. "You have removed it?" I asked.

Charles looked at me with grave eyes. "John, it has vanished into thin air."

At first, I didn't know what to make of Charles's revelation. "It has walked?" I repeated dumbly.

"Or, at least, has gone missing?" Holmes suggested.

Charles's fingers brushed a photograph of a large black shrine-like box.

"He was there," he eventually said, "within a series of coffins, each more ornate than the last and all perfectly preserved. The linen – it was so fresh, or so it seemed to my untrained eyes. Sir Benjamin was beside himself with excitement, slapping me on the back and declaring this the discovery of the age.

"And then it happened."

"I'm sorry?"

"As we gazed down at the mummy, one of the lamp-stands by the doorway toppled over, its ash spilling across the floor."

"Knocked over by one of your party," Holmes offered.

"Perhaps," Charles replied. "Whatever the cause of the fall, the noise it made – the clatter. I would never be surprised to discover that the damned thing has taken years off my life."

"I can imagine," I said. "Enough to put the wind up anyone."

"And that is exactly what it did, John. From that day on, all we have heard about is the curse of Itisen."

At this, Holmes laughed. "Really, Mr Sprotley . . ."

"You may mock, Mr Holmes, but the locals in our team took fright at the sound."

"What did they think it was? The spirit of Itisen, displeased that his tomb had been breached?"

There was no humour in Charles's reply. "Exactly that. Some even turned and fled. Like you, Sir Benjamin laughed it off, telling me not to worry. 'It is merely the superstition of a primitive people, my boy,' he said. 'Stuff and nonsense.'"

"Quite right," said Holmes. "The world is terrifying enough, without inventing devilry from the dawn of time. The papers at home are full of such bunkum. Every expedition that returns from Egypt seems blighted by misfortune and disease."

"And you do not believe the stories, Mr Holmes," Charles stated.

"I believe in coincidences, Mr Sprotley. Not curses."

"Then Sir Benjamin would agree with you. He said such superstition went hand in hand with the work. Even Schiaparelli had recently suffered a setback when his workforce downed tools over some suspected hex or other."

"Schiaparelli?" I asked, unfamiliar with the name.

The answer came from Holmes. "Ernesto Schiaparelli, the Director of the Egyptian Museum in Turin. Last year, he made an important discovery not far from here, I believe."

Charles nodded. "The tomb of Queen Nefertari, wife of Ramesses II. I've visited the site myself."

"Is it as impressive as they say?" Holmes enquired.

"Quite extraordinary," came the response. "The tomb itself was raided thousands of years ago, but the murals on the wall are simply breathtaking. Sir Benjamin was less than happy that I had dealings with Schiaparelli, but I had to see what all the fuss was about."

Holmes's eyes narrowed. "There is animosity between Sir Benjamin and the Italian?"

Charles let out a wry laugh. "Not on Schiaparelli's part. Between you and me, Sir Benjamin is a little jealous."

"How so?" I asked.

"The discoveries in the Valley of the Queens are all anyone is talking about," Charles revealed. "Sir Benjamin believes that our work has been rather unfairly overlooked."

"And do you agree?"

"It is no concern of mine," Charles admitted, "but, as Mr Holmes surmised, Sir Benjamin is as much a showman as he is a historian. He revels in the theatre and mystery of a dig. If I didn't know better, I would say he even encourages all this talk of a curse."

Holmes shook his head. "A displaced lamp-stand in the dark. Are your men really so weak-minded?"

Charles didn't answer, but instead rose to retrieve a small casket, no bigger than a shoebox, from the corner of the tent. His hands were shaking as he placed it on the table and carefully lifted the lid. I peered inside to see a small clay figure similar in shape to the mummies I had seen on visits to the British Museum.

"What the devil is it?" I asked.

Once again, it was Sherlock Holmes who provided the answer. Without waiting to be asked, he plucked the figurine out of the box and turned it over in his hands.

"This is an *ushabti*," he said, surprising me again with his knowledge of such matters. "They were placed in tombs to act as servants in the afterlife." His grey eyes glanced up to note the amazement on my face. "Watson, you mean to tell me that you didn't read up on Egyptology before we left?"

"Other than what I've seen in *The Times*," I admitted.

"Really, Watson," Holmes continued. "You cannot expect travel to broaden the mind if you fail to give it a push in the right direction. Every journey should begin in the library, ideally before a single step has been taken."

"Yes, yes," I agreed, keen to cut short Holmes's sanctimonious lecture. "That is all very well, but how is this little fellow connected with Charles's missing mummy?"

"A good question," Holmes conceded. "Although if we give him a chance, I'd wager Mr Sprotley has an equally good answer."

Charles swallowed before answering. "The night after we opened the tomb, I retired to the Imperial Hotel in Luxor."

"Where we are staying?" I asked.

"The same," Charles confirmed. "I keep rooms there for myself, Ruth and Sir Benjamin."

"For when the thought of another night sleeping on a camp bed becomes too much to contemplate," Holmes surmised.

"I'm a man who appreciates my home comforts, Mr Holmes," Charles admitted, although one detail of his statement had me confused.

"You mentioned a 'Ruth'?" I pointed out.

"Miss Starkings," Charles replied. "Sir Benjamin's daughter." He paused, a slight flush appearing on his cheeks. "And my fiancée."

"Good heavens, man," I exclaimed, immediately grabbing his hand and pumping it vigorously. It was damp within my grip. "Why did you not mention it before? Congratulations."

"Thank you," Charles said. "She has only recently agreed to be my wife. A fine woman."

"And the *ushabti*?" Holmes prompted, eager, as always, to bring the subject back to the matter at hand.

Charles removed his hand from my clasp and took the artefact back from Holmes, staring at it with a haunted expression on his face.

"When I retired to my rooms, my head still buzzing with the excitement of the day, I pulled back the bedcovers . . ."

"And discovered the object lying in your bed," said Holmes.

Charles laid the *ushabti* back into its casket. "And I was not alone. Ruth found one of the damned things tucked into her bed sheets."

"And Sir Benjamin?" I asked.

"In his pile of fresh shirts back at the camp."

"Good Lord."

"It was as if they were spreading through the camp of their own accord. Every day brought *ushabti* where you'd least expect them. On tables, in our washbasins. I was even breaking fast with Sir Benjamin one morning and retrieved my handkerchief only to find one nestled in my pocket."

"Surely you would have noticed something that size . . ." I began.

"*Ushabti* come in all shapes and sizes, Doctor," Holmes informed me, once again keen to share his new-found knowledge.

"I thought I was going mad. The appearances even began to concern Sir Benjamin."

"The curse?" I asked. "Some kind of warning perhaps?"

Holmes couldn't resist but to roll his eyes at my suggestion. The expression was subtle, but I noticed it nonetheless. "You have another theory, Holmes?"

"The supposition that the unexpected appearances of the *ushabti* might be regarded as a warning has its merit, Watson, but I doubt it is the work of a three thousand-year-old spirit. The perpetrator is somewhat more human than that."

"One you can apprehend, Mr Holmes?" Charles asked.

"Possibly, although I would like to hear more of the facts. When did your mummy disappear?"

"Two days ago. Ruth entered the tomb at first light to continue making her catalogue and it was gone."

"Miss Starkings?" Holmes asked. "Not Sir Benjamin."

Charles shook his head. "Sir Benjamin has been unwell for a number of days now."

"Really?" Holmes said. "Since the tomb was opened?"

"Since the *ushabti* started to appear. Fearing that someone in the camp was behind it all, Sir Benjamin gathered the *ushabti* from the tomb and secured them in a safe within his tent. As he locked the door, he was overcome with the most terrible abdominal pain."

"Has he been seen by a doctor?" I asked.

"Only after much persuasion on my part," Charles replied.

"And the diagnosis?" Holmes asked.

"The local doctor is stumped. The poor devil is blighted with such cramps. He is doubled over in pain."

"Perhaps Watson can have a look at him?" Holmes suggested.

"I would be happy to," said I. "Is he in his tent?"

Charles smiled at the suggestion. "I very much doubt it. He hasn't eaten properly for days, but can we get him to rest? Ruth has pleaded with him to slow down, but to no avail. He is in the tomb every day, as before."

"And one can guess what the locals are making of Sir Benjamin's mysterious illness," Holmes commented.

"The curse of the mummy?" I suggested.

"A delusion that will continue until the truth of the matter is uncovered," said Holmes, turning his full attention to Charles. "Mr Sprotley, may we examine this tomb of yours?"

The relief on Charles's face was clear. "I would be so grateful. If anyone can see a clear path through this mess it is you. I am sure you appreciate the importance of recovering that mummy. The treasures of the tomb are exquisite."

"But if a museum is to purchase them, the presence of the body itself will only add to the price they are willing to pay?"

Charles looked uncomfortable for a moment. "I wouldn't have put it so boldly myself, but yes, that is the long and short of it. I did not get into this business for the pursuit of knowledge alone."

"You are a businessman, Mr Sprotley," Holmes noted, "who requires a return on his investment. I see no shame in that, so there is no need to apologize for the fact." With that, he turned to me, his eyes positively gleaming with delight. "Watson?" he asked. "Are you ready to step into history?"

★     ★     ★

Charles led us across the site, towards the ominous hillside ahead. As we walked, I became aware of dozens of eyes resting on us. All around were locals, regarding us with undisguised suspicion. Holmes had suggested that the *ushabti* were distributed by human hand. Could it be one of these men, I asked myself, angry that the ancient tomb had been desecrated? What then of Sir Benjamin's stomach pains. If this was the work of a disgruntled local, then the implications were all the more sinister. Had Sir Benjamin been poisoned?

I hoped an examination of the man himself would bring answers, but the archaeologist was not in his tent as we passed.

"He must already be in the tomb," Charles said, indicating a flight of roughly hewn steps cut into the hillside. "This way, gentlemen."

As we began our ascent, I soon found myself longing for the cool air of the tomb itself. The midday sun was almost intolerable, draining my meagre resources in minutes. My knees ached and my shirt was drenched in sweat. Even Holmes was struggling as we reached the top, where two large wooden doors awaited us. These were not the work of the ancients but constructed by Sir Benjamin's team, a sturdy lock barring entrance to the treasures within. Charles fished around in his pocket and took out a key. He had barely slipped it into the lock before a woman's voice called out behind us.

"Charles!"

We turned to see a handsome woman wearing a long khaki dress, matching tunic and a large straw hat climbing the steps behind us. "What are you doing? Who are these men?"

"Ruth, darling," said Charles, greeting the newcomer. "May I introduce my guests? This is the friend I mentioned, Doctor John Watson and this is—"

"Mr Sherlock Holmes," the woman replied, barely even out of breath.

Holmes inclined his head in greeting, although Charles's fiancée failed to extend her hand.

"Charmed to make your acquaintance, Miss Starkings," Holmes said, an amused smile on his lips.

"Likewise," she replied, her face like flint. "I am sorry, Mr Holmes, but we do not stand on ceremony here. Social niceties have a habit of being forgotten in the desert." Finally, she turned to me and nodded. "Doctor Watson."

I smiled warmly in response. "Miss Starkings."

"I was about to give the guided tour," Charles said, apologetically. "Mr Holmes is going to cast a professional eye over our little collection."

"Professional?" Miss Starkings repeated, giving Holmes a quizzical glance.

"In the field of detection, rather than archaeology," Holmes countered. "I believe you have lost your mummy."

"My father has agreed to this?" the lady asked, a note of caution in her voice. "No one is to enter the tomb without his say-so."

"Or mine, for that matter," Charles responded, a little too curtly. "Besides, your father is not in his tent."

"And the doors to the tomb are locked from the outside," Holmes observed. "Could Sir Benjamin have spent the night at the Imperial?"

Miss Starkings's brow creased beneath the brim of her hat. "I doubt it," she replied. "He hasn't wanted to leave the site since . . ." Her voice trailed off.

"Since the *ushabti* started to walk," Holmes suggested.

"Quite so," Miss Starkings confirmed, barely even looking at the detective. "Very well, if you are sure . . ."

Charles's only answer was to turn back to the lock.

"And it appears you are," Miss Starkings muttered beneath her breath.

"We will endeavour not to disturb any of your discoveries," I tried to assure her, although she failed to look convinced.

"There are gas lamps in the passage," she merely commented, as Charles swung open the door.

Our lamps lit, we followed her fiancé into the tunnel. As I had hoped, the temperature inside the hillside was considerably cooler, although much of the chill came from the eerie calm that seemed to emanate from the very rock. Charles led us down the passage in silence, Holmes at his heels and Miss Starkings following close behind. We unlocked and passed a second set of recently hung doors before reaching the entrances to the burial chamber itself. Standing there, with the corridor lit by the flickering glow of our lamps, I was convinced the others could hear the sound of my heart hammering away in my chest. It felt as if we were about to cross the threshold to another world, another time. I am not a nervous man, but with all this talk of curses and wandering corpses, it was all I could do not to turn and flee myself.

"Gentlemen," Charles said, still struggling to form his words, "I welcome you to the tomb of Itisen."

Charles pushed open the door and ushered us inside.

The chamber was exactly how it had appeared in the photographs, although many of the artefacts had now been removed. I had expected the air to smell stale, but there was an almost fragrant scent to the chamber, exotic spices from forgotten days.

In front of us, lay Itisen's open coffin, its many lids carefully stacked to the side.

Miss Starkings brushed against me without apology, as she stepped towards the large box. "We were due to remove the mummy at the weekend," she explained, as she reached the coffin. "But first we wanted to—"

Her voice descended into a choking gargle as she looked inside the casket.

"Ruth?" Charles said, rushing forward, as she began to stumble back. The lady was falling into a swoon.

"Catch her," I said, although Charles needed no encouragement. He was beside her in a few steps, and lowered her to the cold floor. I knelt beside her, instinctively checking her pulse. Her eyes had rolled up into their sockets and her face was deathly pale, even in the weak lamplight.

"What's wrong with her?" Charles asked.

"She's fainted clean away," I reported. "But what on earth brought it on?"

"I believe I know," intoned Holmes. He was standing above us, looking gravely into the coffin.

"What is it?" I asked, grabbing the side of the casket to haul myself back to my feet, my knees protesting from the climb.

Holmes did not respond. There was need to. There, in the coffin, lay a body, but not one wrapped in linen. The corpse, because there was no doubt that the fellow was dead, was that of a large man in his early sixties. His mouth lolled open revealing rows of tobacco-stained teeth, while a prestigious moustache smothered his upper lip. There was no way of telling whether his sightless eyes were open or closed as they were covered by two round, onyx stones.

I heard Charles gasp beside me. He had removed his jacket to cushion Miss Starkings's head and was staring down in horror at the body.

"Sir Benjamin," he wheezed, confirming the identity of the poor unfortunate. "Is he?"

This time there was no need to check for a pulse.

"Everyone step back," Holmes ordered, his voice sharp and commanding in the silence of the tomb.

Used to both his method and tone I did as he requested, although Charles remained where he stood, frozen to the spot.

"Mr Sprotley," Holmes barked. "I must insist . . ."

Charles turned, as if waking from a dream, and looked at me in confusion. Without speaking, I took his arm and gently guided him back.

Holmes swung his lamp in an arc, first over the coffin and then above the floor surrounding the casket.

As the light flashed by, Miss Starkings groaned, coming back to us.

"Ruth," Charles said, snapping out of his trance.

"Father?" she moaned, trying to lift her head.

Charles was beside her in an instant, helping her to rise unsteadily to her feet.

"Ruth, please come away," he pleaded, but the lady wouldn't hear of it. Grabbing hold of the side of the coffin, she regarded its grisly contents, a hand flying to her trembling lips as if it could stifle the sob that followed immediately.

"What has happened to him?" she wept, Charles holding her in case she fell into another faint.

Holmes's response was clinical, his well of compassion run dry with the immediacy of the situation. "He has been killed, Miss Starkings."

"Holmes, a little sensitivity, please!" I implored, only to receive a withering glare from the detective.

"That will come, Watson, as well you know, but nothing will be gained for indulging sentimentality at this time."

"Sentimentality?" I blurted out. "The lady's father is dead."

"Which is regrettable, but if we are to find his killer, we need to close our hearts and open our eyes."

He did, thankfully, show a glimmer of humanity when he added: "Miss Starkings, I realize that this is difficult in the extreme, and I am truly sorry for your loss, but time is the enemy of detection. If we wait to mourn, vital details will be lost. Perhaps, Mr Sprotley should take you outside."

"No!" came the lady's response, surprising us all with a steely intensity even through her tears. "I want to hear what you have to say."

Admiration shone in my friend's eyes. "Very well," said he, before returning his gaze to me. "Watson? If I may ask for your assistance?"

"Of course, Holmes," I agreed without hesitation, joining his side.

"I knew I could rely on you," he said, although his eyes were on the corpse as we approached the coffin. "Now, first thoughts?"

I looked down at Sir Benjamin. "The stones, Holmes," I said, indicating the black pebbles. "Why have they covered his eyes?"

"An ancient Egyptian custom," Miss Starkings informed us, her voice shaking. "When a body was embalmed, the eyes were removed and replaced with stones or in some cases onions."

"Removed?" I repeated, appalled at the thought. "Holmes, you don't think . . ."

Sherlock Holmes leant into the coffin and carefully lifted one of the pebbles from Sir Benjamin's face. The archaeologist's daughter let out a whimper as it was revealed that not only was his milky eye still present and correct, it was staring blindly up at us.

"Thank heavens," I murmured, as Holmes examined the pebble.

"No fingerprints," he concluded. "A pity."

"Then you believe . . ."

Holmes let out a frustrated sigh. "Yes, Watson I believe the murderer was human, not preternatural. Would an avenging mummy from the dim and distant past leave a mark such as this?"

Pocketing the stone, Holmes carefully turned Sir Benjamin's head to the left, thankfully ensuring that the second pebble did not slip from its perch and clatter to the bottom of the casket.

"What is it?" Charles asked, as I peered closer.

"A puncture wound," I reported sadly. "A knife."

"Are you sure?" Holmes asked.

"There's nothing wrong with my eyesight," I retorted. "Here, you can see where the blood has pooled beneath the head."

I glanced nervously at Miss Starkings, but she was silent, staring in disbelief at the body. She was either made of strong stuff, or had receded into shock. Maybe both, but Holmes was right. This had to be done.

"Yes, there is a wound," Holmes continued, "and indeed there is blood, but that was not the work of a knife. Look closer, Watson. A knife would leave a long and narrow slash."

"And yet the puncture is small and round," I conceded, looking up at my colleague. "An ice pick?"

Holmes's eyebrow raised. "In the desert?"

"No." It was Ruth Starkings again. She shrugged off her fiancé's embrace and rushed over to a trestle table bearing what looked like a role of a navy-blue canvas. "Not an ice pick," she said, unrolling the fabric. "But a mattock."

I had no idea what the lady was talking about, and said so.

"A miniature pickaxe," Holmes informed me. "Used by archaeologists to dig away at rock."

"It is missing," Miss Starkings reported with frustration, the canvas unrolled to reveal a large collection of small trowels and hammers. "My father's mattock. It should be here."

"Our murder weapon?" I proposed.

"A distinct possibility," Holmes agreed. "Watson, hold your lamp steady."

I did so, and Holmes leant over to examine the wound more closely. "Judging by the size of the wound, the blade would have been forced between the fourth and fifth cervical vertebrae."

I had to concur and turned back to Miss Starkings. "I realize it is little in the way of consolation, my dear," I said, trying to soften the blow of the diagnosis, "but, your father would have been rendered unconscious almost immediately."

"Yes, the spinal column would have been severed as effectively as if his head would have been removed by a guillotine," added Holmes, somewhat counteracting my efforts.

Before I could remonstrate, Holmes asked me a question. "Watson, how long ago do you estimate that Sir Benjamin was lost to us?"

I reached into the coffin and, with as much respect as possible, checked the small muscles of the man's face and neck. "Rigor mortis has yet to set in," I reported.

"Giving us a timeframe of less than two hours."

"Although the relatively cool conditions of the tomb may have slowed the process considerably."

"Agreed," said Holmes, running a finger through the blood in the coffin. "The blood seems to favour a time of death of at least an hour and forty-five minutes."

"How do you know?" asked Charles.

"Approximately fifteen minutes after being spilt, blood will start to congeal," I explained, fully aware that Miss Starkings was looking worryingly pale.

"Indeed," Holmes said, stalking around the tomb, his lamp held low. "It darkens and takes on an almost gelatine-like appearance. However, leave it for longer than two hours and the fat content in the blood will separate . . ." His voice trailed slightly as he scoured the ground, before making a startling exclamation. "A-ha! Here we are!"

"Holmes?"

"Look, Watson," he said, crouching in front of the coffin with his lamp to reveal dark blotches on the chamber floor.

"More traces," said I.

"Forgive me," said Charles, "but if Sir Benjamin was . . ." His voice trailed off.

"Should there not be significantly more blood?" Holmes said, completing the question. "Indeed there should, Mr Sprotley, but not on the floor."

He straightened to his full height and pushed past Charles, heading towards the far wall.

"The blow would have sliced through an artery. I would expect an arc of blood to have sprayed over this wall at force."

He held the lamp near the plaster.

"And yet nothing?" I asked, joining him.

"No, there is something here, if not blood." He snapped his fingers at me. "Watson, Sir Benjamin's tools. A pair of tweezers, if you please."

Too intrigued to be put out by being treated like a common nurse, I turned to the trestle table and returned with the implement Holmes required. He took the tweezers without thanks and proceeded to pull a solitary strand of what looked like silk from the plaster.

"A fibre?" I asked.

"Perhaps from the fabric used to wipe the wall clean of blood," he replied. "See, there are smudges that were missed in the murderer's haste. Whoever they are, they tried to cover their tracks."

"But who were they, Holmes?" I blurted out. "Someone from the rival expedition?"

"From the Schiaparelli camp? Why would they kill Sir Benjamin?"

"If there was bad blood between the two men."

Charles was quick to cut in. "There was rivalry, but nothing like this."

"And what of the missing mummy?" I remembered. "Could it be that a member of Schiaparelli's team stole it away, to discredit Sir Benjamin. He could have confronted them."

"Here, in his own camp?" Holmes asked. "Surely he would have gone to them to make such as accusation."

I was forced to agree. "And the fact that there is blood spatter—"

"Means that the murder couldn't have taken place elsewhere and Sir Benjamin's body returned to be found within the tomb," Holmes concluded.

A thought occurred to me, the suspicions I had felt as we walked through the camp. "The curse," I said, much to my companion's annoyance.

"I have told you, Watson—"

"No, hear me out. What if the curse is another way to discredit Sir Benjamin, or to scare him off? The *ushabti* could have been planted by a disgruntled party—"

"And the mummy stolen," Holmes conceded. "The thought had occurred to me. But to commit murder to manufacture a curse?"

"The locals?" I suggested.

"There has been opposition to our work," admitted Charles. "And Schiaparelli's too, for that matter. There are those who believe that Egypt's ancient treasure should remain here—"

"Rather than transported to Italy or England," Holmes completed. "Interesting."

"Wait."

At the sound of Miss Starkings's voice, we turned to see her leaning into the coffin.

"Ruth," exclaimed Charles, attempting to pull her back out. "Whatever are you doing?"

The grieving woman pushed her fiancé away. "There is something here." She stood again, something small held in her fingers, glinting in the lamplight. Something metal.

"What have you found, Miss Starkings?" Holmes asked, stepping towards her and holding out his hand.

She said not a word as she deposited her discovery into the detective's open palm, but glared at Charles with undisguised malice.

Holmes passed me his lamp and examined the object. "It is a tiepin," he announced. "A regimental tiepin."

"Military?" I said. "But which regiment?"

Holmes fixed Charles with a cold, hard stare. "The 66th Berkshire Regiment of Foot."

"I don't believe it," I exploded, after Sir Benjamin's body had been removed and my friend had been handed over to the local authorities. "Charles would never do such a thing."

"How can you be so sure?" Holmes replied, perched in a chair in the main tent and lighting a cigarette. "You admit yourself that you barely see the man from year to year. Your friendship may be sound, but do you really know him?"

"You could say the same about you and I," I retorted, as Holmes drew smoke into his lungs. He didn't grace my outburst with a response. I sighed, sitting heavily in another canvas seat, which creaked worryingly beneath my weight. "But why would he commit murder, Holmes? There seems to be no quarrel between the men. Charles was worried, I grant you—"

"Due to the whereabouts of friend Itisen."

"But to take it out on Sir Benjamin with an ice pick?"

"A mattock," Holmes pointed out.

"A mattock then," I agreed, my hands balled into fists on my lap.

"A mattock that was recovered from Mr Sprotley's sleeping quarters here in the camp."

Again, I could mount no argument against the facts. The murder weapon had been found stashed beneath Charles's bunk; its point caked with dried blood.

"There is still no motive," I insisted.

"The local police seem convinced," Holmes said.

"Or simply pleased of a distraction from those blessed missing gems, belonging to the French Ambassador's wife. It was all they could speak about. You would not have thought a man had just been—"

I cut myself short as Miss Starkings walked into the tent. Holmes and I rose, Holmes having the decency to stub out his cigarette.

"Gentlemen," she said, her composure as thin as tissue paper. "Thank you for your assistance."

"It was the least we could do," I said, taking a step closer to the lady. I paused as she physically recoiled.

"I am sorry, Doctor," she said. "But, as I am sure you understand, it has been a rather trying day."

"Which is why you should be resting, my dear. The camp is no place for you now. You could come back with us to the hotel."

"No," she insisted. "Thank you, but I would rather lose myself in my work."

"Surely you cannot mean to re-enter the tomb today of all days."

"There is much to catalogue," she said, her voice wavering, "plus the small matter of the mummy." She looked at Holmes with eyes swollen from crying. "I suppose that the—" she paused again to search for the correct word "—events of the morning have meant that you have had little time to ponder our other little problem, Mr Holmes?"

The woman's control was outstanding. One could not help but be impressed.

"To the contrary, Miss Starkings," Holmes said, surprising both of us, "I believe I can lead us straight to Itisen."

"You can?" the lady said in amazement.

"I need only an hour to confirm my suspicions and then you will have your mummy."

Miss Starkings tried to smile, but failed, although no one could blame her. "That is wonderful news. Is there anything I can do?"

Holmes flashed me a look. "Only entertain my friend, Doctor Watson, for a short while," said he.

"Holmes?" I enquired. "What the devil are you up to?"

"Pray indulge me, Watson. I have one line of inquiry to follow, but fear that if we were to move en masse, our quarry would flee."

"You believe that whoever took the mummy is within the camp?" Miss Starkings gasped.

"I do indeed," Holmes confirmed, already striding towards the exit. "I should be no more than ten minutes and then all will be revealed."

He made to exit, but then stopped. "One last question, if you would permit?" he said, turning back to our hostess.

"Anything," she replied.

"Your late father," Holmes said softly. "Did he by any chance serve in India?"

"In the Army?" she replied, confused. "Why no, Father was never a military man."

Holmes frowned. "I see. Thank you, Miss Starkings."

"But my cousin, Frederick, served at Omdurman."

"During the conflict to retake the Sudan?" I asked.

The lady nodded.

"And your father, was he close to his nephew?" asked Holmes.

"He was indeed," Miss Starkings replied, a shadow passing over her face. "The son he never had."

"I see," Holmes simply said, before giving us a sharp smile and pushing his way out of the tent.

"What a remarkable man," Miss Starkings remarked.

"In more ways than you will ever know," I concurred, wondering what Holmes was up to this time.

Sherlock Holmes was as good as his word. He returned within ten minutes, Tarik at his side. The boy looked understandably crestfallen, no doubt reeling from the news about his master.

"Are you ready?" Holmes asked brightly, obviously relishing the look of bewilderment on our faces.

Before long we found ourselves on the back of our camels, traipsing across the sand. Tarik led the caravan, followed by Miss Starkings expertly riding a fine-looking beast, and Holmes and I once again swinging from side to side at the rear.

"Wherever are you taking us, Holmes?" I asked, but the only answer I received was a solitary finger raised to his lips.

"Oh, you really are the limit," I told him, but could do nothing but fume as we were transported to a lonely rock face not more than two miles from the main camp.

"Mr Holmes," Miss Starkings said after we had dismounted. "I do not understand. Why have you brought us here?"

"And, for that matter," I added, "where *is* here?"

Holmes indicated for Miss Starkings to identify our location.

"This is the burial site my father uncovered while we searched for Itisen's tomb."

"The one that had already fallen foul of grave robbers?" I enquired.

"The very same," Holmes confirmed.

"But why bring us here?" Miss Starkings asked.

Holmes turned to Tarik. "Will you show us the entrance to the tomb, as you promised?"

"Tarik?" Miss Starkings enquired.

Tarik looked shamefaced, but led us up a slope of loose scree. I followed the lad close behind, while Holmes let Miss Starkings step in front of him. As we climbed the sharp rise, the lady let out a sharp cry and slipped, but Holmes was there to catch her, although her wide-brimmed hat was not as fortunate. It rolled back down the slope, Holmes springing after it like a gazelle.

"Please, Mr Holmes," Ruth Starkings called after him. "It is not worth the effort." Yet Holmes would not hear of it and returned to her side, proffering her lost headgear. She took the hat gratefully and we continued on our way.

Finally, we reached a cave and, lighting the lamps Holmes had insisted we bring, ventured inside.

Tarik once again took the lead and before long we found ourselves entering a rectangular chamber similar in size to the tomb of Itisen, albeit devoid of treasures or artwork.

However, it was anything but empty.

"Mr Holmes, you have found him," Miss Starkings exclaimed, rushing forward as we spied a solitary figure lying prone on the stone floor.

"Good grief," I said, peering into the gloom. "Is that—"

"Itisen the architect, himself," Holmes announced. We followed Miss Starkings and regarded the bound form, smothered in bandages and wearing an impressive gilded burial mask.

"How ever did you know it was here?" I asked, as Miss Starkings checked her father's precious discovery for damage.

"I did not," Holmes admitted, turning to Tarik who had remained beside the door. "But someone did."

"Tarik?" I exclaimed in wonder. "You stole the mummy?"

Tarik stared at me defiantly and gave a short, sharp nod of the head in admission to his guilt.

"But why?" Ruth Starkings asked, taking my hand as she stood, satisfied that all was well with her ancient charge.

"I believe there is another question to ask, Miss Starkings," Holmes said, regarding the young lady. "Is there not?"

Miss Starkings's voice faltered as she responded. "I am not sure what you—"

"Do not insult my intelligence."

"You?" I said, not quite believing my own words. "You helped this young thief steal your father's treasure."

"I'm no thief," Tarik insisted behind us.

"Then what do you call it?" I said, before another thought struck me. "You wanted to liberate the mummy before it could be shipped to Britain!"

"An excellent theory, Watson, but one that is laughably wide of the mark, as Miss Starkings knows all to well. The late Sir Benjamin was the man behind Itisen's disappearance."

I looked from Holmes to Tarik, rapidly in danger of losing the thread of the conversation.

Ruth Starkings came to my rescue. "My father was concerned that Schiaparelli's many discoveries were diverting the attention away from the importance of Itisen and his riches." Miss Starkings's eyes flared wide as she explained. "I had no idea what he was doing at first. Distributing the *ushabti*, faking his own sickness."

"And then he went to Tarik, with a proposition," Holmes stated.

The lad nodded. "He asked me to help move the mummy here, to this tomb."

"To this *empty* tomb," Holmes added.

"Where no one would dream of looking for it," I realized. "But how did you know, Holmes?"

The detective simply asked Tarik to show his wrist. The boy did so, revealing the strap of leather Holmes had noticed on the drive from the station.

"My father's wristlet," Miss Starkings gasped.

"A present from your cousin, I would imagine," Holmes said. "Soldiers serving General Sir Herbert Kitchener at the battle of Omdurman took to wearing timepieces mounted on leather wristlets. It is becoming quite the fashion back home as well."

"Frederick gave his watch to Father when he returned from service," the lady admitted.

"And your father wore it ever since, according to the ring of pale skin around Sir Benjamin's right wrist. I noticed it as I made my initial examination of the body. The leather had protected the skin from the glare of the sun." The detective turned to address the boy again. "Sir Benjamin gave it to you for helping him transport Itisen, did he not?"

Tarik nodded, unconsciously placing his left hand over the timepiece.

"Your eyesight never fails to amaze me, Holmes, I said."

"And yet I failed to notice a regimental tiepin in the coffin," Holmes admitted. "No doubt knocked from Mr Sprotley's cravat as he lifted Sir Benjamin's body into the sarcophagus."

The thought of Charles performing such a deed made my stomach knot.

"None of us are getting any younger, old boy," I said, trying to help, to which Holmes smiled gratefully.

"Never a truer word spoken, Watson. Indeed, I find myself increasingly concerned about my mental faculties. After all, I should have realized immediately that Mr Sprotley was innocent."

"He is?" I asked, hope welling in my chest.

"I am an old fool, Watson. I see a belt worn upside down and conclude that its wearer was not paying attention when dressing."

"What are you saying, Holmes?"

"Or assume that a man's stutter has been brought about by a guilty conscience. Tell me, Miss Starkings, is your fiancé a religious man?"

Sir Benjamin's daughter gave the merest of shrugs. "I am not sure."

"Watson?" Holmes asked, turning his question to me.

"I believe Charles comes from a Catholic family, although whether he's devout himself is—"

"Largely unimportant," Holmes interrupted. "Yet, his upbringing is not. Many of a religious temperament consider the state of being left-handed ungodly, analogous of the goats that will be cast to the left on the Day of Judgement."

"But Charles is right-handed," Miss Starkings insisted.

"Is he?" Holmes asked. "Or was he forced as a child to favour the right hand? Struggling to write, with his left arm tied behind his back. The trauma of overcoming one's nature is enough, I would suggest, to bring up a speech impediment, easily controlled later in life, but liable to reassert itself during times of stress."

"And the belt?" I asked.

"A common mistake of the left-handed, whether they have been trained to use the right hand or not. In fact, even after such torture as a child, true left-handers still favour their dominant side during extreme circumstances – such as the act of committing murder."

All at once, I realized what Holmes was saying. "The mattock wound. It was on the left—"

"And therefore, delivered by a right-handed assailant," said Holmes, completing my thinking.

"But if not Charles, then who?" Ruth Starkings asked, looking Holmes straight in the eye.

"Who indeed?" my friend responded, moving across to the mummy on the floor.

"No, don't touch him," Miss Starkings snapped, stepping forward to stop the detective, but it was too late. Holmes was on his knees and running his hands across the mummy's bound chest.

"Did you know, Watson," Holmes commented, as he worked a long finger beneath a length of mouldering bandage, "that the embalmers of Thebes inserted charms between the layers of cloth while wrapping a corpse?"

Miss Starkings did not give me time to answer. "You'll damage it," she insisted.

"However, I doubt," Holmes continued, "even considering the great wealth of the Upper Kingdom, that they ever buried such trinkets as these."

He drew out his fingers, bringing with them a gold chain.

"Good heavens," I exclaimed, as Holmes rose to his feet, the chain dangling like a stage magician ready to place a member of the audience under hypnosis. At the bottom of the chain swung an emerald the like of which I had never seen.

"I am sure the French Ambassador would be fascinated to learn how his wife's jewels came to be in the possession of a man who has been dead for three thousand years," Holmes said, returning the defiant gaze of Sir Benjamin's daughter. "Would you like to recover the rest of your loot, or shall I?"

"I owe you my thanks, Mr Holmes," said Charles, raising his glass. Holmes lit another cigarette and added to the already smoky atmosphere of the Imperial's opulent lounge.

"Not at all, my dear fellow," the detective remarked. "I am only sorry that you had to endure incarceration before we discovered the true perpetrator."

Charles took a deep pull on his whisky, before staring into the liquid, lost in his thoughts. I exchanged a look with Holmes, who indicated that we should wait for Charles to recover before continuing the conversation. We sat in silence, enjoying the hubbub of the hotel, until Charles was ready to rejoin the conversation.

"I knew she was far from happy, with our engagement, I mean," he finally commented, placing the glass down on the table in front of him.

"It was arranged by Sir Benjamin?" Holmes enquired.

Charles took no offence at the directness of the question. "Let us say that he encouraged it, and I had no complaints. I thought her a fine woman and I hoped she would grow to love me."

"As you loved her?" I asked.

He gave a sad smile. "It is academic now. She was happy to see me rot in an Egyptian jail for a murder that she committed."

I took a sip of brandy. "Her own father," I said, shaking my head.

"At least we know that the murder was not premeditated," Holmes offered.

"We do?" Charles said. His speech impediment had diminished, but I doubted the sadness in his voice would vanish so quickly.

"You heard her testimony," I reminded him. "Miss Starkings had hidden the gems she had stolen within the mummy."

"Only for the mummy itself to vanish, as part of her father's theatrics," Holmes added.

"I realize all that," Charles said, "but to kill her father?"

"A crime of passion," said Holmes, taking another draw on his cigarette. "When she discovered what Sir Benjamin had done, she confronted him in the tomb. Father and daughter argued and, desperate to retrieve the plundered riches she hoped would finance her escape from an unwanted engagement, she threatened Sir Benjamin with his own mattock."

"We have seen it so many times," I agreed. "A moment of madness, temper overriding sanity."

"And she struck," said Holmes, "delivering a blow she hardly expected herself."

"That is all very well, Mr Holmes," said Charles, "but she had the presence of mind to lift the body into the coffin."

"Or he fell into the grave, as it were," said I.

"Either way, to place the stones over his eyes?"

"Theatrics must run in the family," Holmes conceded. "Although that does not forgive the coldness of locking the tomb and running to your tent to retrieve the tiepin that would incriminate her own fiancé."

"How she must have hated me," Charles said, reaching for his drink once again.

"By the look of her face as she was arrested," I said softly, "I would think that her hate for herself is greater still."

"Or at least that she is disappointed that her plan to smuggle the gems back to civilization has been foiled," Holmes said, seemingly unaware that I was attempting to comfort my friend.

"But how did you know?" Charles asked.

"That Miss Starkings was guilty?" Holmes asked, extinguishing the cigarette in a marble ashtray. "The blood was wiped from the walls of the tomb by a silk cloth, at least according to the solitary fibre snagged in the plasterwork. When Miss Starkings lost her hat, I noticed that the sun's rays had bleached the brim, while the crown retained its original colour. Until recently it had evidently been covered."

"You are right," Charles exclaimed. "Ruth usually wears a scarf pinned around the crown."

"A silk scarf she removed in a hurry, according the stitching it left behind. I must admit that I had yet to make the connection to the missing gems, but when we found the missing mummy—"

"She rushed straight over and checked that they were still in place," I realized.

"Very good, Watson," Holmes acknowledged. "I see that years together have not been a complete waste of your valuable time."

"Not at all, Holmes."

"Her examination of the mummy focused on its chest, as if she was searching for something. The young lady is a fine actress, as her performance beside the coffin bears witness, but even she could not disguise her relief when she realized the gems were still there."

"And what of the expedition?" I asked, keen to steer the conversation away from Miss Starkings's crimes.

A determined look crossed Charles's ashen face. "We continue, in honour of Sir Benjamin's memory. He deserves that as much. The world shall see Itisen and his treasures. It will be Sir Benjamin's legacy."

Helped by the scandalous events that surrounded the discovery of the mummy, I thought to myself. The papers would have a field day. Starkings would be proud.

The sight of Tarik entering the lounge interrupted my musings. He spotted us immediately and made a beeline for Holmes.

"Hello there," Holmes said, greeting the youth with more warmth than any of us expected.

"Mr Holmes," Tarik acknowledged. "Doctor. Mr Sprotley."

"Tarik, very soon Watson and I will be returning to England—"

"Although, I wish you would stay," Charles cut in.

"Unfortunately, that will not be possible," Holmes insisted. "Mrs Watson would never forgive me if I kept her husband from her a moment longer. However, I have a parting gift for you, young man."

Tarik looked as surprised as the rest of us. "Me, sir?"

Holmes reached down beside his seat where he had concealed a small package, tied neatly with string. Without another word, he gave it to the Egyptian lad and watched with amusement as Tarik carefully removed the brown paper.

"A book," I exclaimed, when the nature of the gift was revealed.

"And not just any book," Holmes insisted.

Tarik turned the volume over in his hands and read the title on the spine: "*The Adventures of Sherlock Holmes*, by Doctor John H. Watson."

"Good heavens," I said, completely astounded.

"I always carry a copy while I travel," Holmes explained, reaching for his cigarette case, "and I'm sure Watson can provide me with a replacement. Now, you can complete your education, although try to forgive my associate for some of his more purple prose. The good Doctor does have a habit of getting carried away when a pen is in his hand."

Tarik beamed and expressed his gratitude, which Holmes waved away. "Think nothing of it. Indeed, you are doing me a favour."

"Eager to be rid of it, I suppose." I bristled at the implication.

Holmes struck a match to light his cigarette. "Not at all, my dear Watson. I am merely gratified that I am leaving a treasure of my own on Egyptian soil."

# The Case of the Lost Soul

## Paul Kane

### 1.

Greater and more qualified minds than mine have spent life-times pondering and debating the notion of what makes a human soul. What it is that actually makes us the person we are. Is it our upbringing, our environment, our experiences ... or something more, something spiritual that we cannot define? It was once believed that the heart is the vessel for the human soul. Science insists that it begins and ends with the brain. But, as I grow older, and especially since witnessing the dramatic events of the case I am about to elaborate upon, I have found my thoughts turning time and again to this particular and singular topic. Indeed, more and more of our cases in the run-up to the new century and in the years since its turn – some of which I have not had the heart to set down on paper yet – have forced me to question my own beliefs about the realities and absolutes of this world. Even the time I spent serving my country in foreign climes could not have prepared me for such an adventure as the one I am about to relate to you, dear reader.

It all began on an autumnal morning when I arrived back at the lodgings I share with my friend and companion of more than thirty years, Sherlock Holmes, after attending my morning surgery. Of late, I have limited the number of patients I have on my books, not only due to my work with Holmes, but also because I am not as young as I once was. Although, I have to say, both myself and Holmes remain in fine physical condition for our age and in spite of our many ordeals; we would certainly give someone half our age a run for their money . . . or at least I should like to think so.

In any event, I arrived back expecting to take luncheon with Holmes – prepared, as always, by our wonderful housekeeper Mrs Hudson. (I really do not know what we would do without her; at times she is more like a surrogate mother to us both, and it is comforting to know that whatever life might present, the one thing we can rely on is a welcoming pot of Mrs Hudson's tea.) My plans for dining, however, would have to be postponed, for upon alighting from my cab, I witnessed a couple standing outside our residence, looking up. The lady, who sported delicate features and wore a navy dress and jacket, seemed more hesitant and unsure than the man, himself only a foot or so taller than the woman, older than she (closer to my age in fact) and thin, with an angular face. It was not the first time I had observed potential clients loitering on our doorstep, or across the way on the pavement opposite. Often, I have learned, people find it hard to ask for aid, even in the direst of times.

When they noticed my presence, and that I was bound for the same destination, I doffed my hat and said: "May I be of assistance?" I was vague enough so as to not cause any undue anxiety – or to frighten off anyone who may be in need of our services.

"This is the residence of Mr Sherlock Holmes," said the man in a deep voice. It was more a statement than a question, for he knew full well that the great detective was to be found within its walls. The woman, saying nothing, simply cast her eyes from her companion to myself and back again.

"Indeed it is." I held out my hand. "Dr John Watson, at your service."

His grip was firm, overly so in fact – perhaps to show that his visit was a serious one, or to compensate for an occupation that was not so physical in nature (over the years I have done my best to study Holmes's methods, though I have come not even close to his levels of deductive reasoning). "I wonder if we might see him." Again, it was not really a question and there was a forcefulness to his tone that betrayed his urgency. Neither offered me their names, but that is not unusual when dealing with matters of the utmost delicacy. I nodded, knowing that all would probably be revealed once we were in the company of Holmes.

I entered first, greeting Mrs Hudson and leaving her to see to the couple's outer garments, while I climbed the stairs to Holmes's study – paving the way for their "appointment".

I needn't have bothered, of course.

Holmes being Holmes, he already knew we had visitors. That keen hearing of his showed no signs of waning yet.

"Please, Watson," he told me from his chair, "deliver the lady and gentleman in question to me. And have Mrs Hudson prepare a fresh pot of tea."

I had to smile a little at that; if I wasn't to partake of lunch then Mrs Hudson's tea – and more than likely a plate of her delicious scones – would keep me going a little while, and simultaneously help to calm the nerves of our guests.

I had assumed that my couple were man and wife, simply by the way he appeared to be escorting her to Holmes's abode. But, as Holmes ably demonstrated when they took their places on the sofa, he was indeed my superior when it came to such guesswork.

"Mr Holmes, my name is—"

"Mr Wakefield, of Pattison & Wakefield," Holmes interrupted, standing and striding to the fireplace. There was that look of confusion, the one I was so used to seeing upon our clients' first encounters with Holmes: mouth open, stunned silence. "And this must be Mrs Pattison, widow of the late Arnold Pattison – who was your partner in the international shipping business you own, and best friend since childhood."

Now it was the lady's turn to stare, uncomprehending.

Finally, Mr Wakefield found his voice, though it lost some of its deepness as he answered. "Why, that is absolutely correct. But I sent no word beforehand, how could you possibly . . .?"

Holmes took out his cigarettes and promptly lit one, clouding himself in smoke for a moment. "It is presumably because of these talents that you sought me out, Mr Wakefield. But if I must furnish you with an explanation, so be it." He leaned an elbow on the mantelpiece and continued to smoke as he enlightened us. "The first clue is your accent, traces of American, French, German – the mark of someone well travelled, who deals with clients from around the world. The second was your smell, sir: a distinctive aroma, that certain stretch of The Pool. One blended on this occasion with that of a certain purveyor of penny pies, muffins and crumpets well known to me, who sets out his stall not a stone's throw, I believe, from your main offices. You hastily partook of his wares this morning – there are even traces of the muffin crumbs on your lapel – having worked through the night once more . . . A necessity, I imagine, brought about due to the loss of said partner; though the sleeplessness evident by your bloodshot eyes and the distinctive darkening around them is not wholly owing to such labours. I can also tell from the slight wincing and involuntary touching of the stomach that what you did manage to consume of your 'breakfast' did not sit well with you – nothing to do with the quality of it, but more the result of your unsettled condition."

Even I was impressed by that, though Holmes's talk of muffins and pies did nothing to dampen my hunger. I was therefore delighted when Mrs Hudson knocked and then entered with her tea and scones, one of which never even made it to the table.

Continuing after the interruption, Holmes said: "As for your connection to Mrs Pattison, I could tell from the body language, as it were, of both parties that there were no romantic ties – although it is obvious you have known each other for no small amount of time. Long enough, in fact, for the lady to listen to you about venturing here today, against her better judgement. Therefore, it seems obvious to me that this must be the spouse of your recently departed business partner, one I should add that I read about in the business section of paper just last month, Mr Pattison having passed away quite suddenly of heart failure."

I waited a moment or two and, when it looked like our guests were not going to ask the remaining question, then I did: "And how did you know about Mr Wakefield and Mr Pattison's long-standing friendship? The paper again?"

Holmes shook his head. "Business partnerships of the likes of Pattison & Wakefield's tend to be founded on deep-seated friendships, otherwise they do not last very long – and they are unquestionably not as successful. Most of the firmest friendships begin at school, Watson."

"Ours didn't," I reminded him and he flashed me one of his tight, controlled smiles.

With all that out of the way, I suggested that Mr Wakefield and Mrs Pattison tell us about the problem that had brought them to our door this day.

It was Wakefield who again took the lead. "I was not sure whether to bother you at all with this," he told Holmes. "In the cold light of day such things seem so . . . ridiculous."

"Yet here you are," said he, not meaning to sound dismissive – only to emphasize that the man was present regardless. In all these years Holmes's abrupt manner has not softened any. "Pray continue."

Wakefield nodded. "There have been . . . well, I do not know how else to put it . . . there have been *sightings*," he said, turning to look at me as I settled in a chair not far away.

"What sort of sightings?" I asked.

He paused before answering, bluntly. "Sightings of Mr Pattison."

"The *deceased* Mr Pattison?"

Wakefield nodded. "At first I dismissed them as nonsense. Two members of an exclusive club Arnold and I used to frequent – a place I have not had the heart to return to since his passing – claimed to have seen him late one night upon their leaving. He was on the street outside, but they were so shocked that by the time they came to their senses and went after him he was gone. Naturally, when I heard of this, I put it down to a mixture of grief and large amounts of brandy."

I frowned, looking over at Holmes for some sort of reaction. Typically, he gave none. "And . . . and have others experienced these sightings?"

Another nod. "I have heard rumours that some of our work-force on the docks have seen . . . something . . . early in the morning, long before dawn."

"This 'something' being Mr Pattison?" Holmes pressed.

A further nod.

"Then please, Mr Wakefield, be *specific*," my friend said, inhaling more smoke. "I cannot possibly help if you are not."

"Then yes. It took some coaxing out of them and, in one instance the threat of dismissal, however that is what they maintain. They saw the late Mr Pattison." Wakefield looked sideways at Mrs Pattison.

"But that's not all, is it?" I prompted.

Wakefield sighed. "No. Apparently, he was spotted in the grounds of the Pattison family home, by the groundskeeper, no less, as he woke in the middle of the night. "

"*And* by Mrs Pattison," Holmes stated, turning his intense scrutiny upon the widow, who had tears forming in her eyes.

She gave a nod herself now and collapsed forward, howling. I rushed to her, bringing out my handkerchief, which she accepted gratefully, stemming the flood of saltwater as best she could.

"I thought I was imagining him," Mrs Pattison blurted out and it was actually a surprise to hear her speak. "That . . . that if I spoke of such things, Arnold might never return."

I could sympathize with the poor woman; even now, what might I give for just a glimpse of my beloved wife Mary.

"Mrs Pattison . . . Barbara . . . only informed me of those sightings recently," Wakefield confirmed.

"After you yourself had seen this . . . apparition," Holmes said to him.

"How did you . . .?" began Wakefield.

"You saw him outside your offices. And that's the *real* reason you were there again all night last night, and the past few nights, I'll warrant." Holmes flicked his ash into the hearth, and shifted position. "Hence the redness of your eyes from lack of sleep. You maintained a vigil."

"I . . . yes, I suppose I was hoping to see him again – if nothing else to confirm that I did the first time – but it was not to be. At first I thought I'd fallen asleep, that I was simply dreaming about my old friend; however, he was so clear to me; pale, yes, but dressed in the suit he always wore. The suit he was *buried* in. Only . . . only his shoes appeared quite worn." Wakefield shook his head. "He was looking up at me through my office window, but by the time I reached the ground level, he had vanished."

Holmes finished off the cigarette and tossed it into the flames of the fire beside him. He stood for a moment with a finger touching his lips, then said: "If you are in search of a ghost-finder, then you might find a man of our acquaintance more useful, a fellow by the name of Carnacki?"

Wakefield gave a louder sigh. "Mr Holmes, I do not believe in ghosts – and, if what I have heard of you is to be believed, then neither do you! My friend is dead." This initiated more wailing from Mrs Pattison, but Wakefield pressed on. "I know that. Someone is playing a cruel trick on us, perhaps someone who wishes to sabotage our business? I cannot offer any explanations, which is why I am . . . *we* are here."

Holmes thought for a moment or two. "Very well, then if you both concur . . ." He waited as Wakefield gave one final, eager nod, while Mrs Pattison – still very distressed – followed suit. "Then we shall begin our investigation and report back when we have any findings."

Once they had departed, with the promise that we would do all that we could to clear the mystery up, I asked Holmes what *he* thought was going on. "Mass hallucination perhaps? Hypnosis? Drugs? Or is Pattison actually still alive?"

"There is only one way to find out about the latter, Watson," he informed me, with a twinkle in his eye. "You had best fill up on Mrs Hudson's scones, for we have work to do – and we must begin immediately."

## 2.

Our quest to establish whether Mr Arnold Pattison was deceased involved a trip to the physician who attended to him upon his demise, a colleague I knew through reputation alone; a doctor of good standing by the name of Reynolds. He told us that the man's "heart simply stopped working" – no sign of anything untoward that he could determine. Not the most unusual death I have ever heard of, but Pattison had apparently been in fine fettle, just like Holmes and myself. It gave one pause for thought, if I'm honest.

Our next port of call was the Pattison family plot in a relatively isolated part of Camberwell Old Cemetery, where Arnold Pattison had been interred in an elaborate stone crypt, angels standing guard at each corner. In order to remain inconspicuous, we had both donned muted clothing; dark jerseys and trousers that would afford some cover in the twilight.

"Would it not have been wiser to go through the proper channels?" I asked of Holmes, as he busied himself with the heavy locks on the outside of the crypt.

"That would take too long," he informed me, pointing at the darkening sky. "The cold light of day is rapidly diminishing, Watson!"

"I have to say, I never saw myself as Burke or Hare," I protested, glancing over my shoulder, but Holmes wasn't listening to me. He was opening the door, locating Pattison's coffin, and bidding me to help him carefully remove the lid. And there the man was: white-faced, eyes closed. He looked to have been embalmed, for he had a waxy sheen to his skin and there had been little or no decay. As Holmes held up a lamp, I gave him a cursory examination – all I could do under the circumstances – but, when I was finished, I declared that, yes, Mr Arnold Pattison was indeed quite dead. For one thing, he was stone cold.

Holmes nodded and we replaced the coffin lid. We then left and closed the door behind us.

"So?" I asked, hoping for more information.

"You said it yourself, Watson: Mr Pattison is dead, just as Wakefield acknowledged."

"Then what are you suggesting – that the eyewitnesses *have* been seeing his spirit? Wandering around his old haunts?" I realized what I'd just said and balked at my unintentional pun. "Visiting familiar places like some kind of . . . . of lost soul?"

"Wandering, yes. But, like Wakefield, I still do not believe we are dealing with a shade here."

"All right . . . then what?" I snapped my fingers. "Ha! You suspect some sort of lookalike, then? A long-lost relative, perhaps, bearing a resemblance? Or someone made up to look like the deceased? It would have to be good to fool the likes of Wakefield and Pattison's wife." Then again, I have seen Holmes, himself, adopt many disguises over the years; it was not inconceivable that these so-called sightings were down to mere theatrics, to an actor taking on the part. "For the purposes of driving those left behind into some form of crazed state?" I added. "A revenge, as Wakefield suggested?"

Holmes said nothing.

"And our next step? To patrol those areas where 'Pattison' – or whoever he is – might be seen again?"

Once more, my friend remained silent.

"Holmes?" I urged. "What next?"

"We wait," he informed me.

"Wait? But for what?"

Darkness had fallen fully by this time and we were still in the cemetery, not a place I particularly relished spending much time in – or, for that matter, getting caught in. Fortunately, we did not have to wait long . . .

From our hiding place, Holmes having ushered me behind a nearby tree, I heard a noise, which appeared to emanate from the direction of Pattison's crypt.

"Observe," whispered Holmes.

And I did so, watching as the door to the crypt open wide. I looked at Holmes, bewildered, and he held up the locks that he had pocketed just moments ago. Then there he was again: Mr Arnold Pattison, as "large as life", leaving his crypt. A dead man walking. He moved out of sight behind a line of bushes.

"I don't understand . . . but how?" I asked Holmes, somewhat inarticulately. "You saw him yourself, he was . . ."

"You have been wrong before about this kind of thing," my friend reminded me. "Have you forgotten already about that business with Lord Blackwood and his toxin derived from the nectar of the rhododendron?"

But that had been a different kettle of fish altogether; for one thing, Pattison had been dead more than a month already when I cast my eyes over him. Yet here he was, as large as life . . . or whatever passed for it where he was concerned.

"Come with me," said Holmes, "he must not be allowed to leave."

I followed my friend around the bushes, then watched in astonishment as he stood in front of Pattison and halted the fellow. The former businessman simply gazed at Holmes, unblinking, mouth open, as if my friend had baffled him with one of his leaps of logic. I joined them, calling Pattison's name to see if he would react; he did not. Then I clicked my fingers close to his ear, and waved a hand in front of his face. Nothing again. I even felt his wrist for a pulse, the skin still clammy to the touch. There was none . . . but how was that even possible?

"Here, help me get him back inside," Holmes said to me. Pattison was definitely solid, as I now felt for myself, but easily directed back into his "lair". Holmes replaced the locks he'd taken, fastening them tightly. "It is the only reason the sightings have stopped," he explained. "See here." He pointed to a set of marks on the door and the side of the crypt. "The locks have been replaced, and did you not wonder why there were more than one now?"

"I assumed to keep people out."

"Rather to keep Mr Pattison *in*."

I shook my head. It was impossible, the stuff of fantasy: the dead coming back to life and breaking out of their final resting places, as if there was no more room in Heaven . . . or Hell. What was to stop the rest of the graveyard rising up right now and roaming the Earth?

"This was done *to* Mr Pattison," Holmes said, as if reading my mind. "Note the shoes, polished rather than worn – replaced, Watson, after his wanderings. An unusual crime, it is true, but a crime nonetheless."

"Unusual? How about impossible?" I spluttered.

But again he wasn't listening, he was gazing off into the distance – then suddenly became animated. "Come, Watson, there is work to do!"

"We . . . we cannot just leave him in there like that," I protested, jabbing a finger back at Pattison's crypt.

"There is nothing we *can* do for him at present, and he will be safe enough, assuming he does not break out again. Above all else, it is imperative that whoever did this believe he is still contained."

"But what . . ."

Holmes held up the lamp, regarding me seriously. "There is much I need to confirm, but if I am correct then this business is larger than first imagined. And we may well have a very long journey ahead of us, Watson!"

And with that he strode off into the dark cemetery, leaving me to trail after him.

### 3.

Those confirmations saw us departing on one of Wakefield's ships the very next day, with the man himself in tow. The journey would take more than a week, but was essential – Holmes promised – if we were to help poor Mr Pattison and quite possibly prevent more people from suffering a similar fate.

I had been sent back to Baker Street to pack "for somewhere with a more temperate climate than our own" (rest assured, it was not our first trip abroad) while Holmes went off alone, as he often did.

"Meet me later at the offices of Pattison & Wakefield," he'd told me before disappearing.

It was there, at the offices, that Holmes finally informed me of our destination, having checked the shipping manifests of the company and visited an expert in botany he was acquainted with at the Museum of Natural History.

"To solicit his opinion on this," said Holmes, holding up what looked like part of a dried-up leaf and flower. "I discovered it in the crypt while you were examining Pattison . . . My contact has verified my suspicions that it does indeed belong to the *Datura stramonium*, also known as the Devil's Snare. This particular variety is local to the Caribbean, or more accurately the western portion of the island of Hispaniola, in the Greater Antillean archipelago."

"And?" I said, eager for the rest.

"Pattison & Wakefield have their fingers in many pies, but one of their suppliers happens to be a company called the Helios Corporation – named after the Greek god of the sun, obviously – based in that exact location, trading in sugar and other local goods. Pattison & Wakefield receive shipments from there on a very regular basis."

"So you think whatever did this to him might have originated from there?"

"Whatever or whoever," Holmes clarified. "Perhaps someone working in conjunction with a contact there? Regardless of that, I feel sure we will find our answers further afield. Our client is at this very moment making arrangements for us to depart, appropriating a ship for us, as I knew he would – though he was insistent on accompanying us on our journey. At least he has visited the place before."

"But . . . but *what* place exactly, Holmes?"

"Watson, we are to set sail for Port-au-Prince – Haiti!"

I did not know it then, but the very mention of that place should have filled me with dread. And if I had known the sights I would see, in spite of my loyalty to my friend, I might have thought twice about accompanying Holmes on his mission.

## 4.

The long journey on choppy seas, and with sparse comforts from home – the cabin I shared with Holmes was no larger than our larder – did at least provide Holmes with the time and opportunity to acquaint me with the history of the land we were heading towards. Its great ups and downs rivalling the ocean we bobbed upon, and the political instability that, even now, was threatening to tear the country apart at the seams.

"The French call it 'La Perle des Antilles' or 'The Pearl of the Antilles', due to its natural beauty," Holmes informed me as we took some the air on deck. "But it was originally inhabited by the Taíno Indians, before the Europeans arrived. It was these peoples that Columbus encountered when he landed at Môle Saint-Nicolas in 1492 and claimed the island in the name of Spain. Later on, Hispaniola became a haven for pirates, but it was the French who officially received the western third of the island. They began to set up sugar cane plantations, importing thousands of slaves from Africa." Holmes gripped the rail tightly as the ship made its way over the waves. "There followed years of unrest – and eventually a revolution inspired by that of the French in the latter part of the eighteenth century. The result? An unstable independence – and another attempt by the French to wrestle control from the natives. Various coups have since marred its history in the latter half of the previous century."

It was at this point Wakefield came above decks and joined us. "Gentlemen. I trust all is well?"

"Ah, there you are," said Holmes. "I was just regaling Watson with a little of Haiti's history. Is it not true that over the course of the last fifty years or so they have been crippled by enforced payments to France, with Western nations refusing to even acknowledge their independence?"

Wakefield opened his mouth to say something, but simply shrugged instead. Either he did not know, or did not care about the politics of the place his shipments originated from.

"All of which made it ripe for certain . . . entrepreneurial sorts to take advantage," Holmes added, and I noted the twitch in Wakefield's cheek.

"The Germans predominantly, I have to say," replied the thin man. "But yes, American and British investments are definitely at stake in the region."

"With Pattison & Wakefield having a vested interest, naturally," I broke in.

The man said nothing, but he could see what I was driving at; a motivation if ever there was one for foul play involving his partner.

"But it is their religion that interests me most at this time," Holmes stated, swiftly changing the subject.

"Now *that* is a subject I know very little about," Wakefield assured us. "Not many Westerners do. The whole thing is shrouded in mystery and superstition."

"Nevertheless," my friend said gravely, "I believe this, more than anything else, might hold the key to solving our case . . ."

## 5.

Upon our approach, I saw for myself why this island had gained its nickname. It certainly was a pearl, the landscape simply stunning; the clear cerulean sea meeting sandy beaches, with rolling hills and forest land brushing the horizon.

We docked at Port-au-Prince mid-afternoon, and I was glad of the cooler cotton clothing I'd packed for us both: Holmes in a cream suit with white shirt, still insistent upon a tie, the outfit topped off with a panama hat; and for myself, light greys and a shirt open at the neck, walking stick in my hand (a souvenir of my time in the Afghanistan war). Wakefield had gone on ahead to secure our guide, and returned with a young, dark-skinned lad who was wearing a tatty chequered shirt and trousers cut off just below the knee. In direct opposition to the boots that we wore, he was barefoot, the soles of his feet clearly toughened from walking around like that all the time. I could not help thinking about Pattison and his worn shoes . . .

"This is Philippe," Wakefield informed us, and the boy smiled. "He will show us around and translate for us where needed, then take us to the plantation the Helios Corporation uses as its base. Luckily, it is well within walking distance." There, we were to meet the manager, a representative of that company called Mr Roberts, who Wakefield had met on several previous occasions. Philippe made to take our luggage, and while Wakefield was happy to let him, both Holmes and I said thank you, but we could manage our own, not wishing to overburden him.

As we were taken through the town, I saw first hand the toll its history had had on both the people and the area. The poverty this had caused – though, even when the country had been thriving, it would not have been these folk who benefited. I felt the eyes of men, women and children upon me, all dressed in rags, looking out from their makeshift homes – many made from bits of wood and straw – in this virtual shantytown. The distrust of strangers was palpable (and with good reason, I warranted) especially ones who looked as we did. We would have to tread very lightly here, I thought. It was hard to see from this how the country would *ever* be stable, though there were rumblings that the British, German and American governments might step in at some point; something that would no doubt lead to even greater resentment.

But I could discern something else in their eyes; these were people who were no strangers to hardship, but also – like the poorest of our own city back home – no strangers to loss . . . or death.

"Philippe?" Holmes said as we walked, and the boy turned to him. "Where might I find out more about your . . . local customs?"

The youth looked at him as blankly as Pattison had back in that graveyard over a week ago. Either he didn't understand what my friend meant, or did not wish to.

"Your culture . . . the religion you and your people practise here," Holmes elucidated.

Philippe shook his head. "I cannot. It is . . . forbidden." Whether he meant he could not talk about it, or the practices themselves had been forbidden was unclear, but the fear in his eyes was genuine enough.

It was at that point I noticed a disturbance in the crowd to our left. The swell of bodies parted and suddenly; a man broke free of it and ran at us. Both Holmes and I dropped our cases, readying to fend him off; I myself preparing to pull the blade in my walking stick free.

As it happened, this proved unnecessary. The man just clasped Holmes's left hand in both of his own, mouthing something in the local dialect.

"Let him go!" Wakefield shouted, stepping forward.

"He says you must leave, sir," Philippe translated for Holmes. "You leave . . . or you will die."

"That sounds very much like a threat to me," I said.

"No threat." Philippe shook his head again. "Warning."

The man let go of Holmes and ran away, blending back into the crowd before we could do a thing.

"Gentlemen, I do apologize," said a flustered Wakefield.

"No need," said Holmes, brushing himself down and picking up his case again. "I can understand their unease after everything that has happened to them." He gave the impression that the incident had not troubled him, but I have known my friend longer than anyone and I could tell when he was shaken.

And all I could hear in my head, round and around, were the words of that stranger: *"Leave or you will die. Leave or you will die."*

## 6.

The sugar plantation was an impressive affair, with many men working in the fields, hacking away at the cane with long-bladed machetes. It reminded me a little of one such place we had visited about fifteen years previously, in South Africa at the behest of Henry Baskerville; another unsavoury affair I have recounted elsewhere. We were greeted at the entranceway by Roberts: a sturdy fellow with mutton-chop sideburns, who arranged for our belongings to be taken up to his house, a white mock-Georgian construction, for the duration of our stay.

"Ex-military, Dr Watson?" he enquired of me when we were introduced. When I nodded, he answered: "I thought so. I know my own kind when I see it." He cast a contemptuous glance over at Philippe, who Wakefield was in the process of paying. There was no confusion about what he meant; he had an army background himself, but also thought very little of the locals. We found out why when Wakefield returned to the group.

"I'm sorry," he said, "but we've been having quite a lot of difficulty with them of late. As if we don't have enough to worry about with competition like HASCO, we have to deal with those primitives."

"Er . . . HASCO?" I asked, confused.

"The Haitian American Sugar Company," Wakefield explained without missing a beat.

"There's a lot of unrest out there amongst them lot," Roberts said, getting back to his original gripe.

"I cannot imagine why," said Holmes, and Roberts looked at him sideways.

"Their stupid mumbo-jumbo, interfering with our productivity," grumbled the broad-shouldered manager. "If I had my way, I'd shoot the lot of them."

"But then who would you have to labour for you?" Holmes enquired. He had a point, and I was willing to bet it was a cheap workforce at that.

Roberts ignored the question and asked one of his own: "What exactly brings you out here at such short notice?"

"We think there might be some connection between the death of Mr Wakefield's business partner and their business arrangement with your company," I said, perhaps a little too bluntly.

"That and certain claims that he – or someone who looks very much like him – has been spotted wandering the streets at night-time," Holmes elaborated.

Roberts visibly flinched at that. "Now you're starting to sound like one of these blasted natives!"

"What do you mean?" I asked.

"The dead coming back to life, walking around come night-fall . . . Bloody stupid stories! Trying to scare us away, they are! And some of my own men are even daft enough to believe them."

"Really?" said Holmes. "Now that *is* interesting! Perhaps you would be willing to tell us more?"

Roberts grunted his acquiescence, and beckoned us to the house. It was dinner-time, he informed us – and if he was going to talk, he was going to do so as we ate.

## 7.

We went to our rooms that evening with our stomachs full of roast beef and Roberts's stories and complaints still ringing in our ears. He seemed happy to drone on – at length – about the various problems he'd had with the natives. The notions of "magic, superstitious nonsense and hysteria" that were being whipped up and affecting everything he and his colleagues had been trying to build here over the last decade or so. "Don't they realize that this is all for their own good?" he kept ranting, and would bang the table each time.

After years of slavery and volatility, I doubted very much that the population might see it that way. But it did lend credence to the argument that Mr Pattison's condition was in some way a by-product of this struggle. Maybe they thought that with him out of the picture, or rendered ineffectual by the peculiar state he was in now, it would eventually result in the trade agreement crumbling, and Helios withdrawing?

And if we needed a culprit, then we need look no further than a mythical sorcerer from the outlying regions who was rumoured to be able to give the dead life by performing ceremonies and rituals in the hills.

"I mean, who would bloody well believe that – apart from my idiot men?" Roberts asked, taking another large gulp of his wine. Holmes and I exchanged a look, for we had seen such a "resurrection" back in London with our very eyes. "Them and the primitives who live here, of course. They even put it in their hare-brained law, that anyone attempting such a thing would be accused of attempted murder. Honestly, whatever next?" It was one of the reasons, he told us, why he had no local servants in the house – he just did not trust them.

Roberts could not let us go, naturally, without a tour of the house, including the massive wine and spirits cellar he was so proud of: lit by gaslight. I have to say, I would never have thought this man a connoisseur, but then he had drunk a fair amount at dinner, so perhaps there was another rationale.

Whilst I was getting ready for bed, there was a knock on my door. It was Holmes, who crept inside and quietly closed the door.

"I think it is high time we slipped out and did a little looking around on our own, don't you, Watson? But not dressed as we were today, we would stick out like sore thumbs."

I nodded, agreeing with his suggestion, before saying, "A good job, then, I brought along our *other* outfits." I opened the case to reveal the dark clothing we had worn when visiting Camberwell Old Cemetery. I took out another object, and held it in my hand, smiling. "In addition to my trusty pistol, of course . . ."

## 8.

Not knowing where we were heading, Holmes thought it a good idea to retrace our steps back into town. But in the dark, and without our guide, we soon lost our way. After wandering around in what must have been circles for quite a while, we heard the distinctive sound of drums beating in the distance.

"There!" Holmes said, tapping me on the shoulder and pointing.

I squinted, making out tiny lights off to one side.

"Surely worth a look?" I replied, and we headed off in their direction.

We crawled up the side of a hill to watch what was happening in a hollowed-out section of the landscape below. It was only now that we saw what this place was – we had found ourselves in yet another cemetery, this one just as makeshift as the shantytown we had been making for. As well as jagged headstones marking the graves, there were holes dug out of the side of the hill, into which coffins had been slotted – like pegs placed in a child's game. And scattered all around were candles, some of which I saw now were on top of holders made from human skulls. One in particular was formed from a mound of skulls, with candles in all the eye sockets.

The graveyard was filled with men and women. All were dancing to the rhythm of those drums – much louder now because we were so close – and a few people were shaking instruments, containers filled with rice or something similar that rattled and clearly had some kind of religious meaning.

Then there were those holding lit torches, who were running the flames up and down their arms, but instead of shrieking in pain they were actually laughing, full of joy! All I could think was that their skin must have grown accustomed to such treatment, just as their bare feet were used to walking on stony terrain. Others were dancing with what appeared to be live snakes in their hands, bending to direct them first one way, then another.

It was clear that we'd stumbled upon a funeral of sorts, but it was all a far cry from the reverence and civility of an English burial, I have to say. It was almost as if they were celebrating death, embracing it.

But it was all a prelude to one of the coffins being pulled free from its home; lifted by men who were stripped to the waist – the sweat gleaming on their slick bodies. They placed that long box upon the ground. I frowned; what kind of funeral was it where the coffins were taken *out* of their plots, instead of being placed in them?

Then suddenly all grew quiet, as a figure appeared, sneaking between the graves, naked apart from a loincloth. His limbs were long and thin, so that when he moved it was like some kind of insect, while the bones painted all over his body – white against the darkness of his skin – gave him the appearance of a skeleton.

Gradually, he made his way towards the coffin and nodded for other men on either side – dressed in crimson robes – to remove the lid. Inside, was the body of a middle-aged man, face white, and with that same waxy pallor Pattison had boasted. The skull-faced individual hopped around the coffin, splaying his fingers occasionally and chanting words in a language I could not possibly hope to decipher.

It was at this point in the proceedings that one of the robed men handed him an open pot of sorts, which the skull-faced dancer waved around the man – specifically in the region of his heart – until he was satisfied and placed a stopper in the top. Next, the "skeleton" brought out a plant, which looked similar to the one Holmes had found in Pattison's crypt: the Devil's Snare. It was *all* Devil's work as far as I was concerned. Another robed figure brought out a mortar and pestle, into which the plant was placed and ground up. Our skull-faced man dipped his fingers into the resultant paste, then smeared it onto the lips of the corpse, mouthing more ritualistic sentences.

When the skeleton pulled away from the body, it was almost as if he were tugging on invisible strings – for the man, his lips glossy in the moonlight, sat bolt upright in the coffin.

I sucked in a breath and Holmes looked across at me.

"Incredible," I whispered by way of justification, then added: "But quite clearly our culprit, or one of his ilk!"

The fingers of one hand were curled around the grip of the pistol tucked in my belt, those of the other squeezing my walking stick as I continued to watch the dead man rise out of the coffin. He stood in front of his master, gaping just as Pattison had done with Holmes back in the London cemetery.

So captivated by the sight of all this were we, that we did not notice someone behind us until it was too late. It was Holmes who whirled about first, naturally, his instincts still keen, and grabbed the person who had stolen upon us.

He held the figure down, where I could get a good look at him.

"Philippe!" I exclaimed, possibly a little too loudly, because it forced Holmes to place a finger on his lips – this time not an aid to contemplation, but a sign for me to be quiet. After all, we were supposed to be endeavouring to remain out of sight of the people further down the hillside. The boy looked terrified, eyes wide and staring.

Suddenly, he found his voice. "You not be here," he spat.

"What on earth is happening down there?" I demanded, ignoring his statement.

"Not be here!" Philippe merely repeated.

"Who is that with bones painted on his body? Why is he doing those things to that poor man!" I didn't enjoy threatening the youth, but I brought up the gun to show him. "Answer me!"

"Watson," said Holmes, in an effort to calm me – but I wanted, *needed* answers. Then he turned to our captive: "Nobody will hurt you, I give you my word. But we do need to know."

"Bokor," said Philippe reluctantly, looking away as if he'd just revealed some major secret.

"I do not understand," I admitted.

"Bizango Bokor," Philippe "explained", then when he saw we were both still confused, continued, "Magician. Powerful magician!"

I shook my head. "No magic. He revived him with the plant, we saw that. Probably poisoned him with something else . . . Why?"

It was Philippe's turn to shake his head. "Bad man. Did bad things."

"The Bokor?" I asked.

Another shake. "Punishment."

So that was it: revenge, pure and simple, facilitated by this sorcerer. It was nothing more than vigilante justice as far as I could see.

"Bad man not harm anyone any more. Bokor make him zombi," Philippe stated with a curt nod of the head as if to say "that was that". "His soul is trapped, belongs to the Bokor."

"The pot," Holmes said to himself.

"And what will he do with the poor fellow now?" I asked, but Philippe refused to tell me. Anything the Bokor wanted was probably the answer.

"Watson." Holmes tapped me on the shoulder. "Watson, look."

I turned to see that my friend was pointing down at the crowd; the locals were all gazing up at us.

The magician was as well.

"I think we are about to receive company," Holmes said and even before he'd finished they began to move, almost as one, in our direction. We had witnessed things no outsider should. Heaven alone knew what they would do to us. I stood up, leaving Holmes to restrain Philippe, and fired my pistol into the air. They continued to come, so I fired a couple of bullets over their heads. That seemed to do the trick and they did begin to disperse, to scatter.

All except for the Bokor and his zombi.

The skeletal man said something to his puppet, directing him towards us.

"Holmes," I began, aiming my pistol at the "puppet" of a figure. Holmes knew what I was thinking: that this man was not in his right mind – had *no mind* at all at the moment, it would appear. "Holmes, I can't . . ."

He asked for my stick, but left the sword in its housing. As the zombi finally reached us, Holmes left me with Philippe and used a series of bartitsu defensive moves to keep the "dead" man at bay. His opponent was determined, however, and insisted on lunging at Holmes until my friend crouched and made one last swipe, which took the man's legs out from under him, toppling him back down into the graveyard. It was at this point, as he rose, that Holmes suddenly gritted his teeth and clutched his chest.

"Holmes . . . Holmes, whatever is it?" I shouted. It couldn't be the fight; I'd seen him in more vigorous altercations than this one without repercussions.

"My . . . I think it is my heart, Watson."

I rushed over to him, propping him up. When Philippe looked like he was about to flee, I raised my pistol once more, forcing him to take Holmes under the other arm. I glanced behind us, but the zombi and his master were gone.

"We need to get Holmes back to the plantation!" I said to Philippe. "Take us there, right now!"

All I could hear in my head were Philippe's words about the sorcerer's strong magic, and the words of that stranger who'd rushed out to clutch Holmes's hand earlier.

*"Leave . . . or you will die!"*

## 9.

With Philippe reluctantly pointing out the way, we got Holmes back to the plantation and Roberts's house quicker than I would have been able to otherwise. The noise we made dragging a limp Holmes through the door and depositing him on the dining table drew the attentions of both the homeowner and Wakefield.

"What the deuce has happened?" asked the latter, appearing in his pyjamas and dressing gown. "I thought you two had retired for the evening?" I did not have time to answer him, but rushed upstairs instead to rummage in my case for my emergency medical supplies. When I returned, I found that I was too late.

"He's . . . he has gone, Dr Watson. It's just like Arnold," Wakefield informed me.

I went over to Holmes and pressed my ear against his chest. His heart was silent. "No . . ." It was not the first time the great detective had "died", of course, but not like this . . . Nevertheless, my sense of helplessness was the same – worse, if anything, for I was present and could seemingly do nothing.

Roberts had a rifle by this time and was holding Philippe captive in the chair; yet even as he did this, he gulped wine he'd poured for himself, carrying on where he'd left off at dinner.

"I'm willing to wager that whatever happened was to do with this boy and his kind!" he snarled, taking another drink. "I told you the lot of them should be shot!"

"No," I repeated, not knowing myself whether I was still talking about my friend or Philippe.

"Them and their bloody secret ceremonies; their poison bloody powders."

"Powders?" I asked.

"I've seen this before," Roberts growled. "Seen everything! Their poison can be spread by touch, by a scratch." I recalled the man in the street again, how he had taken Holmes's hand. That must have been the way they had administered the fatal dose. "They wish to kill us all, drive us all out!" the manager argued. "Drive us all *mad*!"

He raised his rifle and I heard Philippe whimper. "Please . . ."

"Wait!" shouted Wakefield; he was moving towards one of the big windows in the dining room. Through the tears that were threatening to break free, I followed his gaze outside. There I saw figures in the field, lots of figures, brandishing those long knives. It had to be the Bokor's followers; that was the only explanation I could think of. We would need Philippe, for a bargaining chip if nothing else. The figures were getting closer, close, and there, behind them, the white bones covering his body, picked out by the moon above, the sorcerer.

But the situation was worse than I first imagined. Something about the way the figures were moving, the fact that their skin was both black *and* white . . . Not followers, but zombi. A small army of them, heading in our direction. The Bokor obviously meant to ensure we did not leave here alive with the secrets that he and his clan had kept hidden for so long. I pulled my pistol – my motivation, Holmes lying dead on the table behind me. I needed the sorcerer to bring him back: reverse what one of his minions had done. Restore Holmes completely; there was still hope. He was my *only* hope, in fact!

Then the figures were at the window, the door. They crashed through, and Wakefield had no time to get away. He was dragged out of the broken window, screams following him. Innocents or not, I fired in an effort to free him – failing miserably. Roberts did nothing but stand and watch uselessly. This ex-military man, when it came to the crunch, was nothing more than bloated, drunken talk.

I turned to the side, seeing several of the zombi there – gazing at me, but not really *seeing* me, following commands I could not hope to countermand. I avoided a machete swing, and finally did fire my weapon – hitting the "dead" man closest to me in the shoulder. He dropped the blade. The man behind that one, I shot in the left leg, and the zombi behind him in the right. The chamber of my revolver finally clicked empty.

Looking over at Roberts, I yelled: "Do something!"

He grinned then . . . an odd grin the likes of which I have rarely seen and I wondered if he had indeed been driven mad.

"I already have, Doctor," he informed me.

And then my friend, Sherlock Holmes, sat up on the table – his lips shiny with grease.

"Holmes?" I called across, but he said nothing, just gazed back at me – right through me actually – responding only to the words Roberts spoke. My friend swung his legs off the table, climbing down from there and scooping up an abandoned machete, brandishing it with malice. I shook my head, confused, but still had the presence of mind to take a step backwards when he swiped at me. I had no choice but to make for my cane and pull my own blade free.

Now, I know Holmes is an expert swordsman, but his movements were clumsy. Ordinarily, I would not have stood a chance, yet I could at least buy myself some time to think.

Time to survive.

"You of all people should realize, Dr Watson," Roberts was shouting. "In war you fight fire with fire, and you must use any weapon you can lay your hands upon, even if it belongs to the enemy!" More zombi were entering through the window, heading towards Philippe. This was not the Bokor's army, but Roberts's. "I know all about their stupid secrets. I have observed them for some time. It was a simple matter to get a couple of the older ones to talk about such things. Almost as easy as it was to add a secret ingredient to your friend's meal tonight."

But I could see no pots in the vicinity. If Roberts had performed the same ritual with Holmes that we had seen in the graveyard, then where was the vessel supposedly containing his essence? It was insanity to even think about such things, and yet . . .

*Think, Watson, think!* I thought to myself. Holmes would have been able to work it out in a moment, and in his absence I was the only chance he – and all these other poor unfortunates – had. The container had to be close by, something Roberts could have used unobtrusively. I scanned the area, anything that might possibly be used in that capacity, any kind of vase or . . .

*There!* The wine bottle Roberts had recently drained; it was now stoppered.

As Holmes swung at me again, I shouted across to Philippe, "The bottle – you must smash it!"

The boy, half out of his mind with fright, managed to grasp my meaning; he knew that this was his only hope. He ducked to avoid one of the zombi that lunged at him, and scrambled under the table just as Roberts took aim and fired his rifle. The bullet splintered a table leg, but it didn't stop the nimble young lad, who surfaced again to grab the wine bottle and smash it against the wall.

"*No!*" bellowed Roberts, but this time it was he who'd been too late.

As I watched, Holmes shook his head, rousing himself. He remained as stony faced as always, but the anger was there – even if only I could sense it. He rounded on the manager, slapping the rifle from his grasp before he could train it on Holmes, and rammed his palm into the man's chest, sending him over the table to land near the window.

More of the zombi army were pouring in through the doors and windows, but Holmes shouted for me to go. "You know where, Watson!" And I did; if smashing the bottle had freed Holmes then I had to do the same for the men he'd enslaved. I had to take a trip down into the cellar.

Housing my blade inside its sheath again, I raced down to the cellar where I began smashing the bottles in the racks with the stick, pulling others from their homes so that they broke on the floor. The resemblance to the coffins inside those holes at the cemetery wasn't lost on me as I smashed more and more, but it was taking far too long – especially as Roberts had hidden the fake ones amongst full wine bottles. So I decided to fight fire with fire myself. Pulling the oil lamps from their housings, I tossed them at the racks where they exploded into flame. It would not take long for those racks to split, to crack open with the intense heat – fuelled by bottles of whisky that were also down there.

And, leaving the blaze behind, I made my way back upstairs once more . . . To find the landscape had changed somewhat. The men, who had only a few minutes ago been zombi, were now shaking their heads, wondering where they were and what they were doing. And to find the Bokor now in the room, standing over Roberts.

Holmes took a step towards them, contending: "This man must stand trial!"

Philippe stood barring his way. Holmes could easily have shifted the boy. But no, something else was holding Holmes back, something he has yet to reveal to this day.

"Bad man," Philippe said. "Magic not belong to him. Now his soul belong to the Bokor."

"Holmes!" I called, and he looked back at me. "We can't just let them . . ."

But it was already too late; the Bokor and Roberts were gone, and moments later Philippe with them. By this time, the fire was spreading to our level, and Holmes and I urged the men, who had now recovered their senses, to flee. Soon there would be nothing left of Roberts's home, and the secrets it contained.

And, I thought to myself, as we both stood watching the conflagration take proper hold, perhaps it was better that way.

## 10.

In spite of the fact we alerted the authorities – such as they were – about the Bokor, about Roberts, neither were seen again. Nor was Wakefield, or our guide Philippe. Upon our return to England, Holmes and I discovered that Mrs Pattison had absconded, and in her house correspondence was found between her and Roberts. It transpired that they had known each other for almost as long as she'd known Pattison and Wakefield, being the sister of one of Roberts's old army comrades. At her behest, Roberts had sent materials to use in the "zombification" of her husband, someone she described herself in her diary as "a hateful old man, who pays me scant attention and spends all of his time either at work or at his gentlemen's club, when he is not off with the ladies of the night who frequent the docks where his ships load and unload their cargoes".

Of the instructions Roberts must have sent there was no sign, quite possibly destroyed at his request – burnt perhaps, as his home had been in the end.

Yet Roberts had played his part not solely out of loyalty, or out of a desire to implicate the Haitians. He had responded to Mrs Pattison's pleas because of promises she made to help lower the prices Pattison & Wakefield were charging to ship his goods.

"It seems reasonable to assume that if she had not been able to talk Wakefield into this scheme of hers eventually, then he too might have suffered a similar fate to that of her husband," Holmes said to me, as we observed Pattison through the tiny window in the door of his room at Bethlem Royal Hospital. "The poisoning part at least; for she would have no reason to 're-animate' Wakefield. That particular revenge was reserved solely for her husband, to make him a slave under her control."

Pattison's condition was being treated as a mental disorder, though we both knew it was much more complicated than that. The fact Pattison was alive at all, if you could call it such, was put down to the sleep paralysis that Poe was so fearful of. A condition, they claimed, Pattison had not yet fully recovered from. Still, nobody seemed able to explain how his heart rate was virtually nil, or why he remained so cold to the touch, became animated only at dusk – or indeed why he needed barely anything by way of food or water (the very reason he had "survived" at all until our return).

"Not that his wife had much luck controlling him," Holmes continued to muse.

That was true; something must have gone wrong in her undertaking for Pattison to ignore her orders, for him to try to escape and continue his life – or what he remembered of it. An instinctual thing, some form of homing impulse that had obviously outweighed Mrs Pattison's commands. Hardly surprising, as he did not appear to have taken much notice of her before all this happened, either.

"Once he had been spotted, of course, and Wakefield had come to her, she had no choice but to play along with the charade of asking us for assistance. Quite the actress she proved, with her tears and wailing,"

I could see he was annoyed with himself for not spotting the deception, her true character. Perhaps the first sign that his powers of deduction were waning with age? I hoped not.

It was only after Mrs Pattison had learned of our trip that she'd vanished, and though the boys at Scotland Yard had spread the word, the chances of her turning up, or being found, were dwindling with each passing day. Maybe she had taken a trip abroad herself, to start another life elsewhere?

"And there is still no sign of whatever Mrs Pattison used as her 'vessel'?" I asked.

Holmes shook his head.

As a man of medicine, I could understand the science behind the whole procedure; an inertia induced by that same formula Roberts had made it his business to discover. A formula that one day in the future might become known to the outside world (though I have to wonder if it ever *should* be, given the small army Roberts had managed to amass with the ultimate aim of tackling the natives). It was a state counteracted somehow by that blasted Devil's Snare, though not fully; something which left people in a highly suggestible condition, especially once darkness had fallen. Perhaps, in time, some medical breakthrough would be able to help Pattison.

But I had to wonder about the magic.

That man's warning when we arrived, for instance. Had he known about Roberts – that he intended to "infect" Holmes, to put him out of action and get him to kill both myself and Wakefield (in the end the other zombi had finished that man off). Or had the stranger been able to "see" it somehow? I've never been one for fortune-tellers, but . . .

And it was not until those bottles had been broken that Holmes recovered fully; those other men under Roberts's influence did too. Coincidence? Or was there actually some form of sorcery involved? Something Roberts had copied without understanding, or even believing? Had those souls, looking for somewhere to go once the heart had stopped working, and the body revived, been tricked into entering the nearest empty container?

I can only relate what Holmes says he experienced whilst under the man's influence. That it felt like he was elsewhere, trapped, not able to prevent his body from operating independently of his mind. Whether he was trapped inside his own frame, or somewhere else entirely, is open to conjecture.

"No one, no matter what they have done, deserves to be in that state indefinitely," Holmes said to me then.

"Not even Roberts, whose fault all this was?" I asked, and he remained silent.

We watched Pattison in silence for a little while, strapped into his straitjacket, twitching and jerking as darkness fell upon the hospital.

I wondered if we would ever find his wife, and even if we did whether she would divulge what she had used in the procedure she had performed. What kind of vessel . . .

And I wondered then, as I do so often since this case came our way, if we would ever find Pattison's lost soul.

# The Lunacy of Celestine Blot

## Stephen Volk

*To Whom It May Concern,*

*I entrust this package to your care in the knowledge that, like the
others, it will be kept from the public eye until the appropriate
time. While the unwashed multitude's appetite for sensation is
insatiable, I need not emphasize the peril of these pages coming
into unscrupulous hands while certain parties are still alive and
could be hurt by such revelations.*

*Furthermore, the literary world would be rocked (as well as my
word broken) if it learned that Edgar Allan Poe did not die in an
American gutter in 1849 as popular belief would have it, but
rather fled to Paris, where he applied his considerable intellect to
criminal inquiry under the* nom de guerre *Auguste Dupin – his
fictional hero of Rue Morgue fame. As you will remember from
the previous manuscripts now in the Black Museum's safe-keep-
ing, it was in this guise he crossed paths with Sherlock Holmes, at
that time in his twenties, resulting in the young man's tutelage in
the art of "ratiocination" before his return to London.*

*The enclosed investigation is no less "grotesque and arabesque"
(as Poe might say) than the others you have under lock and key. If
not for the corroborative evidence, I confess, as a policeman to my
boots, I might reject it as fiction – and if not for the fact that this
account was penned by the greatest mind, and man, I ever knew.*

*Signed, Geo. Lestrade*
*Dep. Commissioner (ret'd),*
*Metropolitan Police*

Hearing the keys rattling in the locks behind us, we found ourselves in the Versailles of Pain. A large and well-kept garden lay before us, which under any other circumstances may have been delightful, even uplifting, but not today, in spite of the warm stillness in the air and the cloudless sky above. Male figures circled the paths, seeming supernaturally mobile in contrast to the females, who stood immobile as statues, only giving sudden and unpredictable spasms as we passed, rolling their eyes or jutting out their chins with the dull, uncomprehending interest of ungulates in a field. By far the most animated was a woman who sat on a swing with her legs sticking out, twirling an umbrella. The rest of the inmates, however, were as stiff and indifferent as the Talrich waxworks on the Boulevard des Capuchines. We were entering Salpêtrière Hospital – the so-called "feminine inferno" – an asylum for the sick of mind in the midst of Paris's colourful Belle Époque. But nothing could have prepared me for the reality as we stepped inside the rundown Sainte-Laure building where epileptics and hysterics were indiscriminately housed with madwomen.

Here swarming residents gesticulated with bizarre contortions, dragged themselves, hurried with indecipherable urgency, scuffled – old women, poor women, some stoically awaiting death on a bench, others howling their fury or weeping their sorrow – none reprimanded or given redress by the sub-warder escorting us, who presumably accepted this as the standard behaviour he saw in his work on a daily basis. Yes, the walls I saw around me in their solemn dilapidation retained the majestic qualities of the capital under Louis XIV, but only as a most disturbing and tragic backdrop to the shattered souls who resided there.

"*Entre, qui que tu sois, et laisse l'espérance,*" said Poe out of the corner of his mouth. *Abandon hope all ye who enter here.* Never has the expression been more apposite.

On entering the consulting room of the great man who had summoned us – a man who was later to earn the somewhat unflattering nickname of the "Napoleon of Neurology" – I was immediately drawn to the painting dominating one wall: Robert-Fleury's

*Pinel Liberating the Madwomen of Salpêtrière From Their Chains.*
Fetters lay in the foreground, telling the age-old story. Pinel had
been chief doctor at the hospital, responsible for instituting a new,
progressive regime, enabling the dawn of the benevolent rather
than punitive care of the mad. With the focus on science and cura-
bility, he had instituted a revolution of sorts, liberating the deranged
from confinement and allowing them to coexist with a degree of
autonomy. Nevertheless, on the day we visited, so-called
"debauched women" rubbed shoulders with convulsionaries and
"women of abnormal constitution". I could not avoid the conclusion that all the female dregs of society rejected elsewhere in the
city, whatever their malady, ended up here.

"Monsieur Dupin, Monsieur Holmes."

Jean-Martin Charcot was not the kind of man to thank us for
coming at his urgent behest. In fact, he made it seem as though
he were doing us a great favour by seeing us. Middle-aged, with
rounded shoulders and slicked-back, slightly greying hair, he
resembled nothing so much as an otter. But clearly saw himself
as somewhere between the Sun King and Caesar.

"Doctor." Poe, over twenty years his senior, gave a polite but
imperious nod. "Or should we address you as Monsieur le
Professor?" He knew, as did I, that Charcot had been made
Professor of Anatomical Pathology by the Paris Faculty of
Medicine, being the foremost expert in *les maladies du système
nerveux.*

"I prefer the latter. Many of my patients think a doctor is
there to cut them up."

"When in fact you want to study them."

"Our purpose here is cure. But study is as important to that
end as day-to-day treatment. The intellectual pursuit and the
medical cannot, and should not, be unconjoined."

Napoleon-like, he stuck his hand in his waistcoat with the
manner of a man deeply sure of his own judgement. And yet we,
two detectives, were here because of a problem he could not
solve. So he was not nearly as all knowing as he might wish.

I felt the need to offer some blatant flattery to ingratiate
ourselves. "I hear that students at Oxford have to read Charcot

now as they read Hippocrates and Celsus for their degrees in Bachelor of Medicine."

He shrugged. An equally blatant display of mock humility. "If I have advanced medical science in any way by distinguishing hysteria from epilepsy in particular . . ." He waved his hands, as if to imply he desired no personal credit for the achievement.

"Especially as one cannot get under the skin of a nervous patient to see how the illness works," said Poe.

"Even less can one pathologize a deranged mind without putting that life to an end. One must restrain one's actions to observing without so much as touching or, often, even communicating. The rigour of my process, my methodology, may seem counter-intuitive, unjustified, a kind of madness of its own to those outside the discipline, and far-fetched . . . But my research needs a clinical eye and the eye is as important a tool as psycho-motor experiments and psychological diagrams."

Poe nodded gently.

I could tell he felt he was in the presence of a man after his own heart – a fellow devotee of cold "ratiocination", and that pleased him. As for myself, I was unsure about this dapper gentleman who reigned over his domain at Salpêtrière – this pensive brow, this sombre visage with searching eyes set deep in shadow of sockets, and lips accustomed to silence. Whereas Poe now cast him as a fellow investigator, in my mind I likened him to Dante: the Dante who descended into *Purgatorio*, where sinners are kept in punishment, where penance is done before judgement is made, and the unfortunates are deemed holy enough to pass to Paradise or else consigned to Hell.

I found myself staring at such "sinners" in the ghostly grey images on the wall of the study, and was reminded of Balzac's remark that bodies, insofar as when they are photographed, become spectres. In stark detail and under unmerciful lighting, here were faces like those we had witnessed en route: distorted, startled, grimacing, eyes rolling heavenward, or with hands gripped in an attitude of prayer. Portraits not of royalty or mili-tary heroes but of twisted musculature, the impossible distor-tion of limbs – yet, as Charcot soon told us in answer to my evident curiosity, his patients seemed to suffer no physical injury, no apparent discomfort from these poses, attacks, "*attitudes passionelles*", "crucifixions", "ecstasy" – all the postures of delirium, all caught by the miracle of the lens. "Photography is invaluable in the examination of neurological cases."

"As it will prove to be in the detection of crime," said Poe. "Which is our area of examination."

"The photographic plate is the true retina of the scientist," agreed Charcot. "Human sight combined with memory is endlessly flawed and endlessly open to misinterpretation. You cannot really claim to have seen something unless it is photographed."

An intriguing concept. We are used to the faces of the corporeal betraying the soul within, yet this art was at the service of a strange and territorial science, like that of Gall's phrenology. But instead of Gall's caressing fingertips on a woman's face, all we saw here was the fall of brutal light on the convulsions of overheated minds. All detail was clear, but all meaning tenuous. To me, these snapshots of the mad, while they appeared to show all, showed nothing – except for the physicians' insatiable desire for imagery of hysterics who willingly participated with their increasingly theatricalized body shapes.

"The gestures are so grand and unnatural," I could not resist saying, "they seem to be acting."

"Monsieur Holmes. Performance is a part of the condition," said Charcot. "Do we know for certain any action, mad or sane, is not committed for an audience, to elicit sympathy, or even shock? For punishment? Even self-punishment?"

"And what is the root cause of such exhibitions?"

"That," interjected Poe, "as Monsieur le Professeur will agree, is the greatest mystery in medicine."

"Indeed so. All the efforts of pathological anatomy through the century have been directed at discerning the configuration of such illnesses by their symptoms . . . and localizing the essence of them."

"Yet the autopsies of hysterics have so far revealed nothing palpable," said Poe. "In other words, hysteria seems to escape the anatomical doctrine of *localization* entirely."

"Until we find it."

"Unless you do *not* find it."

"Which would be a great blow to medical orthodoxy."

"Medical orthodoxy is not the goal. The sickness is a paradox and medicine does not like to confront paradoxes. Perhaps the truth is it has no locality at all, in biological terms."

Charcot grunted. "Are you saying then that it is a disorder of the soul? Or *humours*? Or a malady of *passion*? You may be an educated man, but with deep respect, this is my area of expertise. And those are concepts from the Dark Ages."

"I am saying we are possibly living in the Dark Ages now as far as hysteria is concerned, if we but knew it. Landouzy defined it as 'neurosis of the woman's generative apparatus' – yet when Voison opened up hysterics found nothing in pelvic cavities ... A few years later Briquet said, 'no, it's neurosis of the encaphlon' ... They have looked in the ovaries. Nothing. They have looked in the skull. Nothing."

"Nevertheless, if you had worked here as I have, you would have seen that hysterical women are often tormented by a feeling of heat and acridity in their generative organs. That their menses are irregular. If the disposition is not genital, then is it the effect of a special mode of sensibility?"

"Feminine sensibility?" I enquired.

"Because a female endures the suffering," snapped Poe, "it does not mean that the suffering is somehow female. Even on a semantic level, such a concept is – appropriately – quite insane and deluded. Perhaps the fantasy here is provided as much by the practitioners as the inmates."

"Dupin. Please." I tried to calm my friend's flow of abuse, but to my surprise Charcot simply laughed, allowing Poe to continue unabated, as if he had heard similar attacks many times and was immune to them.

"You yourself, Monsieur le Professeur, seem to have assembled a ragbag of causes into predisposing factors – moral impressions, fears, the marvellous, exaggerated religious practices, rheumatism, masturbation, tobacco, certain professions, certain races, Israelites ..."

"There may be any number of *causes* – the cause is in many ways irrelevant – because the essential *mechanism* of hysteria is heredity. It is a condition hidden until prised out by circumstance. And that circumstance, from person to person, might vary. Monsieur Holmes, your companion is an extremely rude man."

"I am afraid so, Monsieur." I blushed.

"And if you were not here for an important purpose I would have him ejected immediately."

"I would not blame you for a second, Monsieur le Professeur, if you locked him in a padded cell. But indulge him his vice – which is extreme contrariness – and I am sure in time, if you have need of his services, his presence will reap dividends."

"How delightful to be discussed as if a patient," trilled Poe, prowling the room in a distracted fashion. "Likewise I have no more power over my outbursts than the dispossessed in your care. For which I apologize deeply. Consider it my 'supranervous expressionism'. Add the term to your bag of tricks, if you wish."

"Dupin."

Turning back, he fell silent, seeing as I did that the learned doctor was pressing his fingertips to his forehead in a gesture of the utmost perturbation. In the hallowed halls of the perturbed, this was a disarming sight.

"*Messieurs.*" Now Charcot spoke in a small, fragile voice. "I can only say I am determined to try any and every method to illuminate these conditions. Sadly, they cannot be dissected, stitched up, repaired like a cracked shin or cut on the epidermis. These illnesses are far deeper than flesh and bone."

"And that troubles you," I ventured.

"One case in particular troubles you," said Poe. "Her name is Celestine and her photograph is under your right elbow, with her name clear to read even upside down."

Charcot looked at it. "As a detective, Dupin, you know one cannot observe a brain, but we can observe behaviour – reaction, cause, effect – and usually reach a conclusion. But this woman has eluded my classification. I cannot file her as the 'venomous' woman, the 'chlorotic', the 'menorrhagic', the 'feverish', the 'visceral' or the 'libidinosa' ... She evades the grammar of the visible."

Poe took the photograph and examined it intently. It was titled: "*HYSTÉRO-ÉPILEPSIE – ÉTAT NORMAL*" and showed a handsome, square-shouldered girl with a strong, defiant jaw and black eyes staring with an intense air of suspicion into the camera.

"Our patients are generally incapable of giving reports of themselves," said Charcot. "Communication runs dry, leaving gaps unfilled and riddles unanswered. The connective tissue of information is mostly incoherent, even the sequence of events uncertain ..."

"And she?" Poe did not look up.

"Quite the opposite. Her symptoms are only a minute element in a grand narrative tableau."

My friend's nose was almost touching the photographic paper. "Intriguing ..."

"At the very least."

Thus we were introduced, by proxy, to Mademoiselle Celestine Blot – pronounced "blow" for the edification of the English ear – who had been subject to the immense distress of an attack of monomania, incapacitated with ataxia, disorder and confusion, and whose life had changed radically as a result.

"She attacked a man of exceptional repute and good character. It was only by a fluke she avoided trial for attempted murder. Luckily, her family saw that she was unable to return to society and entrusted her to the care of this institution five years ago, during which time her state of delusion has, if anything, worsened."

"And that state of delusion takes what form?"

"Everything related to the moon. She will not have any lunar imagery in her presence. Even a crescent design on a napkin or wallpaper will set her off in a paroxysm."

"How often do these 'paroxysms' occur?"

"It varies. Sometimes she has two or three a week. At times of the full moon, as many as a hundred a day."

*A hundred!* I could scarcely believe that was humanly possible, but the doctor had no need to lie. As if to provide evidence he furished us with a second photograph, titled: *"DEDUT D'UNE ATTAQUE: CRI"* – in this Celestine's face was massively disfigured, her tongue extended, hanging out.

"Before this we see the tremors, like hiccups, sometimes growing to the extent of suffocation, and apparent distress. It's preceded by some sharp guttural exclamations, laryngeal noises that resemble a cock's crow, then when it comes, the cry she utters has an unique quality, piercing as a train whistle."

Another photograph showed Celestine curled up in her bed, twisted and alert. In another she was madly crossing her legs, writhing within her straitjacket. In yet another, wriggling like a ignoble and ridiculous worm. It occurred to me that her cry was the last place to hide. Or lose herself from the pain. But I was not a doctor, of either the body or the mind, and was quite sure at that moment I never wanted to be. And I am not sure whether I admired or found loathsome the cold, dispassionate way Charcot described her anguish.

"After the apparent pain and cries come the spontaneous convulsions." He gave every impression the attending doctors might do little more than adjust their spectacles as they witnessed such a scene. "Then, just as quickly, after the *coup de théâtre*, she will invariably return to her relative normality prior to the attack."

He proceeded to tell us that the word "moon" itself would strike her like a wound, in the belly, or lower generative organs, to the extent that it would have to be banned in her presence. At times of heightened agitation, even a word starting with the same sound – that *might become* "moon" – could engender a significant grimace or spastic movement. Her jaw would lock, her eyes roll, her body jerk, arms stiffly outstretched, legs twisting and locking round each other like a corkscrew, as if fending off a physical attack. None of which seemed to be under her conscious control.

Which prompted me to ask a question.

"What is her attitude to such frightful and disabling displays on a regular basis?"

"She is hardly aware of them having happened. They pass like the wind in the trees. In fact, when questioned on her beliefs, she is convinced her anxiety is entirely justified and cannot understand why we, her carers, are not similarly imbued with her own level of terror and concern. Sometimes this rouses her to a point of anger which tips over into volcanic explosions of violence. To her, the guards represent attackers – she does not even believe their authenticity as humans. This is allied to a wilful obsession over the phases of the moon, "the Orb", as she calls it to avoid the offending word. Needless to add, the full moon is when we see her at her worst – she curls into a ball, insists on being tied to her bed and observed until the crisis period has passed."

"It is not of course uncommon for the mad to be affected by phases of the moon." Poe placed the photographs side by side on Charcot's desk. "They are not called lunatics for nothing."

"She insists on all drapes to be pulled at night-time, as she intensely fears moonshine might fall on her skin, with some kind of elemental toxicity."

"Excuse me, Monsieur." Poe became more animated. I could almost feel the crackle of electricity from his skull when he became hooked by a mystery. "You said she believes her fears to be justified. Kindly elaborate on that."

Charcot sat back at his desk and took out a hefty batch of paperwork, but did not need to consult it.

"The origin of her mania would seem to be an episode in which, horse-riding in the Bois de Vincennes, she was overcome by strange sensations – prickling skin, headache, giddiness. She fell from her steed and says that she saw a light in the sky grow larger. This, she is adamant, took form in a craft like a ship, but metallic and shimmering. She then described figures of the most remarkable kind making their way relentlessly towards her, wearing tight-fitting clothes, or skin – she is not sure which. She is positive she is going to be captured by these 'little men' she calls *farfadets*—" goblins, in English "—or sometimes *lutins*—" night imps "—with their mushroom-white heads and no noses. She describes their teardrop-shaped eyes as brown and mottled 'like of leaves beginning to wither', and she says they emitted guttural squawks from what looked like the mouths of fish. With absolute clarity she knew she was being assessed for a purpose. She felt they were intrigued by her skin colour and began to undress her. She then felt a knitting needle inserted into her navel and soon afterwards some sort of cold, glassy object attempted to extract her vital fluids or to deposit some seed – she is unsure which – via her generative passage."

My mouth was incredibly dry. A jug of water sat on a side table and I helped myself to a glass. Poe, in contrast, was by no means unsettled by these revelations, for all their monstrousness, and remained sedate and attentive throughout.

"Go on."

"In short, she insists these lunar creatures had raped her – though medically there was no evidence of sexual infiltration. Thereafter she felt her mind 'raked' by their thoughts, and was shown a vision of Earth's future ruin. When she awoke, there was no craft, no *farfadets*, dawn was breaking and she had lost twelve hours in what had seemed merely minutes."

"She remembers the incident in detail?" asked Poe.

"Uncommon detail, yes. Some hysterics exhibit amnesia, but most are in slavish thrall to memory – their dynamic outbursts, I believe, are a violent reflux of the 'first scene', the birth scene of the ailment, if you will, which demands a restaging. Many hysterics spout their 'first scene' in simple, honest words, with a wealth of detail. To the listener, the delirium seems too precise to be mere delirium."

Was he implying that he believed her incredible story? I could not credit that he did.

But Poe's focus of interest was elsewhere. "Have you considered the symbolic interpretation of her descriptions?"

Charcot turned down the corners of his mouth. "Symbols are everywhere. Symbols solve nothing. A patient tries to coyly cover her modesty as a woman, and simultaneously attack her sexual organs like a man . . ." Again, the esteemed doctor waved his hands, letting the thought drift away on the air.

"Then, forgive me – your view of the role of this event in her mental history is what?"

"As I have said before, hysteria is, I believe, the result of a weak neurological system which is *hereditary*. Yes, it can be ignited by the trigger of an act of violence, or an accident, or an imaginary assault such as this clearly is – but after that it is progressive and irreversible. The exact catalyst is unimportant."

"So, excuse me, why have we been brought here?" I asked. "If the mystery of her condition is unimportant to you?"

"Her condition is not the mystery I wish you to solve." Charcot leant back in his chair. "I never said it was. That is not a criminal matter, but a medical one."

"Then I confess I too am perplexed," said Poe, not without irritation.

"The story is incomplete. If you will grant me the good grace . . ."

"By all means."

Charcot stood.

"Shortly after the strange episode in the Bois de Vincennes, the nature of which Celestine eagerly shared with her deeply concerned family, her mania took the form of an obsession with the author Jules Verne, who has written, as you know, extensively about an imagined expedition to the moon. Believing him to harbour secrets that would account for her vile encounter and the *farfadets*' obscene intentions upon her, Celestine fired a pistol at him, thinking him in collusion with her interplanetary beings."

"Good grief." I was taken aback.

Poe said nothing.

"Incarcerated here five years later, she has only persisted in her conviction of a conspiracy of Verne with the Moon Men. She reads his work – two novels a year – avidly, as soon as they are published, in search of corroborative signs and clues."

"Fascinating," said my friend, restless now. "But Monsieur Verne, if I am not mistaken, is alive and well. And it seems the cause of the crime is locked in the lady's cranium, from whence we will have great difficulty extracting it."

"Exactly so. But the reason I was so desperate to call upon your special talent, Monsieur Dupin, is that Celestine had a recurrence of her 'Moon Men' experience two nights ago, whilst here on these premises. The guard on duty found her in a state of rare and aggressive agitation. She claimed immediately that her other-worldly *farfadets* had entered the building by means of their craft and she, frozen in horror, had watched helplessly as one of her fellow internees was bundled away and abducted by the savages from space."

I frowned. "Obviously no more than another hallucination."

"Surely this, and nothing more," whispered Poe, and I noticed a slight smile on his face, even a twinkle in his eye.

"But you see Monsieur Holmes, the point is this," said Charcot with the utmost gravity, "Gertrude Socha is still missing. We have no explanation for her whereabouts. There was no way out of that room two days ago. The staff and nurses saw no one enter or leave. There is no possible way she could have left the building, given the extensive security in place. And yet she has totally and completely disappeared – you might say, into thin air."

After ascertaining that the police had searched the building to no avail, and showed little interest or alacrity in pursuing the case, Poe requested to see the room where the "abduction" had taken place.

We were guided there past an avenue of women, treated to the sight of drooping breasts and open gowns, the occasional one prone and writhing on the floor to which the attendants seemed oblivious. This was indeed "a great emporium of human misery" as Charcot called it, whose aim was to make this quasi-city with its seedy areas, secret dens, playrooms and laboratories "the centre of truly theoretical and technical teaching". But I could only think of Dante again: "In truth I found myself upon the brink of an abyss, the melancholy valley containing thundering, unending wailings."

Poe had taught me above all else to be distant, cold and rational: to preserve the scalpel of intellect from being blunted by emotional distractions, but in these circumstances I found it impossible. I realized my distress at my surroundings was due to a memory in my formative years of my brother Mycroft being sent away to an aunt for the summer – even then knowing it was a lie, and being robbed of his company feeling like a punishment. Later, I learnt that his summer had been spent at the Middlesex County Asylum Colney Hatch, an alienist having pronounced that his mind was "too active for its own good" – as indeed we, his family, could testify. He returned not greatly changed, and told me only of the aviary where they bred canaries. Yet it inculcated unnameable fears in my young mind, which re-emerged as I watched a woman whose fingers crawled like spider-legs round her neck and through the curls of her hair, and another with a torn dress and bony legs bursting out laughing like a hyena.

Poe was asking if Celestine had any personal connection with the missing woman, before or after incarceration.

"No. They have rooms in separate parts of the building, and none of my staff have seen them communicate in any way."

"What can you tell us about Gertrude Socha?"

Charcot kept his steady pace. "Ordinary. Unimportant. The wife of a bartender in Montmartre. He left her and she took to drink – and I don't mean the occasional glass of Aÿ, I mean the green fairy, in quantity. She is afflicted by the most profound delusions. I suspect she was mentally defective from early age, and the absinthe did her no favours."

As we approached double doors, I asked: "Were you able to categorize her madness?"

"She was what we define as an *écritomaniac* – her every waking moment obsessed with making marks on paper."

"I've heard of such people," said Poe laconically. "They are also known as writers."

The room we were shown was large, but with no decorative niceties except for a constellation of randomly placed open-arm chairs, a bare mahogany dining table and, incongruously, a harpsichord. We were introduced to the guard, name of Hennetier – the sole cogent witness to what had transpired – who sported the face and moustache of a weathered old *grognard*. He confirmed that on the night in question he had kept the keys to the doors and windows on his person at all times, fastened securely to his leather belt. French windows opened onto a small balcony in front of us. Poe asked for the double doors to be opened, and stepped out into the fresh air as Charcot added that his staff had reported to him that every possible exit was found locked. I stood on the balcony briefly after Poe returned inside and registered the considerable drop to the courtyard below.

"You saw nothing?" Poe addressed Hennetier, who stood to attention.

"Yes, Monsieur – I mean no, Monsieur."

"Tell me what you did see."

"I don't remember. That is, I *do* remember – though it will not be much use to you."

"We shall see about that. Stand where you stood. Do as you did. And be as exact as humanly possible in your description."

Hennetier did as he was bidden.

"This is the point from which I can see every corner of the room, if the sparrows are behaving themselves. And if they're not, I will suppress them in the requisite manner, and if that is not enough, blow my whistle for assistance."

"Did you blow your whistle that night?" I asked.

"No, sir. Not until afterwards. After she was gone, I mean."

"At which moment you were here, facing the French windows?"

"That is correct, sir."

"And where were Madame Gertrude and Mademoiselle Celestine?" asked Poe.

"Gertrude was there, sir, in the rocking chair next to the French windows, facing into the room, and Celestine, here, between the two of us, facing the fireplace. With a candle beside her. You have to watch them regarding candles."

"Anything unusual about their temperaments or demeanour?"

Hennetier shook his head. "If anything they were both unusually calm, sir. I am not used to Celestine being quite so calm. Normally wound up like a twisted wire, that one. Gertrude, on the other hand, is never any trouble. Long as you give her pencil and paper, she's the most contented sow in the farmyard." He scratched his cheek and grinned, until our own seriousness made his smile slide away. "And all . . . all was fine until the clock struck seven and the Moon book fell to the floor with a thud, and I perceived Celestine gasping and jumping to her feet and backing towards me, shaking her head. I caught her by the shoulders to stop her crashing into me, but this only made her turn on me with arms thrashing, so I wrapped her in a bear hug and struggled to—"

"—blow your whistle," Poe completed, impatiently.

"Aye, sir. It was only when Sazzarin and Goyon ran to my aid and were able to apply the strait-waistcoat did I see that poor Gertrude was gone. The rocking chair was still rocking. Her manic scribblings were scattered on the floorboards. I searched the room, as we all did, even yanking up the floorboards when the police arrived, but . . ."

Poe turned to Charcot. "Pertinent information reported from other inmates on the night?"

"They can tell us nothing. Remember, one thinks she is the Empress Josephine. Another, Mary Magdalene. Their fantasies are as many and varied as human imagining can provide. Reality is not their strong suit."

I voiced my frustration. "Then how can we ever discover the facts?"

"By talking to the only other witness we have," said Poe, turning again to the Professor of Anatomy. "Is Celestine capable of being questioned on the subject?"

Charcot blanched. "She is not capable of recalling the incident without the greatest distress. As you can imagine . . ."

"I cannot imagine, Monsieur – and neither can you. But I do wish to find Madame Gertrude – and not because this is an idle Sunday afternoon puzzle: experience informs me every minute she is away from Salpêtrière the potential danger to her mortal being increases."

"That's as may be, but as Celestine's physician I cannot condone the idea of interrogating her about something so disturbing to her consciousness."

"Then we shall have to bypass her consciousness altogether." My Southern gentleman chose not to look at the incipient horror rising on the doctor's face and consulted his pocket watch. "By a method that offers us far more than mere recollection. Hypnosis can enable a subject to recall the smallest detail with vivid clarity, free of the hubbub of our natural, waking existence. And I am not unaccomplished in the art."

Charcot almost choked on his laugh. "This is not a place for art, but for science."

"You yourself use the technique."

"Yes, indeed. But to induce and study the symptoms." The doctor felt the sceptical glare of black, lantern eyes. "I'd go as far as to say the ability to be hypnotized is a clinical feature of hysteria. Both are concomitant abnormalities . . ."

"But its usefulness is only to demonstrate? Preposterous. Forty years ago Professor John Elliotson publicly mesmerized the Irish O'Key sisters and it contained their convulsive symptoms. According to my own extensive researches, if used properly, the practice seems not only to sedate but to *reveal* – in extraordinary fashion."

"That may or may not be so, Monsieur Dupin, but I will not be responsible for the harm such an undertaking might do to my already vulnerable patient." Charcot's paleness became mitigated by a ruddy glow of anger. "I refuse to inflict upon Celestine a potential resurrection of her most abhorred possible fantasy. It goes against my vows as a surgeon and my discipline as a theoretician – I simply will not do it."

"Very well, then," said Edgar Allan Poe. "I shall."

Charcot's silence as he escorted us to his *salle d'examen* let us know he was caught between a rock and a hard place. Though his expression made his misgivings plain, he nevertheless wanted to find his missing inmate, and was perhaps aware that his intellectual stubbornness, or even pride, might stand in the way of that outcome. Still, he was by no means happy. And if he was at all human under that icy, pompous exterior, part of him was fearful. Fearful he was handing over control of his patient to – what? A *detective*? But a detective was exactly what he needed.

Tension locked my shoulders and the dream-like character of our environs was made more peculiar still by the echo of a disturbed woman's cries: "Where's the lion? The lion? The giant lion? Where is it? I'm concerned. It needs to be fed." I was selfish enough to be relieved when the closing door of the examination room shut her ravings out.

Within seconds, Celestine was brought in, and the first thing that struck me was Charcot's manner in the way he greeted her, which was that he barely acknowledged her presence at all. When he did, the merest turn of his hand directed her to a chair, which she sat in like an obedient child.

As for Celestine herself, I saw no face of madness, or even of nervous illness. She was taller than I imagined, by no means filthy or ill kempt, and had taken great care in her *toilette*. Dressed in a plain, coarse shift not unlike that worn by mill workers, she did not act with servility in any way, but conveyed an admirable self-assuredness. None of the inmates wore their hair in chignons, but rather cut raggedly and unadorned with pins or clasps that might, I concluded, be used do ill to themselves or others. The only thing that betrayed her maladjustment was that her hands were bunched tightly in fists, making her knuckles white. This made me smile at her, in an effort to help her relax, but it had no effect whatsoever.

The fact we were strangers did not bother her. Rather, it excited her, and she stumbled over her words, asking us if we were astronomers with news of discoveries, as she had written to several and did so on a weekly basis. She then alluded to the regimen that imprisoned her, but with only the mildest rancour, murmuring: "They keep all news of discoveries from me."

I said: "I'm sure that's because they do not wish you to be upset by such matters."

"Why? What would upset me?" For the first time a flicker of panic in her eyes indicated the scale of terror lurking under the surface.

"Nothing." Poe had immersed himself in a strange activity, using a ruler to tear up the blotting paper from Charcot's desk into a rectangle, punching a hole in it with a pen nib, then holding it up to the his eye. "Nothing at all, my dear." He rolled it into a scroll, slid it over the chimney of an oil lamp, affixing it with red wax used for sealing letters. "Nothing will upset you, I promise. Nothing."

The American slowly knelt on one knee in front of her, old bones creaking, one hand steadying himself on the arm of her chair. His sudden proximity made her flinch slightly. Though he did not touch her, his face was level with hers, and closer than a gentleman was accustomed to get.

"Your eye. I really think there is something in your eye. Is there? Do you mind if I look? Try to be still. That's it. Perfect. Just look straight forward. Don't move. Don't blink. Just relax."

He held the lamp with its pinprick of light off to the side, at arm's length, in her peripheral vision, and gave several passes, which I could see reflected as glimmers like tiny comets on her irises. He told her repeatedly that her eyelids were heavy. Within seconds they closed.

"Just feel completely relaxed and safe." The detective's voice was low, almost tender. "And whatever you say and whatever you see or feel, remember no harm can befall you."

I side-glanced at Charcot, head half buried in shadow. His fingers were splayed in a flying buttress at his temple, but his eyes were fixed on Celestine.

If she harboured any anxiety about our identities or why we were there, it no longer showed on her features. The somnambulistic trance had acted like an extraordinary potion.

She had been "mesmerized" – or "hypnotized", to use the verb invented to separate it from the hucksterism of fairground quackery and mysticism. Though mysticism is not a hundred miles from what it looked like to these eyes. It did not look like medicine. It looked like fakery – though I knew it was not. It was some occult process that disrupted and prised into the functioning of the brain, or the soul, or both. Though Mesmer himself always denied any supernatural element, espousing his skill to be a "peculiarity of observing", I found it incredibly hard to retain control of the idea that what I was watching was entirely scientific and not a peephole to the uncanny. No wonder that Poe, in his former incarnation as "Master of the Macabre", had written about it several times. His *Facts in the Case of M.Valdemar* is, of course, about a mesmerist who uses his specialism to halt death – and fails in the most gruesome fashion. But here we were not toying with characters on a page, but the mental life of a living young woman. And the trepidation of so doing created a knot of dread in my stomach.

"You are in the day room two nights ago, Celestine. Hennetier is standing in his usual place by the door. Why are you smiling?"

"He has an egg stain on his tunic. He is always so fastidious in his shiny shoes. He had an egg for breakfast." She tittered.

"He did. And look around. The sunlight is fading. It is evening. Gertude is in the rocking chair, scribbling away. Do you see her?"

Celestine nodded. Her eyes were still closed. Her head lolled slightly. Her hands lay palm-upwards on the armrests. Poe placed the oil lamp on a drop-leaf table where its pallid flame flickered. I could still not be sure whether this was science or hocus-pocus. A treatment, or a showman's dexterity.

"The clock strikes seven." He counted out the numbers at regular intervals. "Does anything happen?"

"No. It is quiet. Quiet as the grave. Mathurine isn't shouting and that's a surprise."

"How do you feel?"

"I feel bored. My book is boring."

"Why is it boring?"

"It tells me nothing new. Nothing important. Verne irritates me so much. Why won't he tell me what he *knows*?"

"And Gertrude?"

"Gertrude is boring too. Scratch, scratch, scratch with her charcoal and crayons. Nothing but scratch, scratch, scratch . . ."

I had seen a corpse on a slab, even a dissected one, and this was much more unpalatable. It had a weird theatricality in its aspect, and in her lack of resistance, her subjugation, a render-ing naked that made me uncomfortable.

"But I look over at her and I see it." Celestine twitched. "I see it again. The craft."

"Where do you see it?"

"Out . . . outside the French windows. Shimmering. There." Her eyes remained shut, but she pointed, almost striking Poe's cheek with her hand. A hand we all saw was trembling.

"What happened next?"

"No . . ."

"You are relaxed, so relaxed you are almost asleep, but you remember everything. What happened next?"

"No. They are coming. They . . . No!"

"Remember, you will not come to harm or pain while you are talking to me. Celestine, what happened next?"

"I see them. Just like before. They are outside the glass, clinging like bats. Then inside in their tight suits. Standing. Unsteady. Because this is not the earth they normally stand on. This is not their world, but ours!" She thrust both hands between her legs, locking them there with her thighs and tilting forward and back. "They look at me. They see me!" She began panting and her expressions changed with astonishing rapid-ity. "It's happening again! Oh God! Oh God! They're coming *again*!"

I was sorely tempted to look around me and check that the Moon Men were not in the room with us.

"Coming for whom, Celestine? For whom?"

"They have come for me! For *me*!" Her breathing was irregu-lar, the oppression of her lungs obvious. Charcot rose to his feet, feeling an attack was imminent, but Poe held him back with the flat of his hand. "Ah! I feel sick . . . Nnnn . . ." Her belly heaved. She made intermittent chewing motions, her forehead etched into a frown, the eyelids fluttered rapidly.

I could hardly bear to continue watching the extravagant agony of a body in the throes of its symptoms, but Poe presided over this hideous pantomime with utter calm, as if to him the seeing and knowing was all, and the suffering invisible.

"You are in a safe place now. No one can touch you. No one can hurt you."

"Chchchch . . ." She ground her teeth. "Get away, sprites! Damned things! Go back to the stars!"

"Celestine, listen to me."

"Leave me in – ahhhhh – sssss! No! Put away the tube! Not the tube!" I had an awful foreboding that the drawn-out moan she then emitted was escalating towards the despicable "*cri*".

"You see a tube. Where is the tube?"

"Gggggg!"

I recalled the phase of tonic immobility or tetanism I had seen in her photographs, and feared that I would be subjected to the sight of a human being abandoned to contractures that were both fantastic and inevitable – a tensing of the shoulders, the tongue withdrawn, almost swallowed, wrists touching each other on the dorsal side, acute mydriasis – jolts, quakes, cramps, throes . . . But no.

"They have it. They have it. They suck on it. They are like bees with nectar. And they touch. They *touch*."

"Who do they touch, Celestine?"

She froze, perplexed, with an air of abandonment – even disappointment. Her eyes still not open. Or were open only to her internal, persecutory universe.

"Celestine?"

"They touch . . . her." The tone in her breath of a question. Or disbelief. Or relief. Or wonder. "They touch *her*. And embrace her. And wrap her up, so quickly she has no time to protest, or even cry out. And lift her." Her cheeks shone with perspiration and her lower lip quivered. "And – take her."

In my mind's eye, I saw the empty rocking chair, the sheets of paper strewn across the room. The French windows – locked.

"And now?"

"Now their arms are around me and I'm struggling to get free and it's as if I wake from a dream and I'm in the arms of Hennetier and I am screaming, screaming until my throat is on fire. And my head is bursting and my legs feel cut off at the knees. And – as they strap me into the jacket and gag me – I

look over to the French windows. I see the craft hanging in the
night sky beyond the panes of glass. And I am laughing, laughing, laughing, because they have returned to the Orb once
more."

Indeed, she was laughing now. Not with pleasure or amusement but with the kind of animal prattle that accompanies an
inhalation of nitrous oxide. The manic gibber of something
unchained and unchecked.

"And the more I laugh, the more they tighten the straps." I
saw her teeth gnash and the pearl of a tear glisten in the corner
of one eye. "Tighten . . . Tighten . . ."

"And before the warders take you away, what do you see?"

"The room is empty."

"What does that tell you?"

"It tells me the inhabitants of – *that place* – are no longer on
our soil."

"That's correct. Which means what?"

Celestine did not answer.

"It means they can no longer threaten you," said Poe. "While
you hear my voice they are powerless, and you are free, and you
are sleeping, the deepest and most comforting sleep you have
ever known."

Within less than a minute she was becalmed.

"And when I tap the arm of the chair you will rouse from that
slumber without remembering any bad thoughts you might
have had or emotions you might have felt. You shall be refreshed
and as gay as you were as a child in the most beautiful meadow
under the warmest sunshine."

He did so, and her eyes opened.

She looked at each of us in turn, with a bewilderment as if she
had just lifted her head from her pillow.

"Celestine, that will be all." Charcot walked to the door and
opened it. The two guards who had brought her stood waiting.

Celestine gave a light laugh. A laugh that would not have been
out of place at a respectable *soirée*. Not at all like the chattering
she had displayed to us only minutes earlier.

"But, Monsieur. I have just this second sat down."

Charcot merely turned his hand towards the door. Without questioning his authority she rose, gave Poe and myself the most rudimentary curtsey, and obeyed.

"Remarkable." The Socrates of Salpêtrière closed the door after her. "Perfectly remarkable."

My friend was unmoved by his praise. "She is calm because I willed her to be calm. She is sick because you will her to remain sick. You imprison her with your misbegotten quest for a biological cure." At sixty-nine, age had not tempered Poe's ability to speak as he felt. The barbs he once wielded as a literary critic now flew at plentiful targets, invariably making me cringe.

"How dare you, Monsieur!" Charcot was flabbergasted at his effrontery. "You—you are not a medical mind."

"No, but I am a mind. And I hope you will think on what you have seen. You have eyes to observe, and I pray they have done their duty." Poe tidied his cuffs and tugged his sleeves. "Now please direct us out of this labyrinth. We have seen enough."

Thus we bade an ambivalent farewell to the Cathedral of the "Sent-Mad", where a system of measuring and cataloguing souls seemed no less absurd than the fantasia of *Doctor Tarr and Professor Fether*. I could not wait to get to the far side of the gates.

Crossing the courtyard past the fountain, I saw an elderly woman pressing her hands into a pile of sand with all the absorption of an infant. I looked back at the high window, behind which a stern visage looked down, his hand gripping one dark lapel. Doctor Charcot was clearly master over all he surveyed, but I wondered how much his patients' survival depended in some fundamental way on pleasing him? I wondered even if, on both sides, there existed something of an invisible, unknowing pact?

"And much of Madness, and more of Sin, and Horror the soul of the plot . . ."

Madness, of course, was Poe's quintessential subject. His writing told us not to look in the madhouse for such ideas, but within us all. That evening, with pipe smoke thick in the air, we discussed whether a mad person had lost their truth or found it, in grasping something beyond the stifling realm of the incurably sane. "Perhaps the *coup de théâtre* results in a lifting of the veil and seeing reality, in all its dreadfulness, the falsehood being the *entr'acte* of so-called 'normality'."

"A romantic notion," I opined. "There is no romance in diseases of the mind."

"And yet can we fail to see in the mad a failed version of ourselves? Why not a different being, but equal? As one sail may be battered by a storm, but one more tightly bound, stay unmoved?"

Madame L'Espanaye served cardamom-flavoured Réunion coffee as Le Bon closed the curtains across a silver disc hanging in the sky. The manservant was not our gaoler, but after what we had seen I had difficulty shaking the notion that our rooms in the Rue de la Femme-Sans-Tête were a kind of confinement.

Poe crossed the room in his Persian slippers, pipe locked in his teeth, and slid open a plans chest, removing faded manuscripts I had never seen before in spite of living there for years. Proctor's *Chart of the Visible Stars*, the *Globi Coelestis in Tabulas Planas* and, lastly, the 1742 *Tabula Selenographica* of Homann and Doppelmayr, created in full colour to illustrate the lunar mapping of Johannes Hevelius and Giovanni Battista Riccioli. Astonishing me in both detail and beauty, here the moon was seen as it never could be from Earth – at greater than three hundred and sixty degrees and with all visible features given equal weight.

"What is a lie? Merely what we cannot see?"

"Are all things possible, then?" I said with heavy sarcasm. "Surely not, in scientific terms."

"But science has to change, to adapt to what is perceived." He fetched a candelabrum, the better to peruse the surface of the moon, whose whiteness mirrored his thinning hair.

"And what *is* perceived?" The implication of his words stunned me. "Poe, you cannot possibly consider that Celestine's story is true?"

"I have not had it disproven," he said disinterestedly – and provocatively.

"Then let me oblige." I eagerly seized the gauntlet. "There are trees in the Bois de Vicennes. One can postulate, and an experiment might easily demonstrate, that as she galloped through the park in bright sunshine, a stroboscopic effect was created between a low evening sun and the space between the tree trunks, at a certain frequency inducing a seizure in the brain. Or else this: the attack was real, by real men intent on rape, and as a defence mechanism she has retreated into fantasy. To blank it out."

"But, *mon brave*, she has *not* blanked it out. It haunts and plagues her. It gives her no respite. Why would memory do that in an attempt to salve the psychic wound?"

"Because the brain knows not what it does," I said, trying not to flounder. "And pain cannot be eradicated. So the malicious act is transformed into a malevolent fantasy."

"But what of the actual disappearance of Gertrude? That is not a mental aberration but a physical one."

"Then Celestine saw men from the moon?"

"You think it a ludicrous concept?"

"I do!"

"Recall, then, the Aztecs of Mexico who saw the first sailing ships from Spain on their shores and could not conceive of their reality." He circled the esoteric charts. "They thought *conquistadores* on horseback to be exotic centaurs, not two animals but one monstrous hybrid."

I laughed. "Which is only to say those very implements of observation and knowledge – our eyes – can sometimes lie. To protect us from the truth."

"And the truth is what?" He tossed book after book onto the maps. They thudded with the heft of their contents. "Greater minds than mine have found the idea of non-terrestrial life not only credible but likely. The astronomer Flammarion espouses the belief in his *La plurité des mondes habités*—" one of the volumes before me "—and Gottfried Liebnitz, Newton's rival in the creation of calculus, said it must be acknowledged that 'an infinite number of globes have as much right as ours' to hold rational inhabitants – 'through it follows not at all that they are human'."

"But recent calculations show the moon to be too small, its gravity too feeble, to hold an atmosphere. And Julian Schmidt has shown there are no cities or artificial structures."

"My dear Holmes! You are dangerously close to thinking our planet is the centre of the universe! Giordano Bruno disputed that back in *De l'Infinito, Universo e Mondi*, and was burned at the stake for it. For declaring, 'Countless suns and countless earths all rotate around their suns in exactly the same way as the seven planets of our system.' And that these worlds must be no less inhabited than our Earth."

"And if they did exist, these imps or *farfadets*, on the moon or Venus or Mars – what possible desire or inclination would they have to visit us and for what purpose? To abuse us, to examine us with their instruments, to assess our biology, the better to understand?"

Poe shrugged and watched a circle of pipe smoke rise to the ceiling. "Or to play, as we would dangle a ball of wool for a kitten? Which we would just as swiftly drown."

"Human beings also have a capacity for affection."

"Ah, but we are not considering human beings."

Now I sensed the kitten he was playing with was me. Could he really be serious is his assertions? Or like a dutiful defence lawyer, was he simply stating a case that he privately disavowed?

"Please. For these many months your intelligence has impressed me, overwhelmed me – no, transformed me." I could not disguise that I was upset. "I beg of you, do not destroy that gargantuan monument by telling me you believe we are being visited by other worlds."

His hooded eyes looked away from me with supreme nonchalance. "Let me just say, my dear Holmes, that as regards life within our solar system or beyond, I follow the precept or *Tertullion: Credo quia absurdum*. I believe it because it is absurd."

I returned the books to the shelves. "All fancies aside, what we have here on Earth is a room from which a person vanished without trace."

"You are right." He closed the plans chest. "Our satellite exerts an eternal fascination in its confluence with madness, even a mythological power – was it not Aristotle who suggested that the brain was the 'moistest' organ in the body and thereby most susceptible to the pernicious influences of the moon, which triggers the tides? The sun is Helios, giver of life – but what does the moon offer? It is the light by which the nocturnal hunt and their prey cower . . . But we cannot travel there to solve this puzzle."

"We agree at last," I said. "But if the key to unlock the mystery is not in the high heavens, where is it?"

"In Celestine. In her crime of attempted murder." He blew out all the candles save one. "Come, let us take to our beds. Tomorrow we shall need all our wits about us, and more. We are going to seek out the madwoman's nemesis . . . And find indeed if he has secrets to hide."

The next morning, we hastened to catch the first train to Amiens, a two-hour journey via Abbeville. I expected, and found, a sleepy provincial town, near enough to feel a reflection of Paris but without its insufferable racket and agitation. The honeysuckle scent of bougainvilleas drifted on the air from the floating *Hortillonnages* amongst the canals – or *rieux* as they were called in the dialect of Picardy. Willow, alder and the sight of wildfowl combined to give a welcome sense of Eden.

The house at 44 Boulevard Longueville was severe-looking but spacious, and we were quickly greeted by its owner – ruddy tan from striding the jetty at Le Crotoy, hair like an undulating sea frothy with waves, a nautical beard and slightly heavy-lidded eyes that nevertheless sparkled with intense vigour. At the age of fifty, not a line marred Jules Verne's features other than around his eyes: more the product of laughter than frowning.

"Dupin! My friend!" He boomed as he shook my companion's hand. "I feel I know you intimately, even if it was a name only used in the American editions! Honestly, there is not a greater devotee of Poe in France than the man before you!" I now thought his handshake might break bones. "I confess, when I read of his death, I wept like a baby. In mourning a great writer, even one you never met, you mourn a friend."

"Indeed," said Poe, extracting his digits. I could tell he was flattered, even if he dared not show it for fear of revealing his true identity.

"Did you know him, then? I detect the trace of an American accent."

"We were acquainted." Poe coughed. "In Richmond. Briefly. He was good company, but a difficult man. Hard to like. Drove away friends as others would swat away bees."

"But had a sting of his own." Verne grinned. "Albeit delivered with his critical nib."

"Which made him more enemies than friends. I was one of the few."

"And to die by *delirium tremens*. Awful way to go. Dreadful to think of his febrile life, wracked as it was by madness."

"Relieved by periods of horrible sanity," said Poe without inflection.

Verne laughed like a bear, if a bear can laugh. He slapped our shoulders and led us down the hall.

However, the conversation had made me consider Poe's "madness", which I never had before. *Was* he mad? I remember him once imagining the fate of an individual gifted, or rather cursed, with an intellect far superior to those around him. Surely, he said, that person's opinions and speculations would differ so widely from the rest of mankind that he would be considered mad? *And how horribly painful such a condition. Hell could invent no greater torture than being charged with abnormal weakness on account of being abnormally strong.* I had no doubt the individual he was ruminating upon was himself.

At the door to Verne's study, we were intercepted by his wife, Honorine, not a great beauty but a pleasant if homely woman. She offered us soup made from local produce from the market gardens – carrots, turnips, leeks – but we declined.

"My dear, these men have come to discuss business." (Indeed, our pantelegraph message had said – falsely – as much.) Honorine curtseyed and absented herself to elsewhere in the house. Verne shut the door of the study. "Poor darling, she does not understand the writer's life. She complained her husband 'was forever in his balloon', but that same balloon was to make her a wealthy woman."

Poe and I glanced at each other.

I saw one table to write on, another piled with reference books, a comfortable armchair and a camp bed – at peak intensity, Verne desired to be no more than five paces from his work – a pipe rack and, beyond it all, a library. I half expected the riveted metal of the hull of the *Nautilus*, but no. The only concession to his yarns, and his upbringing in the seaport of Nantes with its Cape-Horners docked with exotic cargo from across the world, was a large propeller mounted on one wall. Now his mind was full of the "Cape-Horners" of space, of the future – as attested to by framed illustrations from *Five Weeks in a Balloon*, Verne as Professor Aronnax from *20,000 Leagues Under the Sea* and two scenes depicting Captain Nemo at the helm and the battle with the giant squid.

"Ah, this is my '62 edition of Poe's works." Verne took a volume from his shelves. "But I first read it close to '48 when it first came out in translation. I devoured it! Of course the 'Balloon Hoax' and 'Hans Pfaall' gave me the idea for *Un Voyage en Ballon*, but neither of his stories is particularly convincing. 'Pfaall' is nothing but a humorous fantasy – clearly a flaw."

*Flaw?* I looked at Poe, but Poe remained mute.

"What I do, you see, is to make the fantastic seem *convincing*. What's annoying, as I said in my essay on Poe for *Le Musée des Familles*, is that he could so easily have made his tales more *plausible* had he just respected a few elementary laws of physics."

Poe's mouth twitched into a fixed grin, but Verne was in full flood.

"You see, over the years, I have compiled thousands of data cards, the better to educate a general public who know little of what is happening in the world of science – but you cannot drag a horse to water and expect it to drink! Reading Poe, I immediately saw what could be done if you mix fantasy and *facts*. But in Poe science plays a secondary role, a pretext, a frame for the writer's own anguish by depicting human behaviour in abnormal situations – the *bizarre* for its own sake. Moral deviation was his way of showing his crushing scorn for progress in American society. I wanted to do the opposite! Show that man can achieve fulfilment by tackling the environment, nature, which is both real and hostile – not the escapist cults of Truth, Imagination or Beauty."

"But Poe created a new form of literature, a form coming from the sensitivity of his excessive mental processes." I spoke up on behalf of my friend to avoid him having to do so. "I see in his stories a relentless scrutiny of his own morbid traits, a discussion of obscure facts, sometimes through satire, yes, but with no whiff of the supernatural. Poe saw the fantastic in the real."

The corporeal Poe appreciated my defence.

"But without *scienee* . . ."Verne gesticulated. "A manuscript in a bottle, a decent into a maelstrom – what is it worth? Where is the excitement? Where is the *commerciality*?"

Now, Poe had to sit down. But he also had to take it on the chin. He was, after all, not "Edgar Poe" but "Auguste Dupin" – his literary creation and the identity he chose to appropriate when inventing a new life in Europe. And we had a job to do.

"I do not deny," said Verne, "that he is the undisputed leader of the school of the strange."

"And his characters are eminently human." Poe now spoke. "Endowed often with a supercharged sensitivity. Exceptional individuals, galvanized as if by air with more oxygen than it should have, and whose lives are one long combustion. If they are not mad, they most inevitably *become* mad through the abuse of their minds. They push self-reflection and deduction to the limit. They are fearsome analysts. Starting from the merest trifle, they reach absolute truth."

Far from contradicting him, Verne's face became enraptured with glee.

"Don't misunderstand me! I owe him everything! Look at me!" He gave an expansive gesture, encompassing the room. "He wrote a little concoction about a cosmological oddity called 'Three Sundays in a Week' and I turned the idea into *Around the World in Eighty Days*! The popular edition sold over a hundred thousand copies and the illustrated three times that! It was the novel that made me famous!" He kissed the book squarely on the cover.

Poe's lips tried hard not to tighten. "Then you owe old Edgar quite a lot. And not just in terms of plagiarism."

Verne guffawed. "Novelty of situation. Little known facts. The drama of nature and destruction ... But my heroes are never unhealthy or nervous of temperament."

"God forbid."

"If only Poe could have gloried in human energy. In the positive!"

"And have Man defeat death, perhaps? In what way does that reflect any life actually lived?"

"But to strive, Monsieur Dupin, to *strive*! That is what Man does. And so I push my characters to the extreme – outwards ..."

"Perhaps the real exploration is inwards."

Verne made a face. "I took literature in a different direction."

"Yet at times," I chipped in, "it feels you had to make an effort not to step in his footsteps."

"You're an Englishman. My apologies for not detecting it earlier."

"My name is Sherlock Holmes."

"I saw the Blackwall Tunnel and the Great Eastern being built in Greenwich. Most impressive! More impressive than the *Macbeth* I saw at the Princess Royal." Verne's smile twisted. "But I also saw children in rags and beggars holding out hats beneath the tall London housefronts."

"Alas, that dichotomy is not unique to my homeland."

In a room above I could hear somebody playing the piano. Perhaps one of Verne's married stepdaughters, Valentine and Suzanne, or his son by this marriage, Michel, still a schoolboy.

"Now, the reason for your visit. I understand you have a business proposition."

"If you'll indulge me just a moment longer, monsieur," said Poe. "I'm such a fan of your work." Remarkably, the words did not stick in his craw. "Can I just ask where the inspiration came

from for your astounding books about the voyage to the moon?"
He had slyly opened the door to our investigation.

"I was at the height of my popularity, but still dividing my
time between the capital and the coast. Sailing round Cotentin
and Finistere in the *Saint-Michel*, while travelling to the stars
here." Verne tapped the side of his head. "*De la Terre à la Lune*
drew on all my accumulated knowledge, in exactly the way I've
talked about. I even got my cousin, a cosmologist and mathe-
matician, to establish the correct trajectories. There were problems of excessive initial velocity, overheating due to friction in
the atmosphere, the design of the breaking rockets, and so on.
But I was determined to make the project ballistically
feasible."

Like most of France, I had read Verne's story of the Baltimore
Gun Club, a post-Civil War society of weapons aficionados,
building a sky-facing cannon in Florida to launch a projectile
containing three people (their president Impey Barbicane, his
plate armour-making rival, Nicholl, and a French poet) at the
moon – and land on it.

"Yet they failed," I said.

Verne shrugged. "That is the cost of realism. After a series of
misadventures, they fall short of their target. But I couldn't let
them revolve in orbit forever or go crashing into the surface
below, so in my sequel, *Autour de Lune*, I had Ardan get the idea
of using auxiliary rockets, planned to buffer the landing, to steer
Barbicane and his companions back within the gravitational pull
of Earth."

"The three men discuss the possibility of life on the moon," I
said. "If I remember correctly, they conclude it is barren."

"Absolutely. None of 'Hans Pfaall"s ridiculous two foot tall
Lunarians!"

"And that is the view you maintain, given the current scientific knowledge with which you are at great pains to keep
up-to-date?"

For the first time, Verne sensed he was being interrogated.
"Most definitely and emphatically." His mood darkened.
"Forgive me. What is the *exact* purpose of this conversation?"

Poe remained unruffled. "Please answer the question, Monsieur."

"I am not sure I shall. At all. I don't like your tone of voice, whoever-you-are. And who *are* you? I had thought from the telegram your interest was a 'business venture' – a theatrical one. In my stupidity I'd assumed the signature, *Dupin* – obviously a pseudonym – was a wry way of informing me you wanted my services to adapt a story or stories by Poe for the stage."

"And if we had told you anything else, would you have admitted us?"

"Almost certainly not, without suitable credentials. I am – well, astonished. You . . . you have found your way into my home by . . . by gross deception, Messieurs."

"Deception was the only way open to us, because of the utmost gravity of the situation." I explained. "A life is in peril, and—"

"And I would like an answer to Holmes's question." Poe cut in. "Do you believe inhabitants of the moon visit this planet?"

Verne's demeanour, formerly relaxed and free of airs and graces, now became taciturn and formidable.

"I'm afraid I must ask you to leave." He rang a bell pull.

"Not an unpredictable request," said Poe, "but we are undertaking an inquiry on behalf of Salpêtrière Hospital. And though we are not the police, that inquiry is a criminal one."

"Salpêtrière?" Verne could hardly have looked less horrified if told one of his children had been maimed. "That woman? That harridan. *Mon Dieu!* I vowed never to discuss that event again."

"If there is a prosecution for murder, you may have to. And in a glare of publicity you could do without."

A servant appeared, but with sudden irritation Verne waved him away. When the man was gone he spoke again, through beetle brows: "I have nothing whatsoever to hide. What do you want of me?"

"Firstly and foremost, a simple account of Celestine's attack on you."

Verne wiped his face with meaty hands, took up his pen and held it as if the object gave him some kind of comfort. "I was in the Paris offices of my editor, Hetzel, in the Rue Jacob." Hetzel would be famous for publishing not only Verne but Hugo, George Sand (another "Dupin") and Erckman-Chatrain. "We were revising the final proofs of *Une Fantasie du Docteur Ox.* A woman burst in. She waved a book – *my* book, *The Moon Voyage* – and blathered without pause or breath that I was conspiring with creatures from the moon in their invasion of our planet. That I was deliberately disseminating information to the population of the world that life on the moon was impossible in order to trick us all, to disguise the horrific truth! Before I could even laugh, she fired a pistol at me. Luckily, the bullet only grazed my shoulder, but she was aiming for my head. Then she came at me violently, as if possessed, kicking and screaming, but, having heard the gunshot, Heztel's assistants rushed in and pinned her to ground."

"You are shaking, even now," I observed.

"I was rattled. So was Hetzel. It is rare to encounter the mad. Michel, I know – my boy has his problems – he can be sullen, odious, charming, full of selfish actions, stubborn, impulsive – his mother and I don't know what shall become of him, but this . . ." Forlorn, he looked a different person from the one who had greeted us with such *bonhomie.* "The next day, I was numb and couldn't write a word. I told Honorine I felt I should contact this woman, help her if I could, but she wisely counselled me it was better not to. The girl plainly cannot be shaken in her convictions, and it is better she is left to the care of experts."

"Can you tell us anything more about her temperament or demeanour?"

"Her eyes were glassy, lacking in focus. She had the determination of an animal fixed on its prey."

"You did not report the incident to the police or the press?"

"Strange as this may seem, I did not want to bring undue unpleasantness to her family. My fame brings unwarranted consequences."

Poe examined his lapel distractedly. "Tell me about Hetzel."

"I would trust the man with my life. He is my literary and spiritual father. He took me in when other publishers rejected me. He had faith in me when others didn't. He created me."

I could not help but look at the reclining Poe with his crossed legs – my wonderful, supercilious *Dupin* – and think the same.

"As for his character," Verne continued, "he was a revolutionary. I came to Paris as a student cheering a republic he had helped create." He picked up a sheet of paper full of crossings-out. "From the beginning, he helped me rewrite, to change a sad ending to a happy one, tone down any political messages, to get rid of the pessimism and add sentiment – which always goes down well with the public."

Poe made what I can only call a grimace.

"I never knew a good editor whose instinct was superior to that of a good writer."

Verne shook his head. "I wanted Nemo to be a vengeful Pole sinking Russian ships. Hetzel persuaded me it would be a mistake. So I made him a more general rebel against tyranny."

"Diminishing your character in the process."

"Not according to the sales figures."

"And his death in *L'Ile Mystèrieuse* was somewhat tardy." Poe's nostrils flared.

"You sound like a critic."

"Perhaps I was. In another life."

Verne could never have realized the infinite truth behind such a remark. We sat in the lap of luxury, with servants and surrounded by domestic bliss. Verne had been given the Légion d'honneur, had recently enjoyed a private audience with the Pope, had been embraced by Venice where they put up bunting saying "Eviva Giulio Verne" and let off fireworks. Poe in his lifetime had never had even a glimmer of such success or adoration. His was the struggle of a troubled genius, a narrative of starvation, setbacks and ill health, a reputation, yes, but never reputation enough to keep the wolf from the door.

"I suppose she will now be under lock and key for the rest of her days," said the Frenchman. "I presume she has killed one of the other inmates."

"Presumption is a dangerous thing." Poe stood. "And certainly not scientific. I would think you would have learned that in your years of research." The two writers shook hands. "Now, we shall take up no more of your time."

Verne accompanied us back through the hall, decorated as it was by illustrations from his *Voyages Extraordinaires*, a painting of the aeronaut Tissandier and an advertisement for a "*Panorama de Paris*" ride up into the air in a "*Grand Ballon Captif a Vapeur!*" – "*Tous Les Jours Ascensions Captives de 500 à 600 mètres D'Altitude!*"

"One last thing, Monsieur Dupin. Before you go." Verne hovered on his doorstep. "Did you really know Edgar Poe?"

Poe revolved on his heel, turning back to him. I wondered what he would say. "Intimately."

"Then put me out of my misery, please. Ever since I read it I have been obsessed by the inconclusive ending of *The Narrative of Arthur Gordon Pym*. The giant white female figure barring his way to the South Pole . . . Is she some mythic eternal mother? The symbol of the cosmic breast? An angel? Or some white race superior even to *Homo sapiens*?"

"I think I am safe in saying, nothing was further from the author's intention."

"But he implies it is not of this earth. Did he believe such things possible? What does it mean?"

"To a poet, meaning is a very overrated commodity."

"But the public do not love poetry, they love a good story!" cried Verne. "And the ending is so vexatious, it leaves us perplexed and dissatisfied."

Poe's face was both haughty and pained. "Perhaps that was the intention."

"But surely, had he lived, he would have changed it? To satisfy, rather than baffle the reader?"

"He may have changed nothing," said Poe wearily. "Perhaps he got tired of writing marvel after marvel. The temptation constantly hovers, when to write 'The End'. As we must end this conversation, Monsieur. *Au revoir.*"

After stating that the visit had been entirely wasted, Poe spend the entire sprightly walk to the station – and he could be sprightly when required – grumbling about Verne, thanking the Lord that he had not trapped us into discussing the problem of the Newfoundland dog that conveniently vanishes, or whether the crewmates were "scientific" in their cannibalization of the unfortunate seaman Parker.

I asked if he was by any chance riled by the man. "Not at all!" Yet still he wittered on about the novelist's egregious faults, specifically and generally, arriving at the dismissive summation: "He devises his plots as a bricklayer builds a wall. And the worst of it is that in listening to his self-aggrandizing drivel, we are no closer to solving the mystery of Gertrude Socha's disappearance."

"That may not be true." I saw a plume of steam, announcing our train was shortly to pull into the platform. "I think I have the answer. As we left the house, the final piece of the puzzle fell into place."

Poe looked at me with the delight and astonishment of a proud parent.

His features brightened from his previous all-pervading gloom, but then, just as somebody barged past behind him, became pale, then quizzical, his neck straightening.

"That is most curious." He blinked, leaning with one hand against my chest. "I always wondered what the sensation would be like, and now I know. It is like being hit by a mallet. Now a coldness is spreading through my body. Take note of this for future reference, my dear Holmes. I feel extremely – yes – *faint* . . ."

Frighteningly, his eyes became totally blank and fixed, corpse-like. His head fell forward, but his legs had given way, and he sank to the platform before I was able to catch him.

He lay in a heap, limbs splayed, passengers hurrying by in blissful ignorance, as I fell to my knees beside him. Behind his head and neck, I saw blood pumping out of him, forming a thick, viscous pool to which strands of his long white hair stuck.

The life was leaving his body, as the light had already left his eyes.

"Dupin! Dupin!" I yelled, then cursed myself for not using his real name. "*Edgar!*"

Even as his skin turned from parchment to grey, he lifted a weak hand, feebly, and covered my mouth.

We rushed him, soaked in blood, to Amiens Hospital Infirmary in one of the *barque à cornets*, resembling nothing so much – to my horrified heart – as a funeral barge. He was unconscious when I left him to the mercy of the surgeons. I could not take in what the nurse was telling me, then heard my friend telling me to snap out of it and concentrate on the valuable information. He had been stabbed in the back. A downward swipe at his shoulder blade. I damned myself for not pushing aside the crowd on the platform, for not having the instinct to search for his attacker, but it had all been a blur.

I asked if the wound might be fatal. She said they didn't know yet. I thought: *They will not know until the person dies: then it's fatal all right*. I was ungrateful to her, hated her in fact, though she didn't deserve it. My rage had to target somebody. Again I heard Poe telling me, I must keep my feelings in check. I remembered the first few days and weeks training in "ratiocination", spent learning that emotion is an enemy to logic, that it lures us further and further from the truth. If I succumbed now, all my education would have been in vain.

I caught the next train back to Paris. I knew I had to act swiftly or the Master would never forgive me. Also, sickeningly, there was a possibility I was now seeking the murderer of Edgar Allan Poe, and while the world had mourned the writer many years before, I would have to mourn my friend alone.

Sitting in that railway carriage, I wept far more than when I heard of the loss of my father. But I had to steel my nerves. Apply all the lessons he had given me, crack the crime and apprehend the criminal. And I had to remember not only was Poe's life in the balance, but that of Gertrude Socha. And the clock was ticking on both counts.

I raced to Salpêtrière. Demanded to see Charcot. With no time for his objections, I demanded to see Hennetier, threatening him with the police if he didn't let me. As soon as I saw the guard, and he saw the devastation in my face and a smirk arose,

I lost all reason and grabbed him by the throat, driving him hard against the wall. It was all too obvious he thought "Dupin" was dead. He shoved me away and blew his whistle deafeningly – a woman inmate in our vicinity covered her ears and shrieked like a pig at slaughter – and by the time I got my breath back two gigantic warders were fastened onto my arms.

"He is the one you should be apprehending!" I screamed, as I saw a third gaoler carrying a strait-jacket. "*He* is the one instrumental in the kidnapping of Gertrude Socha!"

Hennetier tried to cover his fear with an air of bravado, showing Charcot the palms of his hands. His colleagues held me firmer still, but I found some of Poe's arrogance and fearlessness had rubbed off on me.

"You can lock me up or throw me out, but you would do well to listen unless you want this institution to descend into extreme disrepute." Now I was certain I had Charcot's undivided attention. "My deductions have led me to the inevitable conclusion. Hennetier 'saw nothing' yet was the sole person responsible for the locks on all the doors and windows – so, eliminating all other possibilities, he *must* be involved. In 'seeing nothing', he sought to divert attention to Celestine's delusion, in order to buy him and his accomplices time. And what he is too stupid to realize is that if they do something reckless, he will go to the guillotine with them."

Hennetier seemed to physically diminish in stature. Openmouthed, he darted his eyes from me to Charcot and back again, as furtive as a rat in a trap.

"I . . . I never knew it would come to this. I am a simple man . . ."

Charcot signalled for the men to let me go.

"What are their names?" I rubbed the bruises on my elbows. "Quickly, damn you."

"Corcoran."

"And the other. One above, one below. I'm not an imbecile."

"Lamiche."

"Where are they holding her?"

"A house in the Rue Maillard, Monsieur. But they will not be there now. Please . . ."

"Where will I find them?"

"Tonight? In the Bois de Vincennes."

How could mention of that place not chill me like ice? It was the very location of Celestine Blot's first encounter with her denizens of the moon.

The Bois de Vincennes . . .

Royal hunting ground, neglected by one King Louis, restored by another, donated to the city by Napoleon III to be made into an "English-style" park: it almost made me feel patriotic. But in the dark of night with a pounding heart, I had room for no such warm thoughts. Unless to keep my teeth from chattering.

The design was by Haussman's landscape architect Jean-Charles Alphand. As I waited, I imagined them as teacher and pupil, like Poe and myself – probably a fantasy. The purpose had been to give green space for leisure to the working class of East Paris – colourful splendour, picturesque landscapes, lawns, groves, flowerbeds and lakes: though there was precious little colour to be seen now under bleak evening cloud. The site had its problems, which Alphand solved by annexing sections of land and creating three smaller parks each with its own artificial lake and surroundings. Lac des Minimes to the north encompassed the original medieval monastery that once stood there, and the Lac de Saint-Mandé in the south-west, while Lake Daumesnil was created as a setting out of a romantic painting, with two islands and sloping lawns. Alphand also planned it to have popular attractions such as a horse-racing track, similar to the Longchamps hippodrome at the Bois de Boulogne, and there were café-restaurants, a bandstand, buildings for vendors and game concessions – all eerily silent now . . .

Through my telescope I could see the Temple of Love: a round Doric edifice placed on a promontory on the Isle de Reuilly, above an artificial grotto. We were stationed facing it.

I had sped immediately from Salpêtrière to the *Préfecture* at 36 Quai des Orfèvres, home of the police *judiciaire*, as had been the Rue de Jérusalem in the days of Balzac. Albert Gigot, the current *Prefet*, had been helped in many cases by

"Dupin" and listened attentively to my story once he knew there had been an attempt on his life – possibly a successful one. Without hesitation, he appointed Claude Bident to be officer in charge – formerly of the *Sûreté nationale* – an Englishman's idea of a Frenchman, a little man with a beard in bowler hat and morning coat. The police in those days were both bureaucratic and sabre rattling, monitoring a city still moody and dangerous, operating amidst enmities and grievances born of the recent struggle resulting in the crea-tion of a new political order.

And so we waited, hidden by shrubbery, under the great orb of a full moon. It seemed inevitable.

The only sound was the water from the ornamental cascades, and the waves splashing the pleasure boats tied inertly to their docks.

Bident, in the shadows, tapped my shoulder. Pointed.

I saw motion on the lake. My lens enlarged it.

A rowing boat, its oars being silently heaved. Two men – the taller one, who would turn out to be Corcoran, sitting at the stern, the other, Lamiche, using the brute force of muscled arms to power it. Between them sat what I first took to be a bundle and then concluded from its shifting movement was the huddled figure of Gertrude Socha, a sack over her head, arms tied behind her back, with a noose round her neck.

They were heading for the island.

I had discussed this eventuality with Bident. I'd told him we could not risk hitting Gertrude if there was gunfire, so we'd initiated a plan for Hennetier to call his fellow miscreants to shore before we pounced. This Hennetier readily agreed to do, in return for a good word in court from the police – anything to diminish the full force of the law, and possible decapitation. As Bident said, it focuses the mind, decapitation.

So, true to his word, once his partners in crime were in sight, Hennetier walked to the waterline and waved his arms in the air. They soon caught sight of his lantern and stopped rowing. The two men looked at each other. Hennetier imitated the hoot of an owl and we watched as the boat slowly changed direction, only one oar spooning the waves, and it made towards him – and, little by little, nearer to us . . .

Suddenly, only yards from running aground, Corcoran made a stirring motion in the air with his hand. Lamiche looked startled, right and left, and paddled furiously. The boat turned in a sharp curve, pointing once more to the island. Corcoran stood up, but only to fire a pistol directly at Hennetier's head, killing the man outright. The gang leader knew somehow by the oddity of Hennetier's unexpected arrival that he had been betrayed.

It was then the police opened fire. Lamiche dived into the belly of the boat and in so doing almost capsized it. Gertrude, being masked and incapacitated by her bonds, could do nothing to rebalance herself, and was thrown into the lake, even as dozens of bullets tore splinters out of wood, and punctured the watery surface in a flotilla of splashes.

I threw myself in after her, hearing Poe in my ear telling me that it was absurd to risk my own life when the chances of saving her were slim, but some part of me equated saving her with bringing the case to a conclusion. Though if I was thinking this, I wasn't aware of it. I just did it, and submerged myself, and swam out, knowing that if I didn't the sackcloth would clog her mouth in seconds, and with her hands tied, she would drown. She had already sunk like a stone.

If it was night above, it was ten times night below the waves. My blood protested as if it were the Arctic, but I went down at the spot where I'd seen her entering the water, and nothing – *nothing* could I find but branches, weeds, everything that could be a barrier to me, not least my own pathetic lungs. I emerged, gasped, descended again, combed and snatched at those hellish fronds. Where was she? There! I felt her. I had her. I grabbed her. What part of her? Her shoulders. Chin. I hooked it with my elbow, bobbed myself to the surface, swam.

Legs surrounded me as I hauled the object onto the lawn, face down in the moonlight. Bident slashed her bonds with a bayonet. I turned her onto her back, trying desperately to eject any water she had swallowed. I saw no movement under the coarse material covering her face, other than the spastic jerks caused by my frenetic beating of her chest. The better to see if she was breathing or not, I tore off the hood.

I did not want to believe she was already dead. I did not want to see that her eyes, gluey with pond water, were fixed half open. I did not want, above anything, to behold that her face was a mass of bruises and contusions caused by incessant and heartless torture. But that is what I saw. I groaned and rocked back, realizing that my actions were futile.

I closed her lids with my fingertips. Perhaps now, at least, she had peace from her madness. Amen, if anything, to that.

The night air was still after the flurry of gunshots. On my knees in the mud, I saw that one of the thuggish individuals had been shot dead by the trigger-happy police. The other struggled in the grip of uniforms, a knife shaken from his fist. This was Lamiche – short to the point of being pygmy-like, shaven-headed and well muscled, stripped to the waist like a boxer. I immediately knew he was Celestine's night-imp, her '*farfadet*' . . . and Poe's intended murderer.

As they bundled Lamiche off, I picked up the weapon and hurled it far into the lake. When I turned back, Bident had extracted something from the dead Corcoran's pocket. He unfolded it and held it up to me. Even by the light of the moon, there was no mistaking it was a treasure map.

"The Gold Bug," Poe croaked. "The deadly bug that infects all men – greed." He was sitting up in the hospital bed, bandaged, with pillows supporting his lower back, but was now out of danger. The sawbones had sewn him up, and to his deep regret he now had to pronounce that he and Verne had *something* in common – if only attempted murder.

"I asked myself, why would Gertrude be abducted?" I said. "As you taught me, I asked, who had the opportunity and who stood to gain? It transpires that her entire time at Salpêtrière she insisted 'Gertrude Socha' was an expedient alias: she was in fact 'the Contessa de Calvi' – of course a delusion. But Hennetier must have overheard her speaking of her fortune, her ramblings about having millions of francs squirrelled away, that she was rich

beyond the dreams of avarice, and took her at her word. He imagined banknotes hoarded under floorboards, chests of dubloons
on a desert island . . . If only he could get the exact location out of
the patient. So that is what he planned, by secreting her away and
interrogating her until she gave the information up. He couldn't
carry this off alone, he knew that, but there was enough money to
go round, the way she was talking. So he approached his acquaintance, Titus Corcoran, an aeronaut who organized balloon rides at
the Exposition Universelles last year in a craft called 'Le Geant'
after Nadar's contraption. Corcoran's background was in the
American use of balloons in combat. In the Civil War, armies
fighting for the Union flag were helped in the Virginia campaign
by Thaddeus Rowe and eight military balloons of the Military
Aeronautics Corps – flying hydrogen balloons for reconnaissance
– powered by a portable hydrogen generator. They were known
as 'Mr Lincoln's Air Force' and here Corcoran learned his skill.

"Their plan was to kidnap Gertrude by rising above the cloud
line. A third party, Lamiche, an acrobat friend of Corcoran from
the Cirque Fernando, would scurry down a rope and enter by
the window opened by Hennetier, scoop up the 'Countess' in
his arms, then speak through a tube – the tube featured so
vividly in Celestine's account – signalling for Corcoran to whisk
him skyward.

"When the latter turned on the air burner, the roar was heard
by one patient who imagined it was a giant lion. And the sand in
the courtyard, too incongruous to be a sandpit, was the deposited ballast to let the balloon make its escape. What Hennetier
did not allow for, though, was the other inmate in the room . . .
Celestine.

"What *she* saw entering and abducting Gertrude was not
Lamiche in his goggles, helmet, straps and leather, but one of
the bug-like space-imps from her damaged mind. She immediately conceived it as evidence her Moon Men having returned.
Consequently, it was the only possible explanation for the magical vanishing of her follow inmate. That is what she saw – *literally*. Even, as the cloud cleared and the balloon dropped, an
enigmatic sphere disappearing into the distance. You see, we

were diverted when you insisted that the answer was in Celestine's madness, and crime, but that was a dead end. The true key was the mania of *Gertrude*."

Poe leaned forward to clap his hands, but agony seared across his shoulders and he sank back in the pillow.

"Excellent work, Holmes." His voice was constrained by a tightness of breath. "Perhaps I should tussle with the Grim Reaper more often. Not only are my methods in safe hands, I should say now, having solved a case entirely by your own diligence – *elle avoit vû le loup!*" She has seen the wolf. He used the old French saying for losing one's maidenhead.

My cheeks reddened. He laughed, but once again twinges of pain inhibited him from persisting with it, like a censorious Puritan.

"The next morning, I returned to Salpêtrière with a heavy heart to give Dr Charcot the news. He was delighted with the arrest of Lamiche, shocked by the death of both Corcoran and Hennetier – I think he still harboured the idea that his warder was an honest man. I told him to sit down before telling him we had lost Gertrude too. He sighed. I showed him the treasure map. He gave a thin little laugh.

"He took me to Gertrude's room. It was full of such maps, from floor to ceiling, none of them the same or even similar. He told me she spent her days drawing diagrams of where her mythical fortune lay buried. This explained the beating the gang had given her in their increasing frustration, thinking she was keeping the truth from them. The truth was, there was no fortune. How many maps had she drawn for them, like these I saw before me? How many places had they searched before the island in the Lac Daumesnil? They would never find it, because the 'Contessa' did not exist, apart from in the head of a poor, abandoned woman wrapped in a fantasy.

"I asked if I could appraise Celestine Blot of the situation, hoping it might be some relief to the woman to know that the invaders were flesh and blood, and human flesh and blood at that. She listened patiently as I spoke of hot air balloons and the three men—"

"But staunchly refused to believe it." Poe's reasoning went ahead of me. Naturally it did. But he was absolutely correct. "She still chose to believe in the Moon Men. I should not say 'choose' because choice is nothing to do with it. She clings to her belief because it is all she has. Sane or mad, we all cling to what we know, or think we know, in order to protect ourselves. To Celestine, the unpalatable truth she cannot face is that there are no Moon Men, only madness."

He gestured to a jug of water. I poured a glass and pressed it to his lips. His eyes thanked me in a way that words could not. I sat and could only listen as he stared at the ceiling and continued speaking.

"In a future written by Jules Verne there may be a Captain Cooke who strides amongst the mysteries of the heavens, conquering our deepest fears and wonder. We may discover non-human things, or they may discover us. But the most frightening voyage is always inside the mind."

His sunken eyes shifted in the dark hollows of his skull, fighting sleep. I wanted to take his hand, and perhaps he knew I did, because he moved it to shield a cough, then lay it flat across his chest.

"We are by nature unstable," he wheezed. "Sanity is not *de rigeur* but a condition of immense irrationality and perverse achievement. It is not our natural state. Our natural state is madness, greed, violence, sexual urges, inner distress. And that is a terrible geography few dare to explore."

I did not realize it then, but I know now that he was giving me, as near as I ever heard it, the root of his fascination with crime.

"Your friend was lucky, Mr Holmes." The lanky young doctor who entered was, to my surprise, an Englishman. "The knife struck a glancing blow on the infraspinous fossa of his left scapula. Fortunately, the blade missed the lung on that side, and the aorta. The muscle's taken a bit of a pounding, which accounts for the rather dramatic loss of blood."

"With a complex anastomosis of arteries running over it," said Poe, "that would hardly be unexpected."

The doctor smiled. "But he's on the road to recovery, and he'll be right as rain if he takes care, a good deal of rest and, most importantly, if he leaves those stitches alone. I used silk rather than catgut, by the way, so they won't dissolve. You'll need a doctor to take them out when you're back in Paris."

His name was Tom Stamford, and I shortly learned he was on his way back to London to work at Bart's. I made him promise to allow me to take him to dinner, by way of thanks for saving my good friend's life, the minute I returned to England.

"*If* he returns," mumbled Poe.

Stamford replied he would be delighted to renew acquaintance on our home shores. That was, of course, not to happen for another two years, at which time I had rented rooms in Montague Street round the corner from the British Museum, and had just begun to embark on my solo career as a consulting detective. It was Stamford who not only gave me use of the chemical laboratory at Bart's, but introduced me to a certain doctor who had served at the Battle of Maiwand.

Within weeks, as a direct consequence of the case of Celestine Blot, Monsieur le Professeur put hypnosis on his teaching programme at Salpêtrière. But not until six years later, did an ambitious young doctor join the hospital, attracted by the great name of Charcot. Sigmund Freud had done a nice job on brain sections in Vienna, but wanted to show them to the Master, little realizing that at Salpêtrière the madwomen were always centre stage, and he the disoriented witness of the hysteria of hysteria. Besotted then critical of Charcot's theories, he went on to devise a markedly different concept of the condition. Hypnosis solidified the relationship between authority and patient: the love affair between madness and medicine was consummated at last. It seemed only fitting that Poe, whose tales foreshadowed psychoanalysis, had a hand in making it the universal idea of the century to come.

I often remember my last picture of Charcot with Celestine, and that last glimpse of her expression, so like a child pleasing her father. He had domesticated this wild beast, this idea of Baroque abandon, this whirlwind. Celestine was his star, his pearl, his masterpiece of exquisite porcelain, taken away to be wrapped up again, until his gaze required her. Perhaps in such unusual circumstances the attention a patient gets due to her illness is all? And the loss of it unthinkable?

By uncanny coincidence, years later, out of the blue and "in a fit of madness", Jules Verne's twenty-five-year-old nephew Gaston – an intelligent and hard-working young man with a job in the Ministry of Foreign Affairs – fired at him twice with a revolver. Luckily, only one shot hit Verne, in the foot, but the wound festered and the bullet could not be extracted, giving him a permanent limp. I could not help wondering, peculiarly, if Gaston, too, had believed in Moon Men – and what Celestine might conclude from the occurrence if she knew. Needless to say, the assault, like hers, was hushed up in the press. Meanwhile, Gaston was taken away for observation, certified insane and spent the rest of his life in a succession of clinics, finally dying in Luxembourg during the Great War.

I next heard of the author when I was investigating "The Dancing Men", and he achieved what he had threatened long before, namely a new, improved version of *The Narrative of Arthur Gordon Pym* in the form of *Le Sphinx des Glaces (The Sphinx of the Ice Realm)*. As I expected and feared, Verne set out to make it "more true to life and more interesting" by rendering mundane everything Poe left in suspense, scrubbing the fantasy elements and laying on his dread realism with a trowel, even explaining away the vast, shrouded giant as an iceberg – and the rest as Pym's hallucinations. The man might have been a prophet to some and a literary hero to many, but I could not help feeling the vast unknowable was reduced immeasurably by his pen.

"It all ends in a mystery, because it has to," Poe told me of his supposedly unfinished novel during our last months together. "Doesn't our own narrative always end in Death? Who is to say that it ends not in darkness but in whiteness?" The whiteness of the blank page, perhaps.

I was quite sure that his tale – *Pym's* tale – is about a journey into Mystery itself. Poe's journey. Always. Unerringly.

"The ending did not evade me," he'd said on the station platform at Amiens. "It presented itself as inevitable."

Poe was the failed romantic, Verne the idealist. The Frenchman's life had been a full one. He'd written millions upon millions of words, enchanting generations. With no more than pen and ink could transport the reader to the slopes of Popocatepetl or the sands or Timbuktu – yet at the end he became disillusioned, fearful of the fate of his beloved science and knowledge against the rise in power of industry and that dark, tentacled creature from the depths, finance.

Thankfully, he died before the monumental horrors that were to consume Europe – machines as a perversion of scientific progress, created for carnage; not for enlightening and liberating Mankind, as he dreamed, but providing ever more ingenious methods of self-destruction.

Now, Lestrade, old fellow, sentimentality has blurred my vision, or the light bulb has – I am not sure which, but it is time I gathered these arthritic bones and took them to bed. When I wake it will be another day, alas, without the company of that formidable brain, that gracious and insufferable poet and detective whose prodigious brilliance moulded me, and whose secret life I have carried as a burden all these years. Hard as it has been, it is but a feather when I think of what he gave me.

You will see appended to this file a letter I received shortly after the case of the missing patient at Salpêtrière. The handwriting and signature will confirm that everything you have read is true.

*A Sh. Holmes*

*Amiens, 26 9ieme. 1879*

*Cher Monsieur,*
*You will forgive me for undertaking my own "detective work" to find your address.*

*I have just read in the press of the remarkable arrest of Lamiche and the fatal shooting of Corcoran in the Bois de Vincennes – and am deeply saddened that the patient from Salpêtrière, Gertrude Socha, was not saved. However my purpose in writing is not to offer my condolences, or congratulate yourself, Monsieur Holmes, or your partner, "Auguste Dupin" in solving the mystery. The article only served as catalyst to express what has been raging in my heart like a tempest.*

*Moments after I closed the door at the end of our meeting at my home, I was overcome by the idea that either I had been in the company of a doppelganger of miraculous accuracy or the gentleman who had stood before me was Edgar Poe himself. Yes, older – twenty or more years older than the famous daguerrotype that now graces every frontispiece of his* Tales of Mystery and Imagination *– yes, without the customary moustache – but the physiognomy, the great forehead, the creased brow, the straight nose, the small lips – and not least, the soupçon of an American accent, almost inaudible but emphatically* there *– was incontrovertible! I almost fainted from the shock! My servants gathered round me – but no, I said nothing of what I knew to be true.*

*And I* shall say *nothing – much as I wish to visit Paris, or rather Olympus, now and embrace my literary god I shall not, and though it wounds me, never will!*

*If there is some reason Poe seeks anonymity, let him enjoy it. If he flees from the limelight, or debtors, or aggrieved women, or aggrieved men – let him. I owe him* worlds *and it is the least I can do to keep my mouth shut on the matter – even if I cry into my pillow, not that there will be no more stories, but tears of joy that he* lives!

*And so it is with astonished excitement but the deepest respect for him, I tell you that no soul will hear of this from my lips. He would cringe at the cliché, and no doubt castigate me for it, but his secret is safe with me.*

*'Dupin' is on his own* Voyage Extraordinaire *now. He is 'Nemo' – he has no name. But he shall always have my love.*

*Votre bien Dévoué,*
*Jules Verne*

# The Crimson Devil

## Mark Morris

For reasons of political sensitivity, it has been politely requested of me on occasion, by certain parties within Her Majesty's government, that I refrain from making public the details of specific cases undertaken by my friend Mr Sherlock Holmes. One such case, which I have now been given leave to recount, took place in the year 1897.

In my mind I have long bestowed the title "The Crimson Devil" upon this singular set of circumstances, an appellation which Holmes has subsequently claimed, in a somewhat dismissive manner, is sensationalistic, but which I nevertheless believe to be apt. Although this case was to take us far beyond our usual stamping grounds, it began, as did so many of our adventures, in our familiar rooms at 221b Baker Street.

It was a murky sort of day, as I recall, the rain slithering down the window and distorting the view of the street beyond, which was, in any case, as grey as slag. I was sipping tea and feeling thankful for the blazing fire, which Mrs Hudson had laid that morning, when Holmes bounded into the room, his dressing gown flying behind him.

"Well, well!" he proclaimed, his normally ascetic features lit up with an excitement I knew only seized him at the prospect of a new case. "What do you make of this, Watson?"

He extended his arm towards me, wafting the telegram he was clutching as if attempting to dispel a vile odour with it. I took the slip of paper from him and read it quickly.

"Why, it's from our old friend Sir Henry Baskerville!" I exclaimed. "Good Lord! He is living in Southern Africa!"

"Yes, yes!" snapped Holmes. "If I had wished you to supply me with the information I had obtained not moments before I would have said so. But what do you make of his request, Watson?"

I scanned the missive again. From its tone it was clear that Sir Henry, who we had last seen in these very rooms some years before, not long after that terrifying business with the hound on Dartmoor, was almost at the end of his tether. Although he did not provide us with specific details, the telegram spoke of "onerous and inexplicable events" that had been plaguing his sugar plantation in the Natal region of Southern Africa, and ended by all but begging for our assistance.

"Well, we must go at once!" I exclaimed.

"Must we indeed?" Holmes mused.

I was taken aback by his seeming reluctance. "Of course! Sir Henry is a decent fellow and he has requested our help! I do not think he would do so idly."

"Nor I," said Holmes. He lit a cigarette and began to smoke it, his eyes narrowing. "And of course we *will* aid Sir Henry howsoever we can. But first I must avail myself of the relevant facts."

"And how will you do that?"

"By dining with my brother Mycroft at his club tonight."

Although I knew Mycroft to be a fount of knowledge when it came to matters of the state, I was mystified as to how he might provide Holmes with information pertaining to a fellow who, as far as I was aware, he had never met. However my friend would not be drawn, and two days later we set sail for Southern Africa.

The three-week journey was an arduous one, though only by dint of the fact that for much of it I was overcome by sheer boredom. For celerity's sake, Holmes and I had sought passage on a trading vessel rather than a passenger liner, which afforded little in the way of creature comforts. I had hoped my friend's company would sustain me during the voyage, but Holmes had lapsed into one of his moods of brooding introspection and spent the majority of the time in his cabin. I availed myself of the ship's library, such as it was, and spent many hours walking aimlessly about the deck, staring out to sea, and offering my services as a doctor to the crew whenever I could. However, I was relieved when we arrived at the bustling port of Durban, from where we caught a train to the interior of what has become known in some quarters as the Dark Continent.

The train would have conveyed us all the way to Johannesburg, if that had been our destination, but we disembarked some considerable distance before then, at a nameless station on the southernmost edge of Natal. Perused with curiosity by rows of silent black faces aboard the train, Holmes and I were the only two passengers to alight upon a platform that was little more than several strips of wood surrounded by thick jungle, from the depths of which issued the strange cries of myriad birds.

It was disconcerting standing there, beset by flying insects, as our means of transportation receded into the distance, but my companion seemed not a bit put out. In fact, our uncertain situation seemed to have revived him from his previous lethargy. He looked about him with obvious relish, his eyes every bit as lively as the insects darting about my head.

Both of us had travelled widely, of course, though Holmes was the more seasoned and confident traveller. For three years after the business with Moriarty at the Reichenbach Falls, he had lived a nomadic life, trekking alone through Tibet and Persia and much of Europe

"Damned flies," I muttered, flapping at the swarm that assailed me. Holmes, for his part, seemed entirely unaffected.

"Shush, Watson. Listen," he ordered, holding up a hand.

Although inclined to make some disparaging remark, I did as he asked. For a moment, I heard nothing but the birds and the insects, and then, faintly beneath this cacophony, came the spluttering approach of an engine.

Less than a minute later, a most extraordinary vehicle emerged from within what had seemed an impenetrable screen of jungle foliage. It was undoubtedly a motorcar, but one which had had its doors removed and its roof replaced by a length of stretched green canvas. What remained of the vehicle's metal shell had been comprehensively scratched and dented – I presumed by the merciless flora, which must have flanked the narrow jungle roads on which it was forced to travel. Despite the parlous state of the vehicle, however, the fellow seated behind its steering wheel was grinning widely at us, his teeth startlingly white in his sun-bronzed and deeply lined face.

"Mr Holmes! Dr Watson!" he exclaimed. "Welcome to Africa!"

He brought the vehicle to a jolting halt beside the wooden platform and leapt out.

He was a lean and wiry man, bow-legged and short in stature. With his weathered, nut-brown skin and his untidy thatch of dark hair, he put me in mind, perhaps somewhat uncharitably, of an ape, which had learned to talk and dress as a man.

"My name is Joseph Villiers," he informed us. "I manage Sir Henry's estate. I trust that you had a pleasant journey?"

I believe we murmured something in the way of affirmation, though even as we were doing so Villiers was bounding forward and, with apparent ease, lifting our various items of baggage into the back of the vehicle. As we climbed aboard, Holmes electing to position himself on the back seat whilst I sat in the front beside the driver, I asked Villiers whether the plantation was close by.

"It's a little less than ten miles from here," he replied, pointing vaguely at the looming wall of greenery from which he had emerged, as if we might somehow be able to penetrate its denseness and view our destination. "Where you come from I daresay that's barely any distance at all, but I'm afraid the road through the jungle is terribly slow-going, and the journey a long and uncomfortable one."

"It is of no matter," drawled Holmes from behind me. "Watson and I are used to roughing it, are we not, my dear fellow?"

"Indeed so," I muttered, though at that moment the prospect of an hour or two spent lurching through a thick and stiflingly hot jungle, with insects bombarding us from all sides, did not appeal in the slightest.

I had no option but to bear it, however, which I did with what I hope was a certain degree of alacrity. Villiers presented me with a length of horsehair attached to a stick with which to repel the flying brutes, which at least helped to ease my ordeal. He further diverted my mind with a ceaseless, though entertaining, commentary on the local flora and fauna that we passed upon our slow and jolting journey. Although I now recall little of the knowledge that he imparted, I believe that for ever more I shall be able to recognize the wild fig tree, the winged orchid and the lucky bean creeper, should such be presented before me.

It was almost dusk when we arrived at Baskerville's plantation, by which time the vibrant colours of the jungle had turned grey with shadow, and the sounds that issued from the darkening landscape had begun to sound ominous and eerie. My first sight of our destination was of a high, encircling fence, twice as tall as a man and constructed of thick wooden poles lashed together, their tips sharpened to points. This forbidding boundary, which appeared at first glance impenetrable, put me in mind of a prison, or a military stronghold, rather than a place in which one might live and work.

"The barrier is to keep out wild animals, I suppose?" said I, indicating the row of wooden spikes, which stood out black and stark against a sky livid with swirls of purple and red.

Villiers was silent for a moment, and then he nodded. "That is one reason."

"What are the others?" I asked him.

He grinned, and I saw his teeth gleaming from within the shadows that were obscuring his features.

"There are many threats here, Dr Watson," said he simply. "The jungle is a dangerous place."

I glanced over my shoulder to ascertain what Holmes had made of this remark, though my friend's slumped form in the back of the vehicle, smothered in shadow as thick and dark as a spider's web, was silent and motionless. I wondered whether he was asleep. It was impossible to tell. I was about to attempt to persuade Villiers to elaborate on his enigmatic statement when there came a sharp and clearly interrogative cry from within the compound in a language I did not understand.

Villiers gave a short response in the same language, and immediately there came the grinding of a key in a lock, followed by the metallic rattle of a chain being pulled rapidly through some aperture. Next moment a part of the wooden fence began to tilt backwards at an angle, whereupon I realized that it was a hinged gate, constructed of the same spiked staves as the fence in which it was set.

We passed through the gate, which I was startled to observe was being held open for us not by an African native, but by an Indian wearing a white turban and a loose white garment, which I knew from my military service in Afghanistan was called a *kurta*. As the Indian closed the gate behind us, I noted that within the compound the jungle foliage had given way to a profusion of tall, straight plants with thick, pale stems topped with feathery green leaves.

"Sugar cane," said Villiers, as if in response to my unspoken question.

I nodded, although in actual fact what occupied my attention were not the regimented rows of crops that flanked us, but the workers hurrying in the same direction that we were driving. To my surprise they were all Indians like the man at the gate. I asked Villiers about them.

"The local tribesmen refuse to work the plantations," said he, with what I am certain was a trace of bitterness. "They think it's servile to provide labour for the white man, in spite of the fact that Sir Henry treats his workers well and pays them a generous wage."

For the first time in perhaps an hour Holmes spoke up from the rear of the vehicle. "The Indian community in Natal is the largest outside India, is it not?"

Villiers glanced over his shoulder and nodded. "It is, Mr Holmes. And we are glad to have them here."

Although Holmes nodded in satisfaction, as if Villiers had confirmed some theory of his, nothing more was said until we reached the plantation house, a large wooden building that had been painted white and built upon a raised platform. In the deepening gloom of twilight, I saw a figure emerge from the front door and stand with his hands clasped tightly together, awaiting our arrival.

It had been some years since we had seen Sir Henry Baskerville, but even so I recognized him from his stature immediately. He was a small man, and sturdily built, and, as soon as Villiers brought the vehicle to a halt at the base of a trio of wooden steps, I disembarked and hurried forward, eager to reacquaint myself with an old friend.

As Baskerville too stepped forward and the light from an overhead lamp fell across his features, I was shocked to see how much he had aged. Sir Henry was still a relatively young man, and yet his face was lined with worry and the hair around his temples streaked with white. Browbeaten though he seemed, however, his relief at the appearance of Holmes and I was instantly apparent.

"My dear Doctor Watson! And Mr Holmes!" he exclaimed. "How wonderful to see you again! I cannot thank you enough for travelling all this way to aid me! It is extraordinarily kind of you! Please, come in."

His effusive greeting was almost pitiful, and yet Holmes accepted it with grace, clasping and shaking Sir Henry's hand with uncharacteristic warmth.

"Rest assured that we will do our utmost to help you howsoever we can, Sir Henry," he murmured.

Over a most delicious dinner that evening, consisting of curried lamb, rice, steamed vegetables and spiced flatbreads, Sir Henry explained his reasons for requesting our presence in Africa.

"My problems, which I was able merely to allude to in my telegram, began some three months ago," said he, toying with his meal as if in imitation of Holmes, who himself frequently ate little during an investigation (suffice to say that I devoured my own repast with gusto).

"I have been resident here for four years now, gentlemen, and all but these last months have been happy and profitable ones.

Admittedly, as a plantation owner, I am reliant on the trends and vagaries of the world market, but the sugarcane industry is a buoyant one, and despite the current situation has all the indications of remaining so for the foreseeable future."

"By your phrase 'the current situation', you refer, of course, to the increasing hostility between the Boers and our own government?" interrupted Holmes.

I looked at him sharply. Despite being the cleverest man I have known, Holmes was not generally conversant with world affairs. If information did not pertain specifically to his work, he was inclined to show little or no interest in it. On the other hand, he was a man of ceaseless contradictions and surprises. For instance, he was often scathing of those who indulged in printed fiction, deeming it an irrelevant pursuit, and yet I had known him quote so frequently and accurately from works of literature that the only conclusion to be drawn was that he had made a detailed study of them.

Sir Henry nodded gravely. "Just so. As I am sure you are aware, Mr Holmes, there has been much recent conflict over the gold mining industry in the Transvaal." He waved a hand. "But that is of little concern to us here in the jungle. We have no gold here, or diamonds, for that matter."

"What, then, is at the root of your recent problems?" I asked.

"And more pertinently, what is the form that they have taken?" added Holmes.

Sir Henry looked momentarily uncomfortable, his gaze sliding away from us and towards the wire mesh screens at the windows that kept the insects at bay.

"It is an admittedly queer story, gentlemen," said he. "I ask only that you bear with me while I tell it."

"We can hardly do otherwise," said Holmes with a smirk.

Sir Henry pushed aside his half-eaten dinner and clasped his hands in front of him. "As I have told you, it all began some months ago. Early one morning, as one of my field workers – a youth barely more than eighteen years of age – was collecting water from the river that traverses the north-western portion of the estate, he was attacked by what he described as a 'crimson devil'. As his account would have it, this creature, its skin a bright, flaming red from top to toe, had the body of a man, the claws of a bear and a wild-eyed face surmounted by a pair of long, curving horns. He said that this 'devil' was utterly crazed, its eyes murderous, its teeth bared and dripping with saliva, and that when it moved it did so in a sort of crouching hop, reminding him of both an ape and a frog."

"Where did this so-called 'devil' appear from?" Holmes asked.

"The boy did not know. He was facing the river, he heard a sound behind him, and when he turned round there it was."

"And was the boy mauled by this apparition?" I asked.

Sir Henry shook his head. "He was so terrified that immediately upon its appearance he abandoned his yoke and his bags of water, turned and fled. When a party of men set out to search for the creature later they could find no trace of it."

"No doubt it had had ample time in which to make its escape," said I.

"Perhaps," said Sir Henry, "though you have seen the height of the fence around the estate. No ordinary man could scale it. And the boundary is inspected daily to ensure that there are no breaches. We cannot afford to risk the ingress of animals which may damage the crop; nor indeed predators, which may prove a danger to my workers."

Holmes steepled his fingers. "I take it that the appearance of this singular creature has not been an isolated incident?"

"Indeed not. The creature, or perhaps others like it, have been sighted several times since that first encounter. My workers live in fear, Mr Holmes. They have been terrorized to the point of distraction ..." He hesitated and, as he took a deep breath, I noted how badly his hands were trembling. "Indeed, after the latest, most terrible incident, which occurred mere days before my telegram reached you, their mood has turned from fearfulness to near mutiny. Already a dozen or more of them have left, never to return. I speak to them daily, try to reassure them, but although I believe they respect me, I fear that we may be on the brink of a mass exodus, and if that were to happen, I would be utterly ruined." His shoulders slumped and his head dropped forward, as if he was exhausted.

Gently, Holmes said, "If you feel able to relate the particulars of the terrible incident to which you have already made reference, Watson and I would willingly give the matter some thought."

Sir Henry rallied himself with an effort, and then nodded. "Of course. As I said to you, the first encounter took place three months ago. Although the boy was clearly frightened by it, I admit I did not take his account too seriously. No evidence could be found of the beast, and my conclusion was that the boy had become spooked by the solitude associated with his task and had imagined the entire affair – after all, it cannot be denied that the Indians, although fine workers, are a superstitious breed. Suffice to say, I thought no more of his story, until a week or two later, when one of my housemaids, walking through the cane rows at dusk, also encountered the brute. Her description of the 'crimson devil' matched that of the boy's before her to the last detail. When I questioned her, she informed me that the creature had sprung out from between the canes and had pursued her for some distance until giving up the chase. Such incidents have happened regularly ever since, each of them spaced some one or two weeks apart. On each occasion the intended victim has been alone and has managed to outrun his pursuer. Then, a little over three weeks ago, there came the first fatality . . ." Sir Henry faltered, and wrung his hands together.

"Pray continue," murmured Holmes.

"I was taking dinner at this very table when my manager, Mr Villiers, arrived to inform me that one of the men had not returned from the fields. Although it was full night, a party which included myself, Mr Villiers and four of my most level-witted and reliable workers, set out, each of us armed with rifles, to discover the fellow's whereabouts. After perhaps an hour had passed, we chanced upon a singularly grisly scene. There was the missing man, his lifeless body spreadeagled among the canes. The flesh of his face and chest had been torn and gouged, as though by the claws of a tiger or bear. It was a most distressing sight, Mr Holmes. We were, all of us, shaken very badly by it."

"It is hardly surprising," said Holmes, looking thoughtful. "Tell me, Sir Henry, was the perpetrator of this appalling crime sighted by anyone in this instance?"

"No one but the victim," replied Sir Henry.

"Though we must assume, judging by the marks on the body, that the murderer was the crimson devil."

Holmes nodded vaguely. "Is that all?"

Sir Henry shook his head. "No, Mr Holmes, there is more. Beside the dead man was a deep pit."

"A pit!" I repeated in astonishment.

"Yes. And neither was it a singular incident. Many such pits – thirty at least – have been discovered on the plantation since this distressing affair began. The Indians are certain that they are from where the 'devil' springs, and to which it returns once its terrible work is done."

Holmes was sitting up straight, his eyes dancing. "Might it be possible to see one of these pits?" he enquired.

"I am afraid not," said Sir Henry. "They are refilled with earth immediately upon discovery. The Indians are afraid that if we leave them, the 'devil' will emerge from the ground with greater frequency, or even that more of its kin will be encouraged to follow it."

"That is a pity," said Holmes, though my friend did not seem unduly surprised or put out at our host's words. He seemed about to say something more when, from within the darkness beyond the house, there came three rapid rifle shots.

Holmes was the first to respond, leaping up from the table and bounding to the doorway.

"Come, Watson!" he cried. "And draw your revolver. You may have need of it."

I followed him from the house and into the stifling darkness, noting that he had drawn his Webley. Aside from the constant chafing of insects and the whisper of the tall canes as they moved in the breeze, all was now silent. Nevertheless Holmes seemed confident of his destination. "This way, Watson!" he cried, plunging into the canes and beginning to weave between them. "And watch out for crimson devils as you go!"

I pursued Holmes with as much vigour as I could muster, though my friend's lath-thin body slipped so easily between the canes that I had a hard time keeping pace with him.

I was mightily relieved when, after several minutes, we burst from between the rows to find ourselves in a clearing, on the far side of which was a rough shack. In the dim light of a lamp that overhung the door, it appeared to be constructed of a combination of tar paper, wooden planks and sheets of corroded metal. I had the partial impression of a profusion of similar buildings cloaked by darkness beyond this first shack, though it was the singular sight of the two bodies sprawled upon the ground in front of it that engaged my attention.

One of the bodies belonged to an Indian, whose white *kurta* was torn and horribly bloody around the chest and throat. The other belonged to a smaller man wearing a light brown shirt, his trousers tucked into long black boots.

It was only when Holmes shouted out the man's name and dropped to his knees beside him that I realized this was Sir Henry's estate manager, Villiers. The sleeve and chest of the man's shirt was ragged and bloody, and I assumed he, too, was dead. But then he gave a groan and half rolled over and opened his eyes.

I knelt beside Holmes as Villiers fixed his gaze upon my friend.

Shooting out a hand to clutch Holmes's sleeve, he hissed, "I saw it, Mr Holmes! I saw the crimson devil!"

I was about to quieten the man, to encourage him to conserve his energy, when Holmes snapped, "You shot at it, did you not? Did you hit it?"

Villiers shook his head. "I don't know."

Holmes looked about him in frustration. We were surrounded on three sides by sugar cane plants taller than we were. "But the creature may be wounded? Tell me, in which direction did it go?"

Here too, however, Villiers was no help. He gestured vaguely and then his head sank back in defeat. "I don't know," he croaked. "The creature attacked swiftly ... I fell ..." A little fearfully he asked, "Am I hurt?"

I examined his wound as best I could in the dim light. "Not badly," I said. "The creature clawed you across the arm, and you have lost some blood, but the wound is not serious."

Both Holmes and I whirled round at a sudden commotion within the canes, but it was only Sir Henry, looking wild-eyed and dishevelled as he burst into the clearing.

"What has happened? Oh, good Lord! Are these men dead?"

"One only," said I. "Mr Villiers is injured, but it is not severe."

"As for what happened," added Holmes, rising to his feet. "I surmise that the creature attacked swiftly, killing one man and wounding another, before either of them could fully react. Mr Villiers let loose several shots, but failed to hit the brute, where-upon it made its escape. Is that about the size of it, Mr Villiers?"

"It is," Villiers said weakly from his place on the ground.

With my aid, he made an attempt to sit up. As I bandaged his arm as best I could, using a clean length of material torn from the dead man's *kurta*, Holmes paced across the clearing and picked up a rifle. He examined it and then carried it across to us.

"This is your weapon, Mr Villiers?" he asked.

"It is," Villiers confirmed.

"Then I shall carry it back to the house for you," Holmes said curtly.

We made a sad and defeated procession as we trooped back to the house, Villiers moving slowly and painfully with my help, and Holmes and Sir Henry carrying the dead man between them. Sir Henry led us in a roundabout route, so that we did not have to push our way through the cane rows. Because of this, and Villiers's injury, it took us considerably longer to return to the house than it had taken Holmes and I to reach the clearing.

When we did return, it was to find that a dozen or more dark and ominous shapes were gathered around the steps in anticipation of our arrival. Spying a number of turbaned heads, my hand crept instinctively to my revolver, which I had slipped into my jacket pocket. Yet although my service in India had made me a little wary of the men of that country, it quickly became apparent that the group meant us no harm. Even so fear had agitated them, and almost immediately Sir Henry became involved in an animated discussion with them, albeit in a language which to me sounded like gibberish, but to which Holmes listened with interest.

Even though I could not understand the exchange, however, it was evident that the Indians were being particularly insistent about something, and that Sir Henry, in response, was close to despair. Only too aware of Villiers's weakened state, and to the fact that I could offer no significant contribution to the discussion, I took my charge inside the house, whereupon Villiers himself directed me weakly to his living quarters, a small ground-floor room beside the kitchen, in the corner of which was a bed, onto which he sank with a groan.

I have already said that the room was small. I should add that it was also neatly and sparsely furnished. Against the wall opposite to the bed was a modest wardrobe for Villiers's clothes and other personal effects, and a washstand upon which stood a water jug and his shaving equipment. The walls were unadorned, aside from a large portrait of Queen Victoria above the headboard of the bed on which Villiers now lay. I must admit it gave me a pang of homesickness, albeit mixed with a modicum of comfort, to see the familiar, serene features of her royal personage looking out at me.

By the time Holmes and Sir Henry entered the room, having wrapped up the body of the dead man in a winding sheet and laid him in Sir Henry's private office, I had cleaned and bandaged Villiers's wound and persuaded him to drink some hot, sweet tea. He was now sitting up in bed, a little weakened and in pain, but much restored.

"A terrible business!" said Holmes, cutting to the nub on the instant. "Perhaps now that Dr Watson has performed his medical wonders upon you, Mr Villiers, you can recall the events of the evening with a little more clarity?"

"I believe I can, Mr Holmes," Villiers replied, and proceeded to recount the incident almost as Holmes himself had surmised it to have taken place.

Even though there seemed little new to be gleaned from Villiers's account, Holmes attended to it with keen interest. "The creature came out of nowhere, you say?"

"That was how it seemed, Mr Holmes," attested the wounded man. "One second it wasn't there, and the next it was, its movements lightning quick. It killed Karamchand and was on me almost before I knew it. I have never seen its like."

"Lightning quick, you say? Quicker than a man then?"

"Much quicker."

"Hmm, that is very interesting."

"You previously believed the creature to be no more than a man?" said I.

"That was my original supposition. But Mr Villiers's account has thrown the matter into some doubt." He stroked his chin and looked thoughtful. "Tell me, Sir Henry, is there a native settlement close by?"

"Yes. There is a Zulu village not more than half an hour's walk from here."

"And are the natives agreeable?"

"They are certainly not hostile. We trade with them from time to time. But for the most part they keep to their affairs and we to ours. It is an arrangement that I believe is satisfactory to both parties."

"But they would not be averse to a visit?"

"I do not believe so."

"Excellent! Then we shall go there in the morning! But first, I think that we are all in need of a good night's sleep. It has been a most tiring—" All at once he started, his words cutting off and his eyes affixing themselves to the portrait above Villiers's bed, as if he had only just noticed it. "I declare! What an excellent portrait of Her Majesty! Is it not, Watson?"

I looked at him curiously, wondering what he meant by the remark. However I nodded, familiar enough with Holmes's methods to play along. "It is indeed."

"Most remarkable," Holmes said, leaning closer to the portrait. He glanced down at Villiers. "Have you had the painting long, Mr Villiers?"

"It belonged to my mother," Villiers said.

"Well then," said Holmes, and straightened up, rubbing his hands as if to denote that the business of the day was at a close. "We shall leave you to your rest. I don't doubt that you are in need of it. Oh!" he added as he went out, and pointed to the corner of the room, between the washstand and a small window covered in a wire-mesh screen. "I have placed your rifle against the wall there, should you have need of it."

We retired to our beds. Although the night was hot, the long journey and that evening's excitement had exhausted me and I fell asleep the instant my head touched the pillow. When I woke some time later, with no inkling of how many hours I had slept, it was to the sound of Holmes sharply calling my name from a nearby room. I came to my senses with a start, and was alert instantly, certain that he was in trouble.

Pausing only to snatch my old service revolver from the pocket of my jacket, I rushed from the room. The house was in darkness and I halted to get my bearings. Within a moment I recalled that my room had been closest to the head of the staircase, and that Holmes's room, although situated behind the next door but one along the upper landing, was a dozen steps away. Barefoot I hurried towards it, clad only in my pyjamas. I wondered what danger my friend was in, and whether I should call out to him and betray my position. But even as I was trying to decide on the best course of action he spoke to me again.

"I hear you approaching, Watson." His voice was quiet now, but urgent. "Enter the room slowly, and with great care."

I did as he advised, pushing the door open with the utmost caution and stepping inside. A lamp was burning on the cabinet beside his bed and instantly I saw what was troubling him.

A black snake, some four feet long, was curled in an S-shape on the floor at the foot of the bed. It had raised the forefront of its body off the ground and was hissing venomously, the hood beneath its mean little head flared in obvious agitation.

"A cobra," I muttered grimly, recognizing the snake from my time in India.

"A Cape cobra," Holmes corrected me. "They are a nervous breed, and therefore highly aggressive. Their venom consists of potent postsynaptic neurotoxins and cardiotoxins that affect the respiratory system, nervous system and heart. If I am bitten, death may occur within one and ten hours if swift and efficient treatment is not administered."

It astounded me that even when subject to appalling peril, Holmes was able to draw calmly upon his comprehensive knowledge of poisons.

"Shall I shoot the brute?" I asked.

Holmes gave me a wry look. "From your perspective, I am standing directly in the line of fire. What would be the likelihood of your missing the creature and hitting me?"

"Pretty high, I should say."

"Well then, I think an alternative stratagem would be more favourable, would it not?"

"Such as?"

Holmes remained motionless, moving only his eyes and lips. "Behind you is a wardrobe, inside which you will find my silver-topped cane and a number of jackets. Select the thickest of the jackets and remove the cane. Your subsequent actions will require swiftness of action and split-second timing. There is no room for error. Can I rely on you, Watson?"

"You can," I assured him.

Holmes explained my part in the proceedings, and then, moving slowly and quietly so as not to arouse the snake, I removed the items he had mentioned from the wardrobe. I readied myself, and then Holmes muttered, "Now."

Immediately, I tossed the cane in Holmes's direction. While the object was still in the air, I opened out the jacket in my hands, stepped forward and dropped it squarely over the rearing snake. Holmes caught the cane, and before the cobra could respond to its sudden incarceration, he brought the cane down with great force on the upraised shape beneath the jacket. Instantly, he raised the cane and brought it down again, bludgeoning the now-thrashing shape until it was quite still. A little flushed from his exertions, he whipped the jacket away to reveal the dead creature, its small skull crushed and bleeding, its hideous black body curled limply upon itself.

"Good work, Watson!" Holmes said almost merrily, sinking down upon his bed, his cane drooping in his hand until its heavy silver top was resting upon the floor.

"Pleased to be of service," I replied, feeling a little faint. I sat beside him, though raised my bare feet from the floor, even now reluctant to place them too close to the broken creature. "Will there be more of these brutes about, do you think?"

"I doubt that very much. I believe the house is effectively sealed against such nocturnal visitors."

It took a moment for his words to sink in, but when they did so I looked at him in horror. "You mean that the creature was introduced into your room deliberately?"

"I believe so. No doubt to incapacitate me and render me incapable of investigating this matter further."

"But who would do such a thing?"

"Whoever is behind this business of 'the crimson devil', I assume."

"You do not believe the 'devil' to be a naturally occurring phenomenon then?"

"No, I do not. Its appearances have been engineered to spread disruption and fear. Why, you witnessed this very evening the effect upon Sir Henry's workers."

"I confess I did not understand their words."

"But you got the gist of them, surely?"

"Their agitation was evident," I conceded.

"They are more than agitated, Watson. They are threatening to abandon Sir Henry and return to India. Indeed, we might have seen them carrying out their threat as early as the morrow if I had not intervened with an assurance that the solution of the mystery was close at hand."

I raised my eyebrows. "And do you truly believe that it is?"

"I do," said he. "The pieces are falling into place. Another day or two, and we should complete our jigsaw." He clapped me on the shoulder. "But now, old friend, let us recommence our night's sleep. Today has been taxing enough, but you may be assured that the days immediately following this one will be similarly so."

Holmes's words proved correct, though the next morning began pleasantly enough, with a stroll in the early sunlight, on which Sir Henry accompanied us. Even though the pits out of which the crimson devil was purported to have sprung had been filled in with earth, Holmes nevertheless wanted to see them – or at least a selection of them, for they were scattered far and wide throughout the plantation.

To my mind the pits were singularly unimpressive, and yielded little in the way of insight, but Holmes crouched beside them and made a selection of sounds, which, although wordless, I had come to associate with his own satisfaction upon the progression of a case. The pits were irregularly shaped, though mostly round-edged rather than square, and although we had no evidence to confirm his words, Sir Henry informed us that they had been deep enough that if a man had fallen down one of them he would not have been able to climb out again.

I was aware, as we walked about the estate, that Sir Henry's Indian workers – who even at this early hour were toiling in the cane fields – were watching us with expressions of both expectation and accusation. I felt most uncomfortable beneath their scrutiny as I wafted at the insects buzzing about my face. If Holmes felt equally unsettled, he gave no indication of it.

After an excellent breakfast we set out to visit the Zulu village, which Sir Henry had mentioned the previous evening. Three of his men accompanied us, though Mr Villiers was not one of them. He was still hampered by his injuries, besides which the mood among the Indians was such that Sir Henry had deemed it necessary to leave behind someone he could trust to oversee the day's work. I will not burden this narrative with a description of our interminable plod through the teeming greenery; suffice to say that our journey was an arduous one, and that the dratted insects assailed me every step of the way.

I was relieved, albeit apprehensive, when we finally broke from the stifling fauna, and found ourselves in a wide, clear space tramped down to dusty earth by the passage of many feet.

Around the periphery of this area was a haphazard conglomeration of rough dwellings constructed of mud, tree bark and local vegetation.

I do not know whether the tribesmen of this community had had prior warning of our arrival, but a large delegation of them was awaiting us when we emerged, blinking and perspiring, into the sunlight. To one unused to their appearance they were a fearsome and arresting sight. To a man (and woman) the skin of these natives was as black as coal, and they were clad, somewhat immodestly, in a combination of animal skins and grass skirts. The women, I was shocked to observe, wore nothing but strings of coloured beads across their bared breasts, and they were all of them daubed with strange white markings upon their faces and arms and bellies.

Despite my apprehension, the natives expressed no hostility towards us. Indeed, they regarded us impassively. At their head was a man who I took to be their chief. He was older and more portly than the rest, and he wore a white beard and an elaborate headdress composed of feathers and leopard skin. It was he who approached us, his mouth widening in a welcoming smile, which revealed large gaps between his yellow teeth. One of the three men who had accompanied us stepped forward, gave a small bow and offered him a gift of several bundles of sugar cane, which the chief accepted appreciatively. The man then began to speak to the chief in a language that seemed to be composed of clicks and guttural sounds in place of words. Presently, the chief indicated that we should follow him, and the silent crowd around him parted to let us through.

The chief led us to the far side of the dusty clearing, whereat the largest hut in the village was situated. We were ushered inside and encouraged to seat ourselves cross-legged on animal skins arrayed about the floor. The interior of the hut smelled pungently of sweetly scented smoke and unwashed flesh. Although no one entered the hut but for the chief and our party of six, I was aware that the entourage that had greeted us were crowded around the doorway, blocking out the light, and listening without expression to the conversation taking place inside.

Of that conversation I confess I contributed very little, though Holmes, through the medium of the man who was acting as interlocutor between the chief and ourselves, asked a series of pertinent questions pertaining to the recent appearances of the crimson devil. The chief, with a great deal of head shaking, denied all knowledge of its existence. Yet although Holmes accepted his claims without argument, I could not help noticing that the chief seemed wary in his dealings with us, and that during his exchanges with Holmes he frequently averted his gaze from my friend's unwavering scrutiny, as if ashamed. I felt certain that he was lying, and on the long walk back to the plantation I took Holmes aside and quietly confessed my suspicions to him.

To my astonishment Holmes said, "Well, naturally he was lying, Watson! The matter was never in doubt."

"But if you knew that," said I, "why did you not call him out on it?" And then immediately it occurred to me why he had not. "Wait, do not tell me – was it because of the threat of repercussions from the natives?"

Holmes shook his head. "The tribesmen are not our enemies."

"Then why would they be so unwilling to help us?" I asked, baffled.

"Our visit today was most instructive – not only for what was said, but for what was seen; or rather, what was *not* seen."

"Whatever do you mean, Holmes?" I asked, but he offered me nothing but an enigmatic smile.

"All will be revealed in due course. In the meantime, think on it, Watson. You have an excellent brain! Or so you often tell me."

For the rest of the day, Holmes retreated to his room to rest, and advised me that I should do the same. "This matter is coming to a head, Watson," said he, as a parting shot. "But we must remain patient and allow our enemies to believe that our investigation has thus far led us nowhere."

The following hours passed slowly. I read a little, took a nap, and at the appointed hour descended the stairs to dinner, only to discover that Sir Henry had received a note from Holmes apologizing for his absence, which he attributed to the fact that he was suffering from a mild case of heatstroke.

Nevertheless, Sir Henry's company was pleasant enough, though it was clear that my host was distracted and anxious. We talked a little of old times, and of his intention to retire to the restful, if somewhat bleak, environs of Baskerville Hall in due course. However, despite our efforts to maintain a degree of normality, our conversation eventually petered to silence, and we both of us went to our beds a little earlier than we might have done if the circumstances had been more favourable.

I lay wakeful for some time, but eventually the darkness and the soothing chirrup of insects from outside my window overcame me and I drifted into sleep. When I awoke, it was to feel a hand shaking my shoulder. I opened my eyes to see Holmes's candlelit face peering down upon me.

"Dress quickly, Watson," he implored. "The fish are nibbling at the bait."

I needed no further urging. I leapt from my bed, and not more than two minutes later Holmes and I were slipping from the room and creeping along the landing. We descended the stairs as soundlessly as we could and hurried out into the night.

Placing a finger to his lips to encourage me to remain silent, Holmes led me on a circuitous route through the trampled-down walkways that intersected the cane rows. There was little breeze this night and the tall feathery plants were mostly still and silent around us. Although we had no lantern, the moon was high and fat, and made an excellent fist of lighting our way. Within minutes I had lost my bearings, but Holmes did not hesitate for a moment, turning right or left at each new junction. Eventually, he halted, raising a hand to indicate that I should do the same. Turning to me, he touched one of his ears with the tip of a finger, and recognizing the gesture I stood still, attuning my senses to the night air. At first I heard only the constant sound of the insects, but then I became cognizant of another sound, a curious and not quite rhythmical chop and scrape. For a moment I was puzzled, and then it suddenly came to me what I was listening to: it was the sound of digging.

We crept closer, the sound increasing with each step. Soon we were close enough to its source to ascertain that it was not one man who was digging, but two. Indicating that I should remain where I was, Holmes slipped into the canes and began to move between them. I glimpsed him as a dwindling thread of darkness in the mass of stalks for several seconds and then he was gone.

For perhaps another minute I stood, immobile, listening hard to the hack and scrape of shovels. Eager though I was to remain at my friend's side, in order that we should face whatever peril might await us together, I consoled myself with the thought that should his presence be detected I would know about it on the instant, and could fly to his aid in seconds.

As it transpired, my fears proved unnecessary. Preceded by a slight commotion among the canes, Holmes was suddenly back, a look of satisfaction on his thin face.

"Come, Watson," he whispered, beckoning me with a crooked finger, "but remain exceedingly quiet. The success of my plan depends upon it."

I followed him into the canes, and instantly it was as though I had been struck blind. The light of the moon did not penetrate the feathery canopy, and I was able to follow Holmes only by the faint rustling of the plants ahead of me, and by the impression of his slim form as a moving blur of darkness upon a mostly black canvas. I knew that he had halted only when such indications ceased, though for a moment I did wonder whether he had simply diverted to another course, leaving me inadvertently stranded. I considered whispering his name, but before I could do so his hand was on my arm.

"Observe, Watson," said he, his voice the barest breath in my ear.

He reached forward and parted several of the canes as though they were curtains. Peering through the narrow gap between them, I saw two heavyset men in shirtsleeves and wide-brimmed hats digging tirelessly, the hole they were creating deepening with each spade full of earth which they tossed over their shoulders. Beside the hole, lying upon the ground, was a wooden ladder, which I supposed would be lowered into the hole when it became too deep for them to climb out unaided (a supposition which later proved to be the case). For almost two hours,

Holmes and I watched the men at work, their efforts unstinting, my friend's face wearing an expression of infinite patience, even as my own mind abounded with questions.

Who were these men? What were they digging for? And how had Holmes known they would be here? I wished I could ask him for an explanation, but he had urged me to silence; indeed, he had intimated that if the men should get wind of our presence his plans might lie in ruins.

Even my hope of procuring some clue from the men's conversation proved fruitless, for they spoke little, and only in low murmurs. Additionally, the deeper they burrowed into the earth the less audible they became.

At length, however, the digging ceased and the creaking of the ladder, only the topmost portion of which could now be seen projecting above the rim of the pit, indicated that the men were ascending. As they emerged from the earth, I noted they were dirtied and scowling and clearly dissatisfied, and could only surmise that they had been digging for something, and had not found it.

As the men collected their tools together, and dragged the ladder from the pit, Holmes indicated that we should follow them. I obeyed without question, though I cannot deny that it irked me to have been left in the dark as to the identity of our quarry. I could only place my trust in the fact that Holmes had his reasons for secrecy, and that he had never let me down. At his command we allowed the men to gain a lead of some fifty yards or more, and then we set off in pursuit.

When the pair reached the main gate I fully expected them to employ their ladder as an aid to scaling the high fence, and so was astonished when the man at the head of the ladder simply reached out a hand and pulled the gate open. Moments later, the two had slipped through the gap and out into the jungle. As soon as they were out of sight, Holmes broke into a run, and I followed.

The game of cat-and-mouse that ensued was even more lengthy and arduous than our tramp through the jungle had been earlier that day. Stumbling through blackness as deep as pitch, with leaves and branches and vines catching at our clothes and lashing at our faces, was little short of a nightmare. The darkness did not even prove a deterrent to the insects, which droned ceaselessly around my head and battered their abhorrent bodies against my face. My misery and unease was further and finally compounded by the constant rustling that accompanied us upon our way, a sound which preyed upon my imagination and encouraged me to imagine fearsome predators stalking our every step.

Although Holmes and I moved in darkness, our quarry did not – which was fortunate for us, as we would almost certainly have lost them otherwise. The instant the two men were outside the gate and thought themselves undetected, they lit up a lantern, which they used to illuminate their progress through the thick vegetation. They moved slowly at first, but once they had concealed their ladder within the dense undergrowth, their pace – and by necessity ours – increased. I sorely envied the men their light, although as Holmes and I trailed its wavering flame through the tropical darkness, I sought consolation in the notion that if a nocturnal predator *was* within the vicinity, it would surely be attracted to the light ahead and to those carrying it, rather than to the two of us.

How long we followed that bobbing flame for I cannot say, but it seemed like an age. Similarly, I can offer no indication of our route, save that it felt as if Holmes and I were drifting far from shore with no hope of rediscovering the safe haven from which we had departed.

Eventually, however, the glow of the lantern was matched by a more distant but expansive glow, as if from a nearby town. This glow was accompanied by a murmur of sound, which slowly grew into a clamour as we approached it. Soon enough the clamour broke into a series of wholly recognizable noises, although there was no reassurance in this fact. I reached out and gripped my friend's arm, and spoke, in a low voice, for the first time since we had plunged into the jungle.

"Good Lord, Holmes! Surely those are the cries of children?"

Our quarry's destination thus evident, Holmes allowed himself to pause. "Do you remember what I said to you earlier today, Watson, following our visit to the tribal village?"

I struggled to recall his exact words. "You claimed that it was most instructive, partly because of what was *not* seen."

"Precisely. And what was not seen?"

For a moment I was puzzled – and then suddenly it came to me. "We saw no children!"

Holmes expressed his pleasure by tapping me twice briskly on the chest. Then, his form now limned by a faint orange glow from the radiance up ahead, he led us cautiously forward.

Presently, we reached an area of undergrowth situated upon the periphery of a wide clearing. Here we crouched in concealment and observed the proceedings before us. Our quarry had led us to a firelit camp, which consisted of several large tents and a roughly hewn but sturdy compound that put me in mind of a cattle pen at a farmers' market. At least two dozen armed men were seated, or standing, or moving around within the camp, each of them similarly dressed to the men who had led us here.

It was not these men, however, that commanded my attention, but the poor creatures contained within the compound. There must have been at least forty native children huddled together for comfort and protection, ranging in age from babes in arms to youths of fifteen or sixteen years. Some of the older children were standing very still and gazing stoically ahead of them, clearly determined to be brave, but many of the younger were wailing in fear, tears streaming down their faces. It made my blood boil to see the armed men laughing and jeering at their captives as they passed by the compound.

I gripped Holmes's sleeve. "We must do something!"

Holmes's face was grim. "And so we shall. But at the right and proper time."

I felt a protest rising to my lips, but almost instantly stymied it. Holmes was right, of course. There was nothing the two of us could do on our own to relieve this situation.

Presently, Holmes murmured, "Come, Watson, I have seen enough – more than enough, in fact."

How he found his way back through the darkness of the jungle I have no idea, but find it he did. When we arrived back at the plantation, it was to discover that the gate, which had been unlocked earlier, had now been closed and locked behind us. We beat upon it and cried out until a sleepy and bemused Indian arrived with a key. Upon gaining admittance, we went straight to the house and upstairs to Sir Henry's bedroom. Holmes tapped on the door, and upon hearing our host's sleep-laden response opened it and entered. Sir Henry was sitting up in bed.

"Whatever is—" he began in confusion, but Holmes waved him to silence.

"I am pleased to inform you that the affair of the crimson devil has almost reached its conclusion, Sir Henry. I thought you would wish to be present to see it out?"

As Holmes's words sank in, the sleep fell away from Sir Henry's face and he came fully awake. Jumping from his bed and pulling his trousers and jacket hastily over his nightclothes, he said, "I would, Mr Holmes! Indeed I would! But can it be true? Have you really solved the mystery?"

"I believe so," said Holmes. "Light a lantern and follow me, and all will be explained."

Sir Henry did so, and then he and I followed Holmes downstairs. Upon reaching the ground floor, Holmes led us to the back of the house, halting at the door to Villiers's room. Drawing his Webley, he pushed the door open without knocking and entered. Striding across the floor, he pointed the gun at the sleeping figure in the bed and bellowed, "Rouse yourself, Mr Villiers! I am afraid the game is up!"

Spluttering and gasping, as though emerging from water, Villiers was startled awake. Clutching his injured arm, he struggled into a sitting position.

"What is this?" said he angrily. "Are you quite mad, Mr Holmes?"

"I think you will find me perfectly cold and reasonable, Mr Villiers," Holmes replied. "Sir Henry, would you be kind enough to bring that lantern over here? Watson, would you remove the portrait of Her Majesty from its place on the wall?"

At Holmes's words, Villiers slumped back against the headboard of his bed, his swarthy, lined features becoming slack with resignation. As Sir Henry held up the lantern, I did as Holmes had asked, reaching out to grasp either side of the heavy portrait and lifting it with a small grunt of effort from its hook.

"Heavens!" Sir Henry exclaimed, staring at the portion of wall that had hitherto been concealed. He brought the lantern closer to it, in order to examine it more carefully.

Etched upon the plaster was a map, crudely done but recognizable as the layout of the plantation. Upon the map myriad crosses had been marked.

"What does it mean, Mr Holmes?" asked Sir Henry, turning to my friend.

"The crosses represent the pits from which your so-called 'crimson devil' is purported to have sprung," Holmes replied. "In truth, however, the pits are not gateways to some fearful netherworld, but merely holes dug out with spades by compatriots of Mr Villiers here – compatriots which he himself has aided by sneaking from his bed in the dead of night to unlock the gate and thus allow them entry."

"How did you know the map was under the portrait, Holmes?" I asked.

Holmes pointed at the wall. "Observe these scuff marks on the plaster at the point at which the two bottom corners of the portrait touch the wall. The only way such an object would create such marks would be if it were in frequent motion, rubbing against the plaster. And the sole reason for it to be in frequent motion would be if it were constantly being taken down and put back up again. I surmised, therefore, that beneath the portrait was something that Mr Villiers did not wish us to see."

Villiers shook his head in disgust. "You're a sharp one, all right, Mr Holmes. I feared you would be a danger to me."

"Which is why you tried to remove me from the equation, is it not, by releasing a venomous snake into my room?"

Sir Henry gasped. "You fiend, Villiers! Mr Holmes could have died from such a bite."

"Oh, I think Mr Villiers is fully aware of the potential consequences of such an action, Sir Henry. But I fear he has no such
scruples in that respect. After all, he had already killed poor
Karamchand earlier that same evening."

On this occasion Sir Henry's mouth dropped open and his
eyes went wide. "*You* killed him?" said he, gaping at Villiers. He
turned in bewilderment to Holmes. "But surely the crimson
devil . . ."

"There is no crimson devil," Holmes said curtly. "At least,
not as you perceive it."

"But Villiers's arm . . . he himself was injured in the creature's
attack."

Holmes looked at Villiers coldly. "Will you have the decency
to relate to your employer a true account of the events of yesterday evening or shall I offer my own conjecture?"

Villiers sighed. Nursing his injured arm, he said, "Mr Holmes
speaks the truth, Sir Henry. But let me say that Karamchand
was not killed in cold blood. He died out of necessity, and that I
regret."

Bathed only in the light of Sir Henry's lantern, and with
Holmes's revolver trained unerringly upon him, Villiers told us
the rest.

"Karamchand made it known to me that he had discovered
my secret – how I don't know. I can only surmise that he had
awoken one night, or perhaps had been unable to sleep, and had
spied me unlocking the gate and admitting my 'compatriots', as
you call them. At first he considered exposing me, but later
decided to turn the situation to his advantage – a decision that
proved his undoing. He demanded financial recompense from
me in return for his silence, and so, in order to discuss the
matter, I arranged to meet him in the clearing where you, Mr
Holmes, discovered us.

"His demands were high, ridiculously so. I tried to make him
see sense, but he was adamant. We argued, and in the heat of the
moment I shot him through the throat. He fell to the ground,
whereupon I acted swiftly to make it look as though we had
been attacked by the crimson devil. I shot twice more into the

air, then used the devil's 'claw', a metal implement, to mask the bullet wound. I tore gashes in my own arm to make it appear as though I too had been a victim of the 'devil', and then I threw the claw into the canes, marking its location so that I could retrieve it later." He shrugged. "And that's it, gentlemen. As I say, I regret Karamchand's death."

Holmes shook his head. "No, I won't have it, Mr Villiers. I don't believe that you regret the poor fellow's death in the slightest. You claim to have had no prior intention of murdering your victim, and yet you arrived at your meeting place already armed with the claw. Such an action would indicate that in your mind the unfortunate man's fate was sealed even before the meeting had taken place." He waved a hand disdainfully. "But that is for a court to decide. I shall simply present the evidence to the relevant authorities as I see it."

I thought of the men that Holmes and I had observed in the clearing tonight, and tried again to contain my anger at the callous manner in which they had tormented their terrified captives.

"But who are these 'compatriots' of Villiers's, Holmes?" I asked.

"They are Boers," Holmes replied. "Indeed, are you not one yourself, Mr Villiers?"

When Villiers failed to respond, Holmes, with a jerk of his head, indicated the rifle propped in the corner of the room. "I suspected it when I retrieved Mr Villiers's weapon from where he had dropped it in the clearing after the staged 'attack' in which Karamchand died. It is a .450 Westley Richards, is it not?"

I crossed to the rifle and examined it. "It would appear so. But what of it?"

"Such rifles were heavily favoured by the Boers in their war against the British almost two decades ago," Holmes replied. "And from the wear on both the stock and the barrel, I suspect that this very weapon was employed in the conflict."

"It belonged to my father," Villiers replied. "My family are from the town of Kimberley in the Orange Free State, and proud to be so."

"I am sure that you are a very proud people and that you feel your cause is a just one, but that does not condone your odious tactics in this matter. As to the information regarding your origins, that would reinforce my theory as to why your fellows have been digging these pits on Sir Henry's land, and why you have been keeping such a careful record of their location."

"I'm not certain I understand, Holmes," said I. "What has Kimberley to do with it?"

"I think *I* know," said Sir Henry. "Kimberley is renowned for its diamond mines." He looked at Holmes with wide eyes. "Is that it then, Mr Holmes? Could there be diamonds on my property?"

"I suspect that Mr Villiers believes there are," Holmes said, looking at the man on the bed.

Villiers let loose another deep sigh. "My father was a diamond miner. He fought in the War for Independence, but was badly injured in the conflict, whereupon my mother cared for him, until, some years ago, he died. On his deathbed he informed me that not long before the outbreak of war he had unearthed a fortune in diamonds, but that if he had declared his find the British would have taken it from him and left him with only a fraction of their true worth. He travelled, therefore, south to Natal, to this region, and buried his haul in the jungle, with the intention of retrieving it at a later date, when the situation between my people and the Uitlanders was not so volatile.

"However, for him, the opportunity to retrieve his buried fortune never arose. Upon his death he left me a crudely drawn map, together with written instructions on where to find the diamonds.

"It took me some considerable time, but eventually I calculated that the diamonds must be somewhere within the borders of Sir Henry's estate. Naturally, the plantation had not been here when my father had visited the area. I bided my time, and eventually heard news that Sir Henry's estate manager was moving on, whereupon I applied for the position. Once I had secured it, and was situated permanently within the boundaries of the plantation, it became simpler to put my plan into operation."

"A plan involving the kidnapping of children and the murder of innocents," said I bitterly.

Villiers held up his good hand as though to deflect my accusation. "I admit the plan was a desperate one – some might even say ruthless – but it was never my intention that anyone should be harmed. I wanted only to spread dissent among the workers here, to such an extent that they would take flight, abandon the plantation—"

"And in the process ruin a good man," I barked, indicating a pale-faced Sir Henry.

"I would have compensated Sir Henry for his loss, once the diamonds were in my possession," Villiers said airily. "In the meanwhile, I concluded that the most effective manner in which to achieve my aims was to seize upon the superstitions and fears of the Indian workers within Sir Henry's employ."

"And so you coerced the local tribesmen to aid you by holding their children to ransom," said Holmes. "But your countrymen were never so patient as you, were they? They were forced to endure the hardship of jungle living, and so insisted upon digging for the diamonds during the dead of night, while the plantation workers were sleeping. But you have a cunning mind, Mr Villiers; it is almost admirably so, in fact. You considered how to turn the impatience of your fellows to your advantage, and thus came upon the explanation that the pits appearing around the plantation were the means of ingress by this 'crimson devil' of yours, this mythical denizen of the underworld. However, upon examining the pits, even though they had been filled back up with earth, I noticed that on one side of each of the holes was a pair of indentations, which it did not take me long to realize must have been caused by the weight of a ladder leaning against the rim of the pit from within. I knew immediately, therefore, that the pits were made by man and not by beast. It was but one piece among several of what at the outset seemed a most complex puzzle. Once those disparate pieces came together, however, they began to form an image, whereupon the remainder of the picture gradually, and inevitably, took shape."

There is not much more to tell. Due to the absence of adequate policing within the vicinity, it was a combined force of Indian plantation workers and Zulu tribesmen, armed with rifles and spears, which routed the Boers' camp the following day and successfully freed the captive children. Caught by surprise, the Boers were swiftly overwhelmed, three of them dying in the melee and the remainder fleeing into the jungle.

Villiers was conveyed under armed guard to the nearest town and handed over to the authorities. What ultimately became of him I know not, though my hope is that he paid sufficiently for his crimes.

As for Sir Henry, he remained in Southern Africa for a further two years, but eventually, upon the outbreak of what has since become known as the Second Boer War, returned to England, where he now resides happily at his ancestral home, Baskerville Hall. I am delighted to say that at the age of forty he took a wife, Constance, and the couple now have a pair of delightful children.

Holmes has never revealed to me the particulars of the dinner he shared with his brother, Mycroft, two nights before we embarked upon our voyage, but I have often wondered how much he knew of the affair prior to our arrival in Africa. Of the diamonds, which were supposedly buried somewhere in the plantation grounds, and which presumably would have greatly aided the Boer cause had they been found, not a trace, as far as I am aware, was ever discovered.

# The Draugr of Tromsø

## Carole Johnstone

*Dear Mr Sherlock Holmes,*
*You will forgive, I am sure, my coming straight to the heart of the matter, for I believe that you are a man as well engaged as myself, and thus certain to appreciate an economy of words. Though, I must confess that I hardly know where to begin.*

*Despite having not resided there for many years, I am a man of some means and considerable influence within my home country of Norway, and this can be the only explanation for a recently received anonymous telegram imploring me to secure your help for the citizens of Tromsø, a northern charter town in Troms county. The telegram spoke of its inhabitants being plagued by a creature known as a* draugr, *the old Norse meaning of which is a revenant. I have some knowledge of the subject, having written of it on occasion, though no more than that. When my own humble investigations uncovered that there had indeed been a spate of unexplained attacks, and even a violent death, I will confess to some measure of cruel curiosity, and having already intended to return home for a visit, I merely brought forward my plans and proposed destination.*

*I am intolerant of both hyperbole and sensationalism, Mr Holmes, but upon arriving in Tromsø, I found a town paralysed by fear and, so it seemed straight away to me, truly besieged by malign influence. In the surrounding countryside, animals are nightly slaughtered and terrible, alien cries are heard. Even in town, people venture outside only when needs absolutely must, and otherwise hide away in silence, cowed by terror.*

*The very night after I arrived, there was a terrible commotion on the main street, and when I hurried to find the cause, discovered a crowd gathered around a wooden gig. Within it was the bloodied corpse of a man quite savaged, his eyes wide and wild, face contorted beyond, I imagined, all recognition and reason, as if he had glimpsed the Devil Himself before death delivered him.*

*Upon meeting with the chief of police and county selectmen, it became clear to me at once that no one had any idea as to what to do; indeed, that no one sought to do anything at all. My own presence was just as ineffectual, for I am a writer and not a man of either action or investigation.*

*I have heard that besides being a detective of great repute, you are also one of reason and not fancy. I am therefore of exactly the same mind as the anonymous author of my telegram in extending a most heartfelt invitation to travel to our country and free this town of its terrible siege. I appreciate that such a journey would be long and arduous: Troms county is three hundred and fifty kilometres inside the Arctic Circle and midwinter approaches, but you may name your price and I will guarantee it.*

*Yours faithfully,*
*Henrik Johan Ibsen*

"Well then, what do you make of it, Watson?"

"Henrik Ibsen!" I cried, quite beside myself. "Why, he is truly brilliant: a profound poetic dramatist; the best, it is said, since Shakespeare!"

"Indeed, Watson," Holmes said, putting down his newspaper and reaching for a half-finished glass of burgundy, "That I have ascertained for myself. As ever, you have missed the point of my enquiry."

"Only two years ago," said I, still enthralled by the letter's author, "I attended the Princess Theatre to watch a most wonderful adaption of his *A Doll's House*. I had very much wanted too to see *The Wild Duck*, arguably his most acclaimed—"

"No matter, no matter," Holmes interrupted, agitated enough now to stand up from his easychair and begin pacing. "You know how uninterested I am in the theatre. What of the letter, Doctor, the letter?"

"It sounds a most interesting case," I answered carefully. "But Ibsen is doubtless correct. I have never chanced to travel to Scandinavia at this time of year, but I imagine that the journey will indeed be arduous."

"Nonetheless, should we accept his invitation?"

"You are asking my opinion?"

Holmes ceased his pacing at once. "Do I not always?"

"You do always ask for it," I conceded dryly, "though rarely does my answer—"

"Watson, dear fellow, you are driving me to nervous distraction!"

"Yes, then," I replied. "My answer is yes."

In truth, I was very glad of the letter's opportunity, for not since the theft of a piece of the famous Beryl Coronet, had anything come close to Holmes's keen interest, and that case had been a full winter ago. He had become increasingly vexed and then melancholic. I had grown quite despairing of his neither speaking nor moving for days, and of the morocco case upon the mantlepiece and its syringe within; the countless puncture marks dotting his pale, thin arms.

Thus, I comforted myself with the eager pinprick of his pupils and his quick returned enthusiasm as we travelled first to Newcastle, and then east to Bergen aboard a passenger steamer. Though I freely confess to a dampening of my own, when thereafter trapped aboard a tiny wind- and snow-swept vessel on the Norwegian Sea, in the too close company of hunters and trappers and timbers, the decks still thick with the stench of dried cod and skins.

When we finally arrived, by means of a low-bellied rowboat, at the otherwise deserted Tromsø dock on the island of Tromsøya, I was quite exhausted. Though it was not yet five in the afternoon, the dark was absolute; the lights of the town were the only sign of life or comfort.

Holmes disembarked with no trace at all of either tiredness or trepidation, turning back to our skipper with a quick smile. "Good sir, will you not alight?"

"I will not," the man muttered, already preparing to put back out to the strait.

"Come, Watson! The wire instructed us to repair to the local beer hall. Your great playwright awaits our arrival!"

The main street beyond the dock was entirely empty save a fresh blanket of snow; its gaslights few and far between, its fewer residences shuttered and dark. I will confess that it was something of a relief to come upon the swinging sign of the Ølhall, and gratefully followed Holmes down its steep stone steps.

The hall was blessedly warm and well lit by high candles. Our arrival attracted the immediate attentions of a huddled group of men close to a healthy wood fire, and it was only when we reached as far as the long timbered bar that I realized that this place too was otherwise empty.

"Sherlock Holmes and Doctor Watson!" a man cried, standing up from the huddle, already extending a hand as he rounded the table and marched towards us, his cane tapping loudly against the floor. I recognized the exuberant and straight-edged sideburns straight away, the luxuriant grey hair, small round spectacles, stern thin lips. Despite both my exhaustion and trepidation, I found myself shaking Ibsen's hand as fiercely as he did mine, suddenly remembering to be glad that I had come at all.

"Mr Holmes!" Ibsen said, turning to shake my friend's hand as enthusiastically. "It is a great pleasure to make your acquaintance at last."

"Indeed," Holmes replied. "And I would very much like to say the same, but I have no idea who you are."

"Why, I am Henrik Ibsen." He blinked. "I sent to you first a letter and then a telegram—"

"My pardon again, good sir," Holmes said. "But you are not."

"Holmes!" I cried, immediately mortified.

"Watson." He smiled, quite unperturbed. "Henrik Johan Ibsen is, I believe, sitting directly behind you."

A man that I had not previously noticed at all stood up at once from the shadows. He was dressed in dark clothing, his face hidden inside a white-furred hood. His chuckle was eclipsed only by the sudden laughter of our nearer companion.

"Bravo, Mr Holmes. Bravo!" the former said, pushing back the hood as he came towards us, revealing nearly the same face again. "You must forgive us the ruse, as impolite as it must seem."

"I am long used to having to prove my singular skills," Holmes replied mildly.

"You are no performing seal, sir," Ibsen said, suddenly sober. He shook Holmes's hand hard between both of his own. "My apologies are heartfelt, you can be certain of that, though you acquitted yourself admirably. And Doctor Watson! A pleasure, a pleasure. Come sit near to the fire. Ludwig, some more beer, if you please?"

Once we were seated on wooden stools next to the hearth, the other men drifted away, until only Holmes, I, Ibsen and his impersonator remained.

"If it is not too great an imposition, how did you know that I was not who I claimed to be, Mr Holmes?" asked the latter, as he removed his sideburns and wig to reveal an altogether younger, handsomer face.

"Ah, that was no great imposition either," Holmes said. "I have long known that it is difficult, if not impossible, for a man to avoid leaving his unique imprint upon any object within his daily use. Your cane, Ibsen, is just such an item. And your companion—"

"Ivar." The man in question smiled. "Ivar Brovik."

"Very well," Holmes said, "Mr Brovik utilized your cane upon his right side, and favoured its flank, when its purpose is to be a companion to an opposing limb. In addition, the cane's inside extremity was scratched and scarred, where it should have been its outside. And I have long made careful study of the influence of a man's trade upon his hands; I have a great many lithotypes, for they are an invaluable aid to body identification. And you, sir," he said to Brovik, "most certainly do not have the hands of a writer. They are calloused and bear the score-burns of rough stone handling – sandstone, I believe?" When Brovik only blinked in answer, Holmes nodded his satisfaction and turned to Ibsen instead.

"Also, I have, I must confess, done some research upon you, good sir, and you are a man of certain composure and abstention. Your eyes and nose are not likely to be bloodshot with drink. Nor would your cheeks be pink with a barber's razor, or squinting against the intrusion of spectacles that ill match your sight. I know too, that you have lived these past few years in Munich, while Mr Brovik has the skin of a man lived somewhere far more exotic."

"Afghanistan!" Ivar Brovik exclaimed. "And you are quite right on all counts: I must confess to having suffered some recent misfortune – a few good investments gone bad – and the only means by which I could return to Norway was by working some months on the sandstone ramparts of the Citadel in Ai-Khanoum. I finally returned to Kristiania not two weeks ago, and only found out about this bad business upon my arrival on Tromsøya. Why, if Ibsen is not impressed than I certainly am! Bravo again, sir!"

Holmes inclined his head as though in dismissal, but I knew well his easy susceptibility to flattery. "As entertaining as this diversion has been, we must address the reason that Watson and I are here, gentlemen," he said, draining his beer and leaning over the table to steeple his long, thin fingers.

"Of course," Ibsen conceded, "though I must confess that nothing more untoward has occurred since my letter to you, save more rumour and livestock slaughter."

"Rumour of the *draugr*?" I asked.

"This town is but a newborn," Ibsen answered obtusely. "Less than a hundred years ago, it boasted a population of only a few dozen, yet now it is the 'Paris of the North', the 'Gateway to the Arctic', attracting socialites and hunters in equal measure. But it is a place ill equipped for either population or revenants—"

"Revenants!" scoffed Holmes. "Quite impossible!"

"Impossible?" Ibsen enquired benignly.

"You do not fool me again even for an instant." Holmes smiled. "Because only a simpleton would believe in animated corpses returned from the grave to terrorize the living. It is a nonsense! Would that there were a crime scene or victim to examine, I should be able to prove so irrefutably. But you mentioned in your letter that you had written of these *draugar* yourself?"

"Indeed, I have, Mr Holmes." Ibsen smiled. "In Norse mythology, the draugar were described as the cruel and savage undead, who returned from death to avenge those who had wronged them in life. They can increase their size at will, are said to possess superhuman strength, and being of corporeal body, are much decomposed. They slay their victims either by crushing them with their heavy forms, or devouring their flesh and drinking their blood. They are also credited with driving some victims quite mad with terror. Any unfortunate animals feeding near a *draugr* grave drop dead in their dozens."

"Ah," Holmes said with a smile, "formidable opponents!"

"Might you perhaps have read any of my works, Mr Holmes?" Ibsen enquired with a sudden frown.

I had to repress a somewhat knowing chuckle at this, for here were two formidable opponents indeed: only perhaps a celebrated writer and *littérateur* could match the great detective for entitled self-aggrandizement.

"I have not, good sir," Holmes answered, quite unabashed. "I have long held a belief that a man's mind is like a storage shed. One can cram it full of lumber, or of items carefully considered and chosen. The distinction matters little to an ordinary gentleman, but a man such as myself must be certain only to store within it those items that will aid me in both my methods and philosophy. I have no room at all to spare for detritus."

"Well," said Ibsen, thin lips pulled thinner, "I have never before had my writings described as either lumber *or* detritus."

"Do not construe it as any stain upon your talent, sir," Holmes said with a smile. "I have only passing interest in any kind of literature whatsoever."

"Well, what then of the study of character, of motivation? How, otherwise, can a detective such as yourself begin to know what is pertinent and what is not? Surely that skill alone requires at least a small corner of your shed?" Ibsen muttered.

"Perhaps," Holmes replied, "but I consider that a singularly acquired skill and not one stolen from the scribbled analyses of another."

I am certain that I was not alone in my considerable relief when the beer hall's stairwell door banged open, admitting both a gust of Arctic air and a stout, short man dressed head to toe in black. He marched towards our table, thrusting a folded note into Ibsen's hand.

"If you are ready to leave, gentlemen," Ibsen said, "then this man has been sent with a carriage to take us to a residence in Bjerkaker, a few kilometres south of Tromsø. Herr and Fru Lundestad have been kind enough to extend an open invitation to their home for the duration of the investigation."

"You are coming also?" I enquired in surprise, when Ivar Brovik got up from the table.

"I am!" said he, draining the last of his beer. "It is how good Ibsen and I made our acquaintance this night. Erhart Lundestad and I are childhood friends, long considered brothers in arms. He has been kind enough to grant me asylum, while I seek to recover my fortune and previously good name."

As we ascended back into the dark and empty street, an icy wind whistled through its hidden extremities and fresh flakes of snow fell from a moonless sky. I was more than dismayed to realize that our carriage was, in fact, little more than a gig cart drawn only by one horse.

"Ha!" exclaimed Holmes, nudging my shoulder with ill-disguised glee. "Not quite a hansom, eh, Watson?"

"Indeed, no," I replied, too exhausted for either objection or feigned enthusiasm.

As the narrow streets of the town gave way to open flatland and fierce whips of Arctic wind, the four of us huddled too closely together in the tight, bone-shaking space permitted us.

The dark grew ever more absolute. The land and the water alongside were little more than twinned shadows beyond the thick golden glare of the gig's oil lamps, its driver sitting high above the level of the cart's shafts as the snow eddied around us in a thick, white fog.

"If I may ask, Ibsen," Holmes bellowed, over the wind and the hooves and the gig's thunderous rattle, "have you discovered from whom that first telegram came?"

"I have not," Ibsen shouted back. "I know only that it originated from my hometown of Skien, in the south-east. No more than that."

And then, from out of the alien darkness – its strata of alternate shadows and cruelly savage slaps of wind – came suddenly the most terrible cry. Halfway between a scream and a roar of malign fury, it reverberated around our muddily lit space, growing almost immediately louder – closer – as if attracted by our intrusion. Above and ahead of us, I heard the driver curse, following its sentiment with the swifter snap of his whip.

"Ha!" Holmes cried again, clapping his hands once and showing his teeth, while I and the remainder of his travelling companions looked to one another with ill-disguised fright.

On we rattled – and now too fast. One of the gig lamps dislodged and shattered hard against the uneven road, leaving in its wake only more impenetrable spectres of black. There came another terrible scream – this time, I was certain, one of absolutely singular malevolence – and I recalled Ibsen's description of the *draugar* with dread reluctance.

"Upon my word!" I shouted, because I hardly knew how else to contain my growing and unwieldy terror. Brovik's expression mirrored that which I imagined was my own, while Ibsen displayed only a thin-lipped grimace born of either consternation or reproval –

I could hardly tell or care which.

When we finally ground to an undignified and hoof-stamped halt alongside a well-lit, two-storey house, we four alighted in some haste, and the black-clad driver had hardly allowed us our disembarkment before he took off into the night.

"Well!" exclaimed Brovik. "I must confess now to better understanding both Ibsen and Tromsøya's consternations. Assure me now, good fellows, that I was not alone in hearing those terrible cries, those evil screams?"

"As easily attributed to the furious wind and cruel moorland!" Holmes exclaimed, brushing snow from his shoulders.

"Do you think so?" Brovik muttered hopefully, some colour returning to his cheeks.

"I think not, Holmes!" I protested. "Why, it was—"

Light flooded at once upon our crouched huddle and, as we turned towards the opened doorway of the house, a man of some considerable height and girth appeared within it.

"Erhart!" Brovik cried. "My good friend! It is wonderful to set eyes upon you once again!" When he hastened up the short stone path towards the house, we all followed swiftly, seeking only warmth and light and, on my part, a door barred against the unsettling night.

Erhart Lundestad was as solid and perfunctory as his home, though the latter, at least, showed signs of having once been far grander than its present aspect: its high, cobwebbed ceilings were painted with intricate though faded designs, its wooden beams a splendidly linear display of varnished dark oak. Lundestad, however, was ruddy and unkempt and fair-bearded; well over six feet tall, and wearing an ill-fitting grey walking-suit and an uglier scowl. Around his head plumed impenetrable clouds of cigarette smoke. Though he greeted Brovik with some enthusiasm, he eyed the rest of us with ill-disguised suspicion.

"Ivar!" a lady's voice cried before its owner, dressed in a long black habit, emerged from a reception room to kiss said gentleman upon both cheeks. "And you must be Mr Ibsen and Mr Holmes!" The feathers in her hair moved within a hidden breeze as she greeted both, and a gold-patterned brooch at her neck caught the lamplight. When she turned to me, I looked upon a complexion that was pale and opaque, her eyes a pleasing shade of grey.

"Doctor John Watson," I provided.

"Doctor Watson! Of course. And I am Ella Lundestad. You must forgive me any offence, Doctor. It has been so very long since we've had guests of any kind to stay." She clasped her slim fingers together. "Why, to have you all here under our humble roof is a wonder indeed."

"They are not here for our entertainment, wife," Lundestad muttered, and she stepped back into the hall's shadows as if struck. I frowned, for no gentleman wishes to see a wife so publicly chastised by her husband, especially not a wife of such obvious refinement and distinction.

Lundestad swept an arm towards those standing alongside. "My mother, Hilde Lundestad." A severely dressed woman nearly as large and disagreeable as he stood forward and gave each of us a sharp nod. "And our two servants, Jörgen and Freda Ekdal. Should you require anything, they shall endeavour to provide it."

By way of apparent greeting, Jörgen frowned lingeringly at each of us in turn. Lundestad nodded once and, as he marched away towards a reception room, I noticed that he held his left leg stiff and straight as though his knee had suffered some long ago and badly healed injury.

"We've prepared you a warm supper in the dining room." Ella Lundestad smiled, though twin spots of ill colour had appeared high upon her cheeks. "Please, gentlemen, if you would follow—"

An almighty banging quite startled us all into frozen silence. When it came again, this time shaking the heavy entrance door inside its frame, Lundestad swore as he lumbered past us to open it wide, admitting a gust of angry wind.

"Herr Lundestad!" shouted a young fellow with a wild expression. "It has happened again!" He ill advisedly clutched at Lundestad's lapels. "My father – he is killed by the *draugr*!"

"Calm yourself, Nils," Lundestad growled. "Freda, take the boy to the kitchen. Jörgen, fetch me my gun, and then send word to Morten Tönnesen to dispatch some men from town. I'll go to the Stockmann farm, see if the boy's story is true."

"I should like to accompany you," Holmes said.

"You?" snorted Lundestad. "I am a trapper and tracker, sir. And, first and foremost, I am a hunter. I work far better alone."

Holmes smiled, entirely unperturbed. "As do I, sir. And I can assure you that my qualifications in all three fields well exceed your own."

Lundestad snorted again before snatching his long-rifle from his servant's hands and marching out into the night.

"Be careful, husband!" Ella cried after him. "Please, Mr Holmes, if you've a mind to go after him then do. He is out all hours of the day and night looking for the monster. Why, he had only just returned from the last patrol when you arrived. I am not sure that I can stand much more worry!"

"Calm yourself, girl," Hilde Lundestad said, pulling her back from the door.

"I know the farm," said Brovik. "It is not far."

"Do you have your revolver, Doctor?" Holmes asked me, producing his own.

"Of course," I replied.

Thus, the three of us followed Lundestad out into the wild, dark night with little more than two revolvers and a muddy oil lamp for company.

The dark was indeed absolute and the terrain contrary. Beyond the gravel road, it grew more contrary still, until I abandoned all pretence of watchfulness, and instead concentrated only upon not losing sight of Brovik's light, and neither breaking neck nor limb in negotiation of the rocky boulders and deep drifts of snow hell-bent upon getting in my way. Though the wind had dropped and the snowfall had ceased, I will admit to having one ear out for the dreadful cries and screams that we had heard earlier – and while none came, I still fervently wished for the moon and a swift end to our too speedy trek.

Finally, the lights of the farmstead came into view, and Brovik led us into its yard. There was no sign at all of Lundestad.

"Who other than the boy and his father live here?" Holmes asked, as we drew closer to its thrown open door.

"None," Brovik said. "Fru Stockmann died in childbirth many years ago."

"Very well," Holmes said. "If you two gentlemen would follow close behind me."

The farmhouse was far more modest than the Lundestads' home. Its front room was small and humbly furnished. At its heart was a large stone hearth, whose fire burned and spat too brightly; some ashes had singed a blanket lying upon a nearby wooden stool. There was a vaguely offensive smell, perhaps that of spoiled, rotting flesh, though perhaps too it was only my trepidation and the memory of Ibsen's decomposing *draugar* that encouraged the association.

Revolver drawn, Holmes ventured further inside, swiftly disappearing into shadow. When he made either an excited or alarmed cry of discovery, I sped past Brovik with a shout of my own.

"Do not enter!" Holmes cried, stopping me dead upon the threshold.

"Good Lord," said I, for I hardly knew what else to say. The bedchamber resembled far better an abattoir: its white-painted walls were liberally splashed with blood and gore, while upon the floor next to the bed lay the body of whom I presumed was Nils Stockmann's father, his throat ripped open and bare torso slashed in too many places to count. The whole room reeked of putrid meat, yet the man could have been dead no more than a few hours at most, his skin neither livid nor shrunken.

"Watson," said Holmes, "have Brovik stand guard inside the house's entrance lest someone should come along and disturb that which I haven't yet had the opportunity to see. After my own observations, I should like you to examine the body if you are willing?"

I nodded my assent to both, and after dispatching a rather pale-faced Brovik to the front yard, I returned to find Holmes crawling around the floor upon his hands and knees with his double lens fixed to one eye. He lifted the heavy quilt and peered under the bed; he skirted around the room for many minutes, drawing closer to the victim in ever decreasing circles. Knowing better than to enter or interrupt, I merely watched as he rose and paced before kneeling again, peering, sniffing, and all the while chattering animatedly away to himself. Once, he paused for many minutes before picking something up from the floor beside the body and placing it inside his coat pocket.

When he finally bade me enter, he continued to pace up and down the room, head down and brows drawn, while I examined the farmer's wretched body.

"What are your immediate observations, Doctor?"

"At first glance," I said, "it would appear that he has been attacked quite ferociously. His throat has been torn rather than cut open; the edges of the wound suggest something other than a knife or sharp implement."

"Teeth?" Holmes asked, his eyes bright as though he already knew the answer.

"Perhaps," I said. "As to the slash wounds upon his torso—"

"Indeed, indeed!" he cried, as if I had already finished my sentence. "I have observed just such results whilst experimenting upon cadavers in St Bartholomew's dissecting rooms. There is not enough blood, is there?"

"No," I replied. "There is not. These wounds were almost certainly perpetrated after death. But I don't see—"

"Ah, but I do! Come, Doctor, there is nothing else to learn here. To the farmyard!"

Brovik balked upon our return, uttering a muttered curse. Still there was no sign of Lundestad, which suddenly struck me as strange indeed. When Sherlock began pacing around the doorway at a crouch and then snapped his fingers towards Brovik, the man visibly started again and looked to me.

"He requires your light, sir," I said. "Would you prefer me to take it?"

He shook his head and stepped quickly down into the yard, and it was while I was watching their slow, lighted progress that I glimpsed the arrival of a vehicle beyond the low moorland adjacent to the farm.

"Ah," Holmes said, straightening and fixing me with a dry smile. "The cavalry, I believe."

Perhaps as many as a dozen men eventually came over the hill, carrying better oil lamps of their own.

"Herr Stockmann is quite dead, sirs," Holmes said, putting away both his lens and his measuring tape.

"And you are?" a bearded and uniformed man asked with a frown.

"I am Sherlock Holmes. I was invited here by—"

"Well, I am Morten Tönnesen, county governor and chief of police, and this—" his light moved to expose a small, rotund figure dressed in sombre black "—is Haakon Brendal, the magistrate of Troms. I would ask all of you gentlemen to step away from the building at once."

Holmes smiled and nodded his acquiescence, and both Brovik and I followed his lead, stepping into the deeper snowfall of the farmyard, while the new arrivals disappeared inside the house. When presently, four of their number came back out to march back and forth around its perimeter, Holmes began to chuckle.

"Well, Watson, I hardly expected to meet the Scandinavian cousins of both Lestrade and Gregson, but here we are all the same! And to think that I attributed such investigative prowess to Scotland Yard only."

"Holmes," I said, already knowing that my entreaty would fall upon deaf ears, "perhaps you would do well not to antagonize—"

"Tönnesen!" Holmes said, as the county governor stepped back over the threshold, face pinched and pale. "And what do you make of this atrocity?"

"The *draugr* has—"

"*Draugr!*" exclaimed Holmes. "Ha! Good grief, man, we are less than fifteen years from the beginning of the twentieth century. What possible place for ghouls and ghosts in that?"

"I do not know who you are, sir, but I know what I have seen and heard these past few—"

"Again: I am Sherlock Holmes, *sir*, and I can assure you that while it is true that I prefer to confine my investigations to the material world, it is also irrefutably true that what murdered Herr Stockmann was no revenant."

"Is that so?" Tönnesen growled. "Perhaps you might seek to enlighten us as to why you believe not?"

"Ah, you are doing so well it would perhaps be a pity to interfere." Holmes smiled.

"Holmes," I warned, both his sarcasm and Tönnesen's animosity sitting suddenly too ill in my belly; I was bone tired and nearly undone.

"Very well," Holmes said, briefly meeting my eye. "These then are my observations. Before your men ran roughshod over the entire crime scene, there were three distinct sets of footprints leading right up to the farmhouse entrance. Both Nils Stockmann and his father are of relatively small stature – little more than five and three-quarter feet I would estimate, while the third set belongs to a man of at least six feet and four inches. The latter is between twenty-five and thirty-five years of age, and although he heavily favours his right leg, he is nonetheless able to move with absolute stealth."

"How on earth can you tell either a man's height or age from his bootprint?" Tönnesen asked.

"The height of a man can be measured from the length of his stride," Holmes replied dismissively. "And his age from both its certainty and agility. See over here, the smaller prints of Stockmann Junior and Senior? The former leaps over a ditch, and the latter steps around it; while the larger man's right foot merely steps over, its subsequent impress neither more nor less than the ones before it. He wears boots with a rounded heel, and he smokes cigarettes, specifically Player's Gold Leaf Navy Cut." As he said so, he reached into his pocket to draw out a small powder of grey-dark ash pinched between finger and thumb.

"How the devil do you know that, Holmes?" I exclaimed. Though I knew that he'd made extensive study of tobacco ash, the deduction still remained extraordinary.

He smiled, and in it I recognized the wry humour that was all too often the preserve of his attempts to educate me in the science of deduction. "I found this near to the body also," he said, producing from the same pocket a cigarette box stamped with the familiar sailor logo. He ignored both my heavy sigh and the selectmens' scowls.

"So, you have decided in mere minutes that everything the good people of this town believe is a nonsense?" Tönnesen growled, although even I could see that the county governor was as uncertain. "This is no more than the wilful conjecture of an outsider!"

Holmes appeared hardly perturbed. "We are *supposed* to believe that a beast or monster murdered Stockmann, yet, as the good Doctor will attest, all of the farmer's wounds were delivered posthumously. In addition, the dead man's lips smell sour, and his features are set in a rictus that reminds me of poisoning by either belladonna or strychnos – I am unable to determine which without my equipment, though it is certainly one or the other."

"Sir," Brendal, the magistrate, grimaced, "I hardly know why we should believe—"

"Because," interrupted Holmes, with the satisfied air of a matador delivering the final killing blow, "the stench of decomposing *draugr* comes instead from the putrid entrails of a slaughtered pig secreted underneath Stockmann's bed. Or is that, too, mere wilful conjecture?"

A giant figure loomed out of the darkness and into the circle thrown by our light. Erhart Lundestad shouldered his long-rifle. "Herr Stockmann is dead then?" he asked gruffly, though it was hardly framed as a question. And then he reached into his pocket and shook free a cigarette from its battered Player's Navy Cut box.

When I awoke, it was to more darkness. I rose from my bed, reached for my pocket watch, and was appalled to discover that it was well past ten – I had slept for nearly twelve hours.

I found Holmes in the parlour, his back poker-straight as he stared out into the impenetrable dark. Ibsen was sitting at an ornate writing desk, reading through a sheaf of papers.

"Ah, Watson!" Holmes smiled, his expression showing none of the tired concern that I am certain was in mine. "You are arisen. I had feared you were sleeping the sleep of the dead."

It was an observation made in bad taste, but Holmes did not realize it; his animated eyes were fixed inward.

"While you, I am sure, have been awake for many hours?"

"A few," he conceded. "Perhaps no more than six."

Ibsen chuckled. "Good morning, Doctor. It was certainly an eventful night, was it not?"

"When does the sun rise?" Holmes suddenly asked.

Ibsen blinked. "It does not."

"The sun must always rise." Holmes frowned.

Ibsen chuckled again, though this time with some measure of surprise. "Indeed it must, but here we will not see it again until late January. Tromsø lies inside the polar circle; there will be a brief twilight in an hour or so, but no more than that."

"Extraordinary," Holmes muttered.

"Holmes has little patience for matters of astronomy," I said.

"They are of next to no importance," Holmes said.

"Unnecessary detritus?" Ibsen enquired mildly.

Holmes smiled. "Quite so, although I can admit that in this case its manifestation is entirely pertinent. What better circumstance for rumours of a vengeful *draugr* to take fearful root?"

The stooped and still sullen figure of the servant, Jörgen Ekdal, appeared behind me in the doorway. "An early luncheon is served in the dining room."

Though the dining room's splendour was as neglected as everywhere else, its dimensions were vast. At the table's head, Erhart Lundestad sat more than three feet from both his wife and his mother, while our places, alongside a very weary looking Brovik, were further away still.

"I trust you spent a comfortable night?" Lundestad asked, though he began piling his plate high with pickled fish and cheese and flatbread as if we had already answered, while the Ekdals bustled fore and aft to serve us the same.

As we ate by flickering candlelight, its mirror heralding the dark blue rise of an eerie twilight through high-paned windows, Holmes inclined his head towards Ella Lundestad. "I hear from Brovik that your father was a military man of some repute?"

Lundestad's wife had grey shadows under her eyes, and her fingers shook against the stem of her wine glass. Though her gown was another of faded black, her hair was still painstakingly pinned with bright feathers, and she wore upon her delicate arm a beautiful cuff bracelet inlaid with turquoise stones.

"Indeed," she murmured, trying to smile. "My father was Ragnar Vaeradal. He used to be one of Tromsø's selectmen before he rose too high in army ranks. When he became a general, we had to leave Norway."

"I imagine that you saw a great many fine societies," Holmes said gently.

Ella ventured another small smile. "I enjoyed the balls immensely. Though my father was a great soldier, Mr Holmes – I don't mean to suggest—"

"Of course not," I said, for her distress was all too palpable, as was the thunderous disapproval of both her husband and his severe mother. "What brought you back?"

"He died," she whispered, "and his last wish was to be buried upon the island. When I returned, I renewed my childhood acquaintance with Erhart, for the Lundestads and Vaeradals have been estate neighbours for generations—"

"And after a few months of renewed acquaintance, I proposed," Lundestad interrupted gruffly. "I'll wager there were a few envious mutters in town upon my making her my bride."

"Though she was pleased to accept you," his mother said, looking only across at her daughter-in-law's bowed head.

"Indeed, indeed!" Brovik smiled, raising his half-filled wine glass. "You have done admirably well, Erhart!"

"The wine is no good," Lundestad barked. "You should try the farmhouse ale instead."

For my part, I felt nearly incensed upon the behalf of poor Ella Lundestad, discussed as if she were a prized heifer successfully bartered for at market. When Holmes recognized my outrage, he allowed himself a tight smile before looking towards Lundestad again.

"And what of your own family's estate?" Holmes asked.

"What of it?" Lundestad asked, eyes narrowing in suspicion. "My wealth is in land. The Lundestads own near two hundred hectares from Bjerkaker in the south to Tromsø in the east." He drained his stein of beer. "Though in truth, I care naught for any of it."

"Erhart!" his mother fiercely admonished, while Brovik openly chuckled from the opposite end of the table, toasting his friend with a newly filled stein of his own.

"It is only the truth," Lundestad said, at once becoming animated. "I am a hunter at heart. I have led more than two score expeditions to both Svalbard and Jan Mayen, in the pursuit of walrus, seal and polar bear."

"We are waiting only upon the settling of General Vaeradal's estate before making the necessary improvements to our own," Hilde Lundestad snapped. "Ella is his only heir."

Ella Lundestad gave a suddenly pitiable cry, and the sound of her chair crashing to the floor as she stood stalled us all. "Why is no one speaking at all of last night's horror?" she cried. "Ivar told me what Mr Holmes said to Tönnesen and Brendal and near a dozen of the town's selectmen. Why does no one care that Mr Holmes has all but implicated my husband in the murder of at least three men?"

"Wife, be silent!" Lundestad bellowed.

"By now, the whole of Tromsø will know it!" she cried.

"That was never my intention, Fru Lundestad," Holmes said, though his brow had furrowed in unusual consternation. "I merely furnished Tönnesen and his men with my most elementary of observations. It is indeed a very base error to arrive at any kind of conclusion before you are in possession of all of the evidence."

"But perhaps Tromsø's selectmen do not realize it," Ibsen said dryly, spearing some mackerel.

"Maybe it would be wise if you left Tromsøya for a time, Erhart," Jörgen Ekdal suggested, sitting down alongside Lundestad, and I was again struck by the curiously informal relationship between servant and master.

"Indeed I will not!" Lundestad spat. He sought out the fierce gaze of his mother. "I am not guilty, and the townspeople will know it. Why, only a few days ago, I heard rumour of a transient named Sigerson newly arrived from Kristiania, spreading rumour through Tromsø and Breivika that the *draugr* is naught but a product of their poor Christian living!" He thrust his empty stein towards Holmes. "The Norwegian capital is rife with your English revival of the spiritualist and occult movement. Fresh suspicion will fall elsewhere soon enough."

The rest of the day passed in uneasy inactivity. Ibsen and I read, while the women played cards. Many times I happened upon Lundestad deep in heated though hushed argument with either Brovik or Ekdal, though each exchange ended as abruptly as my presence was noticed. For his part, Holmes retired to his room, where I imagined him pacing back and forth, caught inside more intense arguments of his own: the lunge and riposte of his ever sharp mind.

When all of us retired early after a nearly silent dinner, Holmes sought me out close to my bedchamber. "How do you fare, Watson? You appear quite out of sorts."

"What she sees in him I can hardly fathom!" I found myself protesting before realizing the extent of my escaped fury. "He, a gruff, sullen trapper, and she, the refined daughter of a Norwegian general!"

"Ah, Watson," Holmes chuckled, "always you judge a book by its cover. The beautiful wife, the boorish husband, the crone of a mother-in-law, the drunken jester of young acquaintance, the queer familiarity of a servant."

"And you do not judge a book at all," said I, still unaccountably infuriated, "for, as you freely admit, you do not read them!"

"Ha!" Holmes barked, hitting my shoulder with the heel of his palm. "Well played, Doctor; Ibsen would be undoubtedly proud. You must recount to him this conversation over breakfast."

"Perhaps I shall!" I said, still hardly knowing why I felt so enraged. Perhaps it was the alien darkness and the rumours of the *draugr*; the ill spots of colour on Ella Lundestad's high cheekbones.

"One should always be on the lookout for that which is out of the common," Holmes said, with a thin smile. "The most obvious conclusion is, it is true, most often the correct conclusion, but one should never discount either internal bias or external influence."

"Does that mean that you have your answer?"

Holmes's smile grew teeth. "A good sleep to you, Watson."

"At breakfast then," I muttered, suddenly exhausted.

But by the morning, he had gone.

When Holmes had not returned by mid-afternoon, I began to feel uneasy. Though I searched both his bedchamber and mine, I found no left note explaining his disappearance. As the brief noon twilight gave way once more to the inky dark of perpetual night, my unease grew. Where had he gone? *Why* had he gone? Perhaps, as there was no note, he had merely stepped outside for a stroll and then fallen foul of whatever monster – alive or dead – stalked the island of Tromsøya. Though for Holmes to have fallen accidentally foul of anything at all seemed impossible indeed.

I expressed a most urgent desire to return to Tromsø, even just to make enquiries at the Ølhall or in the market square, but both Lundestad and his mother were quite rudely insistent that I stay. Indeed, it was only when the main entrance door banged open in the early evening, admitting both Hilde Lundestad and her servant, Freda that I understood they had gone into Tromsø without me. My anger was tempered only by my ever-growing concern, and my curiosity for news of town.

"Have there been any sightings?" I asked.

"Of whom?" Hilde Lundestad barked, though she appeared quite out of sorts.

"Holmes, of course," I said, to which she violently shook her head.

Both Brovik and Lundestad had come out of the parlour and into the hallway, and it was to the latter that she immediately turned.

"There was quite an extraordinary sight in Kirkegata Square," she muttered. "The spiritualist was standing on the steps of the Domkirke, warning of the evils of both religion and ritualized thinking."

"Sigerson?" Lundestad enquired, his face suddenly unaccountably pale.

"He appeared quite mad," Hilde Lundestad exclaimed. "Quite, quite mad."

"It is of no matter!" Lundestad cried, taking the groceries from his servant's arms and hurrying his mother away towards the kitchen alongside him. "No matter at all!"

"Most peculiar," Ibsen observed at my shoulder.

"No more than anything else," I answered, though my thoughts had grown darker and my mind ever more uneasy.

When, after dinner, there sounded suddenly a most violent assault upon the house's entrance doors, all of us – women and servants included – rushed into the hallway. The heavy oak doors shook vocally inside their thick frames, the high-ceilinged space lending an almost monstrous aspect to both the sight and sound, and none – not even Lundestad, furnished once more with his long-rifle – made any approach towards admitting whoever or whatever was upon their other side.

Ella Lundestad let escape a tiny scream when, after a moment of brief silence, the assault began again in earnest. "What should we do?" she cried, gripping hard to my arm as I took out my revolver.

"We should open the doors," said I, feigning a confidence that I hardly felt. "We have guns and we have men. Whatever is on the other side should be quickly faced."

Lundestad appeared suddenly incensed by my words, as though they had been meant as a slight upon his character, and before I realized his intention, he had rushed forwards and thrown wide open the entrance.

Ella Lundestad screamed again when a ragged figure barrelled in from the night, knocking Lundestad and his rifle quite out of the way before crashing headlong into my pelvis and sending us both to the floor in a tangle of limbs and shouts.

"Apologies, Watson, apologies! But I know how true your aim can be."

I looked askance at my dirty, long-haired assailant. "Holmes?"

"Indeed! My apologies again, but I'm afraid that this is neither the time for explanation nor conversation." He sprung to his feet and hauled me back onto mine. "We must away immediately."

"Holmes?" I said again, still stupefied by the stranger stood before me.

"We must away!" he cried. When he ripped free both his fat nose and copious beard, and then threw off his ugly long coat, I found myself returned somewhat to my senses. Holmes held my shoulders inside a fierce grip. His eyes were wild. "Watson, I fear that I have made a grave mistake."

"You?"

"It was from a desire only to hold my hand close to my chest until such time as hard proof bore out my certain deductions, but look at what I have made come to pass!"

"Holmes—"

His fingers pressed deeper. "So often I forget that others are incapable of seeing things as clearly as I—"

"Holmes!" I shouted. "*What* has come to pass?"

"The townspeople believe that Lundestad is responsible for the murders. They are mere minutes behind me!"

"The town selectmen are coming to arrest my son?" Hilde Lundestad exclaimed, a hand at her throat.

"The *town!* The town is coming for your son!" Holmes cried. "For the third and last time, we must away!"

When no one replied, Holmes let go my shoulders and fixed me with the fiercest of stares. "John, please. We must away."

"Lundestad, have you any place far from the house where we might hide you?" I asked, but the man merely stood stock-still, his rifle dangling from his arm as he looked out into a darkness suddenly alive with distant shouts and bobbing light.

"My son has a trapper hut to the south-west, upon the edge of our estate," Hilde Lundestad said, her face quite drained of colour.

"Good!" said Holmes. "The ladies and the Ekdals must stay, for they will not be harmed." He quickly thrust a folded paper into Hilde Lundestad's hand. "Give this note to Tönnesen and to no other, understand?"

"I do *not* understand," Lundestad said, his voice still dull with shock.

"Come then, men!" Holmes cried. "We must leave now!"

"I go with my husband," Ella Lundestad said, suddenly fierce.

"No, madam," I started to protest.

"Let her come if she will not stay," Holmes said, already running for the kitchen door.

Again, the way was fiercely treacherous: windy and icy cold; rocky and slippery with snow. Made all the more unsettling by the nearing fury and lights of the townspeople below, and Holmes's insistence that we escape by no light at all of our own.

By the time we reached the trapper hut, I was quite exhausted and quite terrorized, having no idea at all as to what or whom I should be most wary of: the *draugr* or Lundestad; the town: its people, police, or selectmen.

The hut's dimensions were tiny; it struggled to accommodate the six of us, though had as much choice in that as we did. Once Lundestad had secured shut its thin wooden shutters, Holmes lit the gas lamp that he'd brought from the house and squatted down inside its wan glow. We all of us blinked expectantly back at him: myself, Brovik, Lundestad and his wife, and a considerably out of breath Ibsen.

"What do we do now?" I asked. "Surely we are hardly safe here?"

"We are safer certainly than we were inside the Lundestad homestead," Holmes dryly replied. "Though I would suggest that we keep our guns at the ready." He leaned close to Ella Lundestad with a concerned smile. "How do you fare, madam?"

"I am fine," she replied. "Though I'd feel considerably finer if in possession of a gun of my own."

"That's the spirit!" Holmes chuckled.

"Holmes," I said sharply, "what is this all about? And where in the deuce have you been?"

"Very well," he replied, suddenly sober once again, although I'd glimpsed only too clearly the pleased light in his eye that always heralded the solving of a case. In this instance, I did not mind at all that I had skirted nowhere near to the same. I longed for escape from this place; for the bellow and bustle and warmth of London and our Baker Street rooms.

"To answer your last question first, I have been in Tromsø this past day and a half, loudly extolling the virtues of both séance and transcendence."

"*You* were the mad spiritualist on the steps of the Domkirke?" I exclaimed.

"Indeed so." Holmes smiled. "I realized immediately that Sigerson was a blind – a desperate construct created by Lundestad and his mother in order to deflect attention from his all too obvious guilt."

When Lundestad immediately began to protest, Holmes pressed a finger to his own lips.

"But how did you know—"

"Because, Doctor, when a person seeks to lie or mislead, they put altogether too much detail and too much simplicity into the lie. I can assure you," said he before I could do more than raise my hand, "both can be entirely synchronous."

Holmes then turned his attentions upon the still weakly protesting Lundestad. "I decided to take advantage of your mistake, Lundestad, because I was still appalled that I had so inadvertently incriminated you in the eyes of both your kith and kin. My own first mistake had been in forgetting that most minds are only capable of reasoning forwards rather than backwards. And my second," he said with a quick flashed smile, "was in little realizing how far my own infamy had spread, for, with the notable exception of Tönnesen, my mere observations were assumed as absolute truth nearly immediately."

"Holmes," interrupted I, because I was worried about the long-rifle still slung across Lundestad's torso. "Are you saying that Lundestad is absolutely not the guilty party?"

"Indeed, he is not," Holmes chuckled. "Even Ibsen is more likely a suspect than Lundestad."

"I?" Ibsen cried.

"You before accused me of dismissing matters of literature out of hand, but in recent days I have read several of your works, and it seems to me that your play, *An Enemy of the People*, describes exactly what has come to pass here tonight: an innocent man hounded and vilified by his fellow kinsmen—"

"I can assure you, sir," Ibsen angrily exclaimed, "that my *own* infamy requires no such malign validation!"

"I did not say that it was so," Holmes replied mildly, "only that it appeared to be so. Many things are thus engineered. There are a great many fallacies, both intentional and unintentional. The red herring is a plausible but diversionary tactic. For example, Sigerson was an unintentional fallacy, whereas the crime scene at the Stockmann farm was entirely intentional, devised only to make me believe that Lundestad was its perpetrator."

"By whom?" I cried, entirely at my wit's end.

In answer, Holmes carefully drew out his revolver. "By Ella Lundestad."

Immediately, the lady cried out in protest, though it was Brovik that lunged for Ibsen's cane before Holmes was able to snatch it free. Without thinking, I brought the butt of my pistol down hard upon Brovik's crown, and when he dropped to the ground unconscious, Ella Lundestad fell to her knees beside him with a pitiful cry.

"During my time in Tromsø," Holmes said, "I discovered that while the Lundestads had been much loved by the locals for many generations, the Vaeradals had neglected their estate and squandered much of their fortune. Indeed, it seems that the general was quite destitute when he died." Holmes looked down upon Ella Lundestad's bowed and sobbing head with no vestige of pity at all. "His daughter, however, had been brought up in the comfort of falsely earned privilege. She was used to high society and all of its advantages, and was not about to surrender either.

"She returned to Tromsø not to honour her father's dying wish to be buried upon his estate, but to renew her old acquaintance with the Lundestads, in order to once more secure her position. Lundestad was quite blinded by his childhood love for her, and all too eager, I imagine, to make her his wife. But, as he told to us at dinner, the Lundestad fortune is in land. The only means by which Ella Lundestad could again become rich was by her new husband's death, and what safer means than by lawful firing squad?"

"And Brovik?" Ibsen muttered, staring down at the unconscious man.

"Brovik was doubtless just as in love with her as Lundestad. Consider that he had already told to us that he and Lundestad were childhood friends, as too were Lundestad and Ella. It then follows logically, does it not, that Ella Vaeradal was also known very well to Brovik?"

"I hardly think that evidence enough for murder," I protested, for I had too much enjoyed the company of both Brovik and Ella Lundestad to countenance Holmes's savage suggestion.

"Dear Watson," Holmes said, "always you see only the best in people. Very well, draw your own conclusion thus: you cannot deny that Ella Lundestad's gowns were old and much mended, and all of her jewellery paste – bar that exquisitely beautiful cuff bracelet inlaid with turquoise stones."

I had noticed nothing of the sort, but nodded all the same. "What of it?"

"Did you not recognize the make of it?" Holmes asked.

"The make of it? No, indeed – why should I?"

"Think carefully, Watson!" Holmes exclaimed. "Back to your army years."

The answer came to me at once. "Why, it was Bactrian gold!" I cried. "Of course!"

"From?" Holmes prompted.

"Afghanistan," I said. "Ai-Khanoum! A gift from her lover while he worked for his passage back into Europe!"

"Indeed," Holmes said. "Indeed. In the Ølhall, Brovik was very careful to tell me that he had arrived back in Norway only two weeks before, and had not heard rumour of the *draugr* until he had reached Tromsø the very same day as ourselves, thus making certain that he could never be implicated in the murders. But Skien is not so far from the main port of Kristiania. Almost certainly, Brovik is the author of the telegram sent to Ibsen from his home town."

"But to what end?" Ibsen muttered.

Holmes gave a thin smile. "As a means to lure me to this island. Who, after all, would challenge my infamous expertise? Quite aside from the staged crime scene, Ella Lundestad made certain that I knew her husband had been out all hours of the day and night trying to track the *draugr*; even that he had only just returned moments before we heard the news of Herr Stockmann's murder. And you will doubtless recall Brovik's eagerness to accept my dismissal of the *draugr*'s cries as a trick of the wind. He wished us all to believe that the *draugr* was the biggest blind of them all, created by Lundestad as a cover for his crimes."

"But, Holmes," I said, "if Brovik was in Afghanistan and then in Skien, then that can only mean—"

"Poison," Holmes mildly observed, "is rarely the preserve of men."

"Do not talk about me as if I am not here," Ella Lundestad hissed, her grey eyes suddenly dark. When she snatched a hidden revolver from the coat of the still insensible Brovik, the four of us shrunk immediately back against the hut's flimsy walls.

"How I have hated the crowded hours of my subservient life," she said with a smile. "How I have hated the endless ennui; the ebb and flow of my own fortune at the mercy of only contemptible and weak men." She thrust straight her arm, aiming the pistol at Holmes's torso. "I am Ella Vaeradal, for I am my father's daughter before I am my husband's wife."

"You are undoubtedly one of the most keenly critical and intelligent minds that I have thus far ever met," Holmes entreated. "If you surrender yourself to my care, then I swear to do all within my considerable power to protect you from any likely sentence of death."

She smiled again, and although I tried not to glimpse the fearful beauty in it – in her – I saw it plainly all the same. "Life has no such charm for me that I would seek to prolong it any further," she said, and then she turned the pistol from Holmes before pressing it hard against her temple and letting go the trigger.

Four years later, and not long after I had finished writing up the rather bizarre case of the "Red-Headed League", Holmes announced that he wished to take me to the theatre. I was profoundly surprised, and even more profoundly suspicious, for aside from violin-led concertos, Holmes showed no interest at all in the cultural mores of London society.

It was only once we had arrived at the Vaudeville that I realized why we were there. Henrik Ibsen's name was emblazoned above the entrance, and when I turned to Holmes in ill-disguised delight, he merely smiled his restrained smile and ushered me inside.

But even then, I did not truly understand. Holmes remained tight-lipped throughout the entire performance of *Hedda Gabler*, with the wonderful Elizabeth Robins in the titular role. It was only during the final act, when the manipulative and fiercely intelligent Hedda, realizing that all was lost, killed herself with a bullet to the temple that I realized why Holmes had wanted me to see it.

"Good God!" I exclaimed, as the curtain fell. "She is Ella Lundestad!"

"Ella Vaeradal," Holmes admonished with a smile. "Though I must confess, I am somewhat disappointed that neither you nor I made any kind of appearance at all, however oblique."

"Holmes, I can hardly believe—"

"Nor either the enigmatic Sigerson," he interrupted as mildly, standing up after the final curtain call had ended and the gaslights had been revived.

"Extraordinary," I muttered.

Holmes shot a quick smile into the forgotten dark and then laughed loud and long. "Indeed. Perhaps, Watson, if all is ever again as bleak and desperate as an Arctic town held inside the fearful fist of polar night, I shall seek to revive good Sigerson, just as if he were a vengeful *draugr* awoken fast from his grave." He clasped a hand against my shoulder, but never quite caught my eye. "What do you say to that idea, good friend?"

# The Contributors

**Simon Clark** has written many short stories and novels, including *Darkness Demands*, *The Fall*, *Secrets of the Dead* and *The Night of the Triffids*, which continues John Wyndham's classic, *The Day of the Triffids*. *The Night of the Triffids* has also been adapted as an audio drama by Big Finish.

2014 saw the publication of *Inspector Abberline and the Gods of Rome*, a crime mystery, featuring the real-life Inspector Abberline, who led the hunt for the notorious serial killer Jack the Ripper, and who went on to become head of the Pinkerton National Detective Agency in Europe.

Simon lives in Yorkshire, England. Visit his website at www.nailedbytheheart.com.

**Andrew Darlington** is a renowned fiction writer and poet. He's also a music journalist and critic whose work has been widely published in newspapers and magazines. He lives in West Yorkshire, England.

Andrew is a dedicated blogger and maintains a blog at www.andrewdarlington.blogspot.co.uk where he writes about books, music and anything else that appeals to him.

**Paul Finch** is a former cop and journalist, and, having read History at Goldsmiths College, London, a qualified historian, though he currently earns his living as a full-time writer.

He cut his literary teeth penning episodes of the British TV crime drama *The Bill* and has written extensively in the field of children's animation. However, he is probably best known for his work in thrillers, dark fantasy and horror, in which capacity he is a two-time winner of the British Fantasy Award and a one-time winner of the International Horror Guild Award.

He is responsible for numerous short stories and novellas, but also for two horror movies (a third of his, *War Wolf*, is in pre-production), and for a series of best-selling crime novels featuring the British police detective, Mark "Heck" Heckenburg.

Paul lives in Lancashire, England, with his wife Cathy and his children, Eleanor and Harry. His website can be found at www.paulfinch-writer.blogspot.co.uk, and he can be followed on Twitter as @paulfinchauthor.

**Nev Fountain** has worked mainly in television and radio comedy. He is chiefly known for being a head writer on the *Dead Ringers* sketch show in both its radio and television incarnations, which was the recipient of a Gold Sony, a British Comedy Award and a political studies award, among others.

Nev has also contributed to many other programmes, including *Have I Got News For You*, *The News Quiz*, *Rory Bremner, Who Else?*, *The Impression Show* and *2DTV*. He helped devise and co-write the CBBC show *Scoop* and his co-written radio sitcom *Elephants to Catch Eels* ran for two series on BBC Radio 4.

He was given the Radio Comedy's Peter Titheradge Award for new writing, and last year won the IAMTW "Scribe" Award for his *Dark Shadows* story "The Eternal Actress".

A principal gag writer for the satirical magazine *Private Eye*, he contributes to every issue. Nev has written three humorous detective novels, collectively called *The Mervyn Stone Mysteries*, which also spawned a podcast, an audio and a Twitter novel. He has just completed his first "serious" thriller, *Painkiller*.

**Carole Johnstone**'s "Signs of the Times" recently won the 2014 British Fantasy Award for Best Short Story. Her fiction has appeared in numerous magazines and anthologies, published by ChiZine, PS Publishing, Night Shade Books, TTA Press and Apex Book Company, among many others. Her work has been reprinted in Ellen Datlow's *Best Horror of the Year* series and Salt Publishing's *Best British Fantasy 2014* and *2015*.

Carole's debut short story collection, *The Bright Day is Done*, is available from Gray Friar Press, and she has two novellas in both print and e-book format: *Cold Turkey*, which is part of TTA Press's novella series, and *Frenzy*, published by Eternal Press/Damnation Books. She is presently at work on her second novel, while seeking fame and fortune with the first – but just can't seem to kick the short story habit.

More information can be found at www.carolejohnstone.com

**Paul Kane** is an award-winning author and editor, who has worked in the fields of SF and Dark Fantasy (most notably the bestselling *Arrowhead* trilogy, a post-apocalyptic reworking of Robin Hood gathered together in the sell-out *Hooded Man* omnibus) and the YA market (*The Rainbow Man*, as P. B. Kane), plus he penned the Sherlock Holmes story "The Greatest Mystery". He is also the author of the critically acclaimed serial killer chiller, *The Gemini Factor*. His most recent co-edited anthology is *Beyond Rue Morgue* (Titan), all new stories revolving around Poe's detective C. Auguste Dupin. He has been a guest at many events and conventions, and his work has been optioned for film and television (including Lions Gate/NBC, who adapted one of his stories for primetime US network TV). Several of his stories have been turned into short films and he is currently adapting his novel *Lunar* into a feature for a UK production company.

His website www.shadow-writer.co.uk has featured guest writers such as John Connolly, Dean Koontz, Thomas Harris, Steve Mosby, Mo Hayder, Charlaine Harris and Stephen King.

**Alison Littlewood** is the author of *A Cold Season*, published by Jo Fletcher Books, an imprint of Quercus. The novel was selected for the Richard and Judy Book Club, where it was described as "perfect reading for a dark winter's night". Her second novel, *Path of Needles*, is a dark blend of fairy tales and crime fiction, and her third, *The Unquiet House,* is a ghost story set in the Yorkshire countryside.

Her short stories have been picked for *The Best Horror of the Year* and *The Mammoth Book of Best New Horror* anthologies, as well as *The Best British Fantasy 2013* and *The Mammoth Book of Best British Crime 10*. Other publication credits include the anthologies *Terror Tales of the Cotswolds, Resurrection Engines, Where Are We Going?* and *Never Again*. She has also contributed to the *Zombie Apocalypse! End Game* mosaic novel created by Stephen Jones.

Alison was raised in Penistone, South Yorkshire, England, and went on to attend the University of Northumbria at Newcastle (now Northumbria University). Originally she planned to study graphic design, but "missed the words too much" and switched to a joint English and History degree. She followed a career in marketing before developing her love of writing fiction.

Alison now lives in Yorkshire with her partner Fergus, in a house of creaking doors and crooked walls. Morocco is, to date, her favourite place to visit.

Her website is at www.alisonlittlewood.co.uk.

**Johnny Mains** is a British Fantasy Award winning editor, author and horror historian. He is series editor of Salt's *Best British Horror* series, the first volume published in 2014. The *Guardian* called it "never less than entertaining".

He has also co-edited *Dead Funny* with Robin Ince, an anthology containing original horror stories by Britain's best comedians, including Rufus Hound, Reece Shearsmith and Sara Pascoe. He is the author of two collections of short stories, which are very much in the old *Pan Book of Horror Stories* tradition: *With Deepest Sympathy* and *Frightfully Cosy and Mild Stories for Nervous Types*. Johnny Mains was also responsible for writing the liner notes and other additional material for Odeon Entertainment's blu-ray reissue of Michael Reeve's *The Sorcerers* and has also edited a book on the film's screenplay, originally written by John Burke and published by PS Publishing.

**William Meikle** is a Scottish writer, now living in Canada, with twenty novels published in the genre press and over three hundred short story credits in thirteen countries. He has novels, novellas and collections available from a variety of publishers including Dark Regions Press, DarkFuse and Dark Renaissance, and his work has appeared in a number of professional anthologies and magazines. He has a Holmesian collection, *The Quality of Mercy and other Stories*, and a trio of novellas, *The London Terrors*, both available from Dark Renaissance.

Willie lives in Newfoundland with whales, bald eagles and icebergs for company. When he's not writing he plays guitar, drinks beer, and dreams of fortune and glory.

**David Moody** grew up on a diet of trashy horror and pulp science fiction. He worked as a bank manager before giving up the day job to write about the end of the world for a living. He has written a number of horror novels, including *Autumn*, which has been downloaded more than half a million times since publication in 2001 and spawned a series of sequels and a movie starring Dexter Fletcher and David Carradine. Film rights to *Hater* were snapped up by Guillermo del Toro (*Hellboy, Pan's Labyrinth, Pacific Rim*) and Mark Johnson (*Breaking Bad*).

David Moody lives in Birmingham with his wife and a houseful of daughters and stepdaughters, which may explain his preoccupation with Armageddon. Find out more about David at www.davidmoody.net and www.infectedbooks.co.uk.

**Mark Morris** has written over twenty-five novels, among which are *Toady, Stitch, The Immaculate, The Secret of Anatomy, Fiddleback, The Deluge* and four books in the popular *Doctor Who* range. He is also the author of two short story collections, *Close to the Bone* and *Long Shadows, Nightmare Light*, and several novellas.

His short fiction, articles and reviews have appeared in a wide variety of anthologies and magazines, and he is editor of *Cinema Macabre*, a book of horror movie essays by genre luminaries for which he won the 2007 British Fantasy Award. He has also edited its follow-up *Cinema Futura*, and *The Spectral Book of Horror Stories*. His script work includes audio dramas for Big Finish Productions' *Doctor Who* and *Jago and Litefoot* ranges, and also for Bafflegab's *Hammer Chillers* series. Mark's recently published work includes the official movie tie-in novelization of Darren Aronofsky's *Noah*, a novella entitled *It Sustains* (Earthling Publications), which was nominated for a 2013 Shirley Jackson Award, and three new novels: *Zombie Apocalypse! Horror Hospital* (Constable & Robinson), *The Black* (PS Publishing) and *The Wolves of London*, book one of the *Obsidian Heart* trilogy (Titan Books).

Upcoming is a new short story collection from ChiZine Publications, two more novellas (for Spectral Press and Salt/Remains Publishing), and *The Society of Blood*, book two of the *Obsidian Heart* trilogy, which will be released by Titan Books in October 2015.

**Cavan Scott** has written numerous books, audios and comics based on such cult favourites as *Doctor Who*, *Blake's 7*, *Highlander* and *Warhammer 40,000*. As well as writing extensively for children, he is the co-author of *Who-ology*, the first Doctor Who book to become a *Sunday Times* best-seller.

A lifelong devotee of both the Great Detective and Mummy movies, Cavan's first full-length Sherlock Holmes novel, *The Patchwork Devil*, is published by Titan Books in 2016.

You can find him at www.cavanscott.com or on Twitter at @cavanscott.

**Denis O. Smith**'s first venture into recounting those cases of Sherlock Holmes that Doctor Watson had previously neglected to mention was "The Adventure of the Purple Hand", published in 1982, which was subsequently included in Penguin's *The Further Adventures of Sherlock Holmes*. Since then, he has published numerous other such accounts in magazines and anthologies both in the UK and the USA. In the 1990s, four volumes of his stories were published under the general title of *The Chronicles of Sherlock Holmes*, and he contributed a new story to Mike Ashley's *Mammoth Book of New Sherlock Holmes Adventures*. More recently, in 2014, a dozen of his stories, several never previously published, appeared as *The Lost Chronicles of Sherlock Holmes*.

Although Yorkshire born and bred, Denis Smith lived and worked in London and other parts of the country for some time, and has now lived in Norfolk for many years. His interests range widely, but apart from his dedication to the career of Sherlock Holmes, he has a passion for historical mysteries of all kinds, the railways of Britain and the history of London.

Award-winning author, **Sam Stone** began her professional writing career in 2007 when her first novel, *Killing Kiss*, won the Silver Award for Best Novel in the *ForeWord Magazine* Book of the Year Awards. The series is now on its fifth novel, with a sixth planned for later this year. Over the past few years Sam has written several novels, three novellas and many short stories.

Sam loves all types of fiction and enjoys mixing horror (her first passion) with a variety of different genres including science fiction, fantasy and steampunk. Her works can be found in paperback, audio and e-book. Sam's latest Epic Fantasy Horror novel *Jinx Town* is the first book in a new post-apocalyptic trilogy. For more information check out her blog at www.sam-stone.com.

**Stephen Volk** is best known as the writer of the notorious BBC "Halloween hoax" *Ghostwatch* and creator of the paranormal ITV drama series *Afterlife*, starring Lesley Sharp and Andrew Lincoln. Other screenplays include *The Awakening* (2011), starring Rebecca Hall, Dominic West and Imelda Staunton, Ken Russell's trippy extravaganza *Gothic* and *The Guardian* (co-written and directed by William *The Exorcist* Friedkin).

He won a BAFTA for *The Deadness of Dad* starring Rhys Ifans and has contributed to the Channel 4 horror series *Shockers*. For the stage, he penned a segment of Kim Newman and Sean Hogan's *The Hallowe'en Sessions* and his play *The Chapel of Unrest* was performed at London's Bush Theatre in 2013, starring Jim Broadbent and Reece Shearsmith. His short stories have been selected for *Year's Best Fantasy and Horror*, *Mammoth Book of Best New Horror*, *Best British Mysteries* and *Best British Horror*, and he has been a finalist for the Bram Stoker, British Fantasy and Shirley Jackson Awards.

His first single-author collection was *Dark Corners* (2006) while his second, also from Gray Friar Press, *Monsters in the Heart*, won the 2014 British Fantasy Award for Best Collection. Stephen Volk's highly acclaimed book *Whitstable* was also short-listed for Best Novella. His website is at www.stephenvolk.net.